WHAT DREAMS MAY COME

XENON

Matador
9 Priory Business Park,
Wistow Road, Kibworth Beauchamp,
Leicestershire. LE8 0RX
Tel: 0116 279 2299
Email: books@troubador.co.uk
Web: www.troubador.co.uk/matador
Twitter: @matadorbooks

ISBN 978 1838592 677

British Library Cataloguing in Publication Data.
A catalogue record for this book is available from the British Library.

Printed and bound in Great Britain by 4edge Limited
Typeset in 11pt Adobe Garamond Pro by Troubador Publishing Ltd, Leicester, UK

Matador is an imprint of Troubador Publishing Ltd

For Jenny, as always.
And for John.

Introduction

W*hat Dreams May Come* is the second in a series of ten novels that cover a period of about seventy-five years. Each stands alone, though with references to events in earlier books, and some characters appear in more than one.

The series is set in an imaginary world based loosely on a Classical Greek milieu, though transported to a northern temperate zone and with women playing a much more independent role than in Classical antiquity. The military side is largely based on Alexandrian and Macedonian Successor models.

The land of Gea is mainly an ethnic, linguistic and cultural unity, though not a political one. Its history has been one of intermittent warfare between its fifteen independent states and with the surrounding countries. However, for the last quarter of a century, the inexorable rise of Troia has welded the states, now provinces, into a formidable Empire. Insurrection, civil wars and foreign conflicts nevertheless remain common.

What Dreams May Come is set in the year 510, ten years after the events recounted in the first novel, *None So Blind*. Gea is groaning under the tyrannical rule of the usurping Emperor, Laomedon.

The Geans are culturally and militarily advanced. Their strength is in the hoplite, a heavily armoured, close order infantryman, fighting in a disciplined line with shield and long thrusting spear.

Cavalry is relatively unimportant, generally used for scouting or pursuit of a defeated enemy.

Light javelin armed infantry, called peltastes, and missile troops, or psiloi, with bow and sling, play a supporting role.

The army has a complex command structure, based on ektatoi, equivalent to modern non-commissioned officers, of whom the most important is the feared hyperetes, best regarded as a sergeant-major. Above the ektatoi are line officers of various ranks, culminating in strategoi or generals.

Many cultural and military terms are left unexplained, as the context should suggest the basic meaning, and more is unnecessary.

At the end of the book, information can be found under the following headings:

What Dreams May Come

Perhaps it will be so. Perhaps one weary night,
delight in this insipid world long fled,
a night of frost and stars and pale moonlight,
alone in cold and vastness of my bed
I'll wake to you, and know you warm and by.
I'll once more hear the soft exhale of breath
and feel your loving arm across me lie,
in desperate dream that I but dreamed your death.
From clinging night hag claws I'll frantic fight,
afeared it be delusion, turn to you.
Your face moon-spun and smoothed by soft half-light
brings surety that it be surely true.
Concerned, you reach for me to soothe my fears.
Whisper me to calm, to take no care.
'Twas but a dream. You'll kiss away my tears.
No need for such despair, for you are there.
And real. All's well. To sleep once more. But then,
however could I bear to wake again?

ONE

26th day of Mounichion, Year 510.
Bogazkoi. Mykerenos.

THE GIRL WAVED cheerfully from the open window. She was a pretty little thing, and Troilus raised a nonchalant hand in response but added his best winning smile. He had learned that it had a most satisfactory effect on the young women of Bogazkoi. She glanced behind him and promptly disappeared. With a guilty start, he looked round, but, to his relief, there was no Phoebe in evidence; only Elissa coming down the dirt track that passed for a road. The priestess of Herakla, she was dumpy and apple-cheeked, clad, as always, in a spotless, pure white chiton, with a small golden pomegranate hanging round her neck. Troi liked her. She had a cheerful, maternal manner and a no-nonsense approach to life that appealed to him.

'Troilus,' she hailed. 'I was just coming to see your father.' He waited for her to catch him up. She glanced at the roe deer slung over his shoulder. 'I wanted to ask him about the wild boar he promised for the Lady Herakla's Day of Birth Feast.'

'We know where they're lying up, Revered One, so it will be there. Don't worry.'

She smiled. 'Thank you. Well, that's saved my old legs a little bit of walking.' She looked up speculatively at the window. 'Phoebe not around, then?' There was a definite twinkle in her eye.

'It doesn't seem so,' he said with a straight face.

'Perhaps as well. Take care, Troilus. Sometimes the exuberance of youth can be a trap for the unwary.'

'I can't think what you mean.'

She raised her eyebrows, but her lips quirked slightly. 'Oh, I think you can.' She turned to go. 'May the blessings of the Lady Herakla fall on you.'

'And on you, Revered One.'

'Don't forget the boar,' she said as she set off back to the town.

'I won't.' He hitched the carcass up to sit more comfortably on his shoulder and walked on. He lived with Aias in one of the small collection of rude huts and ramshackle houses that had overleapt the boundaries of the town to trickle out towards the surrounding semicircle of woodland. It was the haunt of outdoorsmen: shepherds and woodsmen, hunters and farmers scratching a living on their smallholdings. A community within a community.

He walked through the open door of one of the sturdier and better-crafted buildings and dumped the deer on the scarred work table. Aias was sitting by the hearth, one leg propped up on a low stool, carefully fixing a new hand grip to a bow. A small ceramic pot sat in a bowl of warm water before the fire, and the air was thick with the rotting smell of animal hide glue. He glanced up at Troi and then the deer.

'Could have done worse,' he grunted.

That was high praise from Aias. He did not throw compliments round like nuts and fruit at a wedding. Troi took the flensing knife down from its hook and began to skin the deer.

'Elissa picked up my spoor. She wanted to be sure there would be wild boar at the feast.'

Aias groaned. 'Bloody woman's a witch. Waits until a man's feeling halfway right with the world after a few kylixes of decent red and then pounces. Then you're out there hunting wild boar and getting bugger all for it.'

'I thought all women were witches.'

'They are,' grumbled Aias, carefully trimming the last bit of leather thong. 'Some's just bigger witches than others.'

Troi laughed. 'Anyway, it's me that'll be doing the hunting. That ankle still needs resting.'

'Just make sure you take the juvenile with the torn ear. She hasn't farrowed.'

Troi nodded, then looked up to a howl of grief from across the low wall of their small courtyard. He glanced across at Aias questioningly.

'Ourania's eldest. Dog's died.'

Troi listened to the wail degenerate into heartfelt sobs. 'Poor kid. She loved that old fleabag.' He indicated the door with a nod. 'Should I...?'

'Leave her be. Let her get it out of her system. That's what tears are for.'

Troi continued to look through the open door for a few heartbeats, then turned back to work on the deer for a while. 'I know a man in town,' he eventually said. 'His bitch has just whelped. Decent enough dog. Not like some.' He looked meaningfully at Argos, who was laid alongside Aias. The big hunthound opened one eye, thumped his tail on the ground twice, and went back to sleep. 'I think he'd give me a pup for a brace of woodpigeons.'

Aias regarded him appraisingly. 'A soft heart doesn't bend iron.'

'Just thinking of you, old man.' Outside, fresh paroxysms of grief. 'At your age, you need your sleep.'

Aias snorted and reached for the glue pot.

TWO

TROI MOVED DOWN the cool, green aisle between the trees, the gutted carcass of a young wild boar slung over his shoulder. He was pleased with himself. Aias could not have taken the animal more cleanly. It was a heavy load, but Elissa would be delighted.

The spring sun sent ripples of light across the forest floor as the leaves shifted with the slight breeze. A willow warbler sang from a nearby treetop against the insistent murmur of woodpigeons, the harsh call of a jay and the drumming of a woodpecker. A stoat scurried across the thin, almost imperceptible track before him, and he smelt smoke. Faint, but smoke.

He stopped. He was too far from the town for it to be their cooking fires, and it did not have the resinous smell of a forest fire. There were strange overtones to it—not least the unsettling hint of burning flesh. He moved to one side, behind the bole of a large beech tree, laid the carcass on the ground and listened intently. The birds called and sang, and, apart from the flit of a feeding tit flock high overhead, there was no movement. He cautiously took his bow and strung it in one practised action, then plucked an arrow from his gorytus, a combined bow and arrow case.

He took a moment to ensure that his knife was loose in its scabbard, nocked the arrow, ducked low and, with slow and barely perceptible movements, shifted to a position where he could peer through the tracery of leaves along the trail. He watched and listened for some time. The smell of smoke was more distinct. There was nothing else.

He slipped forward, scarcely more than another shadow in the shifting sea of light and shade. His bow at half draw, he followed a sinuous path, sliding noiselessly just beyond the reach of the clutching branches. His ears were attuned to the slightest sound, every bird call, each insignificant rustle in the undergrowth, his eyes drawn to the faintest spoor or broken branch. The smoke was getting thicker, and the breeze was coming from the direction of the town.

As the trees began to thin out, he moved off the trail and through the increasingly dense undergrowth until he dropped to the ground and crawled toward the very edge of the ancient woodland. He wormed his way beneath the trailing branches of a young willow to overlook the hollow in which the small town of Bogazkoi lay.

Or rather had lain. It was a mass of flame. Koi, protected though it had been by a gatehouse and a curtain wall, was burning. He was confused. It had to be wrong.

Some incomprehensible mistake. An illusory spell cast by a woodwose. It would shimmer and clear, and all would be well.

But it didn't, and it wasn't. Belief came hard, but it came. His stomach an awful pit of emptiness, his throat burned by bile, his eyes stung by the curls and wisps of acrid smoke—these were nothing to the vertiginous realisation that his entire world had just disappeared. Swept away as if by the flick of a God's uncaring hand. Of the five thousand or so inhabitants of the town there was no sign of life, just dark, crumpled heaps that lay scattered across the fields like so much discarded rubbish. Everyone was dead. His mind reeled under the blow like a pankration contender caught full and true by the fist of his opponent. Everyone. But not Aias. Aias could not be dead. He refused to accept it.

There were no signs of assault and defence. The thick wooden gates stood wide open and unmarked. Round the walls lay no tell-tale fringe of bodies, broken ladders or stubble of arrows. But within, all was fire and smoke as the town burned. Great sheets of flame erupted upwards, coughing out greasy gouts of thick smoke, collapsing buildings crashed and splintered, and fine ash fluttered down from the grey-streaked sky.

To the right of the town, the perpetrators were drawn up in ordered array. Soldiers. At least a thousand of them, obviously just preparing to leave. Some cavalry were already departing along the winding track that led towards the Borean Way beyond the broad, grey stretches of Lake Imbros. They disappeared past a low wooded rise that thrust out from the forest, ox-drawn supply wagons lumbering after them, with archers and peltastes, bearing diminutive round shields and bundles of javelins, strolling along as flank guards. Many still remained, mostly the leather-jacketed spearmen of a speira, a 'hedgehog' of heavily armed infantry. With them, some light troops and the remainder of the cavalry, waiting patiently on their small, shaggy ponies.

A huge standard of an eagle, wings and talons outspread, dull black on a silver ground, swayed slightly as it reared above their heads. Troians, Imperial troops. But it made no sense. Why would the Troian Empire sack its own town, murder its own people? Troi's eyes were drawn to a short, fat, black-haired man in gilded armour, sitting to one side atop a fine black horse and surrounded by a cluster of officers and aides. Above him flew his personal sigil: the white head of an aurochs on a blue ground.

Before him were ten familiar and desolate figures. They were surrounded by guards, big men wearing triple-crested helmets and distinctive blue cloaks. He had heard talk of the 'Bluecloaks', with their reputation for brutality and savagery, and he knew, with sick certainty, what was about to happen. Even at this distance he recognised all ten of the prisoners, especially the tall, spiderlike figure of Erxandros, the town archon, and the silver hair and unmistakable pure white chiton of Elissa. He could make out the two civic magistrates and five councillors from the boule, along with the ancient and bent figure of the crabbed Priest of Dyaus Pitar.

He looked back at the town. The untidy litter of corpses spread little farther than the outer buildings, so the cavalry must have ringed the place, then slaughtered those attempting to flee. The fact that there were no bodies more than a hundred paces from the last houses told him all he needed to know about the possibility of survivors.

A cry of terror, suddenly cut short, dragged his eyes back again. The headless corpse of Erxandros lay in a dark spreading patch, and Elissa was being forced to her knees by two of the Bluecloaks. Some of the others struggled violently against the firm grasp of their captors, but Elissa quietly stretched her head forward as if making an offering on the altar of her beloved Herakla. An officer lifted his sword high and brought it down with sickening force. Her head bounced away like a child's toy, and the next man was hustled forward. Troi could watch no more, but closed his eyes and fought to subdue his frantic breathing, the blood throbbing in his temples and his nails gouging into the heels of his hands.

Coherent thought was lost to him. The surge and undertow of emotion, and the flash of images stamped onto his reeling mind, ripped away all control. He was not the strong, self-contained and disciplined hunter-warrior of his youthful imagination, but a small, petrified boy, suddenly lost in a mad and fearful world, helpless and alone. Terrifyingly alone.

He finally opened his eyes. Ten bodies and ten heads lay in an untidy row. There were shouts of command, and the straggled ranks of the speiroi fell in behind the livestock being herded along after the supply train. They were followed by the fat man with his personal escort of hated Bluecloaks. Finally, the rest of the cavalry moved out, and the long column of men dwindled away and eventually disappeared from sight.

Troilus still did not move. The flames licked at the sky, and the dark cloud of smoke rose ever higher. He clung to one thought. If anyone had survived, it would be Aias. Aias was indestructible. A force of nature. Death and defeat were not options. He had to have survived. Troilus could not, would not, imagine him dead. But he still could not move. His body simply ignored him, refusing to leave the shelter of his beloved woods and to go down, alone, into that horrific reality.

A distant screaming began. An incessant wail of terror and agony. Someone was trapped and burning to death. He instinctively scrambled to his feet. The scream tore through his brain and savaged his soul. He had to help. Then, mercifully, the screaming stopped, though it continued to echo in his head. But the trance was broken. Aias could be injured and in need of help, and there could be others alive down there. Troilus could not stand by and do nothing.

He stepped cautiously out from the protection of the trees, his bow drawn and every sense shrieking, and began the long, blood-freezing descent down the open grassy slope where there was nowhere to hide. He feared men hidden in the fringes of the forest, left behind to ensure any survivors who emerged from the ruins would not be survivors for long. He repeatedly spun round to search the shadowed threat, but there was no movement. A sudden fright of rooks froze him to the spot, but they wheeled and cawed and dropped back down to their untidy nests. The sweat cold on his back, his stomach a yawning chasm and his legs feeble and shaky, he stumbled on.

He came to the first of the bodies. A woman. He knew her. Aspasia, an elderly widow who had been a neighbour. Troi had often left a rabbit or a simple woven basket of morels outside her door, and she had brought nut loaf for Aias and him. She was sprawled on her back, her sightless eyes staring skywards, terror stamped on her waxen features, a savage slash across her sternum and flies already crawling over the coagulating blood.

Troilus was suddenly and violently sick. He retched helplessly even after he had voided his guts, the sour vomit rasping his throat. He sat down heavily. He wanted to turn around and disappear back into the cool, clean depths of the forest, to leave this dreadful place behind him and rinse both his mouth and his mind clean in a cold mountain stream. He took a deep breath, stood up unsteadily and continued. He passed more corpses, mostly women and children. Presumably, the men had fought to give them the chance of escape. But there had been none to give. Most of them he knew, as they had lived in the shanty town outside the walls.

Then something stirred, and there was the faintest flutter of a groan. He ran across, and the shock stopped his breath. It was Phoebe. He had walked with her only three nights before, when she had been a pretty, dark-haired girl with laughing eyes and full lips, but her fresh complexion was now pallid and slick with sweat, her hands clamped over her stomach holding in the pale threads of her entrails, and her eyes closed tight. He knelt beside her and cupped her face in his hands. Her eyes flickered open. Then, incredibly, she smiled.

'Troi,' she breathed.

'Phoebe.' He did not know what to say. Helpless and inadequate, he rued the lightness of his sixteen years. He knew what a gut wound meant. Aias had taught him well about such things, but never what to say to someone with one. Only what to do. Troi unobtrusively drew his long knife. Already, part of him was howling that he could not do it.

'What happened?' he asked, forcing the words past the aching lump in his throat.

She shook her head slightly as a tremor of pain crossed her features. 'The Troians. They said… sheltering traitors.' He had to lean forward to catch the words. 'Said to search. Archon let them in. The Trogs just started killing us.' She gave a sob. He gently stroked her cold, damp brow.

'You'll be fine, now, Phoebe,' he lied. 'I'll look after you.' At least, it was a sort of truth.

'They killed Ma,' she whispered. 'Everybody.' She bit her lip and winced. 'Why?'

He shook his head. 'I don't know. Just lie there quietly and don't talk.' She closed her eyes, her breathing shallow and laboured. He brought the knife up into position, though the horror within gibbered and wailed at him. Then he found an excuse to delay the dreadful moment.

'Who was it?' he asked. 'That fat bastard in charge?'

She opened her eyes and looked at him. She knew. He could see it in her eyes. She had never been a fool. 'Marsyas,' she breathed. Suddenly her voice was stronger and vehement. 'Kill him, Troi. Swear it.'

He could not speak at first as he fought the surge of tears in his eyes. He took a shaky breath and nodded. 'I swear it. By the Gods.'

She had not allowed it to go too far that night, but he was familiar with her firm breasts, and he knew exactly where to place the knife. He lifted her slightly, leaned forward and kissed her. As their lips met, he acted, almost without volition, thrusting the knife forward and up beneath her ribs. She jerked and stiffened, then sagged. The light simply went out from her eyes.

He let her collapse onto the ground and then carefully drew her eyelids down and kissed her brow one final time. He stood up, a dreadful emptiness within, scarcely able to see through the blur of tears, and walked on down towards the still-burning town. Marsyas. The satrap of Mykerenos himself. The name hammered in his brain.

Marsyas.

THREE

HE FOUND AIAS. Huddled in the small stone-walled courtyard behind their neighbour's house. He had not gone quietly. Several pools of dried blood told their own story. Two arrows were embedded deep in Aias's chest, though, bizarrely, the flight feathers had been broken off. His body had been hacked savagely, doubtless in retribution. Behind him lay the bodies of Ourania and her eldest daughter, a child of only twelve. They had both been raped and their throats cut. He pulled their chitons down to cover them and closed their eyes with a shaking hand. Ourania's baby lay flung into a corner like discarded rubbish, its small skull smashed to a pulp. Beside it, the broken body of a puppy. There was no sign of the other two children.

What puzzled him was the corpse of an Elean laid untidily against the wall, recognisable by the multiple parallel scars across his cheeks. He had been stabbed in the heart. But not by Aias. The lack of blood and the scuff marks around the corpse suggested that the body had been deliberately dragged there from elsewhere. Yet, despite the substantial blood spatter around the yard, there were no other bodies. Nothing was making sense.

He turned back to the man who had effectively been his father for nearly ten years and who had taught him everything he knew. There was a wooden bucket of water beside the now-empty pigsty. He tore the faded scarf from the neck of the dead Elean, dipped it in the water and carefully wiped the blood from Aias's face. The side of his skull had been caved in, but his face still wore the look of calm certainty that characterised his every word and deed. He had never seemed to doubt anything for a moment. Troi washed more blood from the short, neatly trimmed grey beard and closed those dark, penetrating eyes.

They had not taken the cheap bronze god guard that hung round his neck on a leather thong. He had always worn it, and Troi had never taken any particular note, but it was something of Aias to wear in remembrance. Their own small hut was a burned-out shell, and nothing remained. He untied the pendant, rinsed it in the bucket and regarded it closely for the first time. He had taken it to be the guard of Apollon, but now he saw that it had only ten rays rather than the standard twelve, and the letter beta embossed within the central disc. He did not understand its significance, but it had clearly meant something to the old man. He fastened it round his own neck.

He arranged the body so it lay proud and straight, and resolved to build a pyre that night, to give Aias the warrior's funeral he deserved. The carcass of the Elean would lie at his feet like a sacrifice. He stood up and, in a cracked and trembling voice, sang the threnody for a warrior. There was no growled response from surrounding warriors, no rhythmic clash of spear against shield, no final ululation, only the crackle and spit of flame and the dull echo of a collapsing building. But it was the best that he could offer the old man. He had been a warrior all his life and had died sword in hand, facing his foes. It was enough. Troi abruptly turned and left the courtyard to continue his hopeless search of the still-burning town.

But something had shifted inside him. Somewhere a door had been closed and barred. A part of him floated in uterine darkness and refused to emerge into the pitiless glare of a savage world.

FOUR

TROI WALKED THROUGH the burning town. How could a place so familiar, so much a part of his very being, have become all but unrecognisable? Fire licked out from empty windows, throwing pulses of heat across the littered streets, and rubble lay in tumbled swathes across his way. Discarded spoil and bodies everywhere. Men. Women. Children. Dogs. All with that still, flaccid shapelessness of the dead. Pools of blood glistened in the throw of the firelight, and the air was wreathed in smoke that caught at his throat and carried the nauseous smell of burning flesh on its back.

It was a tableau of horror, but Troi had gone beyond that. To a place where he felt nothing, except for a strange calm, an acceptance. The whole thing had no reality. Either he was wandering through a dream Hades, or he was an immaterial and indifferent spirit passing through a real one.

Then he saw the horses in what was left of the agora. Two ponies tied to hitching rings inset into limestone blocks amidst the burning buildings, tossing their heads and rolling their eyes, snorting and whinnying in their distress. Beside them, a small pile of collected loot; a few coins, but mostly cheap utensils, some bronze kraters, a couple of decent-looking swords and a dump of boots and clothing. Troi slipped into the shadowed gap between two still-standing buildings and drew his bow from his gorytus. He strung it, checked how many arrows he had—seven—and nocked one. The ponies' saddle cloths were old and dirty but had the Imperial Eagle embroidered in one corner. Either Trog deserters or, more likely, outriders who had taken an opportunity to slip back and see what they could loot.

Troi waited patiently, puzzled by his own unemotional reaction. He should be nervous, wiping his sweaty hands on his tunic, starting at every noise, screaming in fear. Yet there was nothing, just a strange tranquillity at the heart of his being. His mind was working, but without feeling, gauging possibilities, rehearsing scenarios, checking everything, the way Aias had taught him. It was as though he was performing an exercise. He ensured that his knife was loose in its scabbard for a second, then a third, time. They would come.

And they did. Suddenly they were there. Walking across the agora from his left. Two men in grubby grey tunics, with long swords hanging from their belts. One was tall with greasy flaxen hair chopped to shoulder length, the other shorter and stockier, wearing a battered straw sun hat. The first carried an amphora of wine; the second, a red cloak. They walked away from him towards their horses, and he allowed them to do so, wanting distance. Lifting his bow, Troi straightened his back and stretched into the shooting stance. They were forty paces away now. He drew smoothly and loosed, instantly reaching for a second arrow from his quiver.

The taller man stopped walking, the arrow protruding from his back. The other continued for a step or two before beginning to turn in the belated realisation that something was wrong. The stricken man dropped down on his knees, then crashed forward. The amphora smashed on the flagged ground, spilling red wine that mingled with his spreading blood. His companion swung round, dropping the cloak, his hand grabbing for his sword hilt, and froze. His eyes were fixed on the broad arrowhead pointing directly at him. His hand opened, and the sword fell back into its scabbard. He was a young man with a podgy and pasty face, the sparse beginnings of a moustache on an upper lip that, even at this distance, Troi could see had sprung with sweat.

'No,' he said, his voice strangled. 'We had nothing to do with this. We were on patrol. We just…' His eyes widened, and he gave a little gasp. He looked down at the feathered shaft sunk deep in his chest and made a feeble clawing movement towards it, then collapsed in a sprawling heap.

Troi knew he was dead before he hit the ground. He put away his bow, drew his heavy hunting knife and walked over.

The first man lay face down, still alive. Troi yanked the arrow from his back—they were too valuable to waste—and the man cried in pain. Troi pushed him over with his boot.

The trooper stared up at him, his face tight and strained, horror in his eyes, a dribble of blood from his lips. He did not seem able to move.

'Please,' he said. 'Please.' A bubble of blood popped at the corner of his mouth.

Troi slit his throat, retrieved his other arrow and walked on.

Amazingly, he found survivors. Two seriously wounded men and three more who were too badly injured to survive, to whom he gave their quietus, now without a qualm. Then there were seven women, six children and a snivelling, useless young man called Diocles. All unhurt, as they had managed to find secure hiding places until driven out by the encroaching fire, but scarcely undamaged: they ranged from blank-eyed incomprehension, through wailing grief to panic-stricken delirium.

Troi had no response to their distress, finding it irrelevant and unnecessary. He guided them to the small, untouched Temple of Demetra that lay just outside the town. By the time he had collected the boar from the woods and retrieved the two ponies, the survivors' immediate emotions were largely exhausted. He left Diocles to blubber and complain and the women to comfort the children, tend the wounded and prepare a meal, and went back into the Hades of Koi.

FIVE

TROI WAS WEARY, his throat rough and sore, his face grimed with soot and ash. The conflagration had subsided, but fire still flickered and smouldered, the glow of the dying flames seeming to pour a libation of blood over the walls. Wreaths of drifting smoke hung across the town like a shroud, and the occasional crash of a collapsing wall was the funeral drum, calling all to witness and mourn the death of Koi. But there were few to hear. The scattered corpses lay still and broken and took no heed, and Troi stepped over them without thought, even those he recognised, knew as vendors, tutors, acquaintances. Friends. He should have sprinkled a handful of soil on each body, to grant it passage to the Styx, but that had no importance now.

He came across a forgotten Troian spearman, trapped and terrified beneath a fallen beam. At first, the spearman was pathetically grateful that someone had found him, but when he looked into Troi's eyes, his voice died. Troi cut the screaming man's throat without hesitation, but also without any sense of vengeful satisfaction. He had crossed a watershed. He was no longer a youth. He had become a man and a dealer in death. He found no pride in it, but only a grim recognition that, when the moment came and Marsyas was within his sword's reach, there would be no weakness, no wavering, no mercy.

The destruction was so great that he had difficulty finding his way through the once-familiar streets to the postern gate that opened out onto the shanty town beyond. The fire damage was not quite so complete there, but the dead lay just as thickly. He found Ourania's yard, where the log pile remained intact, and from it he built a platform of wood and laid Aias on it with a shield, sword and spear he had gathered as he passed through the town. He then lugged the Elean's corpse across to dump it unceremoniously at his feet.

He fired the funeral pyre and watched the flames take. They licked high into the sky in showers of sparks. He said nothing, trying to grasp at some emotion, a feeling of loss, the release of grief, even the drive of anger. Anything. Nothing. All was cold and dead. It seemed strangely unimportant now.

He turned his back on Aias, clambering over the wall into the backyard of what had formerly been his home. The small house was just a blackened shell, but he gave it no attention, concentrating on carefully pacing out the requisite distances until he was at the spot once identified by Aias. 'If anything happens to me, you must dig here,' he had told Troi.

He began to break up the solid earth with a sharp stick and shovel it out with a piece of broken board. After a while, he struck something. He dug at the soil with his hands and pulled out a black ceramic chest, firmly sealed with pine pitch. He chipped away at the resin and forced off the lid.

Within was a golden god guard of Apollon, a gold ring with an embossed sun disc, and two leather bags closed with drawstrings, one long and cylindrical, the other, from its weight, shape and feel, clearly full of coins. He opened it and poured some out. Gold coins. He stared at them, amazed. How could Aias have come by such a fortune? At least, it explained how he had managed to enrol him with the best pedagogue in town and to persuade a retired swordmaster to take him under his wing. He tipped the coins back and, turning his attention to the second bag, drew out two parchment rolls.

The first was a single scroll securely closed by silver wire, which was threaded through its rolls and then embedded in a block of lead stamped with an ornate seal of a peacock. It was a tamper-proof document sealed at a temple of Herakla. The second consisted of two scrolls rolled together and tied with a black ribbon. Held beneath the ribbon was a scrap of parchment tersely requiring him to read the outer scroll first. He unrolled it and found it to be written in a small, neatly formed and regular hand.

Seventh day of Maimakterion, Year 500.

My beautiful, darling Pyrrhus, my beloved son. This is the most difficult and heart-rending letter I have ever had to write, and the worst thing I have ever had to do. I hope that Aias has told you everything already, but if anything has happened to him, you will be learning the truth for the first time. Please forgive me, my darling, for I will never forgive myself. But I must keep you safe.

Aias will have told you my name is Philomena, that I lived in Argos and died of the bloody flux. That your father had died in the Great Revolt. So Aias adopted you. But that I loved you above all. Only the last is true. The rest was to ensure that you would never know anything that could lead the murdering agents of Laomedon to you. Good and faithful Aias undertook to keep you hidden and safe. I do not know where you are. I do not even know by what name you are now called. No-one does. Thus you cannot be betrayed.

But know, my beloved son, my true name is Aglaia, daughter of Miltiades, onetime Holder of Gla. Your father is Perikles of the Basilides clan, descended from the Thessalian Kings of old and ultimately Apollon himself, and he loves you as much as I do.

When Laomedon rose against Troilus III and there was civil war, my brother, your uncle Antinous, died fighting the traitor at Iron Rock, as did your other two uncles, the brothers of your father. As a family with royal blood who fought against Laomedon, we are marked down. I wished to flee, as both my mother and father have done, but Perikles will not abandon his family and people. In the end, we compromised: I should stay with my husband, but you would be safely hidden until this shadow that has fallen across our land is finally gone.

If you take the sealed scroll to the Great Temple of Herakla at Athen Parthenos, give them the code word Alkibiades and ask for the chest of the Basilides, within you will read how to find us. If we have crossed the Styx, which I fear is all too likely, then the same sealed scroll will prove you to be the inheritor of the Basilides lands and fortune. But do nothing while Laomedon lives. His jackals will be watching.

If you have need of help, your grandmother Kalliste lives in Massalia with Uncle Dio, and your grandfather resides in Thematis. They live beyond our borders, but if you can reach them, they will both do anything to help and guard you.

I pray to Herakla every night that you will remain safe and, if the Gods are good, that I will look upon your face once more. If it is not to be, know how much it hurts me to part from you and how much I love you. There is so much more I want to say, but I have not got the words. May the Gods protect you. Your father wants you to know how proud he is of you and how much he loves you too.

I love you so.

Your grieving mother,

Aglaia

Troi stared at the words. They mostly made no sense. It was too much to take in. The one thing that beat in his brain, like the rhythmic clash of spear on shield, was that his mother lived. He read it through again, this time with more comprehension. He had been about six summers when he had come here with Aias, but he could remember his mother. He had dim memories of happy times, of a large villa and a kind nurse, of his mother and a tall, bearded man, whom he assumed to have been his father, playing games with him. Above all, he had a vivid memory of sitting on his mother's lap as she talked to someone, warm in her arms, feeling a comforting vibration from her chest as she spoke. He had believed what Aias had told him about her death. Why had Aias not told him the truth? He was surely old enough now to have been trusted with such knowledge.

The vision of a vivacious and elegant woman, her hair a mass of black curls, her cheekbones high, suddenly flared in his mind, her hands despairingly outstretched towards him, her large eyes full of tears, as he was carried away. He had been crying, too, he thought.

He looked at the golden sunburst. It bore an embossed beta. It had incredibly tiny and finely wrought hinges along a line across the back. He examined it closely, then clicked open the top half. Within was a small lock of dark hair. He carefully replaced it and closed the lid. That explained the pendant he had taken from Aias. It was obviously the sigil of Clan Basilides. The ring was engraved with the same sign.

He gripped the locket tightly in his hands and stared sightlessly up at the sprinkle of stars beginning to infiltrate the twilit sky. He would find his father and mother. Everything would be made right. He placed the locket carefully in the box and took the second parchment. It was written in crude, archaic characters with the sad lack of punctuation and idiosyncratic spelling of Aias's hand.

THURD DAY OF PINOPSION YEAR 509
BOGAZKOI

IF YOU AR REEDIN THIS THEN I AM DED AND CAN HELP YOU NO MOR I DO NOT NO IF I DID RITE NOT TELLIN YOU THE TROOTH ABOUT YOUR FAMILLY BUT YOU WERE GROWIN UP HAPPY AND SUCH TIMES AR BREEF IN THE LIFE OF A MAN AND I CUD NOT CURDLE SUCH A TIME IF I WAS RONG FORGIV A OLD MAN SADLY UNLERNED IN BRINGIN UP KIDS

I MUST NOW LAY HEVVY NEWS ON YOU AND I WEEP FOR IT TOO YEARS AFTER I BRORT YOU HERE LAOMEDONS CURSED KRIPTIA TOOK YOUR MUM AND DAD I AM AFRADE THER IS NO HOPE FOR THEM YOU AR THE LAST OF THE BASILIDES

YOU MUST NOT SPEEK OF THIS TO ANIONE

I HAV NEVER TOLD YOU THAT I LOVE YOU WURDS LIKE THAT STIK IN THE GULET OF A OLD CAMPAINER BUT I DO YOU HAV BECUM THE SON I NEVER HAD AND I AM PROWED OF YOU I HAV TRYD TO RIASE YOU SO THAT YOU WILL HAV THE SKILLS TO SUVIVE AND BE A GOOD MAN I HOPE THAT I HAV DUN GOOD WITH THE FURST FOR YOU HAV BEEN A GOOD PUPIL FOR THE SECOND I HAD NO PART IN THAT YOU GREW TALL AND

STRATE AS A POPLER BY YOURSEN AND I NOE YOU WILL DO WOT IS RITE

MAY THE GODS WARK WITH YOU AND GIDE YOUR STEPS

FAIR WELL MY BELOVED SON

AIAS

He stared at the words that had strangled his new-born hopes. But they could not be gainsaid. He had found and lost his mother in a few laboriously written strokes of the pen. The same strange calm descended upon him, and the image of his mother seemed to fade into a thick fog until it was lost to his view. It no longer seemed to matter. After all, she had sent him away, abandoned him. Just as Aias had. Leaving him a note instead of telling him the truth. He was best on his own. Safest.

He took a few of the coins and put them in his pouch before replacing everything in the chest. He managed to melt and reform its pitch seal with a burning piece of wood, and reburied it, carefully smoothing over the surface to leave no trace. He rinsed his hands and face in a small puddle of water he found within a leather bucket. Then he returned to the others, just as the first stars disappeared behind the dark roil of an incoming front and a spatter of rain began to fall.

He found, not at all to his surprise, that one of the wounded men had died. The other was injured too grievously to be of use, and Diocles was a weak and indecisive soul, so, despite his youth, Troi found the benumbed and traumatised survivors looking to him for leadership. He considered just pointing them in the direction of the nearest village, but the words in Aias's scroll, 'you will do what is right,' rang in his head, and he reluctantly decided that he should get them there himself.

Over a miserable meal, he managed to piece together the story of what had happened, though Marsyas's manic response to such a trifling event remained incomprehensible. Three se'ennights ago, a small, tired group had come down to Bogazkoi, having crossed the difficult Evinian Pass from the Tirynian Shore. Six men and three women, obviously aristocrats. They had asked to speak to the archon. Erxandros had said nothing of the meeting, but they had left two days later, heading toward Pelium. The consensus was they had been refugees from the doomed rebellion of Kalais in Chalcidike, fleeing the ruthless revenges of Laomedon. It was assumed they had sought sanctuary and been refused. Troi vaguely remembered some talk about it at the time, but he had dismissed it as unimportant.

Many had been sympathetic to the strangers. There was a great deal of unrest in Mykerenos. Laomedon was not a popular Emperor, and there had been mutterings against the archon's decision. But Erxandros had made the sensible call for his town and its people. He had simply not considered, could never have imagined, the savage and deranged response of Marsyas when, somehow, he had learned that the group had arrived at Bogazkoi. Five thousand had died for it. Troi would have to lead the fifteen miserable survivors, through the now-heavy rain, to some sort of safety at the nearest village of Iyalissos.

After which he would resume his interrupted hunt. He would no longer be hunting boar, but bigger game. A white aurochs, to be precise. A white aurochs on a blue ground. Then even, perhaps, an eagle.

SIX

THE INJURED MAN had a cousin in Iyalissos and suspected him of being a member of the proscribed Order of the White Rose, an underground organisation that had sprung up in response to the brutality of Marsyas. Troi left the survivors lying up in a small willow coppice six stadia outside the settlement, then slipped silently through the night. The rain had finally ceased, and the clouds had shredded to reveal the moon, but he was soaked through and exhausted. It had taken them five gruelling dekates to fight their way across the low wooded ridge that lay between Koi and Iyalissos, wrestling a crude stretcher along a glutinously muddy track in the driving rain and thick darkness, the children riding the ponies. In the end, he had promised the complaining Diocles that he would gut him if he said one more word and, in the light of the emerging moon, seen terror in the eyes of the children.

Unlike Koi, the village was unwalled, and it was easy to find the small villa on its outskirts. Overhead, the last ragged clouds scurried after their fellows, and a three-quarters moon shed a pallid light. Troi glanced to his right, where the first faint glow of dawn sharpened the distant peaks. He knocked loudly and incessantly until he heard a shuffling within.

'Who's there?' The voice was old, weak and querulous.

'I wish to speak to Doreios, son of Dymnos, on a matter of urgency. I come with a message from his cousin, Inaros, son of Peithon, concerning the roses he gave him. The white ones.'

There was a long silence.

'Stay there.' The shuffling receded. A dog barked, making Troi start, but it was some distance away. After a worrying wait, he heard the shuffling once more, then the welcome sound of bolts being drawn across. The door opened, spilling the ruddy glow of an oil lamp across the darkness. An old man, stooped and grey-haired, with a long, unkempt beard and protuberant ears, stood there.

'Come in quickly,' he quavered.

Troi slipped inside, and the door was hastily shut behind him. He was in the wide passage that led to a central courtyard lying flat and grey in the pale moonlight. The lamplight threw huge, misshapen shadows on the whitewashed walls. He sensed, rather than saw, the sword that was pointed towards the back of his neck. He turned very slowly, raising his open hands slightly.

A muscular, middle-aged man had been standing behind the door. Presumably Doreios himself. He had a black spade beard, long hair, and an unwavering sword and was regarding Troi in a most unfriendly manner. 'What nonsense is this about roses?'

'Inaros is wounded and needs help. As do the other survivors.'

'Survivors?'

'Bogazkoi has been destroyed. Burned to the ground. Everyone they could find slaughtered. Men, women, children. There are fifteen survivors, one with injuries.'

The sword dropped involuntarily. The man stared at Troi with shock. 'That can't be true.'

'I wish to Hades that it wasn't.'

'We saw smoke but assumed it was a forest fire. Who was responsible?'

'Marsyas,' replied Troi shortly.

'How do you know?'

'I saw it. I was returning from a hunt. I watched from the trees.'

The man's eyes narrowed. 'Impossible. Even that bastard wouldn't wipe out an entire town. You must have been mistaken. It must have been brigands.'

'A brigand band strong enough to sack a town?' Troi's tone was derisory, and he could see Doreios bridle at it. Troi took a deep breath and spoke in more measured tones. 'But that's what Marsyas would like you to believe.' He gestured to his belt pouch and lifted a questioning eyebrow.

The sword rose again, and Doreios jerked his head up in acquiescence. 'Careful,' he warned.

Very slowly, Troi opened his pouch and drew out the fletched end of a broken arrow, handing it to the man, who gestured to his servant to bring the oil lamp nearer in order to study it.

'So, it wasn't Marsyas,' he declared. 'This is an Elean arrow. Though I didn't think they had the strength for this.'

The Eleans were wild mountain tribesmen inhabiting the rocky uplands of Elis between Mykerenos and the Northern Thebeaid. They occasionally raided the lowlands, but they were small nuisance raids, nothing too serious. Running off a few cattle when they could.

'They don't. It was Marsyas. I saw him. Short. Fat. Black-haired. Surrounded by blue-cloaked guards. He had cavalry, light troops and a full speira of spearmen. These arrows were deliberately left scattered around so he can blame the Eleans if he needs to.'

His vehemence seemed to have finally convinced Doreios, who shook his head, puzzled. 'Why should he do such a thing?'

'Apparently he thought some Chalcidikian refugees were there, though in fact they had passed through.'

'But it still doesn't make sense. What good did it do?'

'There were about fifty bodies of Eleans strewn throughout the town. All placed after being killed. My guess is it wasn't deliberate. His troops overreacted to something. Perhaps somebody resisted.'

Doreios was staring at him, his face a shifting battleground over which perplexity and burgeoning anger warred.

'When he realised that they had gone too far, he ordered the systematic annihilation of the place. No survivors to tell the tale. He had the chief citizens beheaded, which is how the Eleans execute prisoners.' Troi made an open-handed gesture of uncertainty. 'He must have had a part-hekaton of Elean mercenary archers with him. He had them slaughtered to provide the evidence. Even he must have realised that this might cause the country to erupt.'

Doreios considered the information with pursed lips and narrowed eyes. Then he nodded slowly. 'That would make sense.' He paused, then looked down. 'I'm sorry,' he said gruffly. 'You must—'

'It doesn't matter.'

'But—' Doreios began again.

'But it'll only work if there are no survivors,' interrupted Troi. 'He'll pile Pelion on Ossa to track us down.'

Doreios gave up on the gruff sympathy and finally lowered his sword. 'Where are the rest? We need to get them as far away from here as quickly as possible, and the truth needs to be spread like a forest fire. So that evil bastard can't stamp out the flames, no matter how he tries.'

SEVEN

IT MUST HAVE been because he was tired. He hadn't slept for well over twenty dekates, and the shock of the massacre had left him drained. He was pleased to be rid of the dragging weight of the small group of survivors and was now making his way back towards Koi to pick up Marsyas's trail. Not that that would be hard. A force that size could be followed by a blind man. The sun was now high in the sky, and it felt pleasantly warm as he ploughed through the lush grass and riot of flowers. The strange whooping call of lapwings and the plaintive whistle of curlews filled the air, and fritillaries bobbed and weaved amongst the thistles and knapweed. It was so normal and soporific that he was all but asleep on his feet, which is why he had simply cut straight across the open pasture instead of keeping to cover. Far too late, he saw the horsemen coming towards him.

He was suddenly wide awake. They were Trog cavalry and must have been left by Marsyas to prevent anyone learning of Bogazkoi or, at the least, to stop any close examination of its ruins. Thank Dyaus for the rain last night that had washed the incriminating cling of smoke from him. He thought desperately. He was only ten stadia from the town and heading directly towards it. He quickly but unobtrusively hooked out the coins from his pouch, dropped them and buried them in the soft earth with his heel as he hastily began to stitch together a story. They closed in on him, surrounding him, spears lowered. He stood very still, his arms outstretched, his hands open. He tried to look surprised and frightened. It wasn't difficult at all.

The officer, a gaunt, hard-faced man, distinguishable by his expensive bronze cuirass, walked his horse up to Troi and looked down at him. Slack-mouthed, Troi gaped back up, widening his eyes, trembling a little.

'And where are you going?' The man's voice was light and cultured, but there was the naked edge of a sword in the tone.

'Bogazkoi.' He had to say that. Where else could he have been going?

'Why?'

'See my nuncle. My da sent me.' A yokel. None too bright. Should be able to manage that.

'What about?'

Troi gestured to his gorytus. 'Want to be a hunter. Like Nuncle Aias.' Troi suddenly beamed. 'He is going to learn me.' Is. Is. He had nearly said was. The sweat trickled cold and clammy down his back.

'Bogazkoi is under interdict,' said the officer.

'Inter...dick ?' He looked appropriately puzzled at the strange term.

'No-one can go there for the moment. There has been an attack by those bastard Eleans.'

Troi allowed his jaw to sag even more, and his eyes darted around feverishly looking for the bastard Eleans.

'So, you can go no farther.'

The man's tone was conversational. For a brief instant, Troi thought he had done it. That he was safe. That he would be sent back whence he had purportedly come.

'Take him,' the officer snapped.

A grinning trooper dismounted with a length of rope in his hand.

EIGHT

THE SUN, HOT as a furnace, hung in the hammered blue steel of the sky, and beads of sweat erupted from his brow in the waves of heat. Troi paused from his work to wipe it from his eyes, and the whip cracked perilously close to his arm. He hastily bent back down and hacked at the tree root with his mattock. Gian heaved, his muscles straining as he tugged at the recalcitrant stump. Troi brought his mattock down again, and it finally gave, lurching from the excavated hole so suddenly that Gian nearly fell backwards. Troi grabbed the stump, and together they wrestled it out and rolled it to one side. He risked a quick glance down the long, labouring line of sunburned slaves; Xarchon had moved away, his back now to them, but was still tapping his coiled whip menacingly against his leg. 'Bastard,' said Gian softly.

'The stump or Xarchon?'

Gian smiled his gap-toothed smile. 'Guess.'

He was a big man, impressively muscled, but with a habitual slouch. His crudely cut mop of vivid auburn hair brought out the pale blue of his eyes, though his round, amiable face was marred by a badly broken nose. He had skin that was dry and leathered, and his body was fretted with whip scars. He had been a slave for seventeen of his thirty years but had never accepted the throw of the knucklebones. Despite an irrepressible sense of dry humour, he had a strength and temper that made even sadistic bastards like Xarchon just a little cautious in their dealings with him. Troi was amazed he had not been flogged to death or crucified years ago.

Gian had befriended the young man and tried to help him to survive this, the first moontide of slavery, especially in the early days when he had stumbled about in a state of confusion from lack of sleep. Gean had proffered good advice, though not always following it himself, showing him the tricks and petty scams of survival.

Troi suspected, from the occasional look, that there was more to his spear cast than friendship. But Gian had not laid a hand on him, and, unless he did, Troi was happy to accept the advice and hard-gleaned knowledge, as well as the fact their companionship deterred anyone else from becoming a nuisance.

They bent to their task again, cutting away at the hard, crusted soil with their mattocks, working their way toward the next stump that thrust, defiantly and obstinately, from the dark earth. The experienced Gian worked just hard enough not to call the attention of the eager whip, but no harder. Two elderly slaves had come and were fastening ropes to their now-defeated antagonist, preparatory to hauling it away to the blazing fire. The whip cracked somewhere along the line, and there was a howl of pain. Troi and Gian neither paused nor looked up. It was the inevitable accompaniment to their daily work.

NINE

THEY SHUFFLED BACK along the dusty road, the fetters rubbing their ankles sore and feeling oppressively heavy and cumbersome. Above them, skylarks rose into the cloudless sky, their cascade of song a cruel jest at the sorry procession stumbling past. There were fifty field slaves. Most of those at the villa were household slaves, trusted with some degree of freedom, but those deemed useful in their strength, yet dangerous because of it, were guarded closely by order of Glycon, their fat, toad-like master, his bloated, glistening face pocked with warts, his small, dark eyes never still and his tongue flicking nervously through his thin lips. He was fond of saying that slaves were too valuable to waste. Which at least meant that they ate adequately and that punishments were rarely extreme. Anything that kept a slave from working was a loss of revenue and a javelin to Glycon's acquisitive heart.

Troi shambled listlessly on, his head lowered, abject resignation evident in every movement. But his eyes were keenly studying the uncleared patch to his right. They were to move on to that next. And it was not far from the dense, mature woodland that constituted the fringe of the vast Dryopian Forest. All he had to do was get into it, and they would never catch him. He would wait until Selenes, when Xarchon always went into town. Xarchon's deuteros was lazy and slow witted, and the guards were noticeably slacker on that day. Troi had been patient for a moontide, observing, analysing, planning; and this was going to be his best chance. Once he had eluded immediate pursuit, he would remain in the wild, surviving on roots, nuts and fruits. And game, of course. He would make deadfall traps and fire-hardened spears and even a bow as soon as he had sufficient animal sinew for the string. It would be slow, but he would survive and eventually be able to work his way north. Across the Sea of Grass and then through Gean Thrake. Towards Mykerenos. Towards Marsyas. Xarchon would be hard on those left behind, but the thought merely flitted through his mind like a dunnock diving for thick cover and was gone.

As they entered their compound, a young, dark-haired woman slipped past them, glancing shyly at Troi as she went. He smiled at her, though knowing full well it was a phantasm. He had managed to have a few words with her, and liked the look of her, but it would come to nothing. Glycon occasionally rewarded the slaves by sending over one of the women. It gave them a glimmer of gold dust in the sludge of dour and tedious existence, some sort of reason to go on living. The slave owner had done the calculations and decided that a strong boy slave was worth more than the negligible cost of his rearing. Most of the baby girls were ruthlessly exposed. But he left the choice of the fortunate male slave to Xarchon. And Gian was not on Xarchon's list, so, it inevitably followed, neither was Troi.

Ahead, surrounded by a thick hedge of thorn bushes and patrolled by guards and dogs, was the large cabin that was their stuffy and malodorous home. It was built on stilts, so there was no chance of digging a way out, and was ill served with windows; what few it had were small and strongly barred. There was just the single solid door, invariably secured on the outside by a heavy balk of wood dropped into bronze sockets. Slave estates were rare in Gea, but Xarchon knew his job. They gratefully climbed the three steps and stood in the requisite double line within its dim interior as the slavemaster's deuteros removed the hated manacles.

The door slammed behind the last retreating guard, plunging the room into even deeper gloom, and the solid thump of the crossbar dropping firmly into place reverberated with an awful finality. There was a moment's stillness, then men stirred, some collapsing wearily onto bunks while a small group coalesced round a table at the far end of the room to begin their interminable game of knucklebones.

A door in the farther wall led to a hole above a stinking cesspit. Even that was surrounded by iron bars driven deep into the earth. The shelves in the recess next to the internal door were piled with wooden bowls, spoons and amphorae of water. Troi got a bowl of stale, tepid water and gulped it down before returning to flop on the lowermost bunk nearest the door. One of the few windows separated his tier from the next, a welcome source of a cooling breeze when the wind was in the right quarter. Gian hauled himself up onto the bunk above and subsided with a huge sigh. The two, along with a young, stringy Keltos called Manannan, red-haired and impressively freckled, had laid claim to this particular set. They had come to an equitable arrangement whereby they exchanged every se'ennight, taking it in turns to enjoy the cooler air of the bottom bed and to endure the enervating heat of the uppermost.

An elderly Eretrian took out his pan pipes and began to play a quiet, haunting tune from the hills of his homeland. Troi lay and listened. He had heard the Eretrian play it many times before. Within the tendrils of its melody, it wrapped the cool green mystery of the forests, the sharp, savage beauty of the uprearing hills, and the jewelled waters of the wooded lakes that hung across his homeland like beads on a string. It sang of a life of freedom that was an aching memory of a happy time. It was a strange feeling, one that seemed at spear point with the flat, unemotional surface of Troi's mind and hinted at something once vibrant and alive that was now lost in the cool, dark depths.

He still lived. That was all that mattered. He had feared that he would just be quietly disposed of, as one more inconvenient irritation, but Marsyas's cupidity had been his salvation. Along with other unfortunates entangled in the sweep net, Troi had been sold to a slaver and thence to Glycon. Now, as always, his thoughts turned to that dream of vengeance. He had deliberately kept his secrets behind his shield, allowing Gian to adopt the role of tutor and guardian and playing the weak, innocent and none too bright acolyte who was clearly no real threat to anyone. He accepted insults and ridicule and an occasional bit of manhandling and had never let his guard slip. Even Gian seemed unaware just how cool, calculating and controlled his young protégé was.

His persona of inoffensive co-operation and total lack of initiative should have quickly brought him out of this dark and dangerous hut as a trusty, but somehow Xarchon had sensed that there was more to this young Mykerenaean than could be seen by the looking and had heeded his instincts.

The Eretrian stopped playing. Gian snored gently. Two men began to quarrel over the knucklebones until a grating voice from somewhere in the thickening gloom told them to shut up. There was instant silence. That was Abantes, a man even bigger than Gian and much nastier. He saw himself as the leader of this troop of lost souls and ruled them with the sadistic enthusiasm of the petty tyrant, a position tolerated, even encouraged, by the knowing Xarchon.

There was but one bone in Abantes' fish, and it stuck painfully in his throat. Gian. He was content to let Abantes play the king, provided he did not interfere with him or those he saw as his. Gian's berserk rage, an unstoppable storm of flailing kicks and punches, totally oblivious of pain or harm, let alone consequences, was legendary. Troi had heard the tale of how Abantes had tried to muscle Gian away from the food pot one evening and paid dearly for the mistake, with half an ear and several front teeth lost. His hatred of Gian was as transparent as the circumspection with which he avoided any subsequent confrontation.

In the silence, the sudden grate of the door bar sounded unnaturally loud. Everybody immediately moved to one side or the other of the hut. Troi climbed from his bunk and shook Gian, who dropped down heavily beside him. The door opened, the painful dazzle of the setting sun streaming in. A guard entered with a long whip and a cudgel. Behind him, stamped dark and depthless against the light, was another with a belly bow. The first guard stepped to his right, and two grey-haired women came in, carrying a large, steaming cauldron between them on a yoke. They lowered it onto a table that stood beside the door and bore innumerable scorch rings from previous visits.

The young girl that Troi had smiled at earlier came after with a basket of coarse bread and a burning oil lamp. Her eyes darted about and locked onto Troi. They flicked urgently to the bread basket. Troi nodded, almost imperceptibly. She gave a smile, but it did not reach her hunted and sorrowful gaze. She placed the basket and lamp on the table, turned on her heel and swiftly followed the first two women. The guard backed out, the door slammed and the bar dropped into position.

TEN

There was a flurry of movement as the slaves moved to the back of the hut to collect bowls and spoons, but Troi went immediately over to the basket. He found a scrap of parchment secreted in the midst of the bread. Gian was at his side, clearly wondering what was going on. Other slaves stopped, their shadows still twisting and contorting in the feeble light of the lamp, and watched him. He angled the scrap to catch the flickering light and read it. For a moment he was disorientated by its message. It was not at all what he was expecting, and he knew all this already. Then his mind was analysing, weighing, predicting, untaxed by emotional baggage, fast as a peregrine plummeting down through a winter's cloudless sky and as sharp and clear as its eyesight. He had a part to play.

He had admitted to hailing from Bogazkoi in a thoughtless moment but had had the sense to make no mention of a massacre. No-one must even guess at what he knew. His debut performance as simple yokel had failed miserably. Now he must play the much more difficult role of shock and devastation. He dropped his hand and simply stared ahead, as if unseeing. He allowed Gian to take the parchment from him, turned and walked back to his bunk where he sat down heavily and put his face in his hands. Perhaps he was being a bit too obvious, he thought. But perhaps not, as Manannan came across, sat beside him and, with a sensitivity that belied his youth, put his arm round Troi's shoulders. Under the cover of his lowered head, Troi held his eyes open against the need to blink until they began to smart, and he was rewarded with a few paltry tears.

'What does it say?' someone whispered.

Gian shook his head in bemusement and handed it to a wiry man standing nearby. 'Here, you can read.'

The man scanned it, cleared his throat, looked around, then proclaimed, 'Bogazkoi has been burned to the ground and everyone massacred. I'm so sorry. Mykerenos is in revolt. The rebels hold Pelium.'

There was silence as they chewed on the news.

Then Abantes hawked and spat. 'Mykerenos in revolt! They hold Pelium! Useless bloody Mickeys! I'll grant you they're fucking revolting, but they couldn't hold their own pricks long enough to have a wank.' He chortled at his own witticism. No-one else did.

Troi stiffened and looked up. This could be trouble.

'As an expert in that particular area, you should know.' Gian's voice was calm. Abantes glared at him, his face suffused with crimson fury, obvious even in the ruddy glow of the lamp. 'They are brave men who deserve respect and honour. They have it from me.'

There was an anonymous, almost inaudible murmur of support, and Abantes spun round, searching in the poor light for the culprits. Then, perhaps realising how ridiculous he looked, he turned back slowly and stared at Gian. 'Blubbering's all Mickeys are good for,' he finally sneered, with a sidelong glance at Troi, Manannan's hand still clasped to his shoulder. 'That, and being affeared to go to sleep.'

'The boy had family and friends there,' said Gian quietly. 'They deserve his tears, and it doesn't make him less of a man. I'll try and explain the concept of a friend to you later, but I fear you'll find it difficult to grasp. That of a man is, of course, beyond you.'

'Are you saying I'm fucking stupid?' spluttered the big man. Someone gave a little laugh, abruptly cut off. Abantes paled and two red spots burned on his cheekbones. His eyes glinted with the reflected fire of the lamp. His shadow on the furthest wall took on monstrous proportions.

'Do I really need to?' asked Gian. This time the laughter spread round the room. It was an affront Abantes could not ignore. They stared at one another. The tension could be felt, as real as the hair-tingling warning that Dyaus sent before he released his fire. No-one moved. Then Abantes shook his head.

'One day, you Thessalian horsefucker,' he muttered.

'Only when I have my back to you,' sneered Gian, 'and not even then.' He deliberately, and with manifest contempt, turned his back on the man to take a crust of bread.

'No,' shouted Troi, leaping to his feet. The bastard had a knife. Where he had managed to get it from, Troi had no idea. Abantes lunged forward and savagely stabbed Gian between the shoulder blades. Everything froze. Even the dancing shadows were stilled. Gian stood motionless, coughed, then collapsed forward and half-rolled to one side. His face was directly towards Troi, and the eyes were open and unmoving. Everyone was pulling back to the walls of the hut, leaving the central area deserted except for Abantes, who turned towards Troi, grinning, the bloody knife in his hand. The look in his eyes said it all. Troi considered a gesture of submission, but that would not stop Abantes now. He had no choice. He stepped forward.

'Well, bugger me. If it ain't the Mickey cry-baby come for the slaughter. The horsefucker's bumboy. Must be my birthday. I get to do two fucking turds in one day.'

'No,' said Troi, 'I think not.' His voice was steady and controlled. 'In fact, it's your death day.'

He felt no emotion. He could read emotion in others, he could respond appropriately, but it was a thing of calculation. He felt nothing. There was, deep beneath the outward show, a turbulent current of rage, but it never caused the slightest ripple on the placid surface. Even lower still, a dark abyss of grief and loss that he refused to acknowledge. He would kill Abantes without hesitation, without regrets, without feeling. Except possibly a grain of satisfaction. Not revenge for Gian. Why should he be concerned about that? Gian had brought it upon himself. But the fleeting and barely conscious thought that, as he could not kill Marsyas, this bastard would have to do instead. For the moment, it would be something. Abantes looked more corpulent than he had thought, and his hair darker. The current shifted nearer the surface.

Abantes merely hefted the knife and laughed. 'Come on then, shitface, and I'll cut your fucking heart out.'

Troi breathed slowly, with no thought except of the huge man and the long blade tracing little circles before him. Emotion was a killer, Aias had always said, but it killed you, not your opponent. And Troi had none. He reached down inside himself for that centre of calm. He felt things slow, his mind crystallising round the single focus of his attention. He could sense Abantes' excitement, his surging confidence, his blood lust. He could read his intentions in his flickering eyes and tensed movements. Troi had no fear, just the clear conviction that he was going to kill him.

It was obvious the man was no knife-fighter. He grasped the knife too firmly, awkwardly, pushed too far forward. He stood flat-footed instead of on the balls of his feet, with his other arm disregarded and simply flailing about as an awkward counterbalance. He believed the knife gave him easy superiority. That it gave him the kill. His fixation on his knife would kill him instead. Troi had learned enough knife-fighting from Aias to outmatch this clumsy ox. But he would have to be swift. From the noises outside, it was obvious that the guards had realised something was going on, and running steps approached the door.

He stepped forward and back again in one fluid motion, swaying away from the clumsy, overly lengthy sweep of the blade with easy confidence, deliberately moving to his right to ensure there was ample space behind him. Abantes lunged forward again, making the expected crude reverse cut. Again, Troi stepped back, but this time his left forearm rose and struck Abantes' arm sideways, adding to the momentum of the sweep, driving the knife safely away and twisting Abantes' body round so that his trunk was square and open to the counter. Troi stepped in and hammered his fist into the man's solar plexus, aiming for his backbone as the imaginary target of his punch. Just as Aias had taught him. The giant doubled up with an explosive exhalation, and Troi jerked his knee up to smash into the descending chin with a jarring blow. Abantes' head snapped back with a sickening crack.

The man went down backwards with a crash, like the sacrificial ox poleaxed at the altar of Dyaus Pitar. It had been surprisingly easy. The bar was being scrambled free and the door flung open to allow a flood of grey twilight to wash across the scene. Abantes was probably dead already, but Troi was taking no chances. 'Never give a downed man the chance to rise,' Aias had always preached. The blade lay on the floor. He knelt swiftly beside the supine figure, picked up the knife and drove it without a moment's hesitation into his heart, just before a cudgel caught him at the side of his head and sent him spinning into a deep, dark place.

ELEVEN

Troi woke with a shock of freezing water in his face. He shook his head and wished he hadn't. It hurt abominably. His arms were pained and numb, thanks to the tight bonds that tied him to a rough wooden chair. His knee, unsurprisingly, hurt, but his side did too. Presumably someone had kicked him. One eye was half closed. His vision was somewhat unfocussed, but he was aware that he was in a room in the villa, and that others were there. Someone was speaking. He wasn't at all sure what they were saying.

'Bastard,' said a voice immediately behind him, and something hit him hard in the side of the mouth. He rocked dangerously but managed to stay upright on the chair. That had been clear enough. He spat out blood. The gravelly voice belonged to Kittos, the biggest and nastiest thug among the guards. 'Hang the fucker.'

Troi wasn't convinced that clarity of hearing had been a positive step forward, although regaining consciousness to begin with had probably been his big mistake.

His vision was also beginning to clear. He lifted his head slightly and looked around. He was plainly in Glycon's office because the fat slug himself, moistening his obscene lips with his nasty little lizard's tongue, sat facing him from behind a marble-topped table. Beyond him was a window through which a shaft of golden sunlight swirled with dust motes.

Something landed on the frame of the window. A beautiful comma butterfly. He gazed at it, at the vivid orange and black patterning in the wings and their intricate wavy edge. Although it was so far away, he could somehow see the quivering of its delicate antennae. He knew that it meant something. It seemed so important that he was not really aware of the voices.

Kittos hit him again. This time on his temple. He sensed it coming and instinctively rode the blow. So Kittos hit him once more.

'Stop that,' said Glycon, with his damp, sibilant voice. 'Whatever we do, we don't want him beaten to death. Not yet.'

'Too bloody easy,' said the figure to his side. That was Xarchon. 'Crucify him.'

Troi stared at Glycon, silhouetted against the shaft of liquid gold, where he could not read his facial expression. The butterfly raised its wings and lazily pottered off into the wide-open sky, into freedom. Troi watched it go. It was all so symbolic. He hurt. He hurt badly. The pain in his temple was searing his brain. If they were going to kill him, let them get on with it. He just didn't care. The butterfly was there again. Growing larger. Breaking into a mosaic of shimmering colour. Becoming…

Something was wrong, but he had no idea what. It was far away and beyond comprehension. He had no sense of where he was or even who he was. There was no self, just a feeling of dislocation and then a sudden coming together, and his bruised cheek was resting on cold, hard tessellated flooring, and he knew where he was. He felt sick. The sour burn of vomit was in the back of his mouth, swamping the iron taste of blood. He must have passed out. He lay there and did not move. At least they were not hitting him.

'…make an example to others,' Xarchon was saying. There was irritation in his voice.

'I've already lost two valuable slaves. What in Hades is the point of throwing a third into the midden? I don't grow money in my bean patch.' Glycon sounded petulant.

'Listen. If you don't make him dance a mid-air jig, he'll become a symbol, a leader. The man who kills and lives, the evidence, in the living flesh, that a slave can take action for himself…' Xarchon paused. '…and survive. He will be a precedent.'

Troi had never regarded Xarchon as a master of rhetoric, but he was impressed. The pause had been masterly. Hades, he was almost convincing *him*.

Xarchon hammered away relentlessly. 'I've seen it happen before. You'll end up having to kill him anyway.'

Glycon sighed heavily. 'I understand Abantes killed Gian first.'

'That makes not the slightest difference. This little shit killed another slave. No excuses.'

'Dangle the bugger,' muttered Kittos behind him, and gave him an absent-minded kick. Troi grunted with pain.

'No.' Glycon had decided. 'I'll sell him. Get something back.'

'Who, by all the Gods, is going to buy a sodding killer?' demanded Xarchon.

'When I got there,' rumbled Kittos, 'he fucking knew I was coming, but he was going to finish off that stupid lump Abantes first.'

'But he wasn't in a rage,' added Xarchon. 'It was calculated. Deliberate. Cold.'

'He seemed innocuous enough,' mused the slave owner.

'They're the most dangerous,' snapped Xarchon. 'He's a natural killer. It means nothing to him. You would have thought the little runt was but thin gruel, but, by all accounts, he took that stupid bugger apart as easy as eating his porridge. Unless you can sell him to the Arkosians, you won't find any takers.'

Troi had heard of the Arkosians. They were a much-feared group of professional assassins about whom legends accreted like moss on a boulder. It was an intriguing thought.

'I won't be so stupid as to sell him here. I'll sell him to a slave trader who can take him far away and make his profit.' Glycon considered the bruised and battered body lying before him and sighed. 'Koronos is due any day now. He'll drive a hard bargain, and I'll lose on the deal, but at least I'll get something back from this balls-up.'

'You'd get something back if you dangled him,' declared Xarchon, refusing to concede defeat. 'It would cow the slaves and no mistake. Less trouble in the future.'

'For you, maybe,' snapped Glycon, 'but not for me. My mind is settled. Throw him in the lockup. And he is to be fed and treated well.' He paused and then corrected himself. 'Well, relatively well. I don't want him marked, or weak. I want him looking strong and healthy. I want some money back from this bloody mess.'

The bloody mess was hauled to his feet. When he had collapsed, they had cut the ropes that held him. He had no strength in his legs, and they half-marched, half-carried him away. So, he wasn't going to die today. That was a bit of a surprise. Perhaps butterflies were divine omens. Perhaps that shaft of sunlight had been a sign from Apollon that he was a true Basilides. Kittos punched him in the back of the head.

Xarchon looked at him questioningly.

Kittos shrugged. 'Won't show there.'

TWELVE

She stopped in front of him and surveyed him. Troi studiously stared ahead, not making eye contact. She was wealthy, if the fine material of her saffron chiton and the delicate silver pendant around her neck were any guide. In her early twenties, she was slightly chubby and large-breasted, with big brown eyes in a round, rather plain, but pleasant enough face. Her long, light brown hair was a complex creation of braids and ringlets.

About him, the agora seethed with the denizens of the small town of Oenone, hawkers shouting their wares and slaves purchasing the early-morning bread and vegetables. Prostitutes passed through with exaggerated hip movements, the studs in their sandals imprinting "Follow me" messages in the ground. Men and women greeted one another, haggled and argued, pushed busily through the throng or dawdled along.

Few took notice of the group of desolate slaves standing in a small pool of silence before the shrine to Dyaus Pitar. Slaves were expensive, scarcely an impulse purchase, and most buyers would go to a proper slave market. But the thin, hawk-faced Koronos, passing through on the way to the Great Market at Leuctra, had set out his wares at a venture. He materialised at the woman's elbow, stooping slightly and obsequiously, with one hand rubbing the other in a characteristic mannerism of his.

'Ah, you have a good eye, my Lady.' He had a strong Phthian accent. 'Only young, but strong, fit and eager to learn. And to please. With stamina to spare. You can mould him to whatever purpose you require.' There was no disguising the salacious overtones to his comment. 'I am Koronos, the fortunate seller of such a fine specimen.'

The woman merely gave him a sidelong glance, then half-turned to the muscular, middle-aged man at her shoulder. He was strong-featured, with short brown hair and a neatly trimmed beard, standing tall and straight as a spear, with brooding, dark eyes. He leaned forward and murmured something in her ear. She nodded.

'Is he servitude-bred?' Her voice was low but clear, her enunciation perfect. She had obviously been coached by a rhetorician.

'Indeed, my Lady. A well-trained house slave too, not a field hand, as will be seen in his manners and absolute discretion.'

Troi had been warned in no uncertain manner as to what would happen if he gainsaid Koronos's lies. He was not really concerned, however. Like Glycon, the man was too much in love with money to risk devaluing his merchandise.

The tall man stepped forward, took Troi's hands and turned them over, regarding them but briefly. He then pulled the shoulder of Troi's tunic down and inspected the sigma branded into his left shoulder.

'Indeed, then why are his hands calloused? And his wrists show the marks of manacles. And why are his arms sunburned and the slave mark two moontides old at most?'

Koronos blanched, wilting under the avalanche of accusations. He had not expected such expertise in a small provincial town.

The man took a cloth from his pouch and rubbed it on Troi's cheek. 'White lead and honey to cover some fairly impressive bruises.'

Koronos just stared, his mouth seemingly refusing to move.

The man looked at Troilus. 'What is the name of your owner?' he asked, indicating the discomfited slaver with a slight tilt of his head.

'Koronos, sir.'

The man smiled fleetingly. 'The burr is unmistakable. You're a Mykerenaean, then?'

'Yes, sir.'

He turned to the cringing Phthian. 'So, this would not be the Mickey slave who killed one of his fellows? There have been rumours.'

Troi glanced up with interest. This might be fun.

Koronos's face hardened. It was not the first time the rumours had preceded them. He strongly suspected that Glycon, that vindictive bastard, was responsible, in retaliation for the hard bargain that Koronos had forced.

The man pursed his lips and looked down his nose at the disconcerted slaver. Troi felt like smiling, but thought an impassive face was probably the safest option.

Koronos did not know what to say. He just might be able to wriggle out of it with stories of the lad being pressed into field service for a short period and the brand just happening to look recent, but if he denied the lad's history that could soon be checked. Glycon would be only too delighted to confirm it. And selling a slave who had killed without revealing the fact was a hanging matter. But if he quickly 'remembered' it, they could immediately drag him before the town archon for manifest dissimulation; to have his nose slit as a visual warning to all that he was a cheat and liar. He glared at Troi. The bastard would probably deliberately land him in it, just out of spite. He opened and closed his mouth, and nothing came out. Sweat beaded his brow.

The tall man smiled grimly. 'Let's ask the boy.' He cocked his head slightly to one side, raised a quizzical eyebrow and said, 'Well, lad?'

Troi nodded. 'I killed another slave, sir, yes.'

Koronos's blood drained from his face, and his hand unconsciously reached for his neck.

'Why?' The woman's large, brown eyes were fixed on his.

Troi risked a very slight shrug. 'He was coming for me with a knife. He'd just used it to kill my friend. He'd stabbed him in the back.'

'Did you have a knife?' asked the tall man.

'No, sir.'

The man made a noncommittal grunt. 'Why did he come for you?'

'I was Gian's friend, sir. That seemed to be reason enough.'

'What was it all about?' asked the woman. She spoke to him naturally, as though to an equal, without the sense of dehumanisation that Troi had found to be the norm among aristocrats and slave owners.

'Status, my Lady.' She looked at him enquiringly. 'The man wanted to be the head wolf. My friend didn't want to be part of such a pack.' She nodded.

'Have you killed anyone else?' the man demanded.

'Yes, sir. Six men and a girl.' He had asked, and Troi saw no reason not to tell him.

The woman looked shocked. The man did not look at all surprised.

She stared at him, wide eyed. 'A girl?' she breathed.

'Yes, my Lady. She had a gut wound. It was the only thing to do.' His voice carried no trace of emotion.

She looked across at her companion, who merely inclined his head in agreement. 'And the others?' she whispered.

'Three the same. They were going to die anyway. Gave them an easy passage over the Styx. One was trapped under a fallen beam and I cut his throat.' He didn't know why he was being so exhaustively, and dangerously, honest. Koronos was now looking positively murderous. But he just didn't care. What importance did it have? 'Two others made the mistake of coming back. They were the bastards who did it.'

'Did what, lad?' asked the man quietly.

'Destroyed Bogazkoi, sir.'

'You were at Bogazkoi?' the woman demanded with the look of horror still inscribed on her face.

'It was my home, my Lady.'

'We have heard rumours,' said the man. 'So, they are true?'

'Yes, sir.'

'The two who came back. You killed them?' Her eyes never left his. She seemed to be searching for something.

'I did.' He said it as though commenting on the weather.

She did not enquire how. Instead, she unexpectedly asked, 'Do you dream?'

That caught him on the hip. He hesitated for just a heartbeat. 'No.'

She regarded him steadily for some time. Then she turned to the man. 'I think so, Ilus.'

He shook his head violently. 'He's a killer, Klio.'

'It seems he had reason for it.'

'Perhaps, if he's telling the truth, but that doesn't make him the less a killer. Look at his eyes. There's nothing in them. I can't allow it. It would be too great a risk.'

'I have looked in his eyes, and I have seen what I expected to see.' Troi was puzzled. She was probably some kind of idiot out with her minder. Her tone suddenly hardened. 'I'm sorry, but it is my throw of the knucklebones.'

'Klio,' the man called Ilus said urgently. 'This is not a good idea.'

'No.' Her voice was iron. He held up his hands in defeat and shook his head. Perhaps not a minder for the half-witted, then. She turned to the slave trader, who was looking amazed but delighted at the sudden wheel of events. 'What are you asking?'

'Nothing,' said Ilus. They both looked at him. 'Or we can take it to the archon to adjudicate.' Koronos looked nauseous.

She laughed. She had a musical laugh. 'It would indeed be just,' she agreed, 'but give him something suitable. I will not take advantage of a poor unfortunate.'

To consider such a sadistic bastard to be an unfortunate seemed a somewhat idiosyncratic view of life to Troi. Perhaps the idiot theory was still viable.

Her companion humphed but drew out a leather pouch and counted some coins for the trader. Koronos looked pleased. It was probably more than he had been going to ask.

'What's your name, lad?' asked Ilus.

'Troilus, sir.'

'You are now in the service of the Lady Kalliope, daughter of Deukalion, of the clan Antipatroi.' He did not look overly pleased about it.

Probably as good as anywhere, thought Troi. He wouldn't be there long.

THIRTEEN

HE WAS GIVEN a small, whitewashed cell in the slaves' quarters which was surprisingly comfortable, furnished with a simple bed with a wool-stuffed mattress, a table and stool, and even an amphora of well-watered wine.

Eirene, the housemistress, was tall and sticklike, with grey hair pulled sternly back from her rather gloomy countenance. She sent him to the bathhouse for 'a forlorn attempt to remove some of the less ingrained layers of filth.' When he returned, she sniffed dismissively, as he had known she would, and then gave him two new tunics with the sigil of the Antipatroi—a coiled serpent—embroidered on the chest, two cloaks, a pair of sandals, some loincloths and a bundle of blankets, and left him to settle in.

He ate with the other slaves and servants in the communal hall, simple fare, but ample and good. He was puzzled. There seemed to be few actual slaves, most being bonded servants, and those that were slaves generally seemed old, cheerful and distinctly unservile in their demeanour. There was much laughter and good-natured banter, and there was no discernible distinction between the slaves and servants. The only way that he could identify the former was by the sigma burned onto their upper arms.

The one sitting next to him was a chubby-faced youth who kept giggling, but did not respond to Troi's attempt to speak to him. A serving woman, with a withered arm, told him that Koinos was a good lad, but a bit simple, so to give him no mind. The solid, competent-looking man to his left half-turned towards Troi. His eyes were strangely unfocussed, and when he reached for his wine without looking, Troi realised that he was blind.

'Where do you hail from, lad?' he asked.

'Bogazkoi,' Troi answered without thinking.

The word fell like a stone and silenced all those around him, and the ripples of quiet spread through the entire room until, except for the chatter and clatter coming from the adjacent kitchen, the room was as hushed as a graveyard at midnight. Troi could have kicked himself. But it was too late.

A man of distinguished appearance, sitting at the head of the long table, spoke, fixing Troi with an intense stare. 'Bogazkoi? Is it true, then, what they are saying? The Holokauston.'

It was the first time Troi had heard it called that. He should have denied any knowledge, continuing to play the long, safe game of silence. But something had changed. The river had broken the final bank and was raging down new courses. There was no stopping it.

'If they are saying that five thousand innocent people were massacred by that bastard Marsyas, and the place burned to the ground, and for no reason, none at all, then that is true.'

A young man rose from the farther end of the long table and slipped quietly from the room.

'Then how is it that you survived?' The man's gaze never wavered. Nobody was moving. A serving woman came in and stopped.

Troi belatedly realised what he had done, but could not stop now. 'I was returning from a hunting trip. I stayed hidden in the trees. I saw the Trog forces just about to march away from a burning town and piles of corpses. They just waited to behead ten of the chief citizens, and then they left.'

'Some say it was the Eleans,' said a large man halfway down the opposite side.

Troi shook his head savagely. 'Marsyas had some Eleans with him. He had them killed as cover. It was Imperial troops.'

'Imperial troops would never do such a thing,' interrupted a white-faced woman.

'They did.'

Ilus came hurrying in. 'Iphiclus.' He nodded shortly at the man at the head of the table. 'May I take young Troilus for a word.' It was not a request.

'Of course,' said Iphiclus, as though it was.

Ilus beckoned, and Troi immediately rose and followed him from the room, which exploded into excited talk behind him. Ilus led him from the servants' block and across to the villa itself, going in through a side door by the washhouse. They entered a corridor and Ilus ushered him through the first door into a spacious and well-furnished andron. From the arms displayed on the walls and the set of finely crafted armour hanging on a crow, Troi assumed it to be his personal quarters.

'Sit,' Ilus said. His voice held iron.

Troi sat on a beautifully carved klismos. He braced himself. Ilus stood over him and glowered.

'You are still very young,' he spoke slowly but intently, 'and should perhaps be permitted a certain degree of latitude. But even allowing for that, that was incredibly stupid.'

'I know.' He did too, but it seemed unimportant.

Ilus sat down heavily in the twin of Troi's chair, visibly composed himself and leaned back against the curved backrest. 'Then why in Hades did you do it?'

Troi thought. 'I suppose I have been hiding the truth for so long, admitting it to you and my Lady broke some sort of dam.' He looked straight at Ilus. 'I just wanted to tell everyone what that bastard did.'

'And what do you think "that bastard" will do when he learns that there is a surviving eyewitness? And one well within his grasp.' His voice suddenly hardened. 'And what do you think he will do to the woman who sheltered him?'

Troi had not thought of that. But she had made her own choices. 'He couldn't,' he said confidently. 'She was not to know.'

'She did know,' pointed out the elder man instantly.

'But they won't know that.'

'The slave trader knows. If there is a profit in it, he will not be slow in casting the discus. And she certainly can't pretend not to know now.' He paused. 'The only sensible thing to do, under the circumstances, is to send you off to Marsyas tied and trussed as a sacrificial goat.'

'I understand,' he said. Strangely, all he felt was disappointment that he would be unable to kill Marsyas.

Ilus looked at Troi keenly. 'But he would then know that she knows.'

Troi managed to stay a somewhat tactless shrug.

'In fact, everyone here now knows. Perhaps we should keep a watch for Eleans.' It was a grim joke, and he wasn't laughing.

Troi suddenly sat upright. 'Perhaps that's the answer,' he said. 'Spread the word as quickly and as far as possible.' He remembered Doreios's words. 'Start a forest fire that he can't stamp out. He couldn't risk attacking this place then. It would be too obvious, and it's not even in his satrapy.'

'Which *he* are you referring to?' asked Ilus. 'Marsyas? The idea may well work. But Laomedon? It was done in his name. He would destroy this villa and all in it with a click of his fingers, merely as a salutary lesson for the rest. He rules by fear alone.' He sat, thinking. Troi watched him.

Eventually he spoke. 'It's partly my fault, I admit. I should have told you to keep your mouth shut. It never occurred to me that you would sound the salpinx at the first opportunity. And to almost the entire household.' There was a sudden flash of anger. 'Dyaus's balls, but you have let the wolves into the sheepfold and no mistake.' He exhaled in a long, lingering breath. 'We have one hope. My Lady engenders fierce loyalty in her household. And anyone who fails to show that loyalty, I quietly get rid of. That is not for my Lady's ears. You will learn discretion, and quickly. I shall speak to the entire household. As for you, you will not mention Bogazkoi again, even if directly asked. Do you understand?'

Troi nodded.

'I just pray that we do not have anyone else so uncaring and careless as to put my Lady in such peril.'

There was a moment's silence. Then Ilus began again, his tone more measured. 'There is more. I would have said this in due course, but now seems to be an appropriate time.' He regarded Troi shrewdly. 'You will have noticed something a little odd about the villa. A strange preponderance of three-legged cats, aged dogs and donkeys bearing old whip scars. Slaves and servants who are too old and decrepit to do useful work, or those like Koinos who are just incapable. We have servants who cannot speak for stammering, deaf-mutes, the blind and the ailing.' He waved his hand vaguely to indicate that the list was too long to enumerate. 'My Lady collects the sick, lame and damaged.' He sighed. 'She can't help it. It's her nature.'

Troi looked up. 'Are you saying that I'm one of the sick, lame and damaged?'

'I am indeed.'

Troi was in a rockslide, tumbling back down the mountain he had so laboriously climbed. 'In what way?' He seemed incredulous, though within him there was something, deep, well hidden, cowed. It knew, and he could not deny it.

'You know in what way,' said Ilus implacably.

Troi almost smiled. 'You think I'm a killer.'

'Rather more than that.' He rose and went across to a highly polished side table, on which were an amphora of wine in an intricate metal cradle and some black-figured kylixes. Surprisingly, he made a gesture of invitation, but Troi shook his head. Ilus poured himself some wine, added spring water from a bronze jug and returned. He remained standing.

'I'm a killer too. I've more men waiting for my spirit to cross the Styx than most. But you've something far more deep and dangerous. Killing to you is nothing. You feel nothing. You have no…' He searched for the right word. '… real contact, no genuine and meaningful relationship with others. No feelings. You are closed in. You have the storm covers in place and the door barred.'

Troi had the urge to protest, but that small voice within was trying to tell him that Ilus had the right of it. He made an effort to silence it, but it would not be stilled.

Ilus looked at him. His eyes were surprisingly sad. 'I've seen others like you, boy. You make good soldiers but bad people. And it can't be cured. I tried to warn my Lady. But she saw hurt in you, and that was enough. I can't see the hurt, just the ice. Anyway, I can't gainsay her. She's far stronger than she seems. But you could bring harm to her. In one way or another.'

There was a different light in his eye now, and Troi did not like it.

'So, I'm warning you. The instant you do anything that could damage my Lady, I'll kill you. And don't think that I can't.'

Troi looked at the man, hard and fit, standing with a swordfighter's perfect balance, and with an air of quiet but indisputable confidence, and he knew that he could.

'I was swordmaster at Gla. For only a short period, until Laomedon replaced the holder with a complete bastard who wanted his own men in position. But I was taught by none other than Diomedes, so do not flatter yourself you could stand in the same arena.'

A sistrum rang quietly in Troi's head at the name, but he could not make the connection and knew nothing of the man. However, Ilus spoke with such assurance that Troi knew it was not good news.

Ilus finally sat down and took a sip of his wine. 'So, what are we going to do with you?' The sudden switch from menace to almost jovial conversation jarred. 'You say you're a hunter?'

Troi nodded cautiously. Never trust a purring lion.

'Well, the lower slopes of the Rhodopians are teeming with game, and a change in diet is always welcome. You can draw a decent bow from the major-domo and fetch in some deer and boar. That would be nice.' He signalled at the door with his eyes. 'You may go,' he said abruptly.

Troi walked back to his room. Those he passed looked at him strangely but did not speak. He collapsed on his bed. His mind was in full gallop. This man was giving a slave weapons and sending him up into the mountains of Gean Thrake, whence he could begin the long trek back to Mykerenos. Was he setting him up as a wand to shoot at, giving himself an opportunity to quietly kill him, or simply opening the door and ridding himself of an inconvenient and dangerous interloper by letting him walk away? Whatever he was doing, it was not stupidity or carelessness. It was premeditated and potentially fatal. This would need very careful handling. After a while, Troi fell asleep. Though he did not want to.

FOURTEEN

THE ENTIRE HOUSEHOLD was gathered in the eating room of the servants' quarters. Fifty souls. Ilus and Troi stood at one end, a circle of space and silence round them. The small crowd shifted and muttered.

'Household,' said Ilus quietly. The noise quickly died away, and everyone stood still and expectantly. 'Household of the Lady Kalliope.' His voice was stronger. He was reminding them of to whom they owed allegiance. 'The slave Troilus is to speak.' He gestured Troi forward with a slight movement of his head.

Troi took a step to the front and cleared his throat. 'My comments of last night were totally untrue. I was not at Bogazkoi and know nothing of its fate. I was just trying to sound important. I'm sorry.'

No-one believed him, he knew that, but that was not the point. The wine could not be put back into the smashed amphora. A susurration of comments passed through the throng.

'Household,' said Ilus again, and the murmurs stopped. 'Listen very carefully. There is no truth in the story the slave told. But there is real jeopardy in it. To tell others of what you have heard is to pass on lies that are a danger to the Empire. They are a canker that will eat at the roots of the authority of our true Emperor. If he decides that such a canker needs to be cut out…' He emphasised the words and paused to let them do their fearful work in the minds of his audience. '…then he has the power and right to do so.' There were several audible intakes of breath, and a woman gave a strangled sob. 'And this will include my Lady, to whom you all owe so much.' He let them think about that, too, for a few heartbeats. 'Fleeing will be no good. You know the reputation of the Emperor's Krypteia.' There was a nervous stirring. Laomedon's hated and powerful internal police force was greatly feared.

'I must therefore warn you to forget this unfortunate slave's stupid and lying words. Under no circumstances must you repeat them to anyone. I emphasise anyone. Not even your best and most trusted friend. It must stay securely locked within the walls of the Villa of the Antipatroi. From this moment, until you are told otherwise, no-one will leave the grounds except with my express permission. No visitors will be allowed.'

He swept over them with a grim look. 'Your lives are in your own hands. Or rather your own mouths. You shall not talk of this, even to one another. If I hear of anyone speaking of this, I will have them whipped, regardless of my Lady.'

People shifted uneasily and glanced at one another. Whipping was unknown in the villa.

'Is that understood?' he barked.

There was a murmur of acquiescence.

'Now, return to your tasks and lock this lie so deep in your minds that you will never be able to find it again. Your lives depend upon it.' He turned and stalked out.

Troi looked out at fifty pairs of eyes staring back at him. They did not look at all friendly. He didn't really care. They would not stop him gutting that fat bastard, Marsyas.

FIFTEEN

TROI WAS SENT to the major-domo.

A taciturn servant, who refused to meet Troi's eyes, escorted him there, taking him through a side door into the villa. They went through the bustling kitchen, the chatter falling silent as he passed, and then through the central courtyard, where beautifully manicured bushes in fine terracotta pots stood about a circular central pool with its mosaic of a dolphin shimmering beneath the pellucid water. A door at the farther side gave access to a corridor which was well lit with horn-covered skylights. An ornately carved oaken door faced him, but his guide turned right and passed down the corridor to a much more workaday door at its end.

Troi scratched and entered. His grumpy escort waited

outside. It was a fairly small box-like office with a single window. A heavily studded door led off to what Troi guessed was a strong room, and every wall was covered in a framework of open wooden boxes individually labelled and full of jumbles of scrolls and piles of wax tablets. Otherwise, all the office contained was a large table and a stool. And the major-domo.

To Troi's complete lack of surprise, he proved to be Iphiclus, the distinguished-looking man who had opened yesterday's disastrous interrogation. He was tall and long-faced, with a fine head of flaxen hair and a pair of unfriendly eyes that surveyed Troi with manifest distaste. Troi guessed that he had received a verbal pummelling for his lack of thought and discretion, and blamed Troi for it.

Iphiclus glanced down at a scroll before him. 'One Troilus, I believe.'

'Yes, sir,' said Troi, standing straight in the customary manner, his hands behind his back, his eyes carefully lowered. He had learned well under the lash of Xarchon.

'No hunting,' declared Iphiclus, without any preamble and with sadistic satisfaction. Then, after a malicious pause. 'At least, not until we have spoken to the local tribal chief. We wouldn't want any unpleasantness, would we?' The curl of his lip indicated that he would actually be quite happy with it.

The Villa Antipatroi lay on the very border with Gean Thrake. Technically, Gean Thrake was another province of the Troian Empire, though no-one seemed to have bothered to inform the wild and bellicose Thracians, who remained a law unto themselves, finding the very idea of a border a thing of bemused incomprehension.

The estate was superbly situated high in the foothills of

the Rhodopians, set within a semicircle of mature woodland and overlooking a small river. In the distance lay the port of Leuctra with the sparkling waters of the Gulf of Scylla beyond. Behind the villa and its cluster of associated buildings rose the craggy and sharp-topped summit of Mount Rhodope itself. Superbly situated, but vulnerably so. Keeping on good relations with the Thracians was a priority.

So, speaking to the local horse lord made sense. Troi didn't want any unpleasantness either. The Thracians enjoyed a reputation for being pretty good at it. The delay would be but a minor inconvenience. Indeed, he needed time to prepare. Marsyas would wait for him. He continued to stare at Iphiclus's chest, stone-faced. The major-domo appeared to be irritated by this disappointing lack of response.

'Whitewashing gang,' he snapped. 'Dismissed.'

Troi's guide, with a distinct smirk on his face, led him off to the group of three men busily engaged in the annual task of whitewashing the villa. They were as sullen and unwelcoming as the rest, but as Troi worked quietly with them in the patchy but warm sun, they gradually began to thaw and to talk to him. When he was instructed to carefully, though speedily, paint round the house martin nests, and not to disturb them at any price, as those were the Mistress's orders, it gave him the opportunity to do some gentle probing.

It was clear that Ilus had been right. They absolutely adored her. They each had a tale to tell of how she had rescued them, one from penury, another from a savage family feud, and had given them a home. Phoebus, the youngest and friendliest, a handsome-looking youth with a mass of golden curls, had the falling sickness. He had been thrown out of his home because of this curse sent by the Gods. He loved scrolls and had been given free access to the Mistress's large library, which resulted in his speaking like a venerable pedagogue, a mannerism at odds with his cherubic appearance.

Troilus was atop a ladder, painting swiftly round a nest as the distracted birds swooped and chattered about his head, when Eirene approached. He had learned that, despite her abrupt manner and her stern and rather forbidding appearance, she was actually a kindly soul. Known universally as Auntie, she was the first person anyone in the household would turn to in case of trouble. She made sure of it. Her mission in life was to protect her beloved Mistress.

'Troilus,' she called. 'My Lady wishes to see you. Phoebus will show you the way.' She surveyed the wall, her arms folded tightly beneath her bosom. Before turning and walking away, she nodded towards a slightly greyer patch and said severely, 'You've missed a bit.'

Phoebus grinned after her. 'Auntie would have been sorely disappointed had we not.' He wiped his hands on an old cloth. 'Come with me.'

SIXTEEN

PHOEBUS SCRATCHED THE silver plate set in the middle of the ornate oaken door.

'Come in.'

The voice was strong and clear and reminded Troi of the flute-like overtones in a blackbird's song. They entered a large and well-appointed andron, the floor vibrantly tessellated and the walls hung with expensive rugs. It was full of lustrously polished and intricately carved furniture. Kalliope was laid on a couch that was covered with a richly embroidered material and possessed of ornate lion legs, the claws inlaid with gold. She was wearing a chiton of rich red, with a gold band through her long light brown hair, the braids and ringlets now brushed out. She smiled, revealing even white teeth.

'Ah, Phoebus. How are you?'

'I am exceedingly well, my Lady, I thank you.'

'No more bouts of the falling sickness?' she asked anxiously. 'No-one has mentioned any.'

'No, my Lady, there have been no occurrences for some considerable time, I am gratified to report.'

'You will tell me, now, if there are?'

He inclined his head. 'I shall indeed, my Lady.'

'Well, get about your business, then,' she said with mock sternness.

'My Lady.' Phoebus turned and left.

She looked at Troi. 'Sit down, please.' She gestured him towards the couch facing her. Troi did so, the softness of the upholstery catching him by surprise as he sank farther than anticipated, and he started.

She laughed easily. 'Don't worry, you're quite safe.'

He didn't doubt it, but kept the smile from his face.

'I hope you're being careful round the martins' nests.'

'We are, my Lady.'

'Good. It would be nice if you would drop all the "my Lady's". They become a bit of a bore, and I want to talk to you.'

'At your command,' he said formally. He wasn't quite sure where this was going and had decided to take the defensive high ground.

'Oh dear, we're not like that, Troi!' He immediately noted her use of the diminutive form of his name. 'I just want us to talk as friends.'

Troi was instantly wary. Friends were not good. They abandoned you. Like family. Best not to have them.

'Would you like some wine? It must be warm work out there.'

'Thank you. I would.'

He was surprised when she rose herself and went to a side table containing a bronze amphora and a silver jug of spring water. She mixed half and half in an expensive-looking red-figured kylix and brought it to him. He thanked her and sipped the wine. It was very good.

She went and sat down on her couch, tucking her legs beneath her. He could not help but be aware of the inviting shadow of her cleavage and her large, well-formed breasts. She seemed to notice his involuntary glance and smiled slightly.

'I see that you can be a little indiscreet,' she said mildly.

For a heartbeat he thought she was referring to his social impropriety, but then realised she was talking of his comments of last night. He lowered his eyes dutifully. 'I'm sorry. I didn't think.'

'That's all right, no harm done.' She wore a mischievous look. 'I had to put up with a great many "I told you so's" and "I did warn you's" from Ilus, but I'm used to that. He has my best interests at heart, the poppet.'

Troi smiled to himself. Calling Ilus a poppet was about the same discus throw as referring to a lion with a sore head as a cuddly kitten. Ilus would have been mortified.

'Are you comfortably settled in?'

'I am, I thank you.' He found it hard to eradicate the formal note from his speech. Nor did he really want to. He regarded all this with a measure of suspicion.

There was a slightly strained pause, then she let out a long breath and looked serious. 'Let me tell you about my father.' She moistened her lips, thought for a few heartbeats, then began. 'He was a kindly and a happy man. Though he grieved greatly when my mother died. He went to fight for his true Emperor, your namesake, Troilus IV.'

Troi was startled. Laomedon had ruthlessly usurped the throne and murdered the young Emperor. He was unforgiving of those who had the temerity to point it out. She was talking treason. To a slave. To do so was to give him power over her, although she had no reason to trust him, as she must have known. All he would have to do was get the information to the nearest Krypteia agent.

'He fought at Iron Rock.'

Troi knew of it, the final desperate battle of the rebellion, in which the numerically superior forces of Laomedon had unsurprisingly emerged victorious, followed by the casual slaughter of Troilus IV. Troi's own uncles had died there.

'I don't know what happened, what he saw, what he suffered, what he might even have done. But he came home a different man. Haunted by ghosts. He no longer laughed. There was no affection in his eyes. They were dead and cold.'

'A killer's eyes,' murmured Troi. He knew where she was going.

'Ilus's description, not mine.' She lay on the couch, propped up on one arm, and was silent for several hekates. Her look was distant. She was elsewhere in time. She shook herself slightly.

'He would wake screaming every night, every single night, his bed soaked with sweat. I'd go to him, but he would not tell me his dreams. He'd get angry and shout at me to leave. But I kept returning. I knew my real father was in there, unable to get out. Unable to reach out to me. Trapped within his memories.'

She stopped for a moment. There was an emotion stamped on her face that he could not identify. Then she began again, her words halting. He sensed she was fighting for control.

'I kept trying, and eventually he began to tell me things. Fragments. Things that often didn't make sense. But it seemed to calm him. And I saw my father coming back to me. Very slowly, but he was coming, step by broken step.'

Troi's leg cramped slightly and he stretched it out to ease it. She was all but oblivious of him. Now totally in a world of her own.

'My father began to smile. Occasionally he would take my hand. Sometimes he slept through the night and was never tormented by the night hag.'

She stopped and swallowed convulsively. Her final words were in a barely audible whisper. 'Then one day Herakla gripped him, and he was dead within the dekate.'

He saw what he assumed to be pain in her eyes.

'He was coming,' she said. Her voice had regained some of its strength. 'But he never made it back. He died still haunted by his ghosts and daemons.'

'And I have the same eyes,' said Troi, amused by the revelation, but careful not to show it.

She blinked, then looked at him. 'You do. And you look tired. Do you wake screaming in the night too?'

That took him aback. 'No,' he said. It was the truth. As far as it went.

But he was not going to tell her of his dreams, when the night hag came and squatted on his chest and poured poison into his mind. How he would be kissing Phoebe, dark-haired, moon-faced Phoebe with the large eyes and the sensuous, mobile mouth, the scent of rosewater in the air, their tongues enwrapped, his questing hands stealing within her tunic to cup and fondle her full breasts, feeling her nipples harden beneath his fumbling touch. Then, how she would draw back with a ghastly death's-head smile that would freeze him to the spot, a mass of maggots squirming and tumbling from her empty eye sockets and surging from her slack-jawed mouth in a sickening cascade. He could feel the tip of the long knife in her desiccated and yellowing hand probing slowly just below his sternum, knew that his death was upon him, and he could not move. He could not blink or breathe. The knife would delicately and unhurriedly penetrate up, parting muscle tissue and slipping between blood vessels, seeking his heart with agonisingly slow deliberation. A heart which beat as wildly as that of any captive bird.

And so he would wake, not screaming, as Kalliope had asked and he had denied, but clamped rigid by the horror and terror of the dream. His bed would be damp and cold with sweat, though—in this she had guessed rightly. Every night, without fail, the dream came. Every night the same, so that he dreaded to sleep. At Glycon's, he had fought it all night, blundering around the next day, eyes red-rimmed, stumbling with exhaustion, only to collapse into a deep slumber the moment he lay upon his bunk. He had learned, in those first two weeks, to accept sleep, for all that his mind screamed and howled against it, knowing that after his waking, he would sleep heavily and untroubled for the rest of the night.

He glanced across at her. She was watching him closely and rightly did not believe him.

'You must be honest with me, Troi. You must talk to me. I can help you. I know I can.' There was an element of desperation in her voice.

He understood. She was trying to save her father again. Perhaps she, too, woke up screaming at her failure. And she could achieve now what she had failed to then. Through him. Arrive at some kind of ease. Assuage some imagined guilt. But this new attempt was doomed to failure in its turn. He had night hags, but so did many people, and, after all, he had cause. Otherwise there was nothing wrong with him. How could he be saved from himself? She seemed to think she could bring him back, but he'd never been away, for Dyaus's sake. It made no sense to him. It was all babble and nonsense. He said nothing.

'All I'm asking is that you talk to me. You don't have to tell me anything that you don't want to. Please, Troi.' She was pleading. The mistress pleading with the slave.

'I'll try,' he found himself saying. He wasn't at all sure why. She visibly relaxed with the relief.

'Thank you.'

This was an exceedingly odd mistress-slave relationship. Troi was both intrigued and wary.

'Would you come and see me every day at the third dekate?'

'Of course, my Lady.' He slightly emphasised the honorific.

She picked up on the subtle signal. 'You may go, Troi. Until the morrow, then.' She smiled again, though this time it did not reach her eyes. Troi guessed that talking about her father had been difficult for her. Perhaps it would help her, at least. He supposed that it could do him no harm.

'My Lady,' he said again, placed the kylix on the marble-topped table at his side, rose, bowed his head, and turned and left.

She watched him go.

SEVENTEEN

For the next ten days he dutifully reported for his interrogation, as he thought of it. It was no hardship. She was kind, patient and considerate. She was focussed on him, and seemed to have an intuitive understanding of what was going through his mind. At first, he felt threatened by this, but her touch was so light and her sympathy so evident that the barriers he had thrown up gradually crumbled and fell. He knew well enough what she was doing, avoiding all talk of the Holokauston but getting him to describe his childhood, his hunting, his juvenile escapades. She was trying hard to gain his confidence and trust, and it was working. He was beginning to talk more easily and freely.

She sipped her wine and regarded him gravely from above the chased silver kylix. The sun shone through the window, and he could hear the screams of swifts as they indulged in a madcap chase round the villa. 'So Aias was one of these very competent men who can cope with everything?'

He began to nod and suddenly stopped when the image of Aias, sitting before the fire and working on his bow, invaded his mind. He instantly thrust him away. It seemed only fair. When Troi had needed him, Aias had left him alone in a savage world.

As usual, she was alert for any hint of reaction and smoothly steered away from the rocks. 'What has Iphiclus got you doing at the moment?'

'Remaking the fish keep. Or, more correctly, restocking. He found out that I could tickle trout.'

She stared at him incredulously. 'Why, by the Horns of Pan, would you tickle fish?'

He explained what it was to her.

'That sounds wonderful. I would love to do that.' She suddenly brightened. 'Would you show me?'

'Of course, my Lady.'

She gave him a reproachful glance. She had prohibited formality when they were alone. He held up an apologetic hand.

'Could we go tomorrow? If the weather is fine, of course.' She spoke to him as an equal, in a way that he could never really get used to.

'I see no reason why not. But you do realise that you'll get wet and muddy, so you must wear old clothes.'

She clapped her hands in glee. 'I haven't played in mud since I was a toddler. This gets better and better. A Thracian tunic and leggings?'

‘That would be ideal.’ He had to smile at her innocent enthusiasm.

A look of concern passed over her face. ‘The fish is not harmed? We can just put it back in the water and it will be fine?’

‘A little surprised perhaps, but nothing else.’ Troi found it odd that she would nevertheless eat fish, but then people were odd.

She nodded with satisfaction. ‘It will get me out of here for a while. I was beginning to feel stifled. I know it’s my fault. I just needed a reason.’

She stood and crossed to a dish of grapes on a side table. She offered them to Troi, who held up an abstaining hand.

Kalliope took one, then looked directly at Troi. ‘Chains of my own making. But then, we are all entangled by chains. Sometimes of our own devising, sometimes those of others. But they are always there. We sometimes need help to free ourselves.’

This was uncharacteristically clumsy and obvious, and Troi stiffened. Making no response. She sat down again. ‘Why won’t you let me help you, Troi?’

‘I don’t need any.’

‘Everybody needs help.’

‘On occasion,’ he conceded.

Outside, the swifts began to scream again.

EIGHTEEN

THE NEXT DAY dawned fine and sunny, and Troi was summoned from his breakfast. Kalliope was waiting at the villa entrance with a grinning Phoebus, who was clutching an osier basket covered with a linen cloth.

'You're late,' she said accusingly.

'I'm sorry, my Lady.' She tolerated the formality in the presence of others. He suspected that she had a similar arrangement with every person of her household. She certainly did with Phoebus. He had told Troi sometime before.

'Come along, then. No dawdling.' They dropped down the track towards the small river. 'Ilus nearly burst a blood vessel,' she told Troi happily. 'He does worry so.' She giggled.'I told him no-one had ever been eaten by a trout.

He humphed a bit, but I think I persuaded him it was quite safe.'

Troi did not think that Ilus had been too concerned about man-eating trout. But nor had he been fully persuaded. Not if the pair of household guards, slipping clumsily from tree to tree behind them in a farcical attempt to stay hidden, was any measure. Phoebus had seen them and winked at Troi. Kalliope was oblivious.

They arrived at the river, and Troi led them to the north, upstream, along a well-trodden path. The stretch near the ford was silty and full of reed beds hung about with the dart of dragonflies and loud with the rasp of sedge warblers. But the river soon became stony, with grassy banks creating overhangs, large boulders, and pools of shade cast by the willows. The water was as clear as the sky, and the silver flash of fish could be seen.

'It's lovely,' said Kalliope, 'I should come down here more often.'

There was a noise behind them as one of the guards tripped up. Kalliope spun round, but they had both gone to earth. 'A wild boar,' said Troi, trying to keep his face straight.

Kalliope was disappointed. 'I never saw it.'

'Never mind,' said Troi. 'This is as good a stretch as any.'

And so they began to tickle. Lying on the grass and feeling along the shady overhangs for the trout. Phoebus, too. There was a great deal of laughter and some none too ladylike language. As they rested after a particularly long and spectacularly unsuccessful session, Troi told them his fisherman joke.

'Two keen fisherman, Eon and Deon, are fishing from the bank when a funeral procession passes by. The mourners weeping and wailing in the front, the priests leading the goat for sacrifice, then the litter with the body carried on the shoulders of strong men, followed by the family. As the litter passes, Eon puts down his fishing pole, stands up and bows his head in respect to the deceased.

'Deon is amazed. "I never thought you did things like that."

'"Least I could do," says Eon, sitting down and picking up his pole again. "Married to her for thirty years."'

Phoebus rolled his eyes, but Kalliope laughed. Then she looked at Troi. 'I've never heard you tell a joke before.'

'I still haven't,' muttered Phoebus.

Troi thought. He used to tell jokes. Aias had a great fund of them, especially after a few kylixes of wine. Perhaps out here, away from the household, he felt more relaxed. 'I promise not to tell any more. Let's catch one of these damned fish.'

But, as long as they tickled from the bank, only he had any success, landing three brown trout, including a sizeable one that would have been ideal for the fish keep, except that Kalliope ordered its immediate release. In the end, he persuaded her to get into the river and wade, very slowly, through the shallow waters. She finally found one lying beneath a natural rock shelf. Her tongue protruding with concentration, she cautiously slipped her hands beneath its tail, Troi quietly instructing her. She very slowly moved one hand forward, lightly touching and tapping the fish's belly until her hands were positioned just before its tail and at its gills. Then she closed her hands to grasp the fish firmly and triumphantly raised it in a silver cascade as the water poured through her fingers. It was only a small one, but she was delighted. She immediately and gently returned it to its natural element, and it darted away downstream and was lost to view.

They clambered out onto the grassy bank, Kalliope and Phoebus laughing. There were times when even Marsyas faded into insubstantiality. Kalliope was flushed, her leggings wet through and her tunic liberally spattered with mud, but she was obviously enjoying herself. She lay down on the grass and sighed.

'That was wonderful. I've never done anything like that before.' She sat up. 'But now I'm hungry.'

Phoebus went for the basket and brought it back. She removed the cloth to reveal a small amphora of wine, three wooden beakers, fresh bread and hunks of cheese.

'Oh,' she said, her tone just a little too surprised and disappointed. 'They've forgotten the figs.' She looked up at Phoebus. 'Be a poppet and run back to the villa for some, would you? Cheese and no figs?' She shuddered. Dissimulation was not her forte, thought Troi.

Phoebus set off immediately, back along the river. Troi smiled as two red and sweaty faces bobbed down into the uncomfortable shelter of a hawthorn thicket. He went and perched on a smooth, moss-covered boulder.

Kalliope shook out her long hair and leaned back on her hands, holding her face up to the sun and closing her eyes. 'Mmm. Haven't enjoyed myself so much for a long time. Thank you, Troi.'

'I'm just glad that you caught one. It is not an easy skill to master.' He actually did have an unfamiliar feeling of pleasure, a relish in her happiness. It made him feel good, and he could not understand why.

She laughed. 'I would lay a drachma or two that there are no other ladies in my circle who have tickled trout. Wait until I tell Hermione. She will be scandalised.' She sat forward and pointed. 'What's that?'

A dumpy brown bird with a startlingly white bib was perched on a boulder in the centre of the river and bobbing comically.

'Dipper. Some call it a water ouzel and some call it a winker. Watch.'

'Its eye goes white when it blinks,' she cried delightedly. The bird plunged into the water and disappeared beneath the surface. She clambered to her feet. 'What's it done? It'll drown!'

He smiled. 'It's feeding. It'll come out in a few heartbeats. It allows the water to press it down against the bed of the river so it can walk upstream and search for food.' As if on cue, the bird hopped out again onto a flat rock, bobbed a couple of times as an encore, then flew off downstream in a whir of wing.

'I've never even heard of a dipper, let alone seen one.' She sat down again. 'Do you know what I would like to do? I'd like to see more things like that.' She gazed around her. 'The trees and the flowers, the animals and birds, the dragonflies. There's so much beauty and fascination in the world, and I've just ignored it.' She looked across at him, her eyes bright. 'Would you show it to me? One day.' She chuckled. 'Perhaps give it a little time first. I'm not sure Ilus will be able to cope. I'll need to work on the poor dear.'

'Could I ask a question?'

She sat down again on the grass. 'Of course.'

'Is it wise doing this? Being alone with a slave? Someone you don't know? Someone whom Ilus, whose opinion deserves respect, regards as a born killer?'

She regarded him thoughtfully. 'No,' she said eventually. 'It isn't wise. But I have found that the wisdom of folly often makes that of the wise foolish.'

'You'll have to fire a second shaft. I lost that one.'

She smiled and brushed some stray hair from her eyes. It looked somewhat the worse for wear after her morning's exertions. 'It's wise not to trust, and yet still folly. For those who are not trusted have no reason to trust you. And so we create the very dangers that we "wisely" avoid.' She considered for a few moments. 'I have found that, if I trust people, if I give them the opportunity of returning that trust, they will do so. I've never been disappointed. It may be that one day I will pay for my folly, but I'd rather have a short life of trust and its return than a long one of fear and suspicion. I'd rather believe in the goodness of people than in their wickedness.'

Perhaps Ilus had more to do with her lack of disappointment than she realised. He thought of the two household guards.

She lay back. 'Now, are you going to rape me, slit my throat and run off into the mountains?'

'Not today.'

'Not any day,' she said comfortably. 'I trust you.' There was a pause. 'Will you trust me?'

'Not to rape me? Yes, I should think so.'

She shaded her eyes and tilted her head to look at him. 'You know very well what I meant.'

'I'm sorry. If there was a problem, I'd be only too happy for you to help. And grateful. But, with respect, you see things that aren't there.'

'You dream. Troi, you know that you do. And they are not dreams of sweetness and light. The man in the room next to you complained. You wake him at the same time every night with your dreams. Auntie had to shift him to another room. And Troi, I've never heard you laugh. Never once.'

Troi stared across the river. He could feel anger beginning to grow within. His simple enjoyment in her pleasure evaporated like autumnal mist. Kalliope looked uncertain, then climbed to her feet and came over towards him. She reached out and put her hands lightly on his shoulders. It was the first time she had ever touched him. He made no move.

'I'm sorry,' she said. 'In my stupidity, I thought you might be more relaxed in your own world. That you might give a little. And now I've made it worse, though I was trying to help.'

'I don't want your help.' It sounded churlish, but he felt churlish. Why could she not leave him alone? They had been having a good time, and she had spoiled it.

Her hands fell away. 'No,' she said sadly. 'I know. I haven't managed this very well, have I?'

He said nothing. She stood there, watching him. He steadfastly refused to meet her gaze.

She eventually spoke. 'Troi,' she said very quietly. 'Look at me, please.'

He thought for a moment and then looked up. There was real sorrow and concern in her face. Not just their signs; he could recognise those as well as anyone, but he could somehow feel them in her. As though they were a part of him too. She sat on a rock, facing him. 'Will you listen to me, please?'

The anger had drained away like waves into the sand. 'Of course, my Lady.' He would make his point, though.

'I'm a silly woman. And I may well see things that are not there. And if it irritates you or upsets you, then I really am sorry.' She thought for a moment. 'Perhaps it's me. Perhaps I'm trying to put something right that isn't wrong for my own reasons. To work out a darkness that still lies within me. So, if not for you, then for me? Will you forgive me, Troi, and still come and see me as before? I promise you that I will not press you again in that way. But it is something I must do.'

Troi looked down. This was beginning to irritate.

'I'll not make you come, Troi, but I'm asking you to. Can we put this behind us? Continue as though it had never happened? Please.' The "please" was very faint. 'I thought that…' Her voice died away.

He got the impression that she was afraid to stop talking, as then he might give a definitive answer, and she could not face it if it was the wrong one.

Troi considered. He did not find the daily trysts uncongenial. The wine was good, and there was still no response to the hunting idea. He did not want to lose the bean crop for lack of watering. It seemed even more important to her than before, which could only be to his advantage. And he actually liked talking to her. Others were unimportant, insubstantial phantoms that appeared briefly, to be dealt with as efficiently as possible and then forgotten. But somehow Kalliope seemed real, another person occupying this world of shades and shadows.

'Of course, my Lady.' But he would drive home his advantage. Make it clear.

She smiled with relief and relaxed. There was movement down the path, and Phoebus trotted into view with a basket of figs.

There was a sneeze from the area of the hawthorn thicket. She looked across.

'Roe deer,' he said blandly. 'They do that.'

NINETEEN

THEY CONTINUED AS before. There was some initial awkwardness that soon faded, but something else had changed. There was a new undercurrent of which Troi could not help but be aware. Each day, it seemed that Kalliope wore ever more revealing and enticing chitons, increasingly subtle and effective cosmetics and headier perfume. When she bent to give him some wine, her hand would often accidentally brush his, and the perfect swell of her breasts seemed invariably present within the compass of his gaze. Her smile, when he entered, conveyed pure pleasure, but when he left, there was a sense of disquiet, of failure. Of sadness. He was sure he was not imagining it.

He idly wondered about indulging her. She was eminently beddable, and it might make his escape plans even easier. Then again, it would complicate matters. It was far too complex to call. There was the minor question of Alexa, the young and pretty slave girl with the clubfoot who crept into his bed every night. She helped with his getting to sleep, and he had made it clear that she had to be gone when he did so. More importantly, the probable reaction of her household. Above all, the response of the formidable Ilus. The rather strange idea even occurred to him that it might cause Kalliope some hurt. He stopped and examined it and then, knowing it had no import for him, put it to one side. Not an insoluble problem, but probably best if things were kept simple.

His self-restraint had no effect on the household's shift in attitude towards him. Once again, he fell into the winter of their distrust. After their initial antipathy, they had begun to soften, to accept him as one of them; but now he was increasingly shut out, the focus of unfriendly glances and even downright hostile glares. There was the solitary exception of Phoebus, who was teaching him the fiendishly complex strategy game of shatang and was delighted to have found a more than competent adversary. So when Troi was sent, with Phoebus, for more fence posts, he decided to grasp the snake by the neck.

'The Mistress, why is she not married?'

'Indeed, she was,' said Phoebus. 'A personage of not inconsiderable status and of advanced years who crossed the Styx some three sun-cycles ago, a little before my time. Not the most felicitous of connubial states, it would appear. He was a man of churlish disposition and somewhat parsimonious by nature. Not at all popular. I would suppose that she has no desire to reprise the experience. He left no surviving family, so she inherited all the money, of which there was a substantial amount.'

Troi had no idea how to do it subtly, so he just threw the discus. 'Does she have a relationship with anyone in the household?'

Phoebus regarded him shrewdly. 'Not of which I am directly aware.' He grinned mischievously. 'Even when there be such impressive candidates for the role as my good self.' The stores building loomed ahead. He stopped, and so did Troi. 'But the situation could well have changed.'

'What do you mean?' asked Troi, knowing full well.

'Most here are convinced that she either has entered such a relationship or is looking to do so. I neither know, nor wish to. But they are not sanguine about its possible ramifications.' He paused, then said with uncharacteristic bluntness, 'You would do well to sleep with one eye open, my friend. Wherever you happen to sleep.'

Troi ignored the insinuation. 'Why should they think that?'

Phoebus looked at him as if he were mad. 'Why should they not? She purchases a handsome young slave who is clearly not at all the proverbial lame dog. She sends for him every day and accompanies him on trout-tickling expeditions, and if that doesn't come to be regarded as a new euphemism, I don't know what will. Then rather clumsily contrives to be left on her own with him. Her ladies report that she is taking uncommon care with her appearance. And that she has started singing in her bath. This, according to the women in the kitchen, who know these things, is an infallible sign and must not be ignored. Now, come along, or the gossip mill will begin to grind as to why you have been so long. And, as the eminent philosopher Pyrrho sagaciously observed in his Seventh Treatise, "What cannot be known can most certainly be invented."'

TWENTY

HE WAS TELLING her about his dog, Amber, and suddenly he was talking of that dreadful day when he had been treed by a bear, and Amber had gone at it. He had sat in the tree, screaming, 'No! Amber, no!' She had rushed in, snarling and snapping, and the bear had crushed her skull, as easily as stepping on a snail, before wandering off, snuffling and growling. He had clambered down and picked up her poor, mangled body, and had cried until he thought his heart would burst.

He had not thought of that day for a long time, but now he was back in that dark wood, made all the gloomier by the overcast skies, clutching the flaccid body of his beloved dog, his throat hurting, his eyes stinging, and such an awful sense of loss that he didn't want to live anymore.

He had forgotten that feeling and was not pleased with its reappearance.

He stopped speaking and realised that his eyes were wet. She was watching him, and he could see pain in her eyes too. He knew it was pain. He did not understand why he knew. Nor why she would feel pain over the death of a dog she had never known.

He swallowed and tried to smile. 'I'll never have another dog like Amber. She never left my side. She never had to be taught anything. She just seemed to know what I wanted her to do, and she did it.' He looked down. 'Except that day.'

'I'm so sorry,' she said quietly. 'You must have loved her.'

He nodded dumbly. He was still trying to deal with the unexpected surge of emotion. It frightened him.

'I cannot comprehend those who dismiss such things as unimportant. "It was only a dog," they say. She loved you, and you loved her. And she gave her life for you. That is the simple, the only thing. Few humans have such love.'

She understood. There was a strange moment when he felt as though they were almost sharing the pain. He no longer felt alone. 'Yes,' he said, his voice still thick. He wanted to say more but couldn't.

'Was that how you felt when you found your father that day?'

The brief, genuine contact stretched and attenuated. 'No, I was more angry then.'

'And the girl?'

He said nothing. The link between them snapped. He could almost feel himself buckling on the armour. He no longer wished to talk of such things. Why relive such trivial matters?

'You knew her, didn't you?' Her usual deft touch had deserted her. She had seen the line beginning to give, to take that first wavering step back, and had flung everything at it, gambling on it breaking.

'I knew lots of people in Koi,' he replied defensively. A little too quickly.

'But you knew her better than most?' He said nothing. 'And you had to kill her.' There was genuine sympathy, even pain, in her voice, but it was rain on a waxed cloak.

She was too perceptive, too intuitive. It was a threat to which he had to react. He looked across at her. The line stiffened, the shields interlocked, and it held. His face was hard, his eyes cold. 'Might I go now, my Lady?'

'Of course, Troi.' She gave him an uncertain smile. She had moved far too far and far too quickly. Again. He rose and, with a slight bow of his head, left immediately. She watched him go and placed her kylix down on a table. It rattled slightly as she did so, and she realised that her hand was trembling.

TWENTY-ONE

As Troi passed through the courtyard, Triopas was clipping one of the bay bushes. He was a big youth, though his muscles were flabby and he was running to fat. He looked up as Troi entered. He had a chubby face with thick, bulbous lips and a simple expression. He spat on the floor and glared truculently at Troi.

The latter was in no mood this day. Kalliope's clumsiness had unsettled him. He stopped and stared directly at Triopas. The young man looked uncertain.

'Clean it up,' said Troi.

Triopas shifted uncomfortably and hastily glanced round for support. There was none. He changed his grasp on the bronze shears in his hand, ineptly pressing the two blades together to make a knife. He took a deep breath.

'Make me,' he said, though there was more nervous wobble than challenge in his voice.

'As you wish,' said Troi disinterestedly. He exploded into movement, feinting with his right hand. Triopas awkwardly flung up an arm to fend off the blow, forgetting his shears, and Troi chopped down with the side of his left hand onto Triopas's wrist, sending them flying. Troi then simply stepped forward, hooked his leg behind the lad's ankles and pushed him backwards. Triopas hit the ground with a real bang.

But Troi was standing motionless. Ilus was just to one side, his sword pointing, as immovable as Pindus, at Troi's jugular.

TWENTY-TWO

TROI STOOD IN the prescribed position, legs slightly apart, hands hooked behind his back, his head submissively lowered. A position that spoke of subservience and regret. A position that lied. Kalliope was upset, her eyes haloed with tears, her hands almost clawing at each other in her distress.

'What have you done?' she whispered.

He said nothing. It was perfectly obvious what he had done.

She shook her head and turned to Ilus, who stood off to one side. He was wearing his sword. 'Don't say it,' she said. 'Please.'

'I won't,' he replied stolidly.

Which was just as good as saying it, thought Troilus.

‘How is he?’ Her mental turmoil was expressed in her physical agitation.

Troi was puzzled. How could she get so worked up about a silly servant, who had asked for all he had got? He just didn’t understand people.

Ilus looked grave. ‘Still unconscious. He hit his head hard when he went down.’

She swung back to Troi, and, for the first time ever, he heard the bite of anger in her voice. ‘Why?’

This was not a good time to shrug, though he had to fight the temptation. ‘He spat when he saw me. I told him to clean it up. He said, “Make me,” and held the shears as a weapon. So, I knocked the shears from his hand and put him down.’

She continued to stare at him. He was conscious of a tear trailing down her cheek. Perhaps more was looked for.

‘I didn’t mean to injure him. If I was a killer, he would be dead.’ He was aware that he didn’t sound at all contrite.

‘I said that you were a killer, not a fool,’ said Ilus angrily. ‘If killing Triopas would have led to your escape, you’d have done so without a second thought.’ Troi thought about that. Ilus was probably right.

‘Triopas is weak-minded,’ she said to Troi. The brief flash of anger had gone like summer godfire. Now there was sorrow. ‘He was reacting as he thought he should. He’s a mimic. He takes his lines from those around him.’

How was I supposed to know that, for Dyaus’s sake? thought Troi, but sensibly left the observation unvoiced.

She glanced back at Ilus. ‘Is he telling the truth?’

Strangely, Troi felt rather hurt at the question.

'He is. I heard the verbal exchange as described and came in to see him chop the shears out of the lad's hand, as he said. The push was clearly not intended to injure, though the possibility could, and should, have been foreseen.'

She nodded. 'I am disappointed in you, Troi. I believe that I can say you have received nothing but kindness here, but you do not repay in kind.'

He fancied he could hear a double message in the words.

There was a scratch at the door, and Auntie came into the andron.

'My Lady,' she said, giving Troi a hard stare. 'I thought that you would wish to know that Triopas has regained consciousness. He has a headache but is talking as much sense now as he ever did before. I believe he will be fine.'

Kalliope gave a huge sigh and sat down on a couch. 'Thank Herakla,' she said fervently.

'He sent a message for you,' said the elderly woman, addressing Troi. 'He said that he was sorry, he would clean it up and please not to hit him again.'

Troi assumed that he was meant to feel ashamed of himself.

Kalliope smiled at the housemistress. 'Thank you, Eirene.' The old lady acknowledged the thanks with a little bow of the head, turned, and left. Kalliope looked up at Ilus. 'What do you think?'

'You know perfectly well what I think.'

'I suppose I do.' She turned back to Troi. 'Can you promise me that you will not use violence against my household in future?'

He thought. Promises were important things and rash ones particularly dangerous. 'I can only promise,' he said carefully, ‘that I will offer no violence to others, except in response to actual violence from them.’

She considered his answer, then nodded briefly. ‘Then we are done here.’

Ilus said nothing, but rolled his eyes heavenwards.

TWENTY-THREE

AT BREAKFAST THE next morning he sat alone, though not disregarded. He knew himself to be the subject of quiet mutterings, the object of malignant stares, the focus of concern and dislike, if not fear and hatred. Though no one was going to put themselves in the arena. He could not blame them. They were an insular group by nature, and not only did they see a threat to their beloved mistress, but they would not be human if they did not worry that their own comfortable lives might be upset by this menacing intruder. He was the anger of Poteidan, able to shift the very ground about them, bringing all they held dear tumbling down. The tremors could already be felt. No wonder they murmured and glared. It was time for him to be gone.

A resentful servant approached. 'Iphiclus wants to see you.'

Troi spooned out the last of the porridge and rose to take his bowl to the cleaning point.

'I'll do that,' the man offered grudgingly. 'Iphiclus said immediately.'

The room was silent as he left to find his way to Iphiclus's small, box-like office. The major-domo was writing on a wax tablet and held up a peremptory hand at Troi's entrance. Troi waited patiently until he had finished. The major-domo did not seem to be hurrying, and Troi guessed it to be a calculated ploy. He was not going to allow such trivial and transparent games to affect him. Iphiclus eventually sat back and surveyed Troi with chill dislike.

'No hunting. Orders of the Mistress. You will stay with the field gang. You are to refence the west pasture.'

Troi kept his face expressionless and said nothing. It had been so long, he had assumed that the idea had been quietly abandoned anyway. Strangely, he felt a sense of betrayal that Kalliope should be the one to stop him. Iphiclus was clearly disappointed at the lack of overt reaction and dismissed him with a disparaging flick of his hand. Troi turned and left, his mind racing. It would make very little difference and certainly not stop him.

The only reason he was still here was that Aias had drilled him to plan, rethink, prepare, check and then think again. It would be difficult and hazardous getting back to Mykerenos, and he could not afford to fail because of sloppy preparation. He had been surreptitiously gathering the needful: knives, boustria, blankets, rope, tinder and kindling. They were well hidden in the wood store.

He had persuaded Phoebus to take him to the library, and there, while Phoebus was myopically preoccupied with a manuscript of Paleius, Troi had found an excellent map of Gea. He had studied it with such concentration that it was inscribed in his memory. He would go due south to cut the river Enkos, follow it to its headwaters below Mount Rhodope, continue west, then north, finding his way through the foothills, until he cut the Goat's Way. This was a narrow, difficult path that traced a tortuous route right through the Rhodopians, beneath the towering summit of Mount Thrax itself. It finally joined the river Phraidos to follow its fall down to the Mykerenaean Littoral. And Marsyas. It would not be easy, but he was confident in his own abilities.

He could go tonight. The weather looked fair. He would go tonight.

As he approached the familiar carved door to Kalliope's rooms, it opened, and one of her ladies emerged. She must have been listening for him because she expressed no surprise.

'My Lady wishes to see you,' she said coldly, and passed on without a backward glance.

He scratched and went in. He knew instantly that it had come to the spear clash.

Kalliope was standing by a side table and arranging some flowers in an elegant red-figured vase. She was dressed in the most diaphanous chiton he had ever seen; it clung to her, revealing every sweep and curve of her body. When she turned to greet him, he could see that, instead of the more usual and more modest breast band, she was wearing a strophion beneath her breasts, accentuating their prominence, the brown blur of her aureoles clearly visible through the pale blue material. Her hair was a complex arrangement of coils and braids and positively shone, and her face had never seemed so beautiful, thanks to the subtle cosmetic ministrations of her ladies. But her eyes held fear and uncertainty and could not be still, flicking to his face and then away again in some desperate game of tag. She smiled, but it was not convincing. She looked awkward and nervous. He actually felt something like sympathy for her.

'Hello, Troi. Thank you for coming. Sit down, won't you?' There was a distinct quaver in her voice. 'Some wine?'

He sat on the usual couch. 'Please.'

She set about pouring out a kylix of half and half. The wine slopped slightly. She stopped for a moment, and he could see that she was getting a grip of herself. She finished with a steadier hand, poured a second, and brought them across to him. He could smell a positively heady perfume. As she handed one to him, her hand brushed his. Accidentally, or so it seemed. Then, to his surprise, she sat down alongside him on the couch. She could not be more obvious. It was getting bloody close to rape, he thought wryly. She looked at him, and there was raw desperation in her eyes.

'I wanted to talk to you.'

He sipped his wine.

She looked away as embarrassment flamed in her face. 'I ordered that the hunting be stopped. Ilus told me last night of his little scheme. He said that it would get you away from the villa and let the…' She struggled for an acceptable term. '…tension die down.' Her head dropped, and she stared into her wine as though it was a scrying glass. What future did she see in it? wondered Troi. There was only one.

Her voice became little more than a whisper. 'I feared that you would take the opportunity to just walk away. Ilus knew what you would do. None better.' She placed her untasted wine on a delicate table beside the couch and finally looked at him. 'I don't want you to go. I want you to stay. It's important to me. You must know… You must have guessed…' She winced. 'I'm sorry,' she muttered, looking down again. 'You do know, don't you? This must be excruciatingly embarrassing for you. It certainly is for me.'

He did not know what he could say, so he said nothing. He was not discomfited, just a little intrigued as to how far she would go. But there was a hope that she would not bring hurt and shame upon herself. Though why it should concern him, he had no idea.

She continued to speak. He assumed she was covering her agitation.

'And I'm sorry about the hunting. When I learned what Ilus had planned, I just reacted without thinking. But it was silly. That's why I needed to see you.' Her voice died away in confusion.

'Ilus has your best interests at heart, my Lady.'

'I know.' She glanced up at him furtively. 'Just this once, could you call me Kalliope? Or even Klio? I would like that.'

'Of course, Klio.' It seemed false and awkward.

She looked down again. She was finding it hard to meet his eyes. 'This isn't going at all as I planned. It's all gone too quickly. It's excruciating. I feel awful.'

'There's no need,' he said. He felt he wanted to make it easier for her, but had no idea how.

'You know what I'm trying to say, so why is it so difficult for me?'

'Shall I say it for you?' His crass attempt to help made her wince and him grimace. If that was the best that he could do, then it was better to remain silent.

She shook her head violently. 'No, I'm in the autumn of your opinion already. If I can't say I love you, then how can I mean it? There, I've said it.' There was a note of triumph in her voice that suddenly changed to a wail of pure horror. 'Lady Herakla, what must you think of me? I sound like a silly girl.'

'Of course you don't.' It didn't convince him, so he doubted that she believed it either.

She breathed out, rather shakily, shook her head slightly and seemed to relax. She looked up at him with a wan smile. 'I could have done that worse, but I would have had to really work at it. As a subtle attempt at seduction, it definitely lacked something. Subtlety, I think.'

Not a great deal of seduction either, thought Troi. He had seen better. But then it wasn't really seduction, was it? Love. That had been the word. It made him shift with unease.

He tried again. 'I think you've got yourself a little too worked up. Relax, and have a sip of wine.' That was no better. He cringed at himself. The irony of the situation was not lost on him.

'I panicked. When I heard of the hunting. I thought that I'd never see you again.' She was breathing slowly and deeply, trying to calm herself. 'I've never felt like this before. Maturity's no guard when Erotes makes you his wand. I'm sorry. I thought, I hoped, given time, that you might come to care for me. I'm not talking about sex.' She coloured slightly. 'I could order you to my bed, but I don't want to do that. If I wanted a bedslave, I could buy myself ten at market; as handsome and athletic as you like and trained to perfection. That's not what it's about. I just want you near. But I know now that you'll go, and I'll never see you again.'

He said nothing. It seemed safest.

'It's not Alexa,' she said. 'I know that. Poor girl.' The apparent sympathy, the real sympathy, surprised him. 'It's that you want to go.'

He could see her tense herself, make her determination iron. He knew what she was going to say.

'But is there… any… chance?' She stared at him, her eyes wide, fear and hope battling it out within the dark brown irises. 'Might you even now stay? I'm not asking that you love me, but, given time, perhaps you might come to care. If only a little.'

There seemed no point in being other than honest. Perhaps, if his obsession with Marsyas did not drive him like a cow to market, he might have considered it. 'I'm sorry, Klio,' he said as gently as he could. She closed her eyes. 'I like you, I respect you, I can't think of anyone who deserves to be loved more than you, but I'm not the one able to do it. I don't think I have love in me. I don't know what it is. It's my fault, not yours.'

'Thank you, but that does not make me feel a great deal better.' She smiled bitterly. 'I'm sorry, Troi. I really thought I could help, that I could get through to the real Troi. And then…' Her voice fell away like the ebb of a wave.

'I'm not sure. I don't feel as others. But that's just who I am. Have you considered that the real Troi is who you see? Not the one you think you see. That you don't love me, but something crafted of your dreams. You would be disappointed in me.'

'No. I don't know how I know, but I do. You'll come through this one day. I can see the real Troi when I look into your eyes. I—'

He interrupted her. 'When you look into someone's eyes, all you see is a reflection of yourself. Or what you want to see. No more than that.'

For the moment, she seemed confounded by his vehemence, then shook her head slowly. 'No. Perhaps for those who choose not to see. And I have no clever arguments; I just know it. I see you. The real you. Emotions cannot be denied. They can be trapped, suppressed, hidden, but they're there. Beating their wings against the bars of their cage like poor, captive linnets. A cage that's locked, and you don't even know that you have the key.'

'I didn't even know I had a cage,' he said, with more than a tinge of sarcasm.

She showed no reaction to it. 'I can see the real you,' she repeated. 'Just brief flashes. But you're there. I know it. I'm convinced that it's your reaction to the Holokauston. It's my father over again.'

Troi grimaced. He wasn't going to convince her. It was a waste of time. 'Perhaps, but I have my doubts.'

'I have none. You were there that day by the river. Just for a few hekates. But it was enough. I knew then… I felt…' She shook her head, then unexpectedly put the helm hard over. 'Will you stay?'

The direct question took him by surprise. He shook his head. A slave telling his mistress that he was just going to walk away. But neither questioned it.

'Why must you go? If you stayed, you could have a good life here. I'd give you your freedom and expect nothing from you. Except to see you, to have you near.' Her voice was wistful, rather than desperate. He got the impression that she had recognised the inevitable.

'Personal reasons.'

'Revenge,' she said. There was no doubt in her voice. He did not answer. 'So, you will go, regardless of what we do.' Again, he said nothing.

She rose and walked over to the table beside her couch. She came back holding a small scroll. There was a moment's hesitation, then she handed it to him. It bore the seal of the Temple of Dyaus at Leuctra. He knew it could only be a certificate of manumission. He was free. It meant little to him, as he felt able to walk away whenever he chose. But he assumed it meant far more to her.

'Thank you,' He tried to sound suitably grateful but suspected that he had missed the mark by an embarrassing margin. He mentally shrugged. It didn't matter.

She turned and went back to the wine on the marble-topped table. She slowly poured a kylix, taking her time. He presumed that it was simply to avoid looking at him. There were two poured already. 'How do you plan getting home?' She was trying to sound casual, but there was a tremble in her voice.

'Walk.'

'I know a trader in Leuctra. A good friend, and trustworthy. He could arrange for a ship to slip you ashore. You may take whatever you need. I shall instruct the storekeeper accordingly.' She paused. 'Please,' she said, 'allow me to do this.' She took a leather pouch and brought it to him. He knew that it would be full of coins. Golden coins. 'Please. For my sake. I need to know that you have everything you might require.'

Exactly what might get me killed, he thought. This much gold calls to murder. But he said nothing. It had never occurred to her. After a moment's hesitation, he rather reluctantly took it. She smiled with relief. A small enough thing in the desert of her despair, but something.

There was one last hopeless throw of the knucklebones. 'Might you come back? Afterwards?'

'I doubt it. I'm sorry.'

'But will you promise that if ever you wanted to come back, that if you needed a refuge, help, just a friend, that you would do so, without hesitation, without embarrassment? No commitments.'

'Is it not better that you forget me?' he asked as gently as he could.

'That's a good idea,' she said. For the first time, he heard bitterness in her voice. 'Now tell me how I do that.'

He spread his hands out in a gesture of defeat. 'Then I promise to contact you, should that ever happen.' It was a meaningless enough concession. 'Though you might well have changed your mind, by then.'

'I will settle for that. I have one more request.' She had returned to the table and was standing with her back to him. Her voice shook even more noticeably. 'Will you send, from time to time, just so that I know that you still live?'

'That might be cruelty rather than kindness,' he said quietly.

'Let me be the arbiter of that. I think you owe me that much.'

'I do. I will send.'

'Now please go,' she said abruptly. Her voice broke.

He stood up. 'I'm sorry I can't give you the love you want and deserve, Klio, but may the Gods walk with you and grant you happiness.'

She nodded, unable to speak.

He turned and left the room for the last time. There was regret and even something like pain as he went. He should have been glad to be going. These were not feelings that he wanted. He fastened onto the image of a fat man with black hair, screaming in agonised terror and clutching his stomach as his entrails tumbled out. He wondered how good the knives were in the storehouse.

TWENTY-FOUR

TROI STOOD IN the prow of the Peace of Poteidan as they rounded the Hook and left the Scyllan Gulf behind. It was a beautiful day, the sky an unmarked blue, the sun warm and comforting on his skin, the sea placid. The wind was full behind them and pushing the Peace along at a good pace, the air full of birds: a gaggle of noisy seagulls following their wake, the brilliant white of the gannets in their impressive vertical dives, the shearwaters speeding past as though riding a cushion of air just above the gently rolling waves. Some distance away, a long line of splashes marked the passage of a school of dolphins. And he was gazing on his homeland again as a free man.

Across the wide straits to his right lay the hazy undulating hills of Thrake, and he could just make out a blotch of white that marked the town of Apamea, but to his left lay the soil of Mykerenos. He regarded the long low promontory that ended in a jumble of dark rocks with its frieze of cormorants drying their wings. From there, the land rose steadily until, at the summit of the gradual incline, the black and blocky fortress of Herea lay stamped against the magnificent backdrop of the distant mountains of the Ring of Mykerenos. It was too far away to see the sigil on the flag flying from its citadel, but a smaller outlying fort built nearby to overwatch the straits flew a banner that uncurled in the wind to display the white head of an aurochs. Anger stirred within.

He forced it down. All his other emotions seemed subdued, weak and puling things that rarely trespassed on his consciousness, and when they did, fled precipitately before his disapproval. But anger ranged free and needed to be controlled. Emotion kills you. Aias's words floated into his mind, though the grumble of anger within the dark caverns below would not be entirely stilled. Not until that whoreson Marsyas lay screaming in a tangle of spilled guts at his feet. And maybe not even then.

Not too long now, and they would be nosing through the Sea Door, the only safe passage through the Great Reef and into the huge bay beyond, for a final long row against the wind into the port of Naupactos. He would disembark there, a Troian-garrisoned town, but he felt safe enough. Unsurprisingly, Ilus had been helpful in devising a cover story for him as a wool trader and even supplying corroborative documentation. He had been more than happy to see him go.

The thought of Ilus brought back the world of the villa. Troi was glad to escape its clutches. Kalliope had unsettled him. Emotions, strange, inexplicable feelings, had begun to wriggle free from their incarceration, troubling him and marring the simplicity and certainty of his world. This voyage and the focus of revenge had stilled them once more. He was himself again.

He grasped the rail tightly and watched the land slide steadily past. He was on his way home in every sense.

Marsyas, you bastard.

I'm coming.

TWENTY-FIVE

TROI SLID A handbreadth farther beneath the tangle of drooping branches until he could look down on the tents, wagons and horse lines of the Troian army, all spread out below him. The wood he was in cloaked the lip of a cliff that loomed high over the site and afforded excellent views of its comings and goings and general bustle, the tiny figures looking like miniature children's toys that he could reach down to grasp and rearrange at his whim.

The Trogs had been there four days now. The large, familiar tent that constituted Marsyas's sumptuous quarters was set up, a separate tent hung within as the satrap's personal living space. It was situated at the very centre of the fortified encampment and was always surrounded by a swarm of the hated Bluecloaks. Marsyas was nothing if not sensible of his own security. But this time, it lay close to a sizeable watercourse that flowed right through the site.

The river was near perfection. Its crumbling shores were cloaked with bushes and trees—alder, willow and the occasional oak—interspersed with a dense growth of hawthorn and blackthorn. The water itself had a deep central channel, and its shallower stretches were thick with long beds and archipelagos of waving reeds. He was sure that he would be able to slip unnoticed into the very heart of the encampment.

It had taken him the best part of a se'ennight to catch up with his prey, and he had been tracking the Trog army for eight days now. Covertly watching their procedures through the night, he'd gained a good grasp of the Butcher's personal protection. At night, he liked his privacy. The delivery of a captive woman every second or third evening, to be dragged out weeping, bloodied and bruised in the early morning, bespoke the sickening rationale. The tent was ringed by a dozen of the household guards, but at a tactful distance of fifty paces or so. They were obviously chosen for nastiness and impressive physique, and therefore probably not for mental acuity. If Troi could penetrate that screen, there would be little to stop him gutting the fat bastard. What happened to himself thereafter was of no consequence.

He glanced up. The thick, grey clouds were hardly moving, and it would be only a quarter moon anyway. That meant darkness. There was always a fire burning at the front of the tent, but there would be little illumination at the back, where the distance from the stream was less than fifty paces, and the ground looked helpfully rough and uneven. As good a chance as he could hope for.

'You've but one chance in a hundred, I estimate. Not worth it.'

He froze. A whisper scarcely more than the sighing of the breeze. How could it be possible for someone to creep up behind him without his knowing? He doubted his own ears until the voice spoke again.

'Don't worry, I'm not a Trog. If I were, you'd be dead by now.'

The man slid effortlessly and silently into place beside him, turned his head and grinned. Troi stared at him. He was in his mid-twenties, thin and wiry, possessed of a long face with well-balanced features and bright brown eyes. His skin was smudged with mud and green moss stains, and he wore a strange cap with ear lappets that was threaded through with twigs and tufts of grass. As were his loosely woven but tight-fitting tunic and trews, dyed an inchoate mix of browns and dark greens. Even this close, it was difficult to pick out the actual shape of his body as he merged into the mosaic of shadows.

He extended a brown and green hand. 'You would be Troilus. I'm Xanthos.' There was an unhurried rhythm to his speech and a characteristic intonation that reminded Troi of someone who hailed from the eastern Thebeaid. Troi guessed him to be a steader, one of the individualists who wrested a harsh living from the inhospitable sea of grass in the Vale of Tempe.

Still in shock, Troi put out his own and they grasped wrists. 'How did you know my name?'

'Not difficult. You've a loose mouth. Luckily, that woodsman you spoke to a se'ennight ago is of our persuasion. I've been watching you track that black-hearted bastard.

Looking at the cloud, I reckoned tonight would be the night you'd go for it. Don't. You won't make it.' His confident assertion brooked no contradiction.

Nevertheless. 'Why not?'

'You obviously don't know about his Daemons.'

Troi just shook his head in puzzlement.

'Well, the Bluecloaks are bad, but these are worse. Dressed the same but cut farther from the hoof and horn. Three of them. Nasty, and bloody good with it. They know every dirty trick in the scroll. They move in and out amongst the others and are always in his outer tent during the night. You'd walk straight into their hands.'

Troi gritted his teeth as a silent scream at his own stupidity and inability to see the obvious ripped through his mind, then he slumped. The cry of rage turned into a howl of anguish. He looked at Xanthos, who was regarding him sympathetically, and felt for the iron within. It could not end like this. 'But I must try. I have sworn.'

'Patience, friend. You're not the only one who seeks his death. And it will come. If the Gods are just, it'll be a bad one. In the meantime, you could be valuable to us.'

'Us?'

'Do you think that Mykerenos will accept the Holokauston? The province is rising. It's the beginning. It'll be bloody, but we'll throw out the Trogs. Perhaps eventually Laomedon himself.'

'But you're not from here. You're not a Mickey. You sound more like a steader.'

'You've a good ear. I happened to be here and do love a good scrap. I'm not the only one. Men are coming from all over the Empire to join.'

'And how could I be valuable?'

'You're a hunter. You clearly have experience with tracking. You move well. And you can use a bow. We've need of such skills. We don't have the strength yet to meet the enemy in the field. It will be a war of bites and nibbles. And for that we need men with special talents.' He paused. 'We can't afford to lose them for gestures.'

A surge of anger made Troi's fists clench. 'It's not a bloody gesture. Bogazkoi was my home.'

There was silence for a few heartbeats. 'I'm sorry. I'm a scout. Tact isn't on the training ground.' Xanthos sighed. 'But gesture it would be. Do you think Marsyas wouldn't be replaced? The rot's higher and needs more drastic surgery.' He looked at Troi, his eyes intense. 'The idea is not to die, but to kill. If you insist on going down there, I won't stop you. But it would be futile. You look for revenge. You won't get it. Be patient and serve it on a golden platter.'

Troi considered. Aias used to say that. Revenge needed to be planned, a thing of the intellect, not emotion. Emotions clouded the judgement. Emotions got you killed. Xanthos was right. Troi nodded, then started to slide unobtrusively back through the screening foliage. But his companion was already gone. When he emerged into the small glade, Xanthos was sitting on a moss-covered tree stump, waiting for him.

'You're a hunter,' he said again. 'What do you see?'

So, he was going to be tested, it seemed. 'Apart from my own footprints, though I'm damned if I can see yours—' The scout merely smiled. '—There are the scratch marks of a bear on that tree, at least three days old. A fox has stalked a game bird.' He took a couple of steps to look more closely at some feathers on the ground. 'Capercaillie. He pounced but missed. Plenty of rabbit signs, old boar rootings, and a couple of fallow deer passed through recently, mother and fawn.'

'Not bad,' said Xanthos.

'Not to mention your friend, up that elm tree, with his bow.'

The young man laughed. 'How do you know he's a friend?'

'Because if I know he's there, you certainly do.'

'And how did you spot him?'

'There's a great tit over there, beak full of caterpillars, refusing to approach its nest. And there's only one climbable route up it.' He shrugged. 'So, I looked. A couple of scuff marks on the lichen and a smear of mud on one of the side branches.'

'And the bow?'

'A fragment of goose feather at the roots. He must have caught one of his arrows as he climbed. I was always taught to fasten my gorytus before shinning up a tree.'

Xanthos inclined his head in confirmation. 'You can come down now, Nicias.'

The faintest rustling, and a tall, long-limbed young man dropped, almost without a sound, before Troi. He was dressed in the same strange outfit as Xanthos and as liberally besmirched with mud and moss. He held a short bow in one hand, and his gorytus was open. He ostentatiously looped the leather thong round the bone hook to close it, raising his eyebrows and pulling a wry face. He had an open, guileless countenance with pale blue eyes and a snub nose.

He held out his hand. Troi took it by the wrist. 'Welcome to the scouts,' Nicias said, grinning infectiously.

Xanthos rose. 'Get your horse. We need to be in Ikaros by dusk. We'll change it there.'

'Change what?'

'Your horse.'

Troi was proud of the fine bay he had bought in Naupactos. 'What's wrong with her?' he demanded.

'Most things. You want a good Thracian pony. Incredible stamina, tough and sturdy, turn on an obol, will survive a moontide on a mouthful of moss and clever little buggers to boot.'

'They haven't got the speed of a Phthian.'

'If a scout needs speed, he's not done his job,' said Xanthos.

As he said it, Nicias chimed in, matching Xanthos word for word and doing a fair imitation of his accent. Then he grinned at Troi. 'Welcome to the scouts,' he repeated. 'Probably going to be the biggest mistake of your short life.'

'I was beginning to wonder,' said Troi gloomily.

TWENTY-SIX

THEY ARRIVED AT Ikaros just as the grey of dusk began to seep out from the shadows and draw the colour from the world. Xanthos told Troi it was the strategion of the Mykereneaen army, though most of the actual forces were out in the field. Surprisingly, there were no defensive walls as they rode in along the main thoroughfare, but Troi was aware of being well watched. He guessed they relied on the scouts and speed to avoid the lumbering Trogs.

It had been a thriving village but was now largely a tumble of ruins and charred skeletons of houses. Marsyas had visited. The news of Bogazkoi had gone before him, and all the inhabitants had sensibly fled. Such of the buildings as had survived more or less intact had been commandeered, and others made habitable by the use of leather tents as temporary roofing.

As they entered it, a man in a linen cuirass and yellow sash stepped out in front of them and held up a hand. They stopped. On either side, several archers with nocked arrows stood behind roughly built barricades. They carried bows a man's height in size, the famous Mykerenaean longbow, a fearsome weapon that could punch an arrow through an oak door. Troi hoped that Xanthos's word would be good enough for them.

He needn't have worried. The officer walked forward, a well-made man with a tight skullcap of black curls and a florid countenance. Xanthos slid easily from his shaggy pony, and they grasped wrists.

'Xan, good to see you, but I thought you were trailing the Butcher.'

'I left Nicias watching him. Looks as though they've gone into a semi-permanent camp.'

'And who's this?' The officer was looking at Troi askance. 'Didn't know we were running a nursery.' The archers had lowered their bows and relaxed, allowing Troi the opportunity to dismount.

'Name's Troilus. He was at Bogazkoi. Wants to fight and has the makings of a decent scout.'

It seemed Xanthos's word was all that was needed. The officer held out his hand. 'Philemon. Pleased to have you with us.'

Troi, rather self-consciously, took his wrist and muttered that he was glad to be there.

'Diomedes will want to see you,' said the officer to Xanthos, turning to walk with them. 'Bring the lad along. The strategarch may have questions about Koi.'

A couple of archers took their horses, and Philemon led them to what had been the agora at the centre of the stricken village. A small party of recruits was practising hoplite drill under the eagle eye of a large hyperetes, who was kindly sharing his considered opinion of their competence, while a group of cavalrymen clattered by, looking tired and dusty, clearly just in from a patrol.

They stopped outside what had been the local tavern. It had not been torched like most of the town, presumably because it would have contained stocks of wine that were busily being plundered, and it was now reborn as the strategion. Two hoplites stood sentry at the door, their shields freshly painted blood red with crudely executed white roses of Mykerenos in the centre. They obviously knew the scout and nodded him and Troi through.

They made their way into the gloomy interior, which already had oil lamps burning against the invasion of twilight. In the centre of the room, five men, in a variety of uniforms, sat round an old, battered table, poring over maps. In one corner, another officer was working with a couple of scribes. A tall, lanky Thracian, marked by his long-belted tunic, baggy trousers and a positive riot of dark blue tattoos, was slumped fast asleep in a chair to one side, his feet propped up on a stool. Three young men, obviously aides, stood by an internal door, waiting patiently. Everyone's eyes turned on them as they entered. Troi felt uncertain, very young and adrift in unknown waters. The oldest of the men, facing them across the table, leaned back and greeted Xanthos brusquely.

'What in Hades are you doing here, Xan? You're supposed to be watching the Butcher.' His dark eyes switched to Troi.

There was a power in them that spoke of authority and confidence, but nothing of welcome or affability. 'And who's the young puppy?'

The man was at least sixty, with grey hair shorn to stubble and two sword scars on his face which did nothing to soften his angular features. He still looked lean and fit and had the unmistakable air of command.

Xanthos, clearly not in the least intimidated, wandered over to a side table where he began to fill two kylixes from a large krater of wine and water. 'The whoreson's bedding down.'

The grey-haired man nodded, as though it came as no surprise to him.

'Left that lazy bugger Nicias to keep an eye on them. Thought it was time I made one of those report thingies you're always going on about.'

The man smiled slightly. 'Good of you to consider us.'

There was some relationship between them, some special rapport that Troi could not grasp. He guessed that no-one else spoke to the elderly officer in that manner. He had already decided that this must be the Diomedes that Philemon had referred to. The name was strangely familiar, but he wasn't sure from where. He turned to accept the wine from Xanthos, nodding his thanks.

'Oh, and the young puppy — I found him preparing to sneak into the heart of the Trog camp and do a bit of butchering of his own devising. And he might have managed it too. He's been taught well, and he's definitely got balls. He'll make a good scout. Name's Troilus.' He paused. 'From Koi.'

Troi looked up to find those disconcerting eyes full on him, scrutinising him, measuring him. There was something odd in his expression.

‘Ah. From Koi,’ Diomedes murmured, as if he had nothing further to say. Nor did he. The inspection did not waver. Then it was done. Xanthos looked puzzled.

‘So, your report thingie, if you would be so kind.’ Diomedes leaned back in his chair.

Xanthos jerked his head towards the door. ‘Philemon’s outside,’ he said to Troi. ‘He’ll find you a billet.’

‘No,’ said Diomedes instantly. ‘The lad stays.’

Some of the other officers looked across at him with surprise, but he made no effort to explain. Xanthos shrugged and went over to the table and its scatter of maps. Troi remained where he stood, not at all sure how to react. So he just sipped his wine. The scout gave a concise and efficient briefing: where the camp was, its layout, and estimates of the forces quartered there. He described the defensive works being prepared and the regular arrival of supply convoys through the Boreas.

Diomedes nodded. ‘So, it certainly looks permanent. Possibly even overwintering.’ He studied the map. ‘Someone has brains. It’s the perfect geographical location. He is well placed to hit most of the Vale, he is on the main traverse routes and is sitting snugly on his supply line. This river gives him good water.’

‘That river’s a way in, as our friend here appreciated. Marsyas is a butcher, not a thinker. But he has a well-developed sense of personal security. I’d lay a talent to an obol that he,’ Xanthos indicated Troi with a tilt of his head, ‘would have sprung a trap halfway down.’

‘But surely they won’t be planning to overwinter yet,’ objected one of the officers, a short, tubby man with red hair and a bushy beard. He reminded Troi of one of the dwarves that Aias claimed lived in the mountains and ate inquisitive young boys.

'Planning for eventualities, Praxis,' replied Diomedes immediately. 'A prepared camp if need be, but always ready to move on if the situation calls for it.'

A younger man spoke, clean shaven with a tangle of blond hair and a sour expression. 'So, what do we do?'

'That's for tomorrow,' said Diomedes, rubbing his temples wearily. 'We think it through and then bring suggestions and ideas to Officer's Call at the second dekate. That will be all for now. Thank you.'

They rose obediently. The sour-faced man shook the Thracian awake. He opened bleary blue eyes and looked at Diomedes, yawned and stretched. 'You finished discussings? When we fight?' He had a thick, guttural accent.

'When we have to, Tereus,' said Diomedes equably. 'But don't worry. There will be enough fighting, even for you.'

'Never enough,' said the Thracian, pulling a grotesque face. 'Sometimes I sleep with boring.' He wandered out after the others. Diomedes glanced across at the officer in the corner, short, stocky and almost totally bald save for two bizarre tufts of white hair above his ears, and made a slight movement of his head in the direction of the tent entrance. The man glowered, gathered his scribes and left without a word. Troi turned to go as well.

'Not you, lad,' said Diomedes, surprisingly gently. 'Nor you, Xan. But you can get to your bed, young Phoinos.' His aide gave him a grateful smile and departed, leaving the three alone.

'Sit you both down.'

They did so, Troi conscious of the bewilderment of the scout. Xanthos glanced at Troi doubtfully, then turned to Diomedes.

'Is there anything wrong, Uncle Dio?'

Uncle Dio. Something stirred, came to the very edge of consciousness, then slipped away beyond recall.

'I don't think so.' Diomedes was looking at Troi again with that intense scrutiny that so discomfited him. 'Tell me about yourself, lad.'

'Nothing much to tell. Brought up in Koi by my father, Aias. He taught me to hunt. We lived by hunting. Until that bastard Marsyas came.' The understandable bitterness thickened his voice.

Diomedes leaned forward, eyes unblinking. 'How come you survived?'

The sharp tone made Troi flinch. He steeled himself. 'Out hunting when it happened.'

'Were you the one who led the survivors to Iyalissos?'

Surprised, Troi nodded. The eyes bored into him unrelentingly. He tried to look back, to meet that granite gaze, but his eyes fell away of their own volition.

'So, where have you been since then?'

'Taken by a Trog patrol. Sold as a slave. Came back.'

Diomedes stretched over and yanked up Troi's sleeve to reveal the branded sigma. He was just about to lean back, when he stopped and pulled the pendant from within Troi's tunic. He glanced at it and let it fall. 'The sigil of the Basilides. What are they to do with you?'

Troi was shocked. Threat hung in the air. 'Nothing. My father owned it. I never asked where he'd got it from. I took it as a keepsake.' He was sweating. This man was going to take his story apart. He knew it.

'Lived in Koi all your life?'

Troi thought quickly. The survivors would be able to give him the lie. This bastard was just the sort to check. 'No, I was about six when we arrived there.' He wasn't sure he was doing the right thing sticking to his cover story, but Aias's final letter had been insistent.

'How old are you?'

Troi felt as if he was in the pankration, staggering under a flurry of blows. 'Sixteen.'

'Where from, before that?' The interrogation was ruthless, and Troi felt the shakiness of the whole edifice of lies. He should have practised his account.

'I don't remember,' he said helplessly. It was true. He had forgotten. He had no idea. But now it sounded weak and suspicious.

'What's your mother's name?'

Xanthos was switching his attention from Troi to Diomedes and back again with a look of amazement on his face.

Troi hesitated, tellingly. 'Philomena.' Then he remembered. 'Argos,' he said. 'I think we lived in Argos.'

'With your mother and father?'

'Yes.'

'So, what happened to your mother?'

'She died.'

'Of what?'

'The bloody flux.'

'What did your father die of?'

He couldn't say Laomedon's murdering Krypteia. 'Herakla's grip.'

'I thought you lived in Koi with your father.' Diomedes was stripping away the layers of lies like onion skins.

'Yes. No. Not my real father. I mean…' Troi felt like a fish out of water, throwing itself desperately around to return to the security of its own element.

'And what did your mother look like?' It was all too fast. A blur of questions.

'I can't really remember.'

'Not even the colour of her hair?' He sounded sceptical to the point of sarcasm.

Black. He nearly said black. There was an agonised pause. 'Brown.'

'So, not black and curly, then?'

He knew. How he knew, Troi had no idea. But the certainty in the man's eyes told him that he knew. Troi remained miserably silent.

Diomedes' voice became gentle. 'And her true name was Aglaia.'

Troi stared at him, then nodded.

Xanthos was staring at Diomedes too. 'But wasn't Aglaia Auntie Kal's daughter?'

'She was,' he said, very quietly. His face was not made for showing emotions, but there was deep sorrow there now.

Auntie Kal. Uncle Dio. Everything slipped into place. 'You're the Uncle Dio from Massalia.' The sense of sudden relief was wonderful.

'And your name is Pyrrhus, not Troilus.'

'Perhaps. I might stay Troilus now.'

'You do know,' Diomedes said carefully and slowly, 'about your mother?' Troi looked down and nodded.

'And her mother?'

There was something in his tone that made Troi look up sharply. He shook his head.

The iron control in Diomedes' voice was worse than any show of emotion. 'She died. A wasting sickness. Two years ago. I'm sorry.' There was a pause. 'Your grandfather is still alive.'

Xanthos finally puzzled it out. 'So, Troilus is Auntie Kal's grandson,' he announced triumphantly.

'Well done, Xan. It was a long journey, but you got there.' Diomedes looked back at Troi. 'Xan's family sheltered and protected your grandmother when she was in great danger. There is much that you don't know. We need to have a long talk. But that's for later.' Dio rose, and the two young men followed him to their feet.

'But tell me one thing,' said Troi. 'How did you know?'

Diomedes looked at him—no, beyond him. He was somewhere else.

'You have her eyes,' he said simply.

TWENTY-SEVEN

THEY TALKED A great deal the next day, in a small back room of the strategion. Troi had spent his years in a placid backwater, far from the surge and ebb of the momentous events beyond. Aias had taken no interest in news of such, or, as Troi now suspected, had simply feigned indifference; and they had always, by the nature of their lifestyle, been largely detached from the social life of the small town. Troi had known little of the outside world and cared less.

But now, Diomedes told him of his family and how entangled they had been in great affairs of state. His grandfather, Miltiades, had been involved in the abortive Monotheite Rising and divorced Troi's grandmother, Kalliste, simply to facilitate an advantageous remarriage.

Then he had ordered, or at the very least acquiesced in, an attempt on her life. Diomedes, as Miltiades' swordmaster, and friend to both him and Kalliste for many years, had spirited Kalliste away from danger, managed to warn the Emperor, and strangled the plot at birth. Only for Laomedon to finally spring his long-anticipated coup. As an old enemy of the usurper, Diomedes, now married to Kalliste, sensibly fled the country.

Diomedes had been like a father to both Aglaia and her brother Antinous, and he told Troi of his mother with real fondness, but the look of desolation when he spoke of his beloved Kal was, even to the detached Troilus, winter, all howling wind, stygian gloom and bone-chilling ice. He had returned to Gea to oppose the bloody rule of Laomedon. Though Diomedes never said so, Troi intuitively grasped that there was nothing left for him to live for, and if he died in the attempt, then so much the better.

In the tough people of Mykerenos, moulded strong and unyielding by their isolated mountain environment, Diomedes had found the seeds of revolt. The granting of the province as a fiefdom to one of Laomedon's whoring cronies was the immediate cause. Marsyas was grasping, cruel and vindictive—the last person to be entrusted with such a difficult and obstinate people. The soil was fertile, tilled with defiance, composted with blood, and sown with resentment. The Order of the White Rose had spread its roots throughout the country, and insurrection had grown like weeds. Mykerenos had only recently been a proud and independent country and now erupted into savage rebellion once more. A rebellion into which Troi was about to immerse himself.

Diomedes stood up and walked to the door. 'I can't teach you how to survive. Only surviving does that. But I can make sure that you have the skills and experience to give you a chance.' He opened the door and asked the guard to send in Sim.

The bald officer who had been working with the clerks entered. He had a bulbous nose, thick lips and humourless eyes. A small, skinny scribe trailed in his wake, clutching his wax tablet and stylus as though they were flotsam to a drowning man, and looking around himself with darting, pale eyes.

'About time,' the officer grumbled, in a voice that reminded Troi of the call of a raven. 'I've been standing around like a bloody barnacle in a foot race.'

He glared at Diomedes, who seemed not in the least disconcerted.

Diomedes introduced Troi. 'This is…' He looked at Troi with a raised eyebrow.

Troi did not hesitate. 'Troilus.'

The little scribe scratched away at his wax tablet. He glanced up with those disconcertingly pale eyes. 'Son of?' he asked in a high-pitched voice.

Troi did not look directly at Diomedes but caught his speculative glance. 'Aias.'

Diomedes did not seem troubled at all by Troi's decision. He gestured towards the officer. 'This is Simonides. He was the best staff officer in the Troian army. Now he's the best in the Mykerenaean. Well, certainly the grumpiest.'

Simonides gave a spectacularly loud humph.

Diomedes winked at Troi. 'And he is going to make sure you are taught by the best. Sword, spear, knife, javelin and bow, not to mention good old-fashioned fists, teeth and nails. Sim knows a man who is going to make you fit. And I mean really fit.' Simonides sighed loudly and glanced at the door as though contemplating an escape attempt. 'When I get the chance, I'll give you a workout. I can still use a sword. You're going to be taught drill and tactics, military history and oratory and how to lead men. You'll have every third se'ennight off. That's when Xanthos takes over to teach you some proper scouting. In your so-called leisure time, you'll learn Thracian, Keltoi and Eretrian. Oh, and when we get a chance, you'll get some genuine fighting. Nothing like the real thing to give a man an edge. Have fun.' He returned to his chair and sat down again.

The young scribe smirked, and Simonides showed his teeth mirthlessly. Troi gave him a sickly smile in response. He didn't think Diomedes was joking.

He wasn't.

TWENTY-EIGHT

THE NEXT DAY, he was introduced to Xenarches, who was to be his military tutor. Thin-faced, sharp-nosed and with a sparse, straggly beard, he had been a tutor at the Military Academy at Megara, but had been banned after an uncomplimentary observation on Laomedon's Stymphalian Campaign. His dust-dry delivery could not detract from his formidable knowledge of military history and battle tactics.

'Never mind about Kratelos and the Battle of Delium,' said Troi as they sat in a scatter of scrolls and tablets like squirrels amongst their cache of nuts. There was no roof on the small, whitewashed room they occupied. 'Tell me how it all started. I never expected to come back to something like this.'

Xenarches leaned forward on the battered old table and steepled his fingers. 'Not exactly planned,' he said. 'It was more spontaneous than anything. The Order of the White Rose formed a secret Council in Pelium; you know what an obdurate lot they are, though all they did was talk. In secret, naturally. But a few began to look for more direct action and gathered on the slopes of Mount Pelion, hiding in the caves and gullies, gradually gathering arms, that sort of thing. Then Diomedes arrived. After his role in stopping the Monotheite Plot, he had a real reputation. He was put in command of a threadbare and ill-trained army, if you can call six hundred men an army.'

'They couldn't take Marsyas on with that,' protested Troi.

'I know. Diomedes knew. Everyone knew. It was hard enough getting them sufficient food. Who said that an army's blood and bone is wine and bread?'

'Not the slightest idea,' admitted Troi cheerfully.

'Kallisthenes of Zagria.' He gave Troi a look of disapproval.

Troi couldn't see how knowing which ancient general had made some trite observation helped when it came to spear and shield, muscle and blood, but apparently it did.

Xenarches continued. 'It would probably have just faded away if it hadn't been for the news of…' He hesitated, remembering the young man's history. '…Bogazkoi.'

Troi gave not the slightest twitch of reaction.

Reassured, his tutor pressed on. 'When people heard of the Holokauston, the place just erupted. They overran the citadel before the Troians even realised there was a problem, and massacred the lot. The naval squadron was largely recruited from the locals, and they went over en masse to the rising. Or over the side.' He chuckled. 'Their navarches, Phormio, joined them with the immortal words, "Fuck it, I'm in."'

The elder man stood and stretched. He was getting old and stiff. 'So, you're Marsyas, what do you do?'

'I know Pelium has good defences, but this was essentially a civilian riot. It not only needed putting down, but it was a good chance to deadhead the White Rose once they'd come out of hiding. I'd have gone in very fast and very hard.'

Xenarches nodded in satisfaction. 'Who said, "Above all, know your enemy"?'

Troi knew this one. 'Iphikrates of Kos.'

Xenarches straightened up and touched his fingertips to his chin. A position invariably preparatory to a formal lecture, as Troi had begun to recognise. 'Marsyas is a man characterised by cowardice, stupidity and no military experience. An opponent sent by the Gods for our amusement.'

'Except that he wields a bloody big stick,' muttered Troi.

'Indeed.' He brushed Troi's comment aside with a touch of irritation. 'But he acts without thought, on impulse. Consider his behaviour at Bogazkoi.' He ticked off the points on his fingers. 'He chooses to send in his Bluecloaks to search the town. When the inevitable conflict erupts, he panics and floods men in. Then he sees it's well out of control and orders a massacre with no thought for the consequences. Somewhat belatedly, realising how this would tumble the boulder downhill, he comes up with the ridiculous idea of blaming the Eleans. Then recognising, or more likely being told, that this wouldn't fool a stoneblind Phthian, he sends back his cavalry to screen the place'—an image of a rider looming above him, faceless against the bright sun, flickered across Troi's mind—'presumably in order for someone to really clean up the place. By then, it's too late.'

Troi felt uncomfortable with the subject. Too many feelings had to be suppressed. 'We were talking about Pelium,' he reminded Xenarches.

'Indeed. Well, Marsyas was dilatory, and by the time he appeared before the port, they were ready for him. He flung his men at the main gates without planning or preparation, no proper siege machinery, no diversions, no organised missile support.' He shook his head at such unprofessional conduct.

'Aias always said you can't beat men behind walls. But didn't Marysas at least attack the walls at various places and times? Stretch the defences? Probe the weak spots?'

'He's not possessed of a military brain and hasn't got the sense to listen to those who have.'

'Then what about Diomedes? Surely that was the time to strike?'

'I'm coming to that,' came the rather testy response. 'Phormio's marines and the townsfolk held the gates, and Diomedes marshalled his army on the slopes of the mountain, waiting until the Troians were fully joined in battle. He gauged the moment well and threw them at the Troians' rear. Good generalship is all about timing.'

'What about the Troian reserve?'

'Marsyas kept no reserve. No reserve at all.' He tutted. 'Diomedes may have had but a small army, poorly armed, largely untrained and with a very rudimentary command structure, but the Trogs broke and fled. A classic collapse of morale. Once it starts, there is no stopping it. Pan is in control.' He looked thoughtful. 'The Troians have the forces to crush us like stepping on a beetle, but I suspect our finest strategos will nevertheless defeat them.'

'Diomedes?'

'By no means. Our best strategos is undoubtedly Marsyas.'

Troi blinked at him.

'He's an arrant coward. He won't use his power in any decisive way. He will be too tentative, too cautious. But above all, his pusillanimity will infect his troops.'

'His what?'

'Pusillanimity. Timidity. Cowardice. It will eat into the very heart of his army like woodrot. They will run. They will run easily. They now expect to be defeated. Mark my words.'

Xenarches shook himself as though coming out of a trance. 'In any event,' he continued, 'Diomedes had no cavalry to turn the rout into a massacre, but it shook Marsyas up, I can tell you. He retreated right across the Vale, falling back on his supply route through the Boreas and ended up, well, you know where better than I. Diomedes has followed him with the best of his troops, but hasn't the forces to face him. Instead, he concentrates on recruitment and training.' He fixed Troi with a stare like the point of a javelin. 'Is he right?'

'Absolutely.'

Xenarches studied the rather strange and distant young man before him. There was something about him, a confidence, a sure and instinctive grasp of tactics, and a quick, analytical mind, that reminded him of a young Parmenio. The best student he had ever taught, and now probably the most effective strategos in the Empire's army. Xenarches would speak to Diomedes.

TWENTY-NINE

A FEW DAYS LATER, Diomedes sent for Troi again. With Xenarches' report fresh in mind, he gave Troi a briefing on the respective forces and their positions. Troi was appalled. Marsyas had the forces to swat them like a fly at any moment he chose. Diomedes rose and went over to a small table to refill his wine. He raised an interrogative eyebrow, but Troi shook his head.

'So that's the situation. Precarious, to say the least. What the White Rose has is a lot of enthusiastic volunteers, unarmed, untrained, untested. What we need is experienced men who can train them. We need even more recruits and volunteers. We need allies and mercenaries, though a lot of Thracians and not a few Aggies have joined us. We need weapons and a whole new infrastructure: logistics, diplomacy, recruitment, an intelligence network. Experienced strategoi. A staff bureau. Spades to dig latrines, for Dyaus's sake. Every bloody thing.' He shook his head in exasperation. 'For that we need time. Above all else, we need time.'

He sat down again. They were in Diomedes' personal quarters. Just a couple of planks on mud brick pillars for a bed, two rough wooden stools purloined from the inn and the small table with a chipped amphora of wine. A terracotta lamp, perched precariously in a roughly excavated aperture, provided a paltry light.

'We have the money, though. When that fat bastard took to his cowardly heels, he abandoned his personal treasury and the army chest, which was, shall we say, substantial. I'll wager that annoyed him. More importantly, the silver mines on Pelion have struck a rich seam. It seems the Gods are with us. We are collecting the annual taxes for ourselves, and Phormio is enjoying himself with a bit of lucrative piracy.' He corrected himself. 'A lot of lucrative piracy.'

'So, how do you buy time?'

'How would you?' asked Diomedes, regarding him quizzically.

'Couldn't better what you're already doing.'

'Which is?' He wasn't going to let him get away with it as easily as that.

Troi began to enumerate on his fingers. 'One, you have your friend Tereus using his Thracians to bottle Marsyas up and effectively blind him. Cavalry is the Butcher's weak spot, and you've now got substantial numbers of the best light cavalry in the world. Or so Xenarches rates them. Two, you're letting him get an occasional glimpse of what you want him to see, and, to that end, you have the poor bloody hoplites scuttling around from place to place pretending to be a massive army. I've heard their complaints. One was telling me he'd been under six different banners in a se'ennight. He said he couldn't rightly remember which was the correct one.' Diomedes gave a slight smile. 'Three, I understand you're hitting his supply trains. I would guess just enough to frighten and weaken him, but not enough to force him to make a move, which is definitely to be avoided at the moment. It's a tight ridgeline you're walking.'

'You have the right of it there.' Diomedes nodded approvingly. 'You've a good military brain, Troi. I doubt there's even one of my senior officers worked that out.'

'Shouldn't Praxis know? What if anything happens to you?'

'He does,' said Diomedes, 'but it took some explaining. So, seeing you're such a clever young devil, what's Marsyas playing at?'

Troi considered. 'He has the superior forces, but he's scared. He's a coward and has probably overestimated your force after the trouncing at Pelium. That's why he's sitting behind those defences and praying that you don't have the guts to attack him.'

'We're feeding him false information. On what he thinks he knows, he's right to be scared. But then, why isn't he demanding reinforcements? They should have been here by now.'

'That's easy. He's more frightened of Laomedon than of you. He's not going to admit to that evil bastard that he got his arse kicked. Laomedon is not the forgiving type, even with his oldest cronies.'

Diomedes nodded with satisfaction. 'My assessment exactly.' He looked at Troi musingly. 'You really do have a good brain. You probably got that from your mother. She was as bright as the Dog Star.' There was that sudden distance in his eyes. 'But your grandmother was the smartest person I ever knew. I never admitted it, but she could run rings round me. She would say that she was trying to teach me common sense, but it was a lost cause.' He smiled sadly. 'She eventually gave up in favour of teaching my horse geometry. She said it would be easier.'

Troi smiled.

'But she wasn't that clever,' Diomedes added. 'She could never get him past the fourth theorem.'

THIRTY

TROI CURSED HIMSELF for a fool the next day.

'How are you holding up to the training?' Diomedes had innocently enquired near the end of his briefing.

'Not a problem,' Troi had airily answered.

Not a problem? This huge brute of a man was attacking him with what seemed like three swords, coming with unbelievable speed from every direction. Sweat poured from Troi's brow. Watch the eyes. Watch the body balance. Don't think. Respond instinctively. Two, three times he blocked a scything stroke and then the wooden practice sword swept under his tardy riposte and hammered into the side of the bronze corselet. He staggered away slightly, and two more blurred strokes punched into his torso hard enough to knock the breath from his body. He fell over backwards with a resounding crash. Aristippus removed his helmet, a broad grin across his homely face.

'Diomedes had a word with you, didn't he?' Troi gasped. His ribs ached.

The grin, if anything, broadened. 'He said I was going too easy on you. Never get cocky, young un.'

'Thanks. I'll take that as sound advice,' muttered Troi, clambering painfully back to his feet.

'Sword arm's held a touch too high,' said Aristippus as he slipped his helmet back on. He pushed his aspis out before him. 'And again.'

THIRTY-ONE

MARSYAS MIGHT HAVE been frightened to admit his difficulties to Laomedon, but that did not prevent the Emperor from knowing all about them, and reinforcements arrived in autumn for the embattled satrap. Two speirai, five eiles of cavalry and some light troops, along with a strategos as 'advisor': a respected tactician called Parmenio who was known to Diomedes and Xenarches and well regarded by both.

Marsyas emerged but the once. Enraged by the loss of a supply convoy, and with the new confidence afforded by his reinforcements, he wrong-footed Diomedes and marched on the nearest Mykerenaean town, sacking it in a deliberate orgy of destruction and killing. Diomedes did not have the forces to bring him to battle, though the Thracian cavalry, now in substantial numbers, made the Troians bleed. Marsyas, encouraged by the savage lesson he had administered, sent a force on to the next small town and unwittingly signed his own death warrant.

THIRTY-TWO

CHRYSAOR PATTED THE neck of his gelding. The horse could hear the distant sounds of battle and was pawing the ground, tossing his head and flaring his nostrils. Chrysaor looked down into the wide flat-bottomed valley where the battle was being fought. At the far end, tucked into the shelter of a scarp slope down which tumbled the silver thread of a waterfall, and surrounded by woods of red and gold, was their goal, a small town, little more than a village of no strategic or tactical importance at all. He was puzzled as to why Marsyas was eager to capture it and, equally so, why the Mickeys were determined to defend it. Though they were doing a good job, by the look of it.

Marsyas had chosen to go for speed and had sent only cavalry and horsed light infantry, and the rebel commander had been obliged to do the same. There just wasn't time for the heavy infantry to get there. The problem was that the rebels had the better cavalry. The reputation of the Thracians was well deserved. Chrysaor watched with increasing agitation as a seeming unruly mob of Thracians, seated on small shaggy ponies, each dressed in a simple tunic and armed with only a bucket full of javelins, a long knife and a small pelta shield, raced up against a heavy cavalry plag and split in either direction, hurling clouds of javelins as they crossed its frontage. Horses reared and fell, men were plucked from their backs, and many of the Troians, without apparent orders, urged their mounts forward in vengeful pursuit of the right-hand wing of their tormentors.

Chrysaor knew what would happen, and he glanced at his deuteros, a brawny, shaggy-haired and bushy-bearded man called Poteidonius, known universally as The Shark, who looked back and shrugged. He knew too. The Thracians kept just ahead of the pursuit, mocking their pursuers, until the tired Troian horses began to slow. No horse could compete with a Thracian pony in terms of endurance. The other Thracian wing had shadowed them and now poured in from the right rear, hurling javelins at the unprotected backs of the Troians. As they turned to face this new attack, the rearward Thracians peeled away, while those in front swung round with impressive alacrity and attacked in turn. Caught between the two, the alarmed Troians urged their horses back towards their own lines. The Thracians instantly turned from irritants into savage killers, working as pairs against the fleeing Trogs, one distracting their victim while the other moved in from the opposite side to plant a javelin between his shoulder blades. Few reached safety.

'It's a bloody massacre,' muttered Poteidonius, 'Onomastus hasn't a fucking clue.'

Chrysaor sighed. Poteidonius's readiness to express an unmitigated opinion about his superiors was the reason he would never rise beyond the rank of plagiophylakes, though he was the best man in a fight that Chrysaor had ever known and no mean tactician.

The Shark swung round to the second plagiophylakes of the eile – a remarkably handsome, golden-haired and swashbuckling young man called Alexandros. 'Tell me again why that idiot's in charge, instead of Parmenio, and why we're sitting on this hill like a carbuncle on a whore's backside and doing bugger all?'

Alexandros answered with the languid air that he had been cultivating for years. 'Because Marsyas doesn't like real strategoi being dumped on him. Cramps his lack of style. He prefers to be surrounded by sycophants and talentless cronies. And because we arrived with Parmenio, we all smell the same to any dog.' He glanced across at his eilarches. 'Do we know who's in command of the rebels?'

'Man called Meleagros,' said Chrysaor. 'They captured some rebels and questioned them.' Anger rang in his voice. 'Tortured them, rather. Then they hanged them. That was stupid. Just feeding fuel to the fire.'

Down below, a group of hirsute little men had just brutally attacked a unit of peltastes on the Troian flank and driven them easily from the small rocky hill they had occupied.

'Agrianians,' said Alexandros. 'They're evil little sods.'

'But why have they done it?' asked Chrysaor. 'It's not tactically significant. They have no support to exploit it.'

He paused. 'Unless…' He walked his horse a little higher up the slope and looked down, shielding his eyes from the sun's full glare. 'Dyaus's balls. Movement. Cavalry. Look like Thracians.' He trotted back down the slope. 'The clever bastard has kept an eile hidden. Possibly more. He's going to come round that hill they've just taken and into our rear.' His eyes scanned the immediate terrain. He pointed to the higher hill to their right. 'Xander, take your second tetrarchia up there and mill around making a show. I want them convinced we're all still up here. Take all the standards and wave them about in a mindless manner.'

Poteidonius grinned. 'He should be able to manage that, Boss.'

Chrysaor gave Poteidonius a withering look, then turned back to Alexandros. 'When you see us hit the Thracians, come down at the ram and join in. Shark. You, the remaining three tets and your irritating sense of humour with me.'

'Hadn't we better check with Onomastus?' asked Poteidonius.

Chrysaor waved the men to follow him. 'No time. And do you really want to?'

Poteidonius grinned again and shrugged, then followed his commander downhill to their left. They quickly dropped out of enemy sight behind a round-topped hill where a dip provided excellent screening from the recently captured hillock. It rose to a slight ridge ahead. Chrysaor quickly gave his orders before he dismounted and crouched low to climb to the top of the ridge, a trooper waiting below him, holding his horse well out of sight.

Upon the signal, Poteidonius was to bring his two tets up over the ridge and charge into the flank of the Thracians. One tet to drive straight in, the second to loop round to take them in the rear. The final tet was to head round the intervening hill to the right and hit the Thracians head on. There was to be no salpinx call. No warning. Boxed in, the Thracians would be ground to dust between the millstones. After they had dealt with them, they would continue round the hill just taken by the Agrianians, reversing the Thracians' manoeuvre and erupt into the rear of the rebel forces.

He had equipped his well-armoured troopers not with the usual javelins, but xystoi, spears with long, wide, stabbing blades and counterweighted with a butt spike, about four paces long. He had then trained them to charge home, putting the momentum of a horse travelling at speed behind that vicious weapon, able to hurl men from their mounts or bring a horse itself tumbling to the ground. He now had a powerful weapon in his hands and knew how to use it.

As soon as he reached his chosen position, he raised his hand and held it there. Every man's eyes were glued to that hand as they tightened their shield straps, settled their helmets more comfortably on their heads and grasped their xystoi at the point of balance.

Then the hand fell.

THIRTY-THREE

CHRYSAOR SAT BY the fire and stared out into the gathering gloom, where a more substantial fire burned. His men sat cleaning their equipment, tending to minor wounds, cooking for their files, surprisingly quiet and dejected. Poteidonius and Alexandros stood a short distance away and watched their commander with worried eyes.

Chrysaor was watching the small town burn. He did not even know the name of the community he had destroyed. The surge and flare of the flames before the darkening sky reminded him of the bonfires built to celebrate the day the sun stood still, when men knew that winter would start to retreat before the promise of spring. The Haloea was a time of celebration, drunkenness and not a little debauchery. But this was no joyous feast.

He could see movement before the flames. Not the suggestive dances of the Haloea, but the scutter of small, dark figures: murderers, rapists, looters and sadists, not just destroying the town but crucifying it. Carrying on the new tradition that had begun with the Holokauston of Bogazkoi. Sickened, Chrysaor had led his eile away from the Hades that had erupted after Meleagros had hastily disengaged and fallen back, leaving the town helpless. Chrysaor had received a rather grudging word of praise from the smug Onomastus, but it only made it worse. He had caused it. He had given them the victory, and this was what they had done with it.

He had rashly demanded to know why they were treating their own people like this. Onomastus angrily responded that it was on orders from Marsyas himself, that the rebels and their supporters must be visited by his wrath until either they submitted or Mykerenos was left an uninhabited desert. Then the strategos had watched, with narrowed eyes, the abrupt departure of an incensed eilarches.

Chrysaor suddenly stood and, without looking back, walked to his horse, threw a blanket over it, quietly mounted and rode off. Poteidonius and Alexandros looked round the camp. Silence had fallen. Everywhere eyes stared back at them, glinting in the firelight. The two officers glanced at one another, Alexandros nodded, and both moved across to their horses. Behind them, several men rose to gather their equipment. More and more stood, without a word spoken, and began to mount up. Soon, over three quarters of the eile were moving out of the camp after their officers, disappearing into the night. Those left stared into the flames of the campfires and would not meet each other's eyes.

And thus, the final shatang piece was in play. Chrysaor and those of his eile who had loyally followed were found by Xanthos and brought to Diomedes. Now Diomedes had been gifted with a military genius. One able to wield the disparate elements of the rebellion into a new and effective fighting force that would prove unstoppable. To protect his friends and family, Chrysaor took the battle name of Harpalycus. The Ravening Wolf. A name that was destined to become known and feared throughout the Troian Empire.

THIRTY-FOUR

THE FALLING LEAF of autumn passed, and then came the drear of winter. Traditionally, men fought the cold and hunger and the treacherous mud and ice of what poor tracks there were, instead of each other. Marsyas moved to occupy and fortify the town of Tenos for his winter quarters, and then remained largely supine behind his defences. But Diomedes was not going to allow him an easy rest. Troi rode and fought with the savage Thracians, stood in the shield line when the toiling supply trains were ambushed in the broken ground of the Boreas and, with Xanthos, slipped through the velvet night like a ghost, taking out the Troian sentinels with ruthless ease to spread alarm and disaffection. He became fit and fast and strong, able to beat Aristippus two times out of five, though he never managed to best Diomedes. The old man always had a trick behind his shield.

The time was not wasted. Ikaros was now a large garrison town, with wooden storehouses and barracks, lines of leather tents and a sturdy defensive stockade. Newly trained units were arriving daily, including the formidable mercenary Cretan archers and Rhodian slingers, paid for with the silver of Mount Pelion. With them, large numbers of volunteers from all over the Troian Empire, derisively called the Chenoi, or Wild Geese, by the Troian loyalists, a name they proudly adopted as their own.

Diomedes had been busy. He had persuaded the receptive Thracians of Gean Thrake that now was the time to regain their recently lost freedom, and many of their free countrymen came across the Athos to join them. They weren't going to let a good fight go to waste. The Troians promptly retired to their strongholds and left the wild Thracians to do much as they had always done; squabble between the tribes, raid the Geans when they could get away with it and throw the odd, rash tax collector down a well. In this case, it was also an opportunity to raise Hades, to participate in their national sport of fighting, take fine revenge on the Trogs and to get paid for it at the same time. It was a Thracian's idea of Elysium.

Diomedes quietly made sure that both the Keltoi and Eretrians, inveterate enemies of the Geans, were kept informed, and they soon began to threaten the frontiers of Gea, drawing away Troian troops. They were happy to do so on the age-old principle that my enemy's enemy is my friend.

In the middle of winter, he journeyed in secret to Agriania. Diomedes' treacherous old blood brother, Neritos, was dead, but his son, Chileos, now ruled in the Kodros and was a much more intelligent man than his father had ever been. He was happy to encourage more recruitment of his troublesome young men and would spread the word to the surrounding kingdoms.

The rebellion had the support of the people, the money, and was beginning to gather the men. It had the commanders and the spirit to fight. An army was being forged in the white heat of insurrection that would be without parallel in the long history of Gea.

THIRTY-FIVE

TROI, DESPITE HIS youth, was now an officer; a lowly tetrarches, perhaps, but a line officer nevertheless.

Gwalchmai, the Skoparches, commander of the scouts, had called him into the four crumbling walls and leather awning that he was pleased to call his office. As befitted that of a scout, it contained little but a table, an eclectic collection of salvaged stools and a chest full of scrolls and maps. A fire burning in the ancient hearth did nothing to dispel the winter's chill.

Gwalchmai was an elderly, one-eyed Keltos who had come to Mykerenos long ago for the hunting, loved the country, and stayed. He spoke Gean perfectly but retained the singsong cadences of his native language. Although no longer active in the field, he knew men and was building up an impressive force of well-trained, self-reliant and extremely effective scouts.

He offered Troi a kylix of wine. Troi added plenty of spring water. He had the feeling that his slightest action was being scrutinised, pondered and weighed. Gwalchmai came straight to the point. His single eye never left Troi's face, and Troi had the uncomfortable sensation that he was looking deep inside him.

'You're a good scout,' Gwalchmai said.

'Thank you. I try.'

Gwalchmai nodded. 'Not just a question of trying. You have an aptitude.'

Troi inclined his head in what he hoped was a graceful acknowledgement.

Gwalchmai took a good drink of his wine and pulled a face of wry distaste. 'Never get used to this bloody Tenedian wine,' he grumbled. 'Horse piss.'

Troi chose not to argue the point.

The Chief Scout studied the young man before him for a few heartbeats, then asked, without further preamble, 'Do you want to be an officer?'

Troi started. The thought had never occurred to him. He considered briefly. 'Yes.'

Gwalchmai nodded with evident satisfaction.

Troi looked back into that slightly unnerving single eye. 'Does this come from Diomedes?'

The man laughed. 'No, by the Black Morrigan. I am the Skoparches. I decide. You have the iron in your back, the fire in your belly and the brains in your head. That is all. The strategarch knows nothing of this.'

'Will the men accept me, being so young?'

'The very fact you ask that question shows that you're older than you seem. Whether they accept you or not is up to you. That's what being an officer is all about. I have no doubts myself.' He took another drink of his wine. 'But one word of advice: Don't ever think you can command Xanthos. He's a law to himself and answers to no-one else. I accept it because he's the best bloody scout I've ever seen.'

'Why isn't he an officer?' asked Troi, intrigued.

'He will not be one. He says that all he wants to do is scout and not track pieces of parchment.' Gwalchmai looked disapprovingly at the pile of wax tablets and scrolls on his desk. 'He has a point.' He looked shrewdly at Troi. 'Are you still interested?'

'Yes.'

Gwalchmai smiled slightly, rummaged in a pouch hanging from a chair and handed him his yellow sash of office, with its bronze clasp of crossed spears. 'Not to be worn while scouting,' he said with a straight face. 'Well, Tetrarches Troilus, a young man is waiting outside, asking to join the scouts. I want a report on my table by first light tomorrow as to his suitability. Dismissed.'

THIRTY-SIX

TROI WAS DUE to be posted to the Boreas Pass, the long but wide gateway to Mykerenos. Cloaked in woodland in its higher, middle stretches, it was more open towards either end, turning and twisting its way through sprawling pine woods and serrated, ice-capped mountains. There were other passes wending tortuously through the ring of mountains that enclosed the Vale and stood sentinel over the outlying fertile strip of the Littoral, but they were all difficult, dangerous, impossible for ox-carts and usually seasonal. None but the Boreas could take the necessary traffic, and it was only rarely blocked.

As such, it was the axis about which the war revolved. As the entire country had risen, Marsyas could not gather in supplies, and dared not send out troops to forage for fear of the deadly Thracians, who specialized in ambush and hit-and-run tactics. But the rebels, faced with an overwhelming mass of heavy infantry, could not, as yet, meet them in the field. It was crocodile against lion. Neither dared venture into the alien territory of its antagonist.

But the supply convoys coming through the pass trundled between sand and tide, and the Boreas became the battleground by proxy, the beauty of its magnificent terrain the stunning backdrop to an arena of death.

Nicias was a local lad. Born not far from Akrai, he knew the Western Boreads well. Winter still held the world in its icy grip, but it was a beautiful day, bitingly cold but sunny, as Nicias rode out with Troi to familiarize the new officer with the area. There were patches of snow on the ground, and ice splintered under the sharp hooves of their ponies.

'Wait until you see the Moesian Gorge,' said Nicias, chattering on in his jovial manner. It rather got on Troi's nerves, but he knew Nicias to be a good scout and controlled his irritation.

'Isn't there a pass there?'

'The Anchises, but it's difficult and blocked in winter. Mostly used by the less reputable members of society who want to slip in and out unnoticed. Must be reasonably well used though, as someone has taken the trouble to throw a rope bridge across the gorge. You used to have to follow the gorge for a hundred stadia to round it. The path's still there, but it's not good. We can follow it though and come back over the bridge.'

Troi studied the terrain. It was bad country: broken rock, craggy upthrusts, thick patches of pine trees. It would take time to decipher this scroll, but Nicias clearly knew how to read it. He led them confidently upwards along what he claimed was a path, but which was only fitfully, and then but barely, recognisable as such. In the mid-morning sunshine, the frozen puddles had a thin sheen of meltwater on them, and Troi took care guiding his Thracian pony, though they were a surefooted breed.

Nicias stopped and grandly proclaimed, 'The Moesian Gorge.'

Troi moved his pony forward and stared. It certainly was impressive. It was as if some God had hacked a huge axe into the entrails of the earth and then riven the two sides apart. Up to a couple of stadia wide, it was a disorientating gash across the mountain extending as far as the eye could see. The sides were all but vertical and plunged down to a savage scatter of sharp rocks far below, bisected by the boiling white water of a mountain stream in spate.

Troi felt an unpleasant touch of vertigo and lifted his eyes to look about him instead. The coniferous forest here descended in places almost to the upper lip of the gorge. The lower side was impenetrable woodland. The path ahead was obvious for once, and sensibly tended to keep well away from the edge, even veering into the trees where it could. They set off along the trail, Nicias still chattering. Crested tits flitted and churred amongst the trees, and high overhead an eagle soared.

After about a dekate, a column of rock forced the path to the very lip. A tiny frozen stream ran across it just before the narrowest part. Troi went first, cautiously keeping as close to the pillar as possible, especially because the path dipped markedly towards the chasm. He reached the other side with some relief. A startling crash of breaking wood, ripping vegetation and a deafening half-howl, half-growl. A horrifying glimpse of a brown bear rising up before him, shaggy fur, startling white teeth and pitiless eyes. The thought flitted bizarrely across his mind that it must have been brought out of hibernation by the recent warm weather, and his pony reared, squealing with fright.

Troi crashed to the ground, and a flailing hoof caught him on the arm. He found himself skating down the slope on a sheet of ice, head first, his hands scrabbling frantically to find purchase, sliding helplessly towards the edge. He could do nothing as his torso slid over, and the rocks below stared up at him, waiting hungrily for the sickening fall. Immediately below him was a small sapling in a fissure, and he instinctively grabbed out for it. His hands closed round the thin trunk just as his legs followed his body, swinging him round like a sling. He was dangling in a void, nothing below him but death, and the tree bending, creaking and giving in its insecure lodgement. Heart. Breath. Time. All stopped.

But the sapling held. His heart commenced to hammer in his ribs, and he sucked in needed air. He gripped tightly, breathing heavily and choosing not to look down. Looking around was bad enough. He was partly facing the cliff and could see that he had fallen from an overhang. It was only a few handbreadths in, but this was enough. He would be unable to climb out. The tree lurched again, then settled. He hung there, scarcely daring to breathe, let alone move.

Above, there were sounds of movement, and Nicias's round face popped into view some way back. Despite the distance, Troi could see the relief in the lad's eyes.

'Thank Dyaus,' Nicias called. 'I thought you'd been given your discharge scroll.'

'Still might be. This tree feels loose and could give.'

'We've another problem. There's a bloody great crack where you went over. The whole lot could go.'

Troi felt something small strike his face and glanced up to see bits of grit and small stones dropping from the underside of the overhang. Dyaus. What a stupid way to die. Falling off his bloody horse. The image of Marsyas, laughing out loud, formed in his mind.

'I've got an idea. Hold on.'

'I've every intention of doing just that,' muttered Troi as Nicias disappeared. The tree moved slightly again, more grit cascaded down, and he tried not to think of those dreadful final heartbeats as he would plummet down, fully conscious, knowing what awaited him.

There were more sounds above, and the overhang began to send positive showers of debris. Nicias's face appeared directly above, tight and beaded with sweat. The overhang could go at any moment, but he seemed oblivious of the danger as he slowly and carefully lowered a rope bridle, the loop of the chin piece at the bottom.

With a supreme effort of will, Troi let go with one hand and grabbed the rope. The tree groaned and sagged. He managed to hook the bridle over a side branch of the sapling to allow him to slide his hand through the loop, twist the rope around his wrist and then grip it just above the knot.

'Don't let go yet,' said Nicias. 'I've fastened the other end to a stump, so it should hold you, but there's slack, so you'll drop. The shock could bring the overhang down.' He paused, choosing not to mention the possible consequences of that. 'Then I'll haul you up.'

If I'm still here, thought Troi, trying not to consider the possibility of a large lump of rock falling on his head.

Nicias disappeared. A few heartbeats later, he called, 'Let go.'

And Troi did. Immediately he dropped, leaving his heart behind as he did so, then stopped with a wrench that all but tore his arm out of its socket. He grabbed the rope with his other hand and kept his head down as he was peppered by a rain of rock particles. Amazingly, the overhang remained, and the shower of detritus died away, leaving him swinging like a pendulum in mid-air.

There were the sounds of mighty grunts, and the rope began to inch up. He could only pray that it did not break or fray against the sharp lip. The process seemed to last forever. Fingerbreadth by fingerbreadth, he edged higher. With some difficulty, he managed to get his hands one at a time over the lip. Nicias, red-faced and sweating, continued to haul him up until he was far enough across the edge to scramble out.

His heart nearly stopped when he saw the crack. It was a handbreadth wide and twice as deep, and how it had not broken away with both his and Nicias's weight on it was beyond him. He hastily crawled across it onto firm ground, collapsed against the old trunk Nicias had been using as a belay, and gave a juddering sigh of relief. The thought occurred to him that it all might mean something. Perhaps the Gods were telling him they would keep him alive until he achieved his goal. But wouldn't it have been easier for them to send their messenger, Eiris, with a scroll?

He sat with his eyes closed for a few heartbeats, simply savouring being alive, then opened them to Nicias's cheerful face. He was unknotting the two bridles he had used and still breathing heavily from his exertions.

Troi rubbed his sore arm where the pony had kicked him. 'What happened to the bloody bear?'

Nicias grinned. 'It ran off. I think you frightened it.'

Troi smiled too. 'Thank you,' he said. 'I owe you a debt.'

'You would have done the same for me.'

Looking back at that ominous crack, Troi wasn't at all sure that he would have done.

THIRTY-SEVEN

TROI ROLLED ONTO his back, breathing rather heavily and slick with sweat. Her fingers massaged his nipple.

'That were lovely,' Danae whispered, with that familiar Mykerenaean burr.

'Good,' he said mechanically. He hoped she didn't want to talk. He had had a hard day, trailing that stupid Trog patrol and wondering where in Hades they were going, until it had transpired that their pathetic officer had simply got himself lost. Permanently lost now. The Thracians had seen to that. She nestled tightly against him. He didn't mind, as the air was cold and the sweat was drying rapidly on his body. He hauled the blankets up over them. She continued to caress his nipple. He found it slightly irritating and pushed her hand away.

'Troi,' she said, lingering over his name. 'Do you love me?'

'Of course I do.' Of course he didn't, but he wasn't going to say that. She was a pleasant-looking enough girl, square-faced, with a small, pert nose, an eminently kissable mouth and a good body, pleasingly solid and curvaceous. She was an enthusiastic love-maker, but she did like to talk.

'Tell me that you love me,' she wheedled, her hand now lightly tracing intricate patterns across his stomach.

'I love you, Danae.'

There were other girls, but each brought her own complications, and this one suited him well enough for the moment. She was the daughter of one of the merchants who had taken the risk of attaching themselves to the army in the hope of rich pickings. Danae was after the same from him, but she was going to be disappointed. 'I think I would like to sleep now,' he said.

Her hand drifted away. 'All right,' she said, with a touch of petulance.

Troi emptied his lungs in a long breath, closed his eyes and relaxed. He could feel the heat of Danae's thigh against his and, from nowhere, came the thought of it being Kalliope's. He would quite like that, he mused. He toyed with the unexpectedness of the thought for a few moments. He ought to write to her. He had promised. Perhaps he would go back there one day. He yawned and felt himself taken by sleep within hekates. Though he knew there would be the waking.

THIRTY-EIGHT

A SE'ENNIGHT LATER, THE two scouts tumbled into the strategion. It looked much more like a proper headquarters than the first time Troi had seen it. Cleaned up, extended, organised. Outside it was a shroud of snow, the smooth sheen of ice, and the stars sparks of fire lost in the cold, cloudless night sky; but within, a large fire burned in the hearth, and oil lamps softened the scene with a warm roseate glow. A group of officers were engaged in animated discussion while two more pored over a map on a large central table. Along one side, a regimented row of tall graphotrapezae, writing desks with clerks attached, stood to attention under the baleful eye of Simonides. He tossed Troi and Xanthos an unfriendly look as they came in, then switched back to harassing a long-suffering scribe. The walls were thick with duty rotas, orders of battle and long lists. But all was not work. Some youthful aides were idly chatting in one corner, and Tereus was fast asleep, as usual, his long legs propped up on a stool.

The guard officer nodded them through. 'The strategarch is in the conference room with Harpalycus and Brasidas,' he said.

They went straight on as a couple of tired-looking arrow riders appeared at the door behind them. Diomedes had insisted on creating an elite squad of expert horsemen to carry messages, and they were proving their value. Xanthos rattled the sistrum hung by the door, and they entered, pulling off their lappet caps in the relative warmth.

'Well, if it isn't the Twins of Terror,' growled Brasidas. He was a balding, middle-aged man, powerful in build and dour of manner, though with a coarse sense of humour. He had been captured in the early days and had volunteered to throw the knucklebones with the Mykerenaeans. He had only been a hyperetes, not officer class at all, but Diomedes had recognised an extremely able tactician and natural leader of men and had promoted him rapidly. Brasidas was justifying the strategarch's opinion. The other man would have faded into insignificance in a crowd of one. Of average height and build, with an unremarkable face, quiet and unassuming, he was easy to underestimate. No-one ever did it a second time. Few got that chance.

'Unc… sir,' blurted out Xanthos. 'We…'

'I know,' said Diomedes urbanely. 'You've caught yourselves an Imperial Messenger.' His seemingly magical powers to know the news before anyone else never ceased to amaze Xanthos, who nodded excitedly.

Troi grinned. 'But you should have seen the doing of it.'

'Oh, that's of no interest to them,' said Xanthos quickly. He gave his fellow scout a hurt look.

Brasidas lifted a quizzical eyebrow. 'It would be to me,' he said, feeling the pull of the current.

'Well,' said Troi, enjoying himself hugely, 'The messenger was good, and careful. We couldn't get close to him. Then Xan had this absolutely brilliant idea.'

Xanthos sighed dramatically and adopted a long-suffering expression.

'He swung down from the trees on a long rope and hit the messenger right in the chest with his feet. Sent him flying. Spectacular. That's the word. Spectacular.'

'So that was that. Good idea, eh?' interrupted Xanthos.

Troi was not in the least deterred. 'Off he soars into the canopy and then returns. Backwards of course.'

Unlike Xanthos, Brasidas had seen what was coming and was smiling.

'The horse never moved, you see,' said Troi.

Brasidas roared with laughter. Harpalycus smiled and even Diomedes' lips twitched.

'I think the branch must have given,' muttered Xanthos. No-one took any notice.

'Arse-over-tip job, was it?' asked Brasidas.

'Several times.'

'Only the once,' objected Xanthos.

'Several times sounds better,' pointed out Troi shamelessly. 'A little artistic embellishment is never out of place. And do you know what his final words were, just before he heroically launched himself into space?'

'Whose fucking silly idea was this?' suggested Brasidas.

'What about what horse?' proposed Harpalycus.

Xanthos opened his mouth to say something, then shut it again and shrugged.

'Nothing can go wrong!' exclaimed Troi triumphantly. There was an outburst of laughter.

'There's a phrase going to follow you for life.' Diomedes chuckled. 'If Marsyas ever gets to know what I've got for scouts, we're finished.'

'It could have been worse,' said Troi seriously, 'I might have died laughing.'

'Where's the message?' asked Harpalycus quietly. The atmosphere shifted.

'Sinon has it. As well as the messenger,' said Xanthos.

Sinon was a small, weasel-faced, swarthy man who had emerged from the shadows of Naupactos, claiming to be the local organiser of Laomedon's spy ring in Mykerenos. Having obviously read the entrails and seen a bright future with the Mykerenaeans, he had promised to deliver up the whole web for a position in the new council set up by the Order of the White Rose. He was as good as his word, and Laomedon's spy network had rapidly ceased to exist in reality, though its carefully nurtured ghost still haunted Troian perceptions.

'But we talked to the messenger,' Xanthos added.

'And?' prompted Harpalycus.

Xanthos became very serious. 'He says that reinforcements are flooding into the Northern Thebeaid, concentrating round Tanagra. It looks like Laomedon has decided to take the stone from his sandal.'

'Shit,' said Brasidas. Diomedes sat down heavily. Harpalycus merely nodded thoughtfully.

'Too soon,' said Diomedes, almost to himself. 'Too soon. We need more time.'

'Did he have an estimate of how many?' Harpalycus's voice was neutral.

Xanthos looked down as though reluctant to make eye contact. 'He reckoned at least ten thousand, with probably more on the way.'

'Shit,' said Brasidas again.

'Are you sure this information was genuine?'

'He was very eager to tell us everything. Once Troi showed him his knife, we couldn't shut him up.'

Harpalycus nodded. 'Thank you, lads,' said Diomedes. 'You've done well, as usual.'

As the two left, the three men looked at one another. Harpalycus spoke first. 'Sinon will soon have confirmation. How much time do we need before we can hope to meet an army like that in the field?'

'Eighteen moontides,' replied Brasidas hopelessly.

'Possibly a year,' said Diomedes. 'Given luck. Too long.'

There was silence. Then Harpalycus spoke again. 'It was foreseeable. I've been playing around with an idea. But it will be a rough road to ride.'

THIRTY-NINE

TROI AND NICIAS, half-buried beneath mounds of damp, partially rotted leaves, peered from beneath a thick bush into the small valley. The Troians had set up camp below them, at the side of a mountain stream. There were about two hundred of them, and they looked sharp and experienced. The guards were well placed, doubled and alert. The cavalry mounts and pack mules were securely corralled at the centre of the camp, and already two patrols had passed within a hundred paces of the scouts.

Troi had, in the absence of his taxiarches, found himself temporarily in command of the scouts in the quadrant. An old woodcutter passing through their camp had reported movement high in the Pass of Anchises, the rarely used and difficult crossing to the west, certainly not suitable for the movement of any supplies or large numbers of men. It had only recently become passable with a very early spring thaw.

Intrigued, Troi had sent the irreverent and cheerful Nicias, along with another young scout, to investigate. The young scout had reappeared in a state of excitement on a horse lathered in sweat. A strong detachment of Trog cavalry was escorting a small mule train down the difficult trail. Troi had immediately set off for the rendezvous Nicias had designated, and he and Nicias were now trying to make sense of the situation. The cavalry was not strong enough to be a viable offensive force, the pack train too small to be carrying vital supplies. Unless.

'Dyaus's balls,' hissed Troi. 'It's only the bloody pay chest.'

Nicias stared at him, his genial face overhung with perplexity. 'The pay chest? They wouldn't send something as valuable as that like this.'

'Wouldn't they, though?' The more Troi thought about it, the clearer it became. 'If they just send it through the Boreas with a supply train, there's a fair chance Sinon will pick up their spoor and they'll be ambushed. If they pack the defence, that will only draw more attention, and Marsyas doesn't know how strong our forces are. He could lose both gold and a significant part of his army. The Boreas is a Hades of a risk.

'But this pass is ignored. Sneak it across here, get it over the Moesian Gorge, and it's just a short dash to Akrai. They've probably arranged for support to come out and meet them. What else would they be transporting over here? And just look at what they're carrying and how well they're guarding it. Nothing else makes sense.'

‘But they haven’t been paid for moontides. There must be thousands of coins in those boxes.’ Nicias’s eyes were huge. Stout wooden boxes bound about with iron reinforcing bars were stacked in a large pile next to the commander’s tent, and ten men stood on guard.

Troi considered. ‘We do this right and we get a windfall of money, while Marsyas’s men remain unpaid and as grumpy as Simonides on a bad day. Two down with one shaft, and a haul of fish to all but sink the boat.’ Troi mixed his metaphors with uncaring abandon. He was silent for a few heartbeats. ‘It could be the deciding factor in the war. What makes the difference. It’s an opportunity we can’t afford to miss. It’s going to be dangerous, but we need to move fast.’

Dusk was falling as they cautiously returned to their well-hidden horses, but it was a clear night, and a full moon provided illumination both useful and risky. They joined the track well below the Troian camp and, balancing caution against the need for haste, followed it down. As they approached the precipitous Moesian Gorge, a place Troi would rather not remember, let alone revisit, Nicias slid from his horse. His pony immediately stopped and occupied itself with munching grass as the scout slipped silently through the shadows to the final bend.

He wriggled forward and cautiously eased round the bole of a tree. He held up a fist, then spread his hand out four times. There were no less than twenty Trogs guarding the rather shaky rope bridge that teetered over the spectacular drop.

Troi joined him and swore under his breath. The Trogs had clearly been sent ahead to secure the crossing, and were bedding down for the night. The approaches to the bridge were devoid of cover, and the combination of doubled guards and bright moonlight made any covert attempt to cross impossible.

Troi thought quickly. To divert and bypass the gorge would take far too long. The enemy would be across the gorge and down the pass before he could get a blocking force in position. And there were too many to take out. There was just one way of possibly managing it, but, if they succeeded, only Troi held the authority to orchestrate the response. He did not hesitate. It had to be Nicias.

'Sorry, Nicias, but you'll have to draw as many away from the bridge as you can, and then I'll just have to improvise.'

Even in the pallid moonlight, he could see Nicias blanch. Pursued up the broken track at high speed, he would be fortunate if his horse kept its footing. If it did, he would somehow have to get off the trail unseen, into difficult countryside, with the bright moon both holding him in its glare and throwing a mosaic of confusing shadows before him. And he must manage this feat before he ran headlong into their main camp.

It was as near an order to commit suicide as could be imagined. Nicias looked at him for several long hekates, clearly waiting for Troi to rescind the order. Troi inflexibly kept his eyes on the bridge. The young man began to slide quietly backwards, but with the faintest sigh.

'At least I've got my gorytus fastened,' he whispered with a brave attempt at nonchalant humour. His voice broke on the final word, and he covered it with a cough.

'The Gods go with you,' murmured Troi in response, and Nicias was gone. Troi waited. It seemed a long time before he heard the sounds of careless hooves clattering down the track.

The guards immediately alerted the other men, and all were on their feet and reaching for their weapons in heartbeats. Nicias trotted into view, his bow in hand. He was going to carry out his orders to the letter.

He drew swiftly and loosed. Before the first man cried out and fell forward, Nicias had nocked a second arrow. Two more men were downed before the first Trogs were scrambling onto their loosed horses.

Nicias paused to bring a fourth man tumbling from his saddlecloth before turning and urging his horse into a foolhardy gallop.

The incensed Trogs were after him en masse and dangerously close behind. He had stayed too long and given himself no realistic chance. The cavalry pounded off up the track in pursuit, and the sounds rapidly faded into the quiet of the night. Hoping they would not catch Nicias too quickly, Troi turned his attention to the scene before him. The stupid officer had left but a single guard who was now kneeling, with his back to Troi, over one of the downed men, very close to the lip of the ravine. The other three casualties were clearly out of it. This was the chance Troi had hardly dared hope for. The possibility of not alerting the returning Trogs that a second scout had crossed.

Troi crept silently across, knife in hand. His moon-thrown shadow was behind him, the slight breeze into his face and the wounded man squealing like a stuck pig. The man had an arrow in his shoulder and the trooper, murmuring reassurance, had worked the missile through and broken the shaft preparatory to removing it.

Troi stooped to pick up a thick length of firewood and hit the kneeling man hard at the back of the head. He collapsed across the legs of the wounded man. Troi hauled the body from him, then stood back. The wounded Trog, grasping the arrow in his shoulder, dragged himself groggily to his feet, staring at Troi, the terror in his eyes clear in the pitiless moonlight. Immediately behind him lay the yawning chasm of the gorge, and Troi simply leaned forward and gave him a push. The trooper teetered horribly on the edge for what seemed like hekates, then fell backwards with a rending scream.

Troi peered down. The body was lying sprawled and broken on an outcrop of rock about fifty paces below. Perfect. He grasped the insensible man under his armpits, dragged him to the edge and rolled him over to fall in the same place. A quick glance confirmed they were lying close together, and he turned his attention to the rest.

One was dead. Another would be in hekates; he was unconscious, his face absolutely bloodless. The arrow had severed an artery in his leg and he was bleeding out, the blood jetting in thick spurts, black in the moonlight. The last man was doubled up with an arrow through his belly.

He knelt behind the man and hauled him up into a sitting position, the trooper crying out with pain. Troi calmly applied a choke hold. His victim gasped for air and scrabbled vainly at Troi's arm with bloody fingers, before finally becoming limp. Troi checked he was dead, then laid him down, listening attentively all the time for any sounds of a return. All was silent except for the distant kivikking of a tawny owl and a sudden shriek as some small denizen of the night met its fate.

He quickly returned to the lip where the first two had fallen, left the broken arrow near the edge and scuffed up the thin soil. There was a good chance that the Troians would read it as an accident and remain oblivious of Troi's passing. He didn't want them taking fright and setting off back across the Anchises on the scuttle.

Well satisfied, he collected his horse and led it across the ominously swaying bridge, then mounted and set off down the track without a backwards glance.

FORTY

IT WAS BREAKING dawn when Troi arrived at the encampment, the grey edges of an encroaching front creeping across the lightening sky. A cavalry patrol angled towards him, then recognised him and simply waved. The guards on the gate, set in the rough palisade of sharpened stakes, saluted as he rode through. He dropped from his tired pony. The officer of the watch, standing to one side, nodded in recognition and began to stroll towards him.

Troi had no time for niceties. 'Sound the alert,' he snapped. 'Everyone rousted and armed. Get Palaemon now.' His commands were authoritative despite his lowly rank, and the officer knew better than to disregard urgent demands from scouts. He bawled orders to his deuteros, and moments later salpinxes were wailing and men tumbling from the lines of leathern tents. Palaemon, the chiliarches in command of this sector, a tall, thin, hook-nosed man, came dashing up clad only in a simple tunic.

'What in Hades—?'

'Command tent,' said Troi tersely, belatedly adding, 'sir,' as he strode towards the large square canvas structure. He snapped his fingers at two nearby hoplites. 'Take the entrance. No-one enters.' Palaemon hurried after him, clearly annoyed. Troi waited for him at the large trestle table covered with maps and scrolls at the centre of the otherwise empty tent.

'This had better be good,' said Palaemon crossly, dropping the entrance flap into position.

'It is, sir. The Trogs are bringing their army pay chest over the Anchises. If we act swiftly, we can take it. They've an eile of cavalry as escort, and that's it.'

Palaemon's bad temper evaporated, and his eyes widened. 'Dyaus's balls.' He was an experienced Chalcidikian officer who had fought the Trogs in the recent revolt and loathed them. He instantly recognised the import of what Troi was saying.

'Have you the roster of units available?' asked Troi, rummaging through the untidy piles of scrolls. Palaemon strode over and grabbed the right document, spreading it out on the table and weighting it down with pebbles. Troi cast a swift eye down it and turned to the large wooden board on an easel, originally painted white but now a grubby, streaked grey.

He took a piece of charcoal and drew a wavy line more or less vertically from the top of the board to halfway down.

'The pass.' He slashed a long transverse line across the lower end. 'The Moesian Gorge.'

He continued the line of the pass in a large double curve all the way down to the bottom, then he scrawled an X well to its right and near the bottom edge. 'Our camp. Here.' Near the top of the impromptu map he cut the vertical line with a short stroke. 'The best choke point on the pass.'

He drew another X just above the horizontal charcoal stroke that represented the gorge. 'Their camp last night.'

Palaemon nodded.

Troi continued. 'Between the gorge and here.' He marked the pass about halfway down its lower course. 'It's thick conifer woodland. If we can catch them in that stretch by blocking top and bottom, we have them. They can scarcely take a mule train through the woods, and certainly can't without being tracked by my scouts as easily as following an elephant across a mudflat.'

Palaemon was looking at the crude map intently, his right fist subconsciously clenched.

'I recommend that you get those peltastes who have ponies to grab some foul weather gear, and send them west to round the end of the gorge. Then head north to hold this choke point as a long stop. One of my scouts knows it and will guide them. Build a defensive wall, set up avalanches. They should be able to stop them if the bastards take it on the scuttle.' He pointed to the roster. 'This heavy cavalry unit immediately available?'

Palaemon grunted assent.

'Order them to follow the others, but then take the northern lip of the gorge to the bridge. I'll allocate a scout. There's still a track along there from before they built the bridge.' A memory intruded, but he pushed it away. 'They must take and hold that crossing at all costs. If necessary, destroy the bridge.'

He straightened and looked Palaemon directly in the eye. 'Drive your hoplites and the rest of your light troops up the pass at ram speed and trap the bastards. I'll get every scout I've got out there in case they manage to give us the slip.'

'That'll leave the camp defenceless.'

'Risk it. Send to Eubalos to rush reinforcements across the Boreas. And ask for every spare scout and arrow rider he's got.'

Palaemon knew when to swallow his pride. He turned for the tent flap. 'Get your men out then,' he ordered brusquely, his only concession to his bruised ego.

FORTY-ONE

A FINE RAIN WAS falling from solid grey skies. The three men stared at the contents in awe. A heaving sea of newly minted silver coins. They had broken open one of the chests and made a rough estimate of its contents. Xanthos picked up one of the coins and inspected the head of Laomedon stamped on its face.

He grinned. 'Never thought the sight of that bastard would be welcome.'

Sitting cross-legged beneath the shelter of a hastily rigged cloak, a small, long-faced man with remarkably pale eyes was busily moving pebbles on a counting board and making notations on a wax tablet. Troi vaguely remembered him from somewhere, but it was unimportant. The Gods had been with them. The sweating hoplites had arrived at the treeline just as the Troian advance patrol emerged from the trees. The Trogs had taken one appalled look and promptly disappeared back along the trail. But the Mykerenaean cavalry were already holding the bridge by then, and the Trogs were well and truly netted. Most of the enemy cavalry had sensibly surrendered. A few had tried to escape through the difficult country off the pass, an ankle-breaking terrain of broken rock and slippery patches of moss, fir and pine, birch and juniper scrub. The scouts were tracking them. They would not last long.

The little clerk looked up. Palaemon glanced at him and nodded to bid him speak. 'I estimate that it will pay our army, as it is now, for nigh on two years.' He had a high, cracked voice.

Palaemon whistled. 'And without loss.'

'Not quite,' said Xanthos, his voice suddenly hard. They had found the body of Nicias tied to a tree and beaten to death. From the Trogs' continued descent that morning, straight into the jaws of the trap, it was obvious that Nicias had told them nothing.

'I spoke without thinking,' said Palaemon contritely.

'He was born not far from here,' said Xanthos. 'Little village just over that ridge. That's why I asked Gwalchmai to post him in this quadrant.' He paused. 'His mother is still alive. He was her only child.'

Troi sensed an obscure criticism within Xanthos's words.

Xanthos dug his hands into the mass of coins and then lifted them out, allowing them to trickle back through his fingers. He regarded them moodily. 'It will be poor comfort, but I'll go and see his mother, and ask Diomedes if a very small part of this wealth could be donated to her to make her final years easy. If not happy.'

Troi said nothing. There was nothing to say.

FORTY-TWO

THE MILITARY COUNCIL was in ferment. Raised voices jarring over each other, stabbing fingers and hammered fists, muttered obscenities. Twenty senior officers and officials sat around two large tables in the strategion, a ring of hoplites on guard at twenty paces from the building. The clerk with the pale eyes was at a writing desk, but he had given up trying to keep any kind of record. Troi sat quietly to one side, more or less ignored, but Diomedes had insisted that he be there. He did not know why, and it troubled him.

'It can't be done,' shouted the short, red-haired Praxis above the uproar. 'They wouldn't last a moontide.' He had been at that first meeting with Diomedes. Troi remembered him well.

'How many men would be needed?' demanded Meleagros.

'Doesn't matter, you'd never get enough volunteers.' Praxis snorted.

'What about food?' That was Themistocles. Eye on the wand, as always. He had been a pedagogue in Priamos and had joined the rebellion in its very early days. Diomedes had quickly recognised the talent under the scholarly and mild-seeming exterior.

Harpalycus looked at Diomedes, who nodded. The young strategos stood up and waited for the hubbub to subside. It did. The little clerk sighed audibly with relief. Diomedes watched Harpalycus closely. His meteoric rise under the aegis of the strategarch may have triggered some underlying resentment, but his abilities were too manifest for it to gain an overt voice. It was his first full council meeting, but he immediately demonstrated a natural dominance, despite his quiet demeanour. He had an instinctive feeling for control and wore the unmistakable cloak of leadership.

'Firstly, the situation. With reinforcements streaming in and Laomedon's orders to lay the country waste, Marsyas has to come out. And we simply haven't the forces to meet him in the field. Nor will have for, at best, a year. We either try and stop him, lose our army and the rebellion is over, or avoid contact and let him burn, destroy and kill at will, thus losing all our support and the rebellion is over.' He looked around and waited for any response to the bleak assessment.

'He might split his forces and allow us to defeat him piecemeal.' Medraut spoke, albeit somewhat doubtfully. A dapper middle-aged strategos, he had arrived recently from Demetrius, one of the Five Fetters of Gea, of which he had been the holder. His brother had been arrested by the Krypteia, and, knowing all too well Laomedon's paranoia and one-slaughter-solves-all policy, he had sensibly defected.

'It's possible,' conceded Harpalycus, 'but that's usually a mistake of the rash and confident, rather than the uncertain and frightened. And we can't risk the rebellion on a knucklebone throw.'

'We harry bastards, hit and run and hit again. Make bleed.' Tereus was, for once, awake.

Harpalycus's answer was immediate. 'You could, Tereus. You could give him a bloody nose sure enough, but you wouldn't beat him.'

The Thracian shrugged.

'What do you think he'll do?' asked Phormio, looking like everyone's favourite grandfather with his tangled bird's-nest of white hair and flowing beard. But his sun- and wind-burned skin was evidence of his natural inclination to lead from the front. He spent as much time at sea as possible and was proving a formidable navarches.

Diomedes leaned back in his chair, his face inscrutable, but obviously leaving the young strategos to take point. The implications were not lost on those present.

'Best guess is the obvious. With those reinforcements coming through, even allowing for garrison troops and protection for his supply line, he'll have an army of twenty thousand or so. Head straight for Pelium or cross the Andros for Plataea. Most probably the latter. Decapitate the rebellion.'

'The Andros is not that easy a pass, Harp. We could block him there.' Meleagros's eyes sparked. 'The terrain is made for my Aggies, and they're flooding in.' He had long since forgiven Harpalycus for the sharp defeat inflicted upon him the day of Harpalycus's defection.

'And I cut supplies,' added Tereus eagerly. 'Change from throats.' He looked singularly disappointed when his joke sank without a ripple.

Harpalycus nodded to Gwalchmai, the one-eyed Skoparches, who leaned forward and spoke. 'Only one place is a good enough choke point, but it can be bypassed by no less than three mountain tracks—difficult, but usable. Diomedes, Harpalycus and myself have looked at it. It does not look possible. They can bring too much weight to bear at too many points.'

'But if Plataea can hold, then his supply line will be incredibly vulnerable,' suggested Medraut.

'Sinon?' Diomedes invited the spymaster to speak.

A little man with sallow skin and hard, bright eyes sat back, put his hands together in a characteristic manner and gazed skywards. 'Merchant cogs are gathering at Leuctra, Carthago and Antenopolis, and the naval forces have been strengthened.' His voice was unpleasantly high-pitched. 'They're going to switch their supply lines to the sea.' His words seemed to continue echoing through the sudden silence.

'They're too strong for us,' muttered Phormio eventually. Then he brightened. 'But Carthago has a narrow anchorage with a wide entrance. Given the right wind and tide, some incendiary ships might wreak havoc.'

'Worth looking at,' agreed Harpalycus, 'but enough to stop them?'

Phormio shook his head with bitter resignation.

'So,' growled Simonides, 'we're buggered.'

‘Our only chance,’ said Harpalycus slowly and distinctly, ‘is to offer Marsyas a target he cannot afford to ignore, a target that can keep his full attention for a nine-moontide as an absolute minimum. We need that much time to gather enough trained men and especially to perfect this new phalanx. And there’s only one place that can draw him and hold him. We’re back to one place and one plan.’

‘But it won’t work,’ repeated Praxis obstinately. ‘How many men will you need?’

‘Four hundred,’ said Diomedes.

‘And you’re going to try and persuade four hundred men to commit suicide. Good luck with that.’

‘As a matter of interest,’ said Harpalycus, ‘we asked two hundred recruits if they’d be willing to accept a suicide mission that meant the survival of the rebellion. No-one under thirty and no-one with children under the age of fifteen. Of course, they had no idea of the nature of the mission, and they had to come individually to volunteer, so there were no false heroics. Fifteen did so.’ He glanced across at Diomedes. ‘I think we’ll be able to do it. I suggest, Praxis, that you’re underestimating the strength of feeling and commitment among those who’ve come from elsewhere to fight, and the passions roused by the Holokauston.’

Praxis was not to be deterred. ‘Food for four hundred men for a year?’ He was incredulous.

A tubby, moon-faced man, bizarrely clutching a large straw hat, looked questioningly at Diomedes. The latter nodded encouragingly, and the man spoke up. ‘We are looking at sources of salted fish and already organising as much suitable produce as we can, boustria, salted meat, eggs in sour wine, honey, dried fruit and so on. We will ensure maximum grain storage. Off the ground. Dried thoroughly. Oh, and plenty of cats. We have done the calculations and can do it. It won't be symposium fare, but they won't starve.' Ladon was a successful merchant from Naupactos who had contacts everywhere and a genius for organisation. Harpalycus had suggested that they invite him to take charge of supplies, and he had donned the sphairai without a moment's hesitation.

'You can't hold for that long. It's impossible.' Praxis was adamant.

Diomedes and Harpalycus glanced at one another. Within the brief exchange, Praxis was relegated to the outer darkness.

'We think we can, if we use every delaying tactic and trick that we can come up with. Aristobulos is already working on some interesting ideas.' Diomedes gestured towards a distinguished patrician with grey hair, the newly appointed chief engineer, who nodded eagerly. 'And we'll harry them from the outside. Use speed and fancy footwork to avoid a full-on spear clash but keep them pinned down.'

Harpalycus spoke again, his tone sombre. 'At the fall of day, we have no choice. Only this brings us time, and without time we lose. As sure as the sun sets, we lose.' There was silence.

Then Brasidas spoke, his sudden parade-ground voice making Simonides, sitting beside him, jump. 'So, who's going to command this suicidal stand?'

Diomedes looked up. 'I am, of course.'

He glanced across at Troi. An understanding flowed between them. Troi realised now why Diomedes had wanted him to be there. Diomedes sought death; life to him now was but a bitter chore, a torment, the desperate tiredness at the end of day when sleep beckons as blessed relief. But he was still proud and needed his death to mean something. This was what he wanted, and Troilus was to be glad for him. Troi understood. He himself felt no strong hold on life. He would readily cross the Styx if it meant that Marsyas would accompany him. All men died. Did it matter when?

Around this still pool of communion, a clamour grew. Distant, unconnected, like the rumble of the faraway anger of Dyaus. Diomedes looked away from Troi and held up a hand. The noise died away.

'It is not negotiable,' he said flatly. 'I am the strategarch, and it is my decision and mine alone. That's the end of the matter.'

FORTY-THREE

In the killing ground of the Boreas, yet another Troian supply train was dying. The first for a while. The Troians had begun escorting them with a half-speira of spearmen, enough to guard against the nimble but lightly armed Thracians and Agrianians. For a while it had worked, but Harpalycus was determined to disrupt the flow. Troian morale was already low, and putting them on half-rations would drive it lower.

The speiroi had formed a sturdy, compact defensive hedgehog around the majority of the wagons, tucked in behind their large oval shields, bristling with spears, against which the Thracians could do little except swirl around them, sweeping in close to hurl their needle-sharp javelins, then jinking out of danger, trying to dodge the arrows from the archers sheltering behind the shield wall.

Harpalycus had timed the attack to hit the rear and draw the spearmen there, leaving several wagons exposed at the front. They remained unmolested for the moment as the attackers were drawn to the hedgehog like wasps to honey. One wagon was of particular interest to Xanthos and Troi. They were up on their feet and heading down towards it. Their task was a snatch and bag. Sinon had received intelligence that the chief Troian logistics officer at Tanagra had been summoned by Marsyas. Both Sinon and Ladon were eager to have a convivial chat with their colleague, and the two scouts had been tasked with his safe delivery.

They had been observing the train for days. At first, they had thought he had not come, until Xanthos had spotted a very ordinary-looking wagon driver disappear into an officer's tent. They watched carefully.

He quietly emerged in the morning and returned to the wagon lines, where he waited, in stately isolation, as the rest bustled around harnessing up the oxen. He climbed aboard when they were ready to move, produced a cushion, which reduced Xanthos to fits of suppressed laughter, and settled himself down for the journey, leaving the driver beside him to do all the work. Even when the wagon stuck in a rut and had to be heaved out, he never got down.

'Do you think that might be him?' asked Troi.

'Him? Don't be silly. He's obviously a common wagon driver. Anyone can see that.' Xanthos's voice was pure incredulity.

'Just throwing a javelin at a venture.'

'But I suppose,' said Xanthos resignedly, 'in the absence of anyone else, he'll just have to do.'

'My thoughts exactly.'

'Thoughts? How long have you been having those, then?' murmured Xanthos as they slid back into the green cover of the trees.

Now they were heading down for their prey, sliding from shrub to hollow, from clump of coarse grass to rocky outcrop, using every scant patch of cover to mask their coming. The wagon drivers and guards were huddled beneath and around the carts, watching the battle boiling around them with understandable apprehension. The two scouts could see the grey-haired man ensconced with the driver and three guards beneath the second ox cart from the front. Three other men stood crouching with sword and shield beside the wagon. If the scouts needed any confirmation this was the right man, that was it. He was too well guarded.

Somewhere a salpinx sounded, and masses of hirsute men with javelins came racing down the grassy slopes opposite like mountain goats. The dreaded Agrianes, come with murder and loot in mind.

'Come on,' urged Xanthos. 'Those savage bastards won't hesitate to stick him like a pig.'

They both took swift aim with their bows and loosed before breaking from cover and running down towards the cart, diverging to either side. Two of the guards slumped onto the ground, and the third twisted to thrust his shield before him and tried to edge back, his eyes on Xanthos. Troi stopped momentarily and thumped an arrow into his exposed side. The driver rolled out from under the farther side and scuttled away. One of the other men beneath the wagon held a belly bow and was trying, with some difficulty, to twist himself into a position to loose it. Without hesitation, Xanthos stopped, drew and aimed in one fluid movement, and the man fell forward and lay still. The grey-haired man was frozen in shock.

The other two, tough-looking veterans, were also scrambling out from underneath, but towards the two scouts. The elder, a muscular man in a breastplate, gained his feet and ran towards Troi.

Troi hastily loosed a shot, but the man twisted, agile and light-footed, and flung his small, bronze-covered pelta before him. The arrow glanced off the conical boss and sheered away harmlessly. The veteran was too close now, and Troi hurled his bow away and drew his sword. The other man was down with an arrow through his thigh and Troi could see, from the corner of his eye, Xanthos with his bow at full draw looking to take out his opponent. Troi, with an open palm outstretched, forcefully gestured to Xanthos and saw the bow lower.

The bodyguard was almost upon him, grinning wolfishly, clearly seeing an immature and feeble victim before him. He swung his heavy kopis in a mighty sweep that would have decapitated Troi if he hadn't stepped back and ducked neatly below its swing. Committed and off-balance, the guard was wide open for the killing riposte to his unshielded side, but Troi simply stepped back again and gave him an ironic salute with his sword. The surprise in the man's eyes was evident.

The guard quickly adopted a defensive stance with his pelta before him. Troi could read caution in his eyes now. The guard jabbed with his sword to test Troi's reactions. Balanced easily on the balls of his feet, Troi estimated it to perfection and merely swayed just out of range.

He watched the man's eyes and sensed, rather than consciously recognised, the second lunge. He beat it away with a swift cross cut, then leapt to his left, keeping to the man's unshielded side. The bodyguard desperately made a reverse cut, but Troi stepped back once more and his sword licked out to merely touch the man's cuirass. His opponent threw his pelta round to try and catch the weapon, but Troi had foreseen the action and lifted his sword, and the shield whirled round without contact.

Troi had the man's measure now and skipped to the right to deliver an insolent stroke with the flat of the blade to the man's buttocks before stepping back out of range.

The guard was now clearly frightened and threw himself at Troi with a fury born of desperation. All skill and guile were lost in a fog of panic. Troi retreated, swaying right and left, avoiding the thrashing sword with ease. Then, the rhythm of the attack obvious, he suddenly stepped up and buried his sword in the man's belly, cutting upwards from below his cuirass. His victim stiffened. Troi mercilessly stabbed again, striking for the heart with savage force.

'That's for Koi,' he said. The bodyguard's brown eyes glazed, and he toppled forward to sprawl at the scout's feet. Troi wiped his sword on the grass and looked up to see Xanthos staring at him with a strange expression. Troi looked back quizzically.

'You were playing with him,' accused Xanthos.

'So?'

Xanthos shrugged. 'So, nothing.' He turned to the grey-haired man still kneeling beneath the wagon. 'You can come out now, Grandpa.'

FORTY-FOUR

TROI SAT ON the wagon seat and watched the battle with professional interest. The Thracians had been joined by hundreds of eager Agrianes, and the speiroi were crouching under a storm of missiles, but remained largely untouched. Those Troians outside the fortress of linked shields were either standing very still with hands high, or lying very still.

A rebel officer strolled across toward the two scouts, loose-limbed, fair-haired and blessed with an amiable face and an almost permanent grin. Two hard-eyed and weather-bitten men, short and stocky and remarkably hairy, followed him. They wore simple belted tunics and carried crescent-shaped peltas, long knives thrust in their rope belts, and bundles of javelins in holders strapped to their backs. They smelt abominably, and Troi was not sure how much of their dark complexion was natural and how much was ingrained dirt. The officer nodded to Troi and greeted Xanthos cheerfully.

'Now then, laddie, who invited you to our convivial little get-together? Scouts shouldn't be pratting about where the big boys play.'

'We sometimes have to put the important things to one side to come and give you a hand, Mel.' Meleagros, despite his lack of any finery or sign of rank, was a chiliarches, but Xanthos simply ignored the military chain of command with its prohibitions and strictures. 'You know you can't find your way from your tent to the latrine.'

Not that Meleagros cared. His grin got even broader. 'Once, laddie. I got lost once. Anyone can turn left instead of right.'

'Down an obviously blind valley?'

'I'd had a skinful the night before. It disorientates a chap.'

Xanthos merely rolled his eyes.

Meleagros commanded the Agrianians, who had become one of the most formidable weapons in the Mykerenaean armoury. He wasn't known as Mad Mel on a whim. Drunk on danger, he was a risk-taker and a natural iconoclast. He and the Agrianian volunteers had bonded like tree and ivy. They adored him, his audacity and effrontery, courage and insouciance, scorn of tradition and sheer exuberance. And he saw in the famously untameable Agrianes what Diomedes had always seen. That with discipline they would make the finest and most feared peltastes in the Gean world. Against all sage prognostications, he had given them that discipline.

'Just came to see the fun,' said Meleagros. 'I think I've got the right valley.' He looked up the pass. 'And here they come.'

Round the bend in the valley had appeared four tags of infantry. The centre two commanded Troi's attention. Clad in white linen cuirasses, leather pteruges, greaves and bronze pilos helmets, they carried small silver-painted shields strapped to their left arms and incredibly long spears called sarissae that wavered above them like a sea of reeds. They marched in close formation in two disciplined sixteen-by-sixteen blocks. On either flank and echeloned back slightly were tags of hoplites, with the usual large bronze aspis shield, Korinthian helmet and relatively short thrusting spear.

Salpinxes sounded, and the Thracians rather reluctantly moved away from the beleaguered speira. The unusual infantry advanced steadily. The two scouts watched with real interest. This was to be the first real test of the new phalanx. There was the double cry of a salpinx, and the leading five rows lowered their pikes with regimented precision so that a hedge of spearpoints preceded them, flickering in and out like the tongues of snakes. They ploughed straight into the spearmen. The Troians crouched behind their shields and tried to hold.

For a while, they stood and tried to fight back, but they could not get beyond the impenetrable line of spearpoints to bring their own weapons to bear, and inevitably the incessant stabs began to penetrate the chinks in the defensive shield wall. Men started to fall or stagger back wounded. Holes appeared in the formation, and the sarissae picked off those within. The Troians began to move back, desperately trying to fend off the inexorable. Even at this distance, the scouts could hear the sharp calls of command. The phalanx stepped forward once, then again, then began to walk forward, maintaining their cohesion. The retreating speira lost its discipline, began to disintegrate, then suddenly broke, frantic men scrambling away in every direction. Round them a circle of Thracians and Aggies eagerly awaited their coming.

'Impressive,' said Xanthos.

'Bloody show-offs,' said Mel. 'My Aggies and Tereus's lads could have taken them without breaking sweat.'

Troi looked round as Harpalycus rode up on a black horse, a couple of aides behind him. Harpalycus nodded to Mel. 'Nice timing.'

'Purely fortuitous. The silly buggers forgot to wake me.'

'I suspected as much,' said Harpalycus with a straight face. He glanced at the two scouts and indicated the prisoner with a throw of his head. 'That him?'

Troi nodded.

'Excellent. Ladon and Sinon will both be pleased. Well done, you two.' He leaned forward on the shoulders of his horse and looked down the valley where the sad remnants of the speiroi were being marshalled by some hoplites. 'What did you think?'

'Unstoppable,' said Troi. 'I presume the hoplites are to guard their flanks.'

Harpalycus looked at Troi appraisingly. 'Indeed. It's their one real weakness.'

'I liked the colour co-ordination. Who's their dancing master?'

Harpalycus ignored Meleagros. It was generally considered the best way to cope with him. Instead, he surveyed the battlefield and nodded in satisfaction. 'Nice to know that the theory works in practice.'

Dejected prisoners were being marched away. The wagons were being ransacked for the most valuable cargo, which would soon be transferred to the train of baggage horses just coming down the valley. The rest would be burned. The incinerated remnants and the Troian dead would be left as a marker for subsequent supply trains. A rich crop of such sites was growing throughout the Boreas. The lightened wagons were to be hidden. There were plans for them.

He glanced at the logistics officer. 'Get him to Sinon, but sweat him first for any urgent information, especially the timing of the next supply train. And what is Marsyas screaming for most? No need to be overly gentle.'

He turned his horse and rode away.

The elderly officer sat down on the rear step of the wagon. He smoothed his tunic. 'No need for any unpleasantness, young gentlemen. What is it that you wish to know?'

FORTY-FIVE

DIOMEDES WAS READING a report in the conference room when the sistrum hanging outside the door rattled. Xanthos entered. He did not look his usual confident self.

'Have a seat, Xan.'

'Thank you, sir. I would rather stand.'

Diomedes laid the scroll on the table. 'Sir? This is serious, then.'

'I think it's a worry.'

'About what?'

Xanthos took a deep breath. 'Troi, sir.'

'Ah,' said Diomedes. He did not look at all surprised. 'Spit it out, lad.'

Xanthos marshalled his thoughts, then began to speak

in slow, measured tones. 'I quite like Troi; he can be fun to be around, when he's in the mood. He's an excellent scout—I've seen better, but not many—and I trust him totally. But.'

Diomedes waited patiently.

Xanthos sighed. 'But there's something wrong with him.'

Diomedes raised one interrogative eyebrow.

'When we netted that messenger, we asked him some questions. He was only too ready to cooperate, particularly once he'd seen the size of Troi's knife, so there was no need to get nasty. But I could see that Troi was disappointed. He was aching to cut the man into collops.' He moistened his lips. 'Don't get me wrong, Uncle Dio, I know sometimes you have to do things to get information, but when you like doing them…' His voice faded away.

He began again. 'In the Boreas, last se'ennight, he killed a man. In fair fight, except it wasn't. He could have killed him quick and clean, or disarmed him, allowed him to yield, whatever, but he was playing with him, like a cat with a mouse.'

Diomedes said nothing. There was more to come and he knew it.

'I've seen him kill before. Cold. Clinical. But this was something else. He's beginning to enjoy it. And the men… don't like him.'

'Any particular reason why not?'

'Well, that business with Nicias didn't endear him to them. But he should be popular. He's hard, but fair. He's strong and decisive, and the men trust his judgement. But they don't trust his care for them. They know he'd sacrifice them if it was to his advantage. Without a qualm.'

Diomedes nodded slightly. 'I had heard.' He looked tired.

'And he always tries to bed down away from the men. They say he wakes every night. From a night hag. I've seen it myself. He won't speak of it.'

Diomedes sat back on the little cross-legged campaign stool. He looked at Xanthos, then lowered his gaze. 'He had a bad experience,' he said quietly. 'A very bad experience. He saw everything he knew and loved wiped from the face of the earth like spilled wine from a table. Everything. Even worse, he had to kill his girl.'

Xanthos's eyes widened.

'Gut wound,' explained Diomedes.

'How do you know? He's never spoken of anything like that to me.'

'He won't. An old comrade of mine joined us. He knew Troi as a slave in Leuctra, and they got to the bottom of the well there. But couldn't do a damned thing about it, and not for want of trying.'

Diomedes did not continue, seeming to withdraw within himself, and Xanthos waited patiently.

Diomedes shook his head, then began to speak again. 'There's never a good time for what happened to the lad, but it scarcely could have been worse. He was old enough to comprehend it, to understand the pain and the loss, but young enough for it to be a total shock. Something he would not even have suspected could exist in this world. The sheer scale of it. I have trouble accepting it myself, even now.'

He looked up again. 'I've seen men like him before. And there is little you can do for them. Their being has been moulded by terror and pain, and to make the twisted straight is an all but impossible task. You will not like what I am going to say, but it makes him a powerful weapon. He has the intellect and the feel for tactics of an excellent strategos, but he also has something more than most. He can make those hard decisions that the majority of men balk at, the ones that need to be made, but often aren't. I should thank the Gods for such a weapon, but I can't. I'll do what I can, but I'm not hopeful.' He looked down and sighed. 'Thank you, Xan. It can't have been easy for you.'

'Sir,' said Xanthos and slipped back out into the dark night.

FORTY-SIX

'WINE?' ASKED DIOMEDES.

'Please.' Troi took the proffered kylix of Rhodian red with a good measure of spring water added.

They sat on wooden stools in Diomedes' command tent, on opposite sides of a small collapsible table. Things had changed. A camp bed stood to one side, with a screening curtain looped back. The other half of his quarters was given over to a graphotrapeza, several chests of assorted scrolls and maps, and a couple of whitewashed boards covered with charcoal scrawl.

The rough-and-ready situation that Troi had seen on his first arrival had long changed. Outside the tent stood tough, uniformed guards, well equipped with arms and armour.

There was the occasional whinny from the nearby horse lines, the measured tread of a unit marching past, the harsh challenge of a sentinel. Though still small in comparison to Marsyas's twenty thousand, the army looked, and was, disciplined, well trained and professional.

Diomedes settled back and looked at Troilus with that rather unnerving, single-minded scrutiny.

'Gwalchmai is going to make you up to taxiarches,' he said without preamble. 'You did very well with that pay chest. Even Palaemon forgot to be offended.'

Troi shrugged. 'There wasn't time for tact.'

'Exactly,' said Diomedes.

Troi wondered what he was getting at. There was silence for several hekates. Eventually, Diomedes began to speak, slowly and quietly.

'I'm not your kin, lad, but I loved your mother, and I loved your grandmother more than you can ever imagine. So I feel a kinship.'

'Thank you,' he said. But he felt ambivalent. He liked and certainly respected the old man, and he knew that Diomedes was the only real link between him and all he had lost, but there was an instant recoil from the idea of kinship. A visceral reluctance to become too close. Especially as, though neither would even hint at it, he recognised this quiet evening as Diomedes' farewell. If he felt such a close kinship, why was he abandoning him as everyone else had done? There was an undertow of resentment.

Be that as it may, this was the last chance for him to learn what he could of his family. Diomedes had talked a great deal to him about his mother, uncle and grandmother, yet things left unsaid gnawed at him throughout the watches of the night. 'Could I ask you something?'

'Of course.'

Troi took a deep breath, then looked away. He felt naïve and embarrassed. Nevertheless, the idea had taken root and was growing and entangling his thoughts like the burgeoning of catchweed, and he needed to know.

'You knew my grandmother for over twenty years. Then, when my grandfather divorced her, you married her.'

He stopped. He did not know how to put the question acceptably.

But Diomedes knew what he was asking. He merely nodded. His eyes never left the young man's. 'I don't blame you for wondering. Many people did. But, in truth, I was an insular man, frightened of relationships. Your grandmother was my friend all those years. Nothing more. Perhaps I lied to myself. Perhaps it slowly crept up on me. I honestly don't know. Even after we fled Gla, I would not accept it at first.' He smiled ruefully. 'Admitting my feelings was more difficult than facing a Dryopian war charge. But it was the best thing I ever did.' He chuckled. 'Xan's mother even threatened to carry us both, one under each arm, and dump us in bed together.'

Troi had to smile. 'Xan says she was a formidable woman. Apparently, she told the Emperor to keep the wedding blessing short and to the point.'

Diomedes chuckled again. 'I never knew that, but I can well believe it. Phyll would stand no nonsense about unwarranted deference, and her idea of subtlety was about on a par with an Aggie's idea of table manners.' His eyes became serious. 'And no, I am not your grandfather, Troi.'

'I don't know whether to be relieved or disappointed.'

'I would be proud to have been,' said Diomedes quietly. 'You're a fine young man.'

There was silence for a few heartbeats. 'Tell me about my grandfather,' said Troi.

Diomedes sighed and took a little time to compose his thoughts. 'I considered him a good friend for many years, and I think he was. I thought him a good husband, and that he and Kal were happy, and for the most part I think they were. Though Kal would never really speak of it after the divorce. She said it felt like a betrayal to do so. But something happened. Whether it was always there inside him but kept well hidden, or whether he changed…' He shrugged. 'We all do.'

Troi sensed an emphasis on his last words that was charged with some implied meaning.

Outside, one of the sentries made a challenge, and Diomedes looked up, expecting a message, but there was a mutter of conversation and all went quiet. 'I said I was not to be disturbed except for the direst emergency. Obviously not dire enough.'

He picked up the thread of what he had been saying. 'What role that damned Monotheite rubbish played in it all, I don't know. But I can't forgive him for what he did to your grandmother. Though, to be honest, I think it was mostly down to a Phthian called Adrastus who was playing the flutes.' He gave a self-satisfied smile. 'We crucified the unctuous bastard.'

There was a tension about Troi. 'So, I have bad blood.'

Diomedes looked at him sharply. 'Not with the blood of your mother and grandmother in you. And until he got mixed up with the plot, I always regarded Milt as a good man. Your Uncle Antinous had your grandfather's blood, but he was as straight and brave as they come. You remind me of him.' His eyes took on that distant look. 'He died at Iron Rock fighting for his Emperor.'

'I know.'

Diomedes nodded, his eyes still elsewhere. He shook himself slightly. 'I don't think that your grandfather was really bad. Misled, maybe. Perhaps you should go and speak to him yourself.'

Troi shook his head. He had had enough of loss. He did not want to add to it.

'Is there anything else you would like to know?' Diomedes did not say that this would be his last chance, but it reverberated in every word.

'I don't think so.'

'Then tell me about the pay chest. I haven't had the chance to really talk to you about it.'

Troi was surprised. They had spoken many times since then, but he had never asked before. Moreover, he always seemingly knew the details even before he was told. But nevertheless, Troi began to recount the whole incident.

He was stopped in mid-canter by Diomedes' mild question. 'Did Nicias volunteer or did you order him?'

'I ordered him.'

'Why?'

'It had to be done. Or, at least, I could think of no alternative.'

'Why not ask him if he would volunteer? He almost certainly would have.'

'And what if he had not?'

'You could have done it and left Nicias to make the report.'

'No. Nicias would not have been able to get things moving. And time was the key.'

'You were confident that you could?'

'I was.' Troi was beginning to get angry at the incessant interrogation. 'And I was right.'

Diomedes nodded thoughtfully.

'Was I wrong?'

'No. You were absolutely right. Considered. Incisive. Confident.' He paused momentarily. 'And ruthless.'

Troi flared. 'It's the job of soldiers to die when necessary. Sending men to die is in the very nature of military command. I did what I had to do.'

'Many men would have balked at it.'

'Then they would have been wrong,' declared Troi obstinately.

'I agree,' said Diomedes equably, 'You have the makings of a very effective officer. Even a great one.' He looked at Troilus with that penetrating gaze again. 'Which is why I want you to transfer from the scouts.'

Troi just stared back at him, completely wrong-footed.

'You're a very good scout, and we need such. But we need men who can make good decisions, quick decisions and hard decisions. We need them more than scouts. We need effective strategoi.'

'We have strategoi.'

'We have men called strategoi. Competent enough most of the time. But not battle winners. We have only four of those. Who are they?' He sat back and waited.

'You,' said Troi immediately.

Diomedes smiled wryly. 'Not counting me. I'm no longer in the shield line.'

'Harpalycus, obviously, Brasidas and…' He considered. 'Possibly Medraut. Can I count chiliarches?'

Diomedes nodded.

'Then Meleagros.'

Diomedes smiled in satisfaction. 'The very fact that you've identified them is evidence enough that you should eventually join them. I shall attach you to the Hetairoi for a moontide as a junior officer, and then let Harpalycus mentor you. He's happy to do so.'

Troi said nothing. His head was whirling. As with his swordplay, Diomedes was always shifting position, coming at Troi from different directions, keeping him off balance.

Diomedes continued, quietly. 'But I would not be meeting my responsibilities if I did not point out one failing in an otherwise impressive armoury. You must learn how to deal with it. One weakness in a city wall is sufficient for its fall.'

Troi stiffened slightly. 'Which weakness?' he asked warily.

'It does not particularly signify when you're a scout. They tend to be naturally insular in any case. But the best line officers have a sympathy, a rapport, with their men. They have the common touch.' He reached for his wine and smiled ruefully. 'Never really my strong point, I must confess, but I make the effort. Harp has it without trying. Meleagros even more so.'

'And I don't have it?'

'You know that you don't.'

And Troi did know it.

'But you learn tricks, techniques. You watch those that do have it and learn. You can get by.'

Troi thought there was more. Diomedes' normally inscrutable countenance was troubled. He sipped his wine and waited.

'How do you feel about Nicias?'

Troi was taken aback by the question. 'He was a good lad, very brave. I feel regret for his death.'

'Do you wake at night thinking of him?'

Puzzled, Troi shook his head. 'No. It was the right thing to do. I thought we had agreed that.'

'We had. But being right doesn't make it easy.'

Troi wasn't quite sure what he was saying.

'When you snatched that logistics officer, you killed one of the guards.' Again, the dislocating switch in attack.

'I killed several, as I recall.'

'You took them out with arrows. This one you fought.'

'Xan has been talking to you.' There was a sourness to his words.

Diomedes did not deny it. 'It seems you toyed with him before killing him.'

Aias's words came unbidden into his mind. *I know you will do what is right.* It had not been right. But a deep undercurrent of shame raised a turbulence of resentment. He crouched behind his shield as the turbidity swirled around him. 'It was for Koi,' he muttered.

There was iron in Diomedes' response. 'It is very unlikely that he was at Koi. He was a hired caravan guard.'

'He was a Trog.' He knew his responses to be feeble, and that made him even more obdurate.

'Your mother would not have approved and—'

'My mother is dead,' Troi interrupted harshly. 'Murdered by Laomedon's butchers.' The atmosphere had suddenly become charged.

'This man was not one of them.' Diomedes sighed and leaned back. 'He may have been a murderer, a sadist, a rapist, I don't know. He could have been a good family man taking on a dangerous task to put bread into the mouths of his children. You could have disarmed him.'

'Yet you don't seem to mind about us killing the others.'

'You kill when you have to, when it is the necessary thing to do within the context of a battle. You don't kill when you don't have to.' He paused. 'And you don't enjoy killing.' His eyes bored into Troi. 'You will become Marsyas.'

Troi leapt to his feet, his hand at his dagger. The stool overturned, the table jerked and his kylix of wine slid from it with a crash. The flap of the tent was flung up, and two hoplites burst in, swords drawn. Diomedes had not flinched but was watching Troilus with a kind of sorrow. He glanced up at the two guards.

'It's fine, lads,' he said. 'A slight domestic tiff.'

They retreated, reluctantly, and the flap fell back into place.

'Sit down,' he said with the honed edge of authority. Troi bent to pick up the stool and sat down again. But his face was white and his posture rigid.

Diomedes pursed his lips. 'I apologise. That was not called for. Kal used to say that I had the sensitivity of a pig at a symposium.'

There was a long pause. Troi could feel the anger ebbing away, his hands uncurling, his heart easing back into its normal rhythm, his breathing slowing. But he still felt tense, defensive, under threat.

'What colour were his eyes?' asked Diomedes.

Troi shook his head in puzzlement. The question seemed so bizarre. 'I don't recall,' he said eventually.

'And what did you see in his eyes when he died?'

'I don't know,' he said, more than a touch of resentment in his voice.

Diomedes sighed. 'I was afraid of that.'

He did not explain this enigmatic comment. They looked at one another, a stone wall between them. It was the last time they spoke.

FORTY-SEVEN

Troilus was duly reposted to Naupactos, to the elite Hetairoi under Alexandros, one of the officers who had defected with Harpalycus.

The very embodiment of the dashing cavalry commander, golden-haired and handsome, with an easy charm, Alexandros was famously the focus of female interest and generously repaid their attentions. His daring and leadership from the front had brought him adulation from his men, but he retained a level head and was one of Diomedes' most trusted subordinates.

He sensibly refused Troi command of an eile, concerned about his youth and lack of experience in cavalry tactics, but made him deuteros to a grizzled old campaigner called Patrobas. The latter held the old-fashioned notion that the deuteros was there to do all the work while the commander just made the big decisions. Like what to have for dinner.

The eile was in training, and Troi learned his trade with them. Patrobas disappeared entirely for the last few days, leaving Troi in charge. He was immediately suspicious and changed and doubled the guard, triumphantly foiling a mock Aggie attack.

Patrobas made a final laconic report to Alexandros. 'He'll do.'

Troi left for the main Mykerenaean camp to join Harpalycus as an aide. It was now sited at the town of Katane, tucked into the foothills of the Boreads. The men had no idea why it had been chosen, but, the town being only two hundred stadia east of Akrai, Troi knew.

FORTY-EIGHT

THE TOWN OF Akrai dominated the mouth of the Boreas Pass as it entered the Vale. Thirty stadia to its north, overlooking the Borean Way itself, hunched the Akroakrai, an ancient fortress, its origins lost to the memory of man. It was not the romantic ideal of a castle, towered and turreted, but simple and functional, with nothing to break its dull and uninteresting outline. It lay squat and low in relation to its length, with but a single gate that looked ridiculously tiny in comparison to the looming structure. It had been built on a large limestone pavement and had immensely thick walls of huge, crudely-worked blocks of stone.

The legend was that it had been made by the Kyklopes, the one-eyed race of Titans who had fought the Gods when the earth was young. There was but a single wall, but it was ten paces high, with an impressively wide fighting platform and substantial parapet. The fortress was roughly circular in plan, boasting no central citadel but enclosing a large area, having a circumference of almost three stadia. Within were a freshwater spring and lots of old stone buildings, many partially collapsed.

Because of its position, it was garrisoned by the Trogs and used as a supply depot, receiving the wagon trains that lurched their tortuous way through the winding and undulating pass, and storing their deliveries to be forwarded, under strong escort, to Marsyas's fortified camp.

One blustery but fine day in autumn, just such a supply train made its slow approach to the fortress, a long, lumbering line of ox carts, piled high with supplies. They were well protected from the mountain storms by leather covers, and from the Mickeys by a strong escort of cavalry guarding the flanks and a large contingent of speiroi marching along, in a rather slovenly manner, in their wake.

The watch officer looked out and swore. They had been expecting the supply train all day and had reasonably assumed that, by this time, it was lying up in a waycastle, or was yet another ghoulish scatter of burned wagons and corpses feeding the kites and crows. It would now have to be unloaded, and the sun was already falling towards the jagged skyline of the Boreads. It would be a late night.

Luckily, the latest reinforcements had left that morning. There was just the usual garrison in place, or they could never have squeezed any more inside. As it was, some would probably have to tent it outside. And that would not be popular. The bloody Agrianes were operating in the vicinity, and that did not make for a peaceful night's repose.

An officer came riding up to the gates ahead of the snail-like progress of the train. A couple of aides trailed behind him, and a hyperetes carried his personal banner of a red crab. He was only a sodding strategos, no less. More grief.

The watch officer stiffened and hissed to the dilochagos beside him, 'Get the bloody guard out and make sure they look smart. Fast. And let the holder know.'

'That'll delight his black and petty soul,' muttered the dilochagos. The officer grinned.

The strategos, a large, balding, muscular man, stopped and glared up. 'Are you bloody well going to open this fucking gate or not?' Despite his having the rough tones of a common soldier, rather than the usual aristocratic enunciation of a high-ranking officer, there was no doubting his air of authority.

'Sorry, sir, the gate cannot be opened without the express command of the holder. I have sent for him.'

The man roared with rage. 'Express command? Express command? I'm giving you a sodding express command, you cretinous wanker. I've been bloody well riding all day and I want to get off this fucking horse.' His voice rose to an almost demonic shriek. 'Now open the fucking gate, or I'll have your apologies for balls fried with mushrooms!'

Such was the force of his command that the watch officer responded almost without volition. 'Open the gate,' he shouted.

The first ox cart was drawing up. The gate began to move with a terrible creaking noise, and the strategos quickly muscled his irascible way within. The watch officer could hear him swearing at the guard with a commendably wide and imaginative vocabulary. The first wagons passed through.

The officer turned around and looked down to where the holder was hurrying from his quarters, then stared in shock. An ox cart had stopped squarely in the gate, preventing it being closed again. The leather covers were thrown back, and armed men erupted from within. He tried to shout for the alarm, but two arrows punched into his back, then a third, and he fell forward to describe a lazy somersault down to the courtyard far below.

FORTY-NINE

KLIO SAT ON the grotesquely carved stone bench in the courtyard, with its satyr-head armrests and the back an intricate gorgon's face in semi-relief. It was not the most comfortable seat, yet she loved it. It was where she went when she was troubled or heavy of heart. She had sat there often recently. It had been warm and sunny when she came, but cloud was beginning to build and it was growing cool.

She opened the scroll and read it again. For the fifth time. There was no need because she knew every word by heart. Nor was there any real comfort in it, unless it be that he had bothered to write to her at all. But it was the faintest wash of dawn after a dark and fearsome night. The scroll had talismanic powers. It was from him. And when he had written it, if only for those few heartbeats, he had been thinking of her.

Her mood was a mix of elation and despair, fluctuating between the two like a wave, surging high, its solid, flawless green sparkling in the sun, and then crashing down into a maelstrom of white water and a hopeless ebb into dissolution.

Twelfth day of Elaphebolion, Year 511

From Troilus

Naupactos

Klio, I was not sure how to address you, but, as you did ask me to call you Klio that time, I thought you would not mind. I am sorry that I have taken so long to write, but it has been difficult to find a conduit. Now that Gean Thrake is more or less cleared, it will be easier, though still a long and uncertain route. Thank you for your scroll. I am afraid that the previous scrolls you mentioned have not got through.

I am an officer now and am to be an aide to one of the strategoi. I am well, thank you, and I hope and trust that you are too.

She sat for a while, staring unseeingly into the clear waters of the pool. She had wondered if time would gradually erode the feelings that she had. If time can wear down the greatest of monuments, surely it could blunt these raw and keen-edged emotions, smooth away forlorn hopes, slowly but persistently erase images from the febrile workings of her imagination.

It could not. The scroll had shown that the mind was mightier than marble.

She unrolled it once more and read.

FIFTY

THE DAY WAS overcast, and light drizzle blew into their faces from time to time. Despite being summer, it was unseasonably cold. Troi shivered. Marsyas was finally coming out.

And the rebels were going to meet him in the field, no matter the disparity in numbers. At the Akroakrai, they were working feverishly, strengthening the defences, constructing Aristobulos's fiendish machines, and packing it with supplies – and they needed time. Marsyas had vacillated as usual – blinded by the Thracians, misled by Sinon's imaginary spy ring and thrown into confusion by the series of spoiling attacks and raids Harpalycus had launched. But with his supply line cut, the satrap had no other choice. He was coming out. And he had to be stopped.

The formidable masses of the speirai formed up outside the main gates of Tenos, and they certainly looked unstoppable: huge, tight formations of men, huddled behind large oval shields, clad in leather cuirasses and open-faced helmets and protected on all sides by a fearsome barrier of spear points. Before them stood a much looser grouping of archers and javelin-armed peltastes with, as always, the cavalry on the wings.

It looked a Hadean mess of men, thought Troi. His eyes searched feverishly for the banner of the white aurochs. He could not see it, and he swore under his breath.

Harpalycus and Brasidas sat on their horses atop the low hill that dominated the track leading to the small town. Simonides stood a short distance away; he loathed horses, hated riding, and dismounted at every opportunity. He was making notes on a wax tablet. Troi, as one of Harpalycus's aides, waited behind them in a cluster of arrow riders and bodyguards. Before and below them, the small Mykerenaean army waited patiently beneath their banners and pennants. No identifying banner flew above the command group. It would later. But for the moment the white rose banner waved behind the substantial force of cavalry massed on the left flank, seemingly identifying it as the planned decisive strike.

Perhaps Marsyas was being equally circumspect and not advertising his presence, but Troi feared that the coward skulked in the safety of the fortified town. His dreams of bringing the Butcher within the compass of his sword remained bright and terrible, but distant.

A young, white-robed priest of Dyaus came clambering up the hill, red-faced and sweating, but beaming. 'My lord,' he called. 'The liver has been read.'

'And?' said Harpalycus. He sat easily, his plumeless helmet crooked within one arm, the reins loose in his other hand.

'The omens are excellent, my lord.' The priest spoke loudly, and all around could hear every word. 'The liver was without mark or blemish. The great fissure was deep and straight and the lobe of Aresia enlarged. Victory, my lord. Victory.'

'The Gods are good,' intoned Harpalycus. Troi caught a glance exchanged between him and Brasidas. 'Let the High Priest inform the men of this good news.'

The priest scampered off. The sneaky bastards have faked it, thought Troi. They must have the High Priest rolled up in their blanket bag. He didn't know whether to be appalled or impressed. He decided upon the latter. He was learning a great deal.

Brasidas had turned his attention back to the distant town, screwing up his eyes to make out the forces. 'Only six speirai,' he growled, 'and he's got ten. Looks like most of his cavalry and light troops, though. What's he playing at?'

'He's seen through us. Someone has finally got the information to him. He knows how weak we really are.' Harpalycus did not sound at all concerned.

'Then why not send out the lot?'

'He, or more probably Parmenio, wants to suck us in, tempt us into engaging. Once we're fixed, like linnets with lime, the rest will emerge and roll over us with sheer numbers. He's had to send out all his supporting troops as he's weakest in that area. And they are who we shall concentrate on. If we can take them out, his speirai are going to be as much use as roasted pebbles at a symposium.'

Brasidas surveyed the intervening stretch of flat ground: fields of beans and barley, interspersed with meadows, now empty of livestock. Only an isolated tree or collection of ramshackle farm buildings presented any impediment to troop movement, but it was minimal. The fields were delineated by simple lines of boundary stones, the grazing land by flimsy wooden fences that would be no more a barrier than the festive ribbons of the Dionysia. It was a battleground made by the Gods for the Troian hordes. They would be able to outflank the smaller Mykerenaean army with ease.

His eyes were drawn to a substantial wood well forward and farther to the left of the extreme Troian left flank, the only stretch of substantial cover in view.

Harpalycus saw his look and nodded. 'Waiting for the scouts' report. There's nowhere else to hide. They'll be in there planning to come boiling out once we're fixed. I would guess strike cavalry with light infantry close support.'

'So, do we accept battle?'

'Oh, yes, but not immediately. We fall back beyond this hill. When Parmenio sees us apparently retreating, he'll have to decide. Does he send his reserves out early and scare us off for good, or does he leave a dangerously wide gap between his first line and his second, hoping we take the bait and he can hook us? He'll do the latter.' His horse tossed its head, sensing the tension, and Harpalycus patted its neck to calm it. 'Moving that army and its supplies with a still intact force nipping at its heels will not be fun.'

He glanced behind him to the open, coarse grassland crumpling into rolls of shallow valleys and low rises. 'And in that lot, we can surprise him.'

'It still sails against the wind to let him take the hill,' grumbled Brasidas. 'Against all the tenets of accepted military wisdom.'

'I know,' said Harpalycus, grinning. 'It'll convince Parmenio that we really are frightened. And what better place to beach a couple of those bloody speirai like stranded whales?'

An arrow rider came pounding up the shallow slope, dragging his horse to a halt before the strategos, and saluted. 'Sir. In the wood. The scouts report a tet of heavy cavalry. No supporting troops.'

'Good work, lad. Get back to Xanthos. Any movement in that quarter, and I want to know.'

The rider hauled his horse round and plunged back down the hill, leaving a shower of grass clods in his wake. Troi wiped a divot of mud from his cheek. He felt confident and unafraid, but just having to sit quietly when a battle was about to erupt was not easy. His whole body rang like a bell with the need to be doing something. How could Harp and Bras be so relaxed? Perhaps they weren't. They just knew how not to show it.

'Just a tet?' mused Harpalycus to Brasidas. 'And no supporting troops? What's Parmenio doing?'

Harpalycus glanced back at Troi and gestured him forward. The strategos pointed to the right flank of the army, held by Meleagros and his Aggies.

'Tell Mel to clear that wood. Just make sure he's got the right one.' Brasidas guffawed. 'They've put unsupported cavalry in there, so he shouldn't have a problem. Then to use his own discretion on that flank. But be careful not to get caught in the open by any cavalry. Whenever possible, he is to hit their light infantry and hit them hard.'

Brasidas grunted something that Troi did not catch.

'Oh, and, as you are returning, just make sure that Alexandros is well concealed in that valley,' added Harpalycus. He pointed behind and half-right. 'We'll probably be on that knoll by then.' He indicated a small rocky outcrop some distance behind. 'Good fortune.'

Troi nodded, wheeled his horse, a fast Phthian with good endurance, and set off at a canter, pleased to be doing something.

The light rain was becoming intermittent, and shafts of sunlight pierced the bunched clouds ahead. A corn bunting called like a jangle of coins, and yellowhammers sang. It all seemed so ordinary and peaceful.

A movement caught his eye, and he looked up. An eagle soared overhead, sweeping towards the Mykerenaean lines. The Gods promised victory. A genuine omen. Unless Harp had a specially trained eagle. Troi wouldn't put it beyond his throw.

He rode across the rear of the army, his aide's red banner streaming proudly behind him. Past the shield lines of hoplites, javelin-armed peltastes, screening archers and the wild, tattooed Thracians. The latter looked like poor relations with their coarse, earth-coloured tunics, tattered horse blankets and bridles of twisted rope, but were the finest light cavalry in the known world.

Behind him, on the hillock, a red standard was lifted, and ranks began to stir and shift to the monotonous calls of salpinxes and shouted orders. Troi curved in toward the very end of the line. The troops there looked even less imposing than the Thracians. Small, grimy men, overly endowed with body hair and clad in simple tunics. They were carrying bundles of javelins and lounging around in no discernible order. He spotted Meleagros, standing with a couple of his officers and wearing his new, bright white shoulder sash. He had just been made up to strategos. Troi cantered up.

Meleagros stretched and yawned as though he had just risen from a sleep. Knowing him, it was not impossible. He glanced round and inclined his head in welcome. 'Young Troilus. Xanthos has had a word. They've got no bloody support, would you believe. This is going to be apple-picking time.'

One of the Aggies with him drew an index finger across his own throat, rolled his eyes dramatically, made a gargling noise and grinned happily.

Troi kept his face straight. 'Harp just wanted to ensure you had the right wood.'

Meleagros looked up at Troi and tutted loudly. 'Hilarious. Can't a chap make an odd mistake without it being flung in his face.' He pointed. 'It's that bloody wood, all right! That thing with trees. In fact, the only thing with bloody trees out there. Tell Harp to bugger off.' He stopped and winked. 'With my compliments, of course. And tell him I've already got three hekatons in that gulley waiting. They'll pop up in the middle of those Trogs before they know they're there. Just waiting for the go.'

'Then, it's a go. Harpalycus says to watch for cavalry, but to operate at your own discretion against psiloi and peltastes afterwards.'

'Got it.' The newly-made strategos noticed Troi staring at a section of Aggies trotting by with fearsome-looking scythe blades on long handles. Meleagros called one across and took the weapon from him, tossing it up to Troi, who caught it deftly despite its weight.

Meleagros was his usual enthusiastic self. 'It's a rhomphaia. The Thraks use them, so we borrowed some. Bloody nasty. Take the front legs off a horse with one swipe. They reckon they'll cut a man in half. Never seen it myself, mind. I remain hopeful, though.'

Troi passed it back. 'The Trogs'll find it a mite unpleasant trapped amongst the trees with these beastly things buzzing around their ears.'

Meleagros grinned evilly. 'Won't be overly happy, that's for sure.' He regarded Troi with a quizzical eye. 'Your first battle, laddie?'

Troi nodded. He hoped he looked confident. His stomach still felt hollow. He considered making a suitably warlike response, but sensibly decided that it would just sound thrasonical.

'Take it easy. There'll be plenty more.'

'I will. May Fortune lead you by the hand.'

'And you, laddie.' He gave him a languid wave and turned back to his two colleagues.

Troi pulled his horse round and angled across towards the well-hidden fold in the ground that lay beyond the Mykerenaean right flank. He scrutinised it as he approached, but could see nothing. Only as he was almost at the lip did he halt and look pointedly at a collection of brushwood near a small thicket of blackthorn.

The brushwood shifted slightly, in an uncomfortable sort of way.

Troi sighed. 'Spread a bit to either side, man. It's too obviously isolated.'

'Sir,' said the pile of brushwood in a decidedly chastened manner.

Troi passed by and to the edge of the low declivity. It was full of horses, laid down, their troopers lying alongside them and stroking their muzzles to keep them calm. At either side squatted units of the Cretan archers, checking their arrows or throwing knucklebones. An officer walked across to Troi. He was tall, athletic and classically handsome, with golden hair and grey eyes. Alexandros. 'Problems?' he enquired.

Troi grinned. 'Nope, Harp just wanted to make sure you were well concealed.'

'Cheeky bastard,' said Alexandros amiably. Troi wasn't sure whether he was referring to him or Harpalycus. 'Well, we are, so task completed. Sod off, then.'

Troi did so. The rebel army, screened by a cloud of light troops, was already beginning a steady retreat. But there was no sign of any disorganisation or nervousness. They knew what they had to do. Following them, the slow, inexorable advance of the Troian speirai. Between the two armies, the psiloi were engaged in a desultory missile duel. Well spread out, they were doing relatively little damage to each other, except on the far left flank, where some Trog archers had the bad luck of clashing with the deadly Mykerenaean longbows.

The battle had begun.

FIFTY-ONE

TROI THREADED HIS way back through the units of heavily armed hoplites. The men seemed to be in good humour. One tag was singing an improvised marching song about advancing backwards, and another was happily engaged in irritating a little red-faced fighting cock of a hyperetes by suggesting that he was leading from the rear.

He looked behind him to see the first Troian light infantry breasting the rounded top of the hillock recently vacated by Harpalycus. Ahead of him, a small group of figures stood atop the rocky knoll with a black flag lifted high over them, snapping in the strong breeze. Towards the Troians' left flank, two eiles of Thracian cavalry about-turned and set off up the smooth, grassy slopes at a canter.

There was immediate confusion in the Troian light troops on the summit. It was not done for cavalry to charge lowly missile troops. Mounted troops traditionally fought it out on the flanks instead. Archers were just not the same social grade. Troi guessed they had rashly pushed too far ahead of their immediate support and would be easily ridden down by the Thracians. Mykerenaean psiloi stopped and turned back to support the cavalry charge with bow and sling.

The enemy commander must have been alert to the threat, as the cavalry force on the Troian left flank began to surge forward to intercept the Thracians. Instead of falling back, the Thracians continued with their advance. Troi watched breathlessly. The Troian heavies would be more than a match for the light cavalry in a face-to-face mêlée. The heartbeats stretched beyond endurance.

Then he could see movement in the declivity to the left of the Troian advance. A salpinx gave an urgent summons, and over the lip, rising like the dragon-born from the earth, came a tide of cavalry, mounted on strong Phthians, the horses' muscles rippling as they clambered from the dip, then bunching powerfully as they sprang into a gallop. The heavily armoured riders streamed long red cloaks in their wake and carried heavy, large-bladed thrusting spears. On their flanks, the Cretans were unleashing a storm of arrows from their powerful bows.

The Imperial cavalry lost all cohesion in their surprise. The Hetairoi hit them with savage force, at full gallop. There was no pause to throw javelins in the time honoured-manner, but they thrust home with the terrifying momentum of a full-blooded charge.

The Trogs shattered like an amphora struck by a rock. Panic-stricken troopers flew in every direction like broken shards, and the Mykerenaeans rolled over them. One of the two Thracian eiles curved round and gleefully took up the pursuit of the fleeing remnants. They harried without mercy, trampling dismounted men beneath their horses' hooves, cutting them down with cruel slashes of their swords, ignoring the supplicating hands and pleas for mercy. It was as if the ground vibrated to the pounding of hooves and the air was hideous with the screams of horses and men, the clash of iron and the blare of salpinxes. The damp air itself seemed to carry a wash of blood and the unmistakable smell of death.

The Imperial psiloi had rashly remained, under the assumption that they were now safe, but the second rebel eile continued its attack, and simply overran and slaughtered the helpless light infantry. Some tried to run, some fell on their knees beseeching quarter that was not on offer, a few tried to fight back; but the Thracians were in their element, and very few Troians made it to the protection of their spearmen. Then the cavalry fell back, with impressive discipline, before the slow and ponderous advance of the sweating speirai.

A Troian trooper in a blue tunic came hurtling towards Troi, looking back over his shoulder, all too obviously terrified. Troi slid his short sword from its scabbard. The man glanced to the front and yanked back on his reins, almost sitting the horse on its haunches. He was only a young lad, scarcely older than Troi himself, but his open mouth and staring eyes said all that Troi needed to know. He had no weapon in his grasp, and he looked beseechingly at Troi.

'Please,' he gasped. 'Please. I surrender. Please.'

Troi nonchalantly turned his sword in his hand, studying the cutting edge. But Diomedes' words pulsed in his head. *You will become Marsyas.*

'Please. Please.' The desperate refrain continued.

Troi sighed. He felt a tinge of sympathy for the young man. Why, he had no idea. He was nothing to him. But Diomedes' words had worried him. He knew that he was different from others, but imagined that he was just that little bit more rational and clear-sighted, that he lacked the weaknesses of others. Perhaps he really was different. In some fundamental way. He came to a decision.

'Dump your weapons.'

The lad fumbled with the straps of his javelin bag and let it fall; then, with his unblinking stare fastened leech-like to Troi, he drew his sword with great caution and dropped that too. His whole body sagged with relief.

'Get down.'

The Troian dismounted, careful not to make any sudden movements, then stood before Troi. He had long brown hair caught up in a ponytail, buck teeth and light green eyes that never left Troi's. His throat apple bobbed as he swallowed.

'Thank you,' he said, and Troi felt a faint wash of gratification. He looked around. A unit of Cretan archers were dropping back fifty paces away, unmistakable in their characteristic large, floppy sun hats and pale green tunics. He called them over.

'Sir,' said their swarthy hekatonarches as he arrived. The red pennant that Troi carried was sufficient authority.

'Take this man prisoner,' Troi said.

'But, sir…' objected the officer.

Troi lifted an eyebrow.

'Yes, sir.'

The boy smiled at Troi and gave him a nod as Troi swung his horse round and headed for the knoll. After a few hundred paces he looked back. The Cretans were marching on. Behind them lay a blue, crumpled heap. He felt a surge of anger, but there seemed little point in confrontation. He shrugged and pressed on, wondering why a brief smile should haunt his mind.

After a few hekates, he got to the top, where Harpalycus calmly watched the battle. Troi hastily took in the scene. A speira remained halted on the summit of the hillock. Beyond, the Troian left was in a state of collapse. Meleagros had emerged from the cleared wood—the Troians there had fled the instant the Aggies appeared—and fallen upon the covering peltastes while the reformed Hetairoi charged what remained of the Troian cavalry. The entire Troian flank was being swept from the field and the speirai left hanging in the air, plagued by a swarm of archers and slingers, with few light troops of their own to shield them. On the other side of the battlefield, the Mykerenaean cavalry had moved forward to engage the bulk of the Troian cavalry in a massive mêlée.

Out of the confusion of the battlefield—as banners advanced and retreated, missiles flew in every direction, and troops of cavalry charged and broke away like waves upon the shore—Troi could see that the plan to refuse the centre and destroy the cavalry and light troops on the wings was working well. And the first rays of the sun broke through the dark clouds and picked out the knoll in a momentary gleam of golden light.

FIFTY-TWO

'DYAUS.' THE AIDE next to Troi urged his horse forward and pointed to their left wing. 'What in Hades...?'

Troi stared. Emerging from a wide valley beyond the savage cavalry mêlée were two large units of Troian heavy horse. Harpalycus didn't hesitate, but swung his horse round and trotted to the farther edge of the knoll. Below it stood two eiles of heavy cavalry under Themistocles.

'We've found them,' he yelled. 'Behind our left flank. Immediate charge.'

There was some sort of response, but Troi could not make it out, and then a salpinx sounded, a flurry of shouted orders and the creak and jingle of harness and thud of hooves.

'The bastard must have snuck them out last night,' said Brasidas, riding over to Harpalycus. 'Those in the wood were just a lure.'

'I'll want to know from Gwalchmai why the scouts didn't find them.' Harpalycus's attention was now fastened on the left wing. Troi pushed his horse forward for a good view. The Troians saw Themistocles coming and counter-charged with one eile while the other continued to crash into the rear of the Mykerenaean cavalry. The whole thing dissolved into chaos as men cut and slashed and stabbed at one another, pressed so close together that they could scarcely move.

'Bras. Get down and bridle our right wing. I want those units under control. If we lose cohesion, we could lose this.'

Brasidas did not waste time on a reply, but was gone.

Harpalycus continued to watch the battle for the left, which pulsed and bulged like a jellyfish, then suddenly swore. 'That new Chenoi unit's just broken.' He turned and shouted to Simonides. 'To Tereus. Immediate. Move two eiles across rear of army to support left wing.'

Simonides scribbled something on a wax tablet and thrust it to an arrow rider, who urged his horse into an immediate gallop. Simonides walked up. 'I said that unit needed blooding.'

'We needed every man. Now the bloody speirai are going to be able to walk away. We won't be able to stop them. But I can't risk Pan taking control. Damn it to Hades.'

The Troian speirai were already falling back under a hail of unanswered arrows and slingshots, leaving a long and bloody trail of dead and dying behind. 'Well, they're not going to get there in one piece, that's for sure,' muttered Simonides.

Harpalycus turned and urgently gestured Troi forward. He pointed to the Imperial speira still on top of the low hill. It hadn't moved. 'Brasidas is down there. There's a gap opening. Tell him to fix that speira, but not to get drawn into an actual spear clash. I want at least one of those bloody hedgehogs to go down.'

Troi didn't even wait to acknowledge the order, but flung his horse down the steep slope in a slide and slither of hooves, gripping tightly with his knees and holding it on a short rein. As soon as the slope bottomed out, he broke into a gallop and thundered across to the lines of waiting hoplites under the running dog banner of Brasidas. They faced the speiroi, who were crouched under a sleet of arrows and the sharp crack of slingshots smacking into their overlocking shields, but even as he arrived, the speiroi stood and began their belated retreat.

Brasidas grasped immediately what was required, and the units of hoplites climbed quickly up towards the Troian spearmen. But the latter were already well on their way. They needed to be held for a few hekates. Troi looked around. Across the stricken battlefield, two eiles of light cavalry were hunting down the wretched psiloi.

He galloped towards them, holding up the long red streamer on his spear that proclaimed him an aide. The commander of the nearest eile saw him coming and angled towards him, his signaller already sounding the recall over and over. The eilarches removed his helmet, revealing a young man with an untameable mop of flaxen hair and a roguish smile despite his large and uneven teeth.

'We've got to stop that hedgehog retiring,' shouted Troi, gesturing towards the solid mass. The other officer came pounding over, his unit beginning to organise behind him. 'I want you to charge them.'

'Charge a bloody hedgehog. You must be mad,' shouted back the second eilarches.

'They'll stop in anticipation of a real charge. Swing right at the last moment across their front and away.'

'You're crazy. Their archers will decimate us as we pass.'

The first officer burst out laughing. 'They haven't got any, you dozy bugger. We've already seen to that.' He glanced at Troi. 'I'll charge first. I want Mardonius four hundred paces behind as a second wave.' He turned to his signaller. 'Form double line.'

Troi was already gone, racing to gather up light infantry units and pull back some of the hoplites following up the rest of the retreating army. They could not stop the other speirai now, but he recognised the catastrophic effect the loss of the separated speira would have upon the Troians' morale. The first eile thundered up the slope, echeloned back at the left. There were sharp cries of command from Troian officers, salpinxes shrieked and the spearmen sank to their knees behind their large shields, spears braced against the ground. At the last moment the cavalry peeled away, racing past their front and then down, hurling javelins as they went. One horse fell and several men ran out from the speira and stabbed viciously down on the screaming trooper before scuttling back to their positions.

The Troians remained in a defensive huddle as the second eile launched its attack. Again, it swung right, the first eile already reforming up behind it. They had pinned the bastards. Troi felt a surge of exultation and whooped with joy. He leaned forward on his horse's shoulders and surveyed the forlorn mass of huddled spearman crowning the hill. Now the rebels could finish them off.

FIFTY-THREE

THE WHITE ROSE banner approached, and Troi trotted over to meet the command group. His horse was flecked with foam, her flanks heaving when he stopped. Harpalycus took in the situation at a glance. Several tags of hoplites now stood about thirty paces from the embattled speira, and the two units of cavalry were back in a threatening position between it and safety. Units of psiloi, both archers and slingers, were beginning to ring the stricken Troians, and heavy infantry were moving back towards them to slam the door shut on their retreat.

The Troians' compatriots had clearly decided to leave them to their fate. They were falling back to the ring of newly emerged reinforcements as quickly as cohesion allowed. They were merely going to ensure their own successful extrication and nothing more. There were few cavalrymen, and even fewer light infantry, accompanying them.

Harpalycus glanced at Troi and nodded. 'The Trogs finally collapsed on the left. Tereus is following up and making them pay. And you've done well here.'

Troi was conscious of a surprising feeling of pride. He had not believed that others' opinions were important beyond the practical and self-serving. A thought struck him. Part of an aide's job. 'That young eilarches,' he said, pointing out the flaxen-haired officer. 'He was impressive. You would do well to have a look at him.'

Harpalycus gave him an approving look. 'Good advice. But already taken. His name's Tros and I have plans for him.' He glanced down at Troi's exhausted horse and turned to another of his aides. 'Get the psiloi concentrated on their right rear as they retire, and as close as we can. Support them with the light cavalry. They can evade and outrun them if need be, but I doubt any Trogs will break formation with that cavalry there. Aimed, not volley. If a gap appears, concentrate on it. If it reforms, make another.' The man nodded and galloped off. Harpalycus beckoned the third aide. 'Get arrow and shot resupply organised. Soonest. Then make sure the longbowmen get here. I want them to concentrate on officers.'

The longbow was a Mykerenaean speciality. Made of skilfully cut yew, with the sapwood on the outside and the heartwood on the inside to maximise its power, its draw was massive. So much so that longbowmen had to be trained to it from an early age, practicing assiduously until their left arms and shoulders were distinctively larger than their right. There were never enough of them, but they were greatly feared by their opponents.

The commander of the speira made his decision and began the slow and lumbering retreat again, the rebel hoplites doggedly following up, the cavalry and missile troops on their flanks. Harpalycus nodded with satisfaction. As the Troians began a cautious descent down the farther slope, the hoplites, now reinforced, took the summit and followed, the advantage of the slope now with them. A line of returning Mykerenaean hoplites formed steadily on the plain between the Troians and the increasingly distant-looking refuge. The rest of the Trog army were gratefully approaching the town, and the lost speira could look for no succour from them.

'Arrow,' Harpalycus shouted. An arrow rider moved forward, holding a long lance bearing a blue pennant. Harpalycus turned to Simonides. 'To charge on green.' Simonides scribbled onto a wax tablet as Harpalycus pointed out the relevant unit, then almost threw it at the arrow rider, who spun his horse round and raced off.

The arrow storm the rebels concentrated on the right rear corner was having its effect, the formation becoming broken and ragged, and the whole of that side, markedly slower than the rest as they watched for incoming missiles, extending into a long and vulnerable tail. The arrow rider arrived, and Troi saw Tros take the tablet, scan it and immediately ride forward to speak to a psiloi commander and then the other eilarches. After a few hekates, the archers and slingers drifted to either side to leave a gap between. The waiting cavalry formed into a wedge. Harpalycus watched and ordered a green signal banner readied and raised. Tros acknowledged with a wave. Harpalycus waited. The lamed creature crawled painfully downwards, losing its shape, its cohesion. 'Now,' he snapped. The banner dropped and a huge salpinx, supported on the shoulder of a man with hands pressed to his ears, boomed out a triple cry.

The cavalry hurtled forward through the gap between two curling waves of arrows and burst upon the stricken troops. Had they been together, shoulder to shoulder, the reassuring press of their comrades behind, their large shields and sharp blades before, they would have stood and the cavalry would have stopped short. No horse will charge an impenetrable obstacle.

But this was no longer impenetrable. It was a fractured mass of frightened individuals. It dissolved in panic, and the horsemen clove deeply into the disintegrating unit, thrusting with their spears and slashing viciously with their swords. At the other side, the hoplites gave their cry of alalalaloi and began their inexorable advance to meet the wilting and hopeless spearmen.

Troi could hear the crash as the two sides collided, and for a short period there was the hideous din of hand-to-hand conflict, the shouts and screams and ring of iron. The cavalry bit deeper, the following hoplites charged into contact in turn, and the banner within the hedgehog, black and decorated with a silver alpha and gamma, rose then fell forward. There was a clatter as shields and spears fell to the ground, the last arrows whirred, and a strange silence seemed to settle over the battlefield. But only for heartbeats before the moans and cries of the wounded fell upon their ears.

The First Battle of Tenos was over. Troi looked around him with a mixture of some disappointment but with more satisfaction. There had been no sign of Marsyas, but the bastard wouldn't exactly be doing jigs of delight. With his light troops and cavalry savagely mauled, his superior strength in heavy infantry was all but useless. And the sight of a speira going down in shameful surrender would live long in Troian memories.

Troi was not unhappy.

He had learned patience. The moment of revenge was getting closer.

FIFTY-FOUR

Marsyas licked his wounds for another se'ennight before emerging again, this time with his whole army. But no Parmenio. Despite having ignored the man's advice and refused him permission to send the remaining speira forward in support, Marsyas had made his most competent strategos the scapegoat and sent him back to Ilios in disgrace. The satrap would command his forces in person. Harpalycus was by no means unhappy with the outcome. He again retreated, refusing combat, the lumbering speirai unable to pin his forces and the supporting troops too sparse to do other than huddle as close to the spearmen as they could.

However, foreseeing exactly this eventuality, Harpalycus had surreptitiously moved the Thracians and Agrianians to the rear of the Troian camp, where they launched a surprise attack that swept aside the few dispirited defenders and began to burn and pillage the vitally needed stores. Marsyas tumbled back desperately, and the raiders melted away, but the hurried and disorganised retreat allowed Harpalycus to launch several devastating strikes, always concentrating on the luckless few remaining ancillary troops rather than the speirai.

Without adequate cavalry and missile support, the hedgehogs could not bring the Mykerenaeans to decisive battle on their own. Eventually Marsyas abandoned his encampment and advanced upon the Akroakrai. Continually harassed by the Thracians, who were growing steadily in numbers, and slowed by his massive baggage train to little more than a crawl, he made grim, tortuous and bloody progress. As he went, he laid waste to the country, putting farms and villages in his path to the torch. It was the best part of a moontide and a half after the rebels captured the fortress before it was actually invested.

FIFTY-FIVE

THE THREAT OF Harpalycus's shadowing force was such that the majority of the Troians were stationed on the defensive. Marsyas created a circumvallation of two stockades round the squat fortress before making his first attempt. The position atop the limestone outcrop prevented the use of assault towers, and the Troians lacked projectile weapons of sufficient strength to do more than scratch the kyklopean walls. They were left with makeshift battering rams and scaling ladders. And numbers. Demonstrating a characteristic ruthlessness and lack of subtlety, Marsyas simply threw his men at the walls. Where they died. Flesh and blood against stone was never a good option. Fortresses fell through treachery or starvation, rarely by assault. And so it proved at the Akroakrai.

With a particularly broad walkway to work with, ample time to prepare and a great deal of ingenuity, Diomedes' men had made the place all but impregnable. The rule was to protect the defenders at all times. To kill but not be killed. To that end the parapets had been significantly heightened and narrow embrasures with angled edges created so that archers could, with relative safety, pick off the attackers as they struggled up the shaky ladders.

If the Troians chose to go for the embrasures, Aristobulos had devised stout wooden pavises, covered with dampened animal skins against fire, that could be rapidly wheeled into position. A long, forked beam hung from a well-supported structure, with transverse handles to provide purchase. Extending it through a hole in the pavise, several men could push away a ladder with ease. A favourite ploy was for other defenders to push it sideways with forked sticks so the tumbling ladder might bring down a whole stretch of others as it fell.

But the device that terrified the attackers and effectively destroyed their morale was the fire-breather. A perforated cauldron of burning charcoal was brought to incandescence by leather bellows. Other bellows inflated several pig bladders, until the pressure was released through a bronze nozzle across the top of the brazier to send a jet of flame blasting through the embrasure. The defenders had five of these, and they could be moved easily along the walkways so the attackers never knew which gap would erupt fire at any moment and turn the luckless leader into a screaming human inferno, cartwheeling down onto the shocked troops waiting below.

The assault on the main gate fared no better. The defenders had channelled gaps through the walls above and were able to rain rocks and burning pitch on the unfortunates toiling to stack brushwood against the gates below. The pitch ignited the half-completed bonfire. When it had burned out, the gates now but crumbling and charred remnants, the Troians were amazed and discomfited to find that beyond them was fire-blackened, but still solid, masonry. Even Marsyas could not stomach such losses, and he pulled his men back. Few defenders had died or been injured, but the losses to the Troians had been horrendous. He settled down to starve them out.

FIFTY-SIX

Over time, Troi had received several scrolls from Klio, telling him what passed for news in the insular community of the Villa Antipatroi. Her only bit of real news was that Ilus, hearing that his old mentor, Diomedes, was commanding the rebel forces, had left to join the rebellion. Troi enquired with the strategarch and learned that Ilus had been placed in command of a unit of hypaspistai at Plataea.

But Troi sent Klio only a couple of cold and perfunctory scrolls in reply. He justified this to himself with the excuses that it was difficult to find someone who could carry such a message from rebel-held territory to Leuctra, and that it was probably unkind to encourage Klio.

However, he was beginning to wonder if he was being honest with himself. He felt surprisingly guilty about his negligence, and other, long-suppressed thoughts were beginning to infiltrate his mind. He had been unable to stop thinking about what Diomedes had said in that final, uncomfortable conversation. Diomedes was now trapped within the confines of the Akroakrai, with the entire Troian army in place around him. Troi would not speak to him again this side of the Styx. And Troi suspected that Diomedes had had the right of it.

There was something lacking in Troi. He could see it in others, but could find no trace within himself. He did have a strange memory of having such feelings, but, when he tried to capture their essence, they dissipated like smoke. He began by assuming they had been some nebulous creation of the immature brain, moulded by social expectations, but ultimately fabrications of gauze and gossamer that could not withstand hard and gritty reality.

Yet, those around him still seemed to feel the pain or the pleasure of others, in some way to resonate with them, almost become one with them. To Troi, everyone was an outsider. He could understand their feelings to some extent, know when they were glad or excited or mournful, have some idea how they would react in consequence. But he could not feel it. It was an exercise in interpretation.

He had taught himself to play the role of someone who cared, even to laugh, if unconvincingly, with those who laughed, to comfort those who cried as best he could, to enquire about their lives, their families, their hopes and fears, to make the effort to recall the small trivial details that seemed to mean so much. But he did not really care. As soon as they were out of his presence, the instant that he had done for them what they had asked, the moment that he had no further need to pretend, they vanished from his consciousness as though they had never been. And they knew it. He was respected but not popular. It worried him.

He thought increasingly of Kalliope, with something almost approaching affection. He even wondered if he might return to the Villa Antipatroi one day. He thought of the caravan guard he'd toyed with before killing. He thought of Gian, who had died defending him. And he thought of Nicias, whose young life had been snuffed out at his order. He still could not feel remorse—it had been the correct decision, and the fact that Nicias had previously saved his life was obviously irrelevant—but he persuaded himself that he ought to go and see the boy's mother. He owed him that, at least.

The only problem was that the small village where she lived was now well within the zone of control of the investing Trog army. Nevertheless, if he was careful, he did not think it would be that difficult. With the Thracians and the Aggies around, the Trogs were understandably reluctant to leave the safety of their camp. And there was no need to tell anyone.

FIFTY-SEVEN

THE SMALL VILLAGE of Tegea was a collection of neat dwellings centred on a ramshackle tavern and a simple shrine to Artemisia. It lay on the bank of a shallow river, clustered around one end of a broad clapper bridge that straddled the clear waters to the meadows beyond. Herds of black, short-legged cattle, the mainstay of the village's existence, should have been grazing there. They had gone now. Snapped up by the maw of the ever-hungry Troian army. But the village was crowded; a hundred or so refugees had come in from isolated farmsteads to its doubtful safety, and an untidy huddle of makeshift shelters lay on the northern edge of the settlement.

There was no sign of the Trogs as Troi approached the bridge through fields thick with sedges and feathered grass and rich with colour: the massed clumps of ox-eyed daisies, the pink of the campions and the blue of the scabious. Skylarks climbed high overhead, spilling song like a sun-drenched waterfall, and the air was a whir of insects and heavy with the heady smell of meadowsweet.

He relied upon his youth and lack of weapons to deflect suspicion. He had only a small knife in a belt scabbard and would simply tell the truth as far as possible. As Sinon was fond of saying, the truth is always the best cloak. Troi had merely come to see Euadne, daughter of Kayx, as an old friend of her dead son, Nicias. His background story was that he was son to a merchant in Leuctra. He still had the documentation Ilus had provided. He could see no problems.

He crossed the flat stone bridge and entered the village. No-one took any notice of him. The inhabitants and refugees alike looked pale, hungry and pinched. He asked after Euadne's house of a woman beating a rug by her front door and received curt directions.

He found the place easily enough, but got a cool welcome from the grey-haired and rheum-eyed old lady who lived there. He was not surprised. Euadne offered him nothing but simply sat at an old wooden table and stared at him as he told her of her son's heroic death.

He deliberately lied to her, saying that Nicias had volunteered. Not to protect himself, he decided, but simply to make her feel better. He wasn't sure how deep the layers of lies went. It seemed to bring no comfort, and the unquenchable grief deep within her tired eyes meant nothing to him. He had the uneasy suspicion that she knew he was lying and was relieved when she asked him to go. Mumbling some meaningless platitude, he left quietly.

FIFTY-EIGHT

TROI STOPPED OUTSIDE the door and stared. Everyone else was still and staring too. A circle of Troian cavalry surrounded the village. Worse yet, they wore the blue cloaks of Marsyas's personal guard. An officer, tall, thin and black-haired, was riding across the bridge with a small escort. Troi's first reaction was one of flesh-freezing panic, the smell of smoke biting into his nostrils, the copper tang of blood and the reek of burning flesh clogging his throat, surrounded by obscene lumps of death and the spit and crackle of flames. He felt himself go cold, yet sweat ran down the small of his back. He needed to run but somehow wrested control back from his instinctive terror, forcing himself to stand as quietly as those about him.

'The village archon. Here. Now.' The officer's voice was harsh and peremptory.

That calmed him. It was not a phantasm that had ridden from the fetches of the night to burst in upon the day, but a real man demanding to see the leader of the small community. A vision rose before his eyes of a tall, spindly figure lying in a dark patch of blood, his head divorced two paces from his body, but he gained command of himself once more. He breathed slowly and deeply, and the sweat began to dry on his skin.

A small, stooped old man went forward slowly, leaning upon a stick. A slim young woman with long, dark brown braids suddenly broke the general spell and ran forward to help him. They stopped before the lanky form of the officer, who looked down arrogantly at them.

'By order of Marsyas, Satrap of Mykerenos, and in the name of the Emperor Laomedon, all inhabitants are required to give loyal assistance to the Imperial Forces in their suppression of the murderous bandits who have dared to foment insurrection.' He paused to look around at the frightened crowd. None dared meet his challenging gaze. Somewhere a child was crying. 'All persons will therefore assemble within the agora. I will be the sole arbiter of those who will have the honour of providing such assistance. You have one dekate to congregate here with a sleeping roll, a spare change of clothing and whatever food you may carry. No weapons will be allowed.' There was no sound, no movement. Everyone was as immobile as masked actors awaiting their cue. Even their clothes seemed to fall in sculpted folds.

'The village will be searched thereafter. Anyone found hiding will be executed as a traitor, as will all in that household. You have one dekate.' Without bothering to await a reply, he turned his horse and rode back across the bridge, followed by his escort. The threatening ring of cavalry remained motionless around them. A stir of movement and a rising tide of voices ran through the crowd.

The old man and the young woman spoke quietly to each other. She turned and faced the now-dense crowd. She was about eighteen, tall but delicately built, with an attractive oval face. Her eyes were fearful, but her voice was strong and carrying, and everyone fell silent when she spoke.

'We must do as he says. We have no choice. Go and collect what you can. Do not try and hide. You will bring death to your families. Do not be afraid. They need us for labour. They will feed us at least.'

'And what about those left behind?' shouted someone from the crowd. There was a murmuring, and it was not friendly. Troi could not fail to notice that the looks thrown at the young woman verged on the hostile.

'I don't know.' Tears trembled in her voice. 'But what choice is there?'

There was further muttering, and then the crowd started to break up as people began to hurry to their houses. The young woman took the old man's arm and helped him away.

Troi thought swiftly. His chances of remaining hidden in some house or other, despite his scout training, were moderate at best, and, if found, they would realise he was a rebel and probably summarily hang him. On the other hand, if he went, he would be but one among many. Further, he might well pick up valuable information, and he was confident that, in the open, he could escape easily when the time came. Civilians would be sloppily guarded. Now was the worst possible time to attempt evasion.

Behind him, the door opened, and Euadne gestured him in with an arthritic finger. She said nothing, so neither did he, as she went into one of the two back rooms. She emerged carrying a thin sleeping roll, an old rope belt and a small bundle of clothing. They must have belonged to Nicias. The elderly woman laid them on the crude wooden table and went to the cooking area, where she produced pieces of boustria, some dried apples and a wedge of cheese, together with a thin cloth to wrap them in.

He began to speak. 'I can't take…'

She shook her head imperiously. 'Nici would have wanted it. Now, make a bundle.' Euadne collected a good leathern water flask from a simple hook on the wall and took it outside to fill it from the well. Troi neatly rolled everything up into a bundle, tying it off securely with the belt. She returned with the flask.

He stood there, awkwardly, for a moment. 'Thank you,' he said.

'No need. Don't forget to leave the knife.'

He nearly had. He rather sheepishly removed both knife and scabbard from his belt and laid them on the table. He took the coins from his pouch and laid them alongside. For a moment, anger crossed her face.

'Rather you than them,' he tersely explained.

She nodded briefly. 'Now go.' Her tone was tart.

He turned for the door, then looked back at the surprisingly straight little old woman. There were tears in her eyes. He gave her a half-smile. She did not respond. The uncomfortable thought came to him that she had guessed his role in the death of her son. He closed the door behind him and headed for the agora.

He was one of the first, but others soon began to arrive, looking understandably apprehensive, clutching their small bundles of belongings. Women holding babies tightly to their breasts, old men leaning heavily on staffs. A legless girl on a small wooden cart. Young and old, men and women, frightened and wailing children, confused and muttering elders, those dressed in good clothes, those in rags. All came and waited. The small market area seethed with people.

Troi stood quietly. He saw the young woman arrive, the old archon steadying himself on her arm. He studied her covertly. She was extremely good-looking, with large, dark brown eyes, high cheekbones, a straight nose and a long, perfectly formed mouth. She was slim and very tall, Troi's height at least, and possessed a natural grace of movement. She glanced at Troi, and he hastily looked away, certain she had sensed the scrutiny. He studied the frontage of the small shrine as though it was of great interest.

Then there was a mutter and a stir, and the spindly officer returned with a squad of hard-faced troopers carrying drawn swords. On the farther side of the bridge stood another squad in a loose semicircle.

'Everyone to my left,' shouted the officer, his voice squeaking comically. No-one laughed. He coughed and lowered the pitch. 'Quickly now.'

The crowd shuffled obediently across, squashing together uncomfortably. A couple of the Bluecloaks stationed themselves on the end of the bridge, others formed a semicircle against the façade of the small shrine and a few remained by the officer. It looked like a well-practised procedure.

'Now,' went on the Troian, his voice deep and manly once more, 'form a line and pass before me. If I say "bridge", then cross the bridge and remain within the line of soldiers. If I say "village", then continue on to the area before the shrine and stay there.'

Two troopers stationed themselves on either side of him, and four more plunged into the crowd and manhandled the villagers into a rough line, pushing them unceremoniously forward. A monotonous litany of 'Village, bridge, bridge, village, bridge,' began.

A vacuous-looking teenager was designated "village" but, bewildered, started off across the bridge. A woman cried shrilly from the crowd that he was a poor simpleton. It did nothing to give the two Bluecloaks pause. They enthusiastically fell upon the hapless soul, beat him unmercifully and then dragged him to the area before the shrine to dump his senseless body on the bare earth.

The dreadful dirge began again, as though nothing had happened. 'Bridge, bridge, village.' Troi realised Euadne was easing her way to his side.

'You have nothing with you,' he whispered.

'Of course not,' she responded coolly. 'They're collecting forced labour. I rather suspect they will pass on me.' The line shuffled forward.

'Bridge, village, bridge, bridge.'

She looked away. 'Nici told me that he saved your life once. So you owe me a life.' Her voice trembled slightly. 'I have a heavy demand of you.' She spoke very quietly.

'Behind,' she murmured and looked back. He did so, too. 'The girl with the long brown braids and the green tunic.'

'The one who helped the archon?'

'He's my brother. She's my great niece.'

'So, she would be Nicias's cousin?'

'She would.' They were still speaking in whispers, barely moving their lips. 'Her father was taken by the Troians. He's a master fletcher.'

Troi nodded in understanding.

'He had no choice, but the Troians deliberately made it look as though he had volunteered.'

He nodded again. They would have threatened his family.

'There's much ill feeling and even silly rumours that all this has been arranged with the connivance of the archon. She'll have no-one to protect her. You will swear, upon the Furies, to do so, to the very best of your abilities.'

He blanched. The Great Oath was not to be taken lightly. Any who broke it would be hunted down by the Furies and never gain the Elysian Fields. The sweat ran cold down his spine.

'But what I can do may be limited by my military responsibilities.'

'You will swear. That is the blood price for my Nici.'

When he glanced at her, she held his gaze in iron hoops. He could not read her expressionless face.

She was implacable. 'In the absence of a sword, this will suffice.' She surreptitiously produced his dagger, half-hidden by the folds of her peplos.

There was a moment's hesitation, then he covertly put his hand across to rest on the hilt.

‘I swear,’ he said reluctantly, ‘by the Furies.’

She nodded in satisfaction and slid the dagger back into concealment. They had drawn much closer to the voice intoning bridge or village now. He found himself pushed forward. “Bridge”. As he walked across the great stone slabs, he heard, “Village,” directed at Euadne.

FIFTY-NINE

TROI SAT ON a smooth boulder by the water's edge and watched the young woman cross the bridge, ever looking over her shoulder at the old man shuffling off in the other direction. As she gained the bank, she turned and came straight towards him, her eyes holding his with adamantine determination. She stopped before him and looked down at him. He felt himself at a distinct disadvantage, but rising to his feet would have been worse, flying his discomfort like a banner. He returned her steady gaze.

'And who are you?' she demanded. Her voice was silken smooth but had iron at its heart. 'What are you doing here?'

'I came to see Euadne. About her son Nicias. My name is Troilus, son of Aias.' He had not thought of Aias for some time.

'Nicias is dead.'

'I know. I came to pay my respects.'

'Nicias rode with the rebels.' It sounded as if she considered it a pejorative term. 'Are you a rebel?' She was nothing if not direct, though she spoke quietly, and there was no-one in the immediate vicinity.

'Would I be likely to tell you if I was?'

She brushed the moss from the surface of another boulder and sat down facing him. He could not help but be entranced by the fluid grace that characterised her every movement, but her hard eyes never left his, and she leaned forward, her hands on her thighs, her body growling confrontation.

'The way I see it,' she said slowly, 'you appear from nowhere, and suddenly the Trogs are here. It seems a big coincidence. I ask myself if they are searching for you and will punish us for hiding you.'

'If they were searching for me,' he said reasonably, 'they'd be separating only the young men.'

'So, if I was to tell that officer that you were a stranger here, there'd be no problem?'

He shook his head confidently. 'None whatsoever.'

She continued to glare at him, then said flatly, 'You're bluffing.'

'Can't blame me for trying.' He gave her a broad grin.

Normally, his grins were pretty well irresistible to most women. Not this one. She did not return it. Instead she glanced up at the nearest guard, and Troi's stomach dissolved, but then she looked back at him.

'Don't worry. I wouldn't give this dogspawn a shit stew.' Her crudity jarred on him. 'But I've little time for you damned rebels either. You have brought this grief down on us.' The sneer on her face was unbecoming.

He was suddenly angry. 'Remember Bogazkoi,' he snapped. 'There were no rebels when they butchered almost everyone and burned it to the ground. I make no apology for fighting the bastards.'

Their eyes clashed. Then she rose. Her green tunic, caught at the waist by a braided belt, swirled enticingly around her long, lithe legs. She saw his furtive glance, and a shadow of anger darkened her face before she turned and walked away. She sat down some distance away, her back to him.

Nearly everyone was gathered in small, supportive groups, getting what comfort they could from the proximity of others. No-one approached her.

It took a good dekate to separate the two groups, but when they had done so, collecting about two thirds of the population across the bridge, the Trogs marched them away, leaving the old, the lame, the sick, the children. Cavalry trotted on either side, not in the least reluctant to use their spears to spur on the laggardly. Women wept as they gazed back at the toddlers and older children lining the opposite bank of the river in silent desolation.

A small party of Marsyas's guard remained behind to block the bridge, and Troi noticed that the cordon of cavalry remained on the other side of the river, but out of the village. He did not like what he saw.

He surreptitiously moved through the despondent column until he was two or three paces behind the woman, where he stationed himself. Even as they walked, there was a ring of emptiness around her. She did not turn, but walked steadily on, her head high.

There was a growing murmur behind him, and he stopped and swung round. Behind them, smeared across the clear blue sky, was a rising pillar of black smoke in the direction of the village. Memories crashed through his frail defences, and he felt sick.

'Someone must have hidden, and they've fired a house,' said a voice without conviction.

A woman screamed. The man next to Troi fell to his knees and began sobbing. The smoke was too thick, too broadly based. A young woman at the rear of the column ran desperately back towards the village. A Troian cantered up behind her and thrust his short spear between her shoulder blades. She tumbled forwards, stretched an arm forward in a last despairing movement, then lay still. The other Bluecloaks moved in and began to beat the villagers forward with the butt ends of their spears. Screams, cries and sobs rose to a crescendo.

Someone lunged at a cavalryman and received his spear full in the face. He fell down, his face a bloody mask. Several others lay where they had been felled, but most started to lurch forward again under the incessant cries of 'Move!' and the merciless pummelling. A Bluecloak stabbed down and skewered an injured woman who was attempting to crawl away, and laughed.

Troi looked over to the thin officer, who was watching with grim satisfaction, and committed his face to memory. Narrow, pointed chin, hooked nose, blue eyes, thin, black slicked-back hair. He would know him again.

The woman ahead of him had turned, her face an ashen white, one hand covering her mouth. He moved quietly closer to her. She did not see him, her horror-stricken eyes fixed on the ominous pillar of smoke that split the sky. The tumult of emotions that surged and broke about him—anger, agonised fear, hatred—made him fear for her safety. But the spirit of the villagers, such as it had been, was broken like a reed carelessly snapped by a child, and they stumbled along in a black miasma of misery. Behind them, the gouts of smoke rose ever higher, but few now looked back.

SIXTY

THE OFFICER CALLED a halt in the early afternoon. Troi sat cross-legged on the ground, positioning himself so that he could see the young woman. She was sitting with her back to him, her head drooped, her body language all desolation. Her long hair was falling out of its braids and hung about her face like a curtain.

Watching her, he felt for her sorrow, and that puzzled him. Why should her sorrow affect him? He was still considering the question when three young men approached her. They had a swagger and a hostility about them that immediately brought him unthinkingly to his feet.

They were in their mid-twenties and all bigger and brawnier than him, but they were farm boys. A bit of crude mayhem in the local tavern from time to time. Possibly an ungainly fistfight or two. They were no threat. Troi had already noted that one was hanging back, his furtive eyes casting around him nervously. He would run the instant anything serious happened. Another had a vacuous grin on his face and lumbered rather than walked. He was watching the front man intently, waiting for guidance. He would be confused, unable to react. The only threat came from the first, a square-jawed, bull-necked thug, with small, unpleasant eyes and an indelible sneer stamped on his porcine features. Troi didn't like him at all.

'Well, if it isn't Miss-I'm-in-Charge.'

The woman's head snapped up. Otherwise she did not move.

'Hello, Evenios.' She moved her head to take in the other two. 'Herm. Cari.' Her voice was strong, but he could see tear stains on her cheeks.

'Hello,' began Herm, the vacuous-looking one, with a happy grin on his face, until a backwards jab from Evenios's elbow hit him in the side. He stopped abruptly, looking confused.

'Ain't you going to do summat about this? Get your Troglover father to have a word with his friends?'

'You know he had no choice,' said the woman wearily, 'and he doesn't have any Trog friends.'

'So, you've no friends at all. Ain't that a shame.' He leered. The long-faced man at the back had spotted Troi watching and leaned forward to tap Evenios's arm. When the thug swung round, he gestured at Troi. The gang leader stared at Troi truculently. 'Summat you want, kid?'

'Not really, though a little less noise might be welcome.'

‘I suggest,’ said Evenios, taking a step forward, ‘you bugger off and find yerself somewhere nice and quiet. We’ve business with the young lady.’

‘I like it here well enough,’ said Troi easily.

The woman turned to look at him. ‘Go away,’ she said. ‘You’ll only get hurt.’

‘See,’ said Evenios triumphantly. ‘Yer only trying to get twixt her legs, but she don’t want you. In fact, she don’t want anyone. Miss Proper-and-Prim. She’s a tasty mushroom that’s better than us dung that surrounds her. So, it would be a hiding for nowt. There’s safer ways of scabbarding your sword.’

‘Not on the agenda. But I think I’ll stay here nevertheless.’

‘On the agenda! Ooooh.’ Evenios glanced over at Cari, who dutifully laughed. As did Herm, though he clearly had no idea what he was laughing about. Evenios returned his gaze to Troi, and the smirk dissolved into something far more sinister. ‘You’ll be here for longer than you planned.’ The threat was unmistakable.

‘Go away,’ urged the woman again. ‘You’re only making things worse.’

Troi simply stood there, watching Evenios, looking into his eyes, reading his stance, his small unconscious movements, knowing his thoughts before they occurred to the youth himself. The long-faced Cari grinned with unpleasant anticipation. Herm patiently waited for some clear direction as to what he should do.

Then Evenios charged, his huge fists balled, throwing two mighty hooks. They certainly had power but were unbelievably crude, long looping punches that could be anticipated hekates before they arrived, and it was all bull-headed offense with no thought of any riposte.

Troi simply swayed back from the right hook, then caught the left fist with his open hand, yanked Evenios towards him and brought his knee up into the man's groin, all in one blur. It was over in a couple of heartbeats. Evenios screamed, clutched his crotch and collapsed to writhe on the ground. Herm gawped at the sight. Cari was already backing off, glancing over his shoulder to ensure his route of retreat.

'Anyone else?' asked Troi evenly. Cari shook his head violently. Herm looked confused. 'Take it away, then,' said Troi, gesturing down at the moaning figure at his feet.

They came forward cautiously, grabbed Evenios under his armpits and hauled him off. Troi glanced around. Those nearby, who had been watching, all hastily averted their gazes. The nearest guard hawked and spat. He couldn't care less. Not so the woman. She was standing, facing Troi, arms akimbo, eyes blazing.

'Who in Hades do you think you are?' she demanded. He was somewhat taken aback. 'It was none of your business. I know them. They wouldn't have done anything beyond crude insults and juvenile threats. But you had to do your pathetic Pterseus riding to save the princess routine. Now I really will be isolated. Thank you so very much.'

'As you may recall, if you actually take the bother, he attacked me.'

'Only because you didn't bugger off when I told you to.'

'Oh, I see,' he responded with distinct bitterness. 'I'm not allowed to get involved in your business, but you're permitted to order me around. Perhaps he was right, Little-Miss-I'm-in-Charge.'

For a brief instant, he really thought she was going to go for him. Then she took a deep breath. 'Just so you know.

It was all for nothing. Beating up on others gets no favours from me.'

'If you think it was for favours, then you flatter yourself.'

She stared at him, then swung round and sat down again. Just then, the guards began to shout at them to start moving once more. He dropped into line a few places behind her. He would need to keep an even closer watch now. Though he was sure that Evenios and his little gang would not come within a hundred paces of him, others might take up the challenge.

The long column crawled across the landscape, leaving behind the empty pastures and heading along a dusty track through an area of scattered trees and hawthorn scrub. Swallows swooped and swirled around them, grabbing the insects they kicked up from the tussocky grass, and some fallow deer started away in sudden panic at the humans' approach.

She looked back a couple of times. Each time he held her eyes but kept his face expressionless. Then she stopped and waited as the column flowed past her until he was alongside. She began walking, but did not look at him.

'I've been thinking,' she said quietly, after a few hekates of strained silence. They both continued to look straight ahead of them. 'I'm sorry I was so ungrateful. You weren't to know that those boys were harmless.'

Troi remembered the huge fists swinging with murderous force, and wondered what her definition of harmless was.

'You did what you thought was right.' She was unable to resist adding, 'Although I asked you to go away.'

Told, thought Troi. Told. He said nothing.

'But I can look after myself, so I would be grateful if you would transfer your attentions to someone else, where you might hope for some recompense.'

She walked faster and pulled away from him. He watched her go. It would not be possible, of course. The Furies could not be ignored.

SIXTY-ONE

IT WAS DROPPING dusk as they arrived at the busy camp near Akrai. The large gates in the crude palisade were wide open, and the villagers were marched straight through, following a merchants' convoy that went similarly unchallenged. So much for him bringing back valuable military information. The place would be crawling with Sinon's men.

Troi glanced at the squat walls of the defiant fortress some distance away, shining in the last rays of the descending sun in a kind of fortuitous symbolism. Within was Diomedes. So near and so far away. Troi wished he could speak to him one final time. He wanted to admit that Diomedes had been right. Troi just did not know how to change himself. The barriers between him and others were too fixed, too impassable, too mysterious.

They were directed into a large open area surrounded by a rough stockade of pointed stakes and lined with bow-armed guards. A rope lay three paces within the perimeter, and Troi knew, even before being told, that it was a kill line. Anyone who crossed it would be shot down. No questions asked.

The place was by no means full, but there were plenty of men and women sitting or lying around. One or two rose and came across, obviously recognising some of the newcomers, but most watched with morose lassitude or simply ignored them. The area was littered with stones and almost barren of grass, with noxious pits in one corner that reeked of human waste. The villagers, physically tired and emotionally drained, almost collapsed where they stood. They had obviously missed what passed for the daily meal, and there was no water.

Most had brought food as instructed, and many carried water flasks, but the young woman had nothing. He guessed she had been too concerned about her grandfather to give it any thought. He walked across to where she was shaking out a sleeping roll. She stood up straight and gave him an unfriendly stare. Troi offered the flask without a word. The woman looked at him, expressionless, then briefly nodded and took it. She drank deeply, closing her eyes to savour it, then, reluctantly, handed it back.

'Thank you.' Her voice was wary.

Troi squatted down and unfastened his roll, taking out the small cloth bundle of food. He could feel her suspicious eyes on him. He unwrapped it and offered her the cheese, dry and hard though it was. Again, the hesitation. She looked him in the eye. 'A piece of cheese does not buy you the right to sleep with me.'

'If you're holding out for the boustria, then just say so.'

The woman glared at him, then said stiffly. 'I'm not in the market.'

'And I'm not buying,' said Troi.

She continued to look at him, clearly trying to determine whether he was telling the truth, then gave up and sighed. 'I'm sorry,' she said. 'Thank you.' She took the cheese.

He began to chew on a piece of the tough, dried beef. It usually took ten hekates of concentrated work to get it into some kind of edible form.

She did not eat. She looked at the cheese but was not seeing it.

'Do you think they might have killed them?' It was scarcely more than a whisper.

He did not know how to answer. Eventually he said, 'I don't know, but they are capable of it.'

Her eyes filled with tears, and she began sobbing uncontrollably.

He reached for her, rather clumsily, thinking it was what he ought to do, but she savagely shook him off. He knew that she was weeping for her grandfather, but his overriding reaction was one of helplessness and even embarrassment.

After a while she quietened down, but the grief still throbbed behind a few sniffles.

No one took any notice. The sound of sobbing seemed to thread the falling night.

Night had finally pushed day over the sharp rim of mountains, and there was only a quarter-moon, but the stars were brilliant in the clear sky. He could scarcely see her face now. Just a pale patch in the gloom.

'Sorry,' she murmured.

'You will have to stop saying that. It limits your conversation terribly.' She said nothing, but finally bit into her cheese, and he recommenced his systematic mastication of the boustria.

After a while, he said, 'I know about your father.'

She stiffened instantly. She did not answer for several hekates. 'He had no choice,' she eventually said with sad resignation. 'He's a master fletcher. But many blame him nevertheless. And, it seems, me.'

'People under stress need someone to blame. They don't care about facts.' He sounded pompous, even to himself, but she nodded. 'Whether you think so or not, I think you need some help in this place.'

He wasn't sure how to phrase what he needed to say. 'You're an attractive girl,' he began awkwardly, 'and I can understand why you think of me as you do.' She began to say something, but he held up a hand and she stopped. 'But I swear by the Furies that I do not offer help with anything like that in mind.'

He had been taught rhetoric, but that was maladroit. It was the second time he had made the Great Oath, and it frightened him. Especially as he had an uneasy feeling that some such idea might nonetheless be lurking in his mind.

She stared into the distance for a while, then clearly made a decision. 'I'm frightened,' she said. 'There have been threats. And people are not reacting rationally after today.'

He wasn't sure how, but he suddenly felt her fear, and he realised that her apparent confidence and poise had all been a sham, a flimsy shield of straw.

'Do you wish me to stay near you? And I don't expect anything, I promise.' He noted his unconscious choice of the word *expect* rather than *want.*

'Would you?' She sounded grateful. 'I'm sorry…' Her voice trailed away in confusion.

He smiled. 'Shall we leave it there before you start being sorry for being sorry? I'm not sure I could handle that degree of complexity. I'm a simple soul. More water?'

'You drink some first,' she said sternly. So he did, then passed it over to her. She only drank a little more and then accepted the proffered dry apple.

'What's your name?' he asked.

'Ariadne, daughter of Mantios.'

'Let's try and get some sleep. We may stand in need of it tomorrow.' He rolled himself up in the thin blankets. 'Sleep well, Ariadne, daughter of Mantios.'

'Sleep well, Troilus, son of Aias.'

But her voice was still guarded. He had by no means laid her daemons to rest.

SIXTY-TWO

THOUGH THE DAY had been warm, and it was early summer, the cloud tumbled away before a chill northerly that had sprung up. The resulting clear, star-hung skies meant that the temperature plummeted. He woke, screaming silently, from the dreadful ride of the night hag. Movement and control gradually seeped back into his paralysed limbs, his breathing calmed and the sweat dried on his brow. It was the middle of the night, and he was stiff and cold. But he was used to that.

Although it was late, the camp was only half asleep, shuffling and twisting in its collective night hag. The murmur of voices, the coughs, and a sudden, sharp complaint as someone trudging to the latrine pits fell over another in the dark. Above all, the incessant background threnody of sobbing.

He glanced across to Ariadne. She was awake, huddled into a tight ball under her thin blankets and shivering. He slid out from his roll and went to crouch beside her.

'Ariadne,' he whispered.

'What do you want?' The tone was part aggression, part fear.

He spread his hands placatingly. 'Not what you're thinking, I promise. Now, listen to me, and think, before you say no. You're cold and not sleeping. I'm pretty cold too. We need to buddy up.'

'Buddy up?'

'A scout's term for sleeping together.' Unfortunate choice of phrase. He hastily explained. 'And I don't mean like that. We'll share the blankets, doubling our insulation, and share body heat. I'll lay down and all you do is tuck in close behind me. You'll be warm, trust me.'

She obviously still didn't, but she considered. He could almost hear her teeth chattering. 'All right,' she said reluctantly, 'but anything untoward, and I shall shout out.'

'Just you try anything, and I'll scream,' he retorted severely. He was surprised by a slight laugh. It felt strangely rewarding. He went back and smoothed out his sleeping roll. 'Come over here.'

She rose, hugging herself and visibly shivering.

'Now lay down there. If you wriggle around a bit, you should find a nice hollow for your hip and one for your shoulder.'

She did so until she was comfortable. He brought over her blankets and small bundle of clothing and slid the bundle under her head as a makeshift pillow, then lay the blankets over her, tucking them tightly in behind her.

'Have you a hat?'

She didn't, so he took his felt cap with the long ear lappets and fastened it snugly round her head. He cleared the ground of stones, stamped a couple of hollows for himself, and carefully lay down before her. He backed up until they were tightly together and drew the blankets round himself. He could feel the press of her breasts against his back and her legs tucked cosily within the bend of his. Already the body warmth was making a difference.

'Can I put my arm over you?' she whispered. 'It would be more comfortable.' He could feel the warmth of her breath on the nape of his neck and was aware of a musky smell.

'Of course.' Her arm crept over him and held him quite tightly. 'Now try and get some sleep.'

'I feel much warmer already.'

Within hekates, her breathing became slower and more regular, and she was asleep. He lay awake, trying to analyse the strange feelings that she evoked. But they made no sense. None at all.

SIXTY-THREE

TROI WOKE AS the stealthy light of dawn gradually suffused the sky. He felt comfortably warm, and her arm hooked over him felt somehow right. She was still asleep. People were already moving, so Troi guessed that the prisoners would be given breakfast, such as it might be, at an early hour. He slipped carefully out from under the blankets. Ariadne mumbled something in her slumber but did not wake.

He stood for a few moments, studying her face smoothed by sleep. He was still puzzled. It was not that he felt no sexual attraction to her. He certainly did. But he was not exactly deprived in that area and felt little for his partners beyond the physical. They passed from his mind as easily as they left his bed.

But Ariadne evoked a feeling of protectiveness, a kind of tenderness, even a disturbing sense of unease. He had misgivings about being vulnerable, of no longer being the master of his own destiny. He was not even sure whether he welcomed or feared this. He shook his head wearily. Whatever these strange feelings, he and Ariadne were now bound together. For better or worse. The Furies were not to be mocked.

He turned and walked over to where people were gathering. A pile of rough wooden bowls and spoons had been dumped just within the kill line. He took a bowl. An elderly man was standing nearby, waiting patiently.

'Water?' asked Troi.

'They'll bring amphorae soon.' He volunteered nothing more, keeping his eyes on a small gate in the stockade. Troi waited. After a few hekates, the gate opened and several men staggered through. They were laden with large ceramic storage jars, which they laid alongside the pile of bowls. People converged upon it, and Troi joined the queue until he was able to fill both the bowl and his water flask. He took them back to Ariadne, who was still asleep, left them beside her, and headed back.

There was quite a crowd by the time he arrived. The same men came through the gate, this time laden with large cauldrons carried on yokes. Several guards accompanied them. They sorted the crowd into some sort of line with the casual assistance of sturdy cudgels, and the men at the cauldrons began to ladle a thin gruel into the proffered wooden bowls.

Troi grabbed another bowl and joined the line. When he had received the meagre and tepid slops, he headed back.

Ariadne was awake, sitting up, still huddled within the cocoon of the blankets. Her hair was a mess, there were dark shadows beneath her eyes, and her face was pasty, but she smiled as he approached, and it gave him the strangest sensation. He smiled back and gave her the gruel. She took it eagerly and began to eat voraciously. Then stopped and looked up at him guiltily. 'Where's yours?'

He glanced across to the feeding area where the line of waiting people had diminished considerably. 'I'll go and get it now. I rather thought they might object to someone appearing with two bowls.'

'I'm sorry,' she said.

He chuckled. 'So, we mean to carry on where we left off last night.'

She gave him a wan smile. Her eyes crinkled when she smiled. 'It's just that we haven't had much to eat for some time. I suppose my stomach demanded precedence.'

He was soon back. 'I managed to get an extra ladle,' he said, 'because I was one of the last. Give me your bowl.' She looked at him for a moment. She clearly did not believe him, but hunger won out. She handed him the bowl, and he scooped most of his paltry ration into it and gave it back to her. Then spent some time pretending to eat what wasn't there. He had acted without any real forethought, and such generosity would seem to demand an explanation. The Great Oath was a perfectly suitable pretext, but it had simply felt the right thing to do and needed no further justification.

'What will they make us do?'

'My guess would be labouring for the men and cooking and washing for the women.'

'So, we'll be separated,' she said.

He thought he detected a note of unease and felt pleased with her reaction. 'Probably, but we'll presumably all return here tonight.' He had been watching the others and noticed that many were rolling up their blankets and just leaving them on the ground. The sun was now well risen. The ground steamed, growing little tendrils of fog, and the low sun threw gigantic, misshapen shadows across the barren compound.

She drank a little water and then, reluctantly, divested herself of her festoon of blankets.

He rinsed out the bowls with the minimum amount of water, left half a bowl of water and their small cache of remaining food under the neatly rolled blankets, and hung the flask across his shoulder.

'If we're separated,' he told her, 'you take it with you.' She nodded. There was nothing else to do except wait, so they sat in the increasingly warm sun.

She glanced at him. 'So, if you're not after my body, why are you doing this?'

'Your aunt asked me to.' Well, it wasn't exactly *asked*, he thought, but it sounded better than *demanded.*

'Aunt Euadne?' He nodded. She considered this new information for some time. 'So, you know that Nicias was my kinsman?' He nodded again. 'I liked Nicias. We were friends.'

'Everyone liked Nicias.'

She spoke carefully. 'But the rumour was that he lost his life unnecessarily, just to capture some Troian gold. That he was ordered to do it.'

How in Hades had she known that? He must have betrayed himself unconsciously, because her eyes suddenly widened and became javelins that pierced him to his very soul.

'You gave that order.'

He lowered his head, took a long breath and then simply said, 'Yes.'

'You deliberately and knowingly sent him to his death.' The surprise had transmuted to anger now. Raw and jagged.

'Yes,' he said again, reluctantly raising his eyes to meet the blaze of accusation. He did not even attempt to qualify it by saying *the likelihood of his death*. He instinctively knew that would make things even worse. He expected her to get up and stalk away, or even hit him, but she remained sitting there, staring at him, breathing rapidly, as taut as a strung bow. Pale red spots had appeared high on her pallid cheeks. Her fists were clenched, the knuckles white.

'Why?' she demanded through gritted teeth. It was amazing how much venom could be squeezed into such a small word.

He thought for some time. 'I doubt I can answer you. Your question is about your love for a kinsman; my answer would be about military necessity. We would be casting our javelins at different targets. All I can say is, it was not a decision I made easily, but it's one I would make again. Because it was the right one. To me. It was important. It'll never be that to you. I understand.'

'It seems simple to me, and there an end.'

'Look at that tree.' An old, withered, dead tree, black and twisted, little more than a stump, stood some distance away in the compound. 'Do you see it exactly as I see it? Wouldn't it look different from the other side, or to a bird flying over it, or a mole looking up from its roots? We see things differently from our individual places. It doesn't make our perceptions wrong, just different.'

'To die for gold?' she whispered. 'How can that be right, however you look at it?'

'What if the gold would save a hundred lives? Or a thousand? Gold is the lifeblood of the rebellion. That gold may well prove to be the difference between victory and defeat.' He sighed. 'Soldiers die. Most die in meaningless skirmishes or on a field far away from where the battle is decided. They die from disease or accident, accomplishing nothing. They die in defeats, or in victories that merely stave off ultimate defeat. A few die achieving something important. Something that makes a real difference. That won't convince you or your aunt, I know that, but always remember that it convinced Nicias.'

'That sounds very fine, but in that case, why wasn't it you that died to make a difference?'

He had been expecting it, but it still came like a sword in the ribs.

'Because I was the only one with the authority to get things done. Without that, then the death, of whoever, would indeed have been meaningless. And never think that it's easier to order someone else to his death than go yourself.' He spread his hands out. 'It was the right decision. I have no doubts, which doesn't mean that I have no regrets. It was a decision I didn't want to have to take. But I had to.'

'I still don't understand how you can order any man to his death.'

'It's the nature of command. Every officer orders men to their deaths.'

‘Then let’s do away with officers. Do away with soldiers. With war.’

Despite her vehemence, he almost laughed at her naïvety. ‘War is part of the human condition.’

‘It isn’t part of my condition.’

‘Then, why are you here?’

‘Because you, and people like you, brought war to us.’

‘Like Nicias.’

She glared at him. ‘He allowed himself to be convinced.’

He closed his eyes and curbed the growing anger. ‘Five thousand died at Koi. Men. Women. Children. You would accept that? Babies smashed against a wall. Men burned alive. Women raped and eviscerated. You would accept that?’

She was white and trembling, but looked down. ‘No,’ she said quietly. ‘I wouldn’t.’

‘You can’t stay out of it. It is the world we inhabit.’

‘We can try,’ she said. He could hear the uncertainty in her voice. Her heart and her head were at war themselves. He refrained from using this as a rhetorical example, simply pleased to see the rage had burned itself out.

He picked up a pebble and idly turned it over in his hand. ‘Perhaps, but I don’t know if there is a way. I suspect not. And I certainly don’t know it, even if there is one.’ He tossed the pebble to one side and stood up. ‘It’s all too complex for me. All I can do, all anyone can do, is to act for what they think is the best.’ He stared into the distance. ‘And people die. They always have done.’ Something caught in his throat, and he knew he was no longer talking of Nicias.

Perhaps she did, too. Her taut face softened slightly. ‘Maybe I’ve been unfair. I was angry and upset, but I understand what you’re saying.’ She rested her hand on his arm, long, elegant fingers pale against his sunburned skin. 'Even though I don't agree with it. There must be a better way. But Nicias chose to fight. It was his decision. I can't really blame just you. You're but one thorn in a bramble bush. If it hadn't been you, it would have been someone else. The world is peopled by idiots.'

'Thank you,' he said with a grimace. 'That's a real help.' He tried to regain his equilibrium. He felt shaken and uncertain.

A salpinx sounded a two-note call, and people immediately began to move, albeit listlessly, to the compound gate, where they gathered. Ariadne and Troi joined them. She gave him a brief smile, and, though it was a weak thing, he was glad of it. After a few hekates, the gate opened and they flooded out, hemmed between two lines of spearmen and stopped by another line at the end. The 'box' was closed by a fourth squad coming up behind, and then the prisoners were marched off, the spearmen cursing, shouting and threatening.

There was no attempt to separate men from women, and they were going directly towards the Akroakrai. Troi felt more than uneasy. Thoughts of human shields or deliberate terror tactics involving the slaughter of unarmed civilians savaged his mind.

They crossed the shallow waters of a small river by a narrow stone bridge, the same river that ran unconcernedly past the blackened ruins of Tegea some distance upstream. He was aware that Ariadne was looking in that direction, and he could feel the wash of grief that surged through her.

He couldn't understand how another's emotions could affect him, nor why he instinctively took her hand. She instantly yanked it from his grasp and glared at him. He raised his hands in apology.

She sighed. 'It looks as though we're not going to be separated after all. You may be an irritating bugger, but I suppose it's not so bad that you're here. At least it's someone.'

'Sometimes, you let your enthusiasm run away with you.'

'That was letting my enthusiasm run away,' she said. 'You should hear what I really think.'

'Perhaps best not.'

'So young, yet so wise.' Then she glanced across and smiled, and it was the sun bursting through the shredding mist on the Ditykoians. 'No, I'm glad that I'm not on my own, and that you're here.' She chanted the child's rhyme. 'If I lie, when it be done, then may the woodwose eat my tongue.'

'Then I'm glad too.' But he was lying, woodwose or not. He wished her anywhere but here. As far away from him as possible. As did she when they arrived.

SIXTY-FOUR

IT DID NOT live up to Troi's worst fears, but was bad enough. As they approached the dour walls, they were assailed by a sickening stench with which Troi was all too familiar. Ariadne was not. She covered her mouth and gagged. Their relentless guards forced them on, nearer and nearer to the rough-hewn walls. There was movement amongst the high parapets. But none from the heaps of putrid corpses that lay piled high round the base of the walls amidst a jumble of broken ladders and discarded equipment, and a forest of arrow shafts. Many of the bodies were badly burned, and the gates were blackened and charred, revealing solid masonry behind.

The smell clawed at their nostrils, clogged their throats and turned their stomachs. Buzzing clouds of flies rose around them. Strutting crows cawed in annoyance, and stray dogs slunk away from their grisly feast. Ariadne bent over and was violently sick. He held her as she retched, unable to stop even after there was nothing left in her stomach to bring up. She was not the only one. Even Troi was feeling nauseous.

But there was elation in him, too. The Imperial Army had obviously received a terrible battering. Then another thought struck him. The Trogs might not care for there to be eyewitnesses to their failure, and the elation evaporated.

He looked at the white-faced young woman as she held her stomach and heaved helplessly. The guards were gesturing and shouting. It was obvious what the prisoners' job was to be. Behind them, great funeral pyres had been constructed. Their task was to drag or carry the decomposing bodies to their cremation.

The stomach-heaving miasma hung sickeningly on every breath. Everywhere horror assaulted their sight: staring eyes, mangled and rotting bodies, faces bloodless and slack or stamped with indelible masks of terror or agony. They slipped and slid on ground thick with the nauseating pale slime of intestines, spilled brains and black, coagulated, fly-ridden blood. The bloated bluebottles settled on their faces and drove them frantic, and fat rats scuttled out from beneath dislodged bodies to make Ariadne scream. He knew this would be the second worst day of his life.

Troi tried to protect her as much as possible. Choosing the least glutinous corpses, avoiding those with maggots spilling from their insides, with eyes pecked out or limbs gnawed by scavengers, doing as much of the work by himself as he could, and insisting that her assistance be minimal and token whenever the inattention of the guards made it possible. Much of the time, though, it was not.

For Ariadne, the day was an endless night hag, a never-ending jumble of obscene images that seared the mind until it could take no more and simply shut them out. A day of weariness and aching limbs, the acid gag of vomit in the mouth and the pervasive stink of corruption, of dreadful thirst and the inescapable hammer of the sun.

She staggered through it, repeatedly retching, working almost mechanically, her eyes distant and unfocussed. She became incommunicative, positively snappish when she did respond, but generally simply ignoring him. He tried to make her drink water, but she brought it back up almost immediately. He fashioned a rough hat by tearing off the hood of a discarded cloak to protect her from the sun and endeavoured to work within what little shade there was from the impassive walls.

Troi kept a careful eye on the guards and made her rest whenever he saw an opportunity. People around them began dropping with exhaustion and the heat. He watched what happened closely. The soldiers made others drag the fallen into the shade of a small copse of trees. Every so often, two or three guards went in and got some moving again with prods and kicks. But they were not the sadistic and murderous bastards of yesterday. Such brutality as there was seemed half-hearted. Troi weighed up the situation and made a decision.

'Look, Ariadne. I want you to collapse. Just fall and stay still. I'll carry you into the trees. Lie there with your eyes closed and don't move. If somebody does start shouting at you, then get up and come back to me, but do it slowly and groggily. I'll try and stay close. Can you do that?'

She gazed at him, almost uncomprehendingly, her red-rimmed eyes standing out in the strained pallor of her face, and then slowly nodded.

'Good girl. Go for it.'

She glared at him, but said nothing, then simply folded up in an inelegant heap. How much was acting and how much was for real, he had no idea. He picked her up and put her over his shoulder, surprised at how little she weighed, and carried her to the trees.

A guard was standing nearby, leaning on a spear. 'Another one?' His tone was not unfriendly.

'Just went down like a stack of shields.'

'Put her in the shade, she'll soon feel better. There's water in there.'

Troi carried her in and carefully chose a spot beneath the thick leaves of a rhododendron, which effectively kept her hidden. It was dim and cool, and even the smell seemed to be less offensive. He laid her down on the bare earth, and she looked up at him.

The relief in her eyes was obvious. Her trailing hand kept hold of his for a moment. 'Thank you. I'm always saying that, aren't I?' She smiled weakly.

He filled the flask and put it beside her hand. 'If anyone comes, keep your eyes shut and don't move. Whenever possible, keep sipping the water. If a guard rousts you, then do exactly what he tells you. Otherwise wait for me.'

'I will,' she whispered. He brushed her hair from her brow, where it had stuck with sweat, then turned abruptly and left.

The bodies were now noticeably fewer, and, incredibly, the end of the horrendous task was finally in sight. Two more dekates, and the last bodies were being dragged away and dumped on the funeral pyres. Troi looked around him. There were none left. He glanced up at the lowering wall. A man was looking down at him. He was wearing an open Boeotian helmet, but his face was in dark shadow. Troi thought it might be Diomedes. The man lifted a hand, and Troi reciprocated before turning and wearily following the others away.

He smiled furtively. Diomedes would undoubtedly be wondering what in Hades his protégé was playing at. Which was apt, as Troi wasn't entirely sure himself. He should be out of here, but had been neatly snared by Euadne's demand. Strangely enough, he was not grinding the bit like a skittish horse, and it was not from dread of the Furies.

He found Ariadne standing by the small wood as the guards cleared everyone out, dragging out two bodies and leaving them at the side of the track. She was looking about her, and her face lit up with a smile when she spotted Troi's approach. Something seemed to lift within him. He beckoned her across to where he stood in a small knot of tired and grim-faced people who waited for the others to gather.

'How are you feeling?'

'Much better, thank you.' Ariadne smiled again. He liked her smile. There was a large bundle at his feet. Glancing around, Troi quickly gave her two leather carrying bags to wear, pulling them round into the small of her back so they were not obvious, then gave her a cloak that would cover them.

'It's hot,' she protested.

'It'll be worth it,' he assured her. He swung a couple of even larger pouches over his shoulder and fastened two cloaks round his neck.

'What's in them?' she whispered.

'Anything I could find that would be useful.'

'Surely they'll search us and confiscate it all?'

Troi shrugged. 'If they do, they do. But I've been watching this lot, and they're sloppy, lazy and obviously consider civilians beneath their notice. I've no doubt quite a few of the more enterprising of the workforce have already absconded. I saw one slipping away myself.'

The young woman regarded him shrewdly. 'So, you could have "slipped away" yourself, without too much trouble.'

'Maybe. But a good opportunity didn't present itself.'

Ariadne gave him a speculative look. He knew what she was thinking, but she said nothing.

The guards were beginning to bawl out orders and marshal the lethargic crowd into some semblance of a column.

Troi picked up two long, thick spear shafts, the heads and butts neatly broken off. 'Walking staffs,' he explained. 'Could prove useful. Now, try and stay as inconspicuous as possible, right in the middle of everyone.'

Ariadne nodded. She looked tired and worn, her brooding eyes dark patches in a pale face beaded with sweat.

'I still feel sick,' she muttered.

On an impulse he reached down, squeezed her hand and gave her an encouraging smile. She smiled wanly in return, though she pulled her hand away.

The officer shouted something, and the shambles of a column began to shuffle forward. A wind had gradually built up, and its cooling presence was welcome.

From his tunic, Troi surreptitiously slipped the knife he had found and put it up his sleeve, trapping it against his body. Any sign of a search and he would simply let it fall and walk away. The column moved slowly, despite the urgings of the guards.

Ariadne said nothing for a while, merely plodding along, seemingly lost in a place of her own. Then she spoke. 'That was awful.' She shuddered. 'I can't go through that again. I can't.'

'You won't have to,' he said. 'It's finished.'

'Unless they attack again,' she sensibly pointed out.

'They won't.' His confidence was not disingenuous. The Trogs had taken a Hades of a beating. Even a butcher like Marsyas could not afford to spend men like that.

Ariadne made a noise of disgust. 'The smell. The feel.' She shuddered again.

'Forget it,' he said. 'It's finished.'

'Words!' She was suddenly angry. Her voice rose and her cheeks burned. 'I can't forget it, and it will never be finished. It may be nothing to you, just some meaningless inconvenience to wipe from your memory like scraping a wax tablet, but it's something I'll carry with me for the rest of my days. The memory of all those poor dead men. That smell will stay with me. I know it.'

Troi was taken aback, especially as he seemed to be the focus of her ire. They walked on in uncomfortable silence.

After a while, Ariadne said quietly, 'I'm sorry. You didn't deserve that. After all that you've done for me.'

'You're just upset.'

'Of course I'm bloody upset,' she snapped. 'You have a remarkable facility for saying the wrong thing at the wrong time.'

'I'm a man.'

Ariadne had the grace to smile. 'That would explain it.'

As they passed a hedge, a sparrowhawk hit a young starling in a spray of feathers and tumbled it into a dry ditch. Troi looked across as they passed. The bird glared at them with fierce yellow eyes, then bent to continue plucking its still-living prey. The world was a cruel place.

SIXTY-FIVE

As he had expected, the guards simply ushered the work gang back into the compound without any attempt to check them. Nevertheless, he breathed a heartfelt sigh of relief. The compound was large, and most people had gravitated to the slightly flatter, grassier and less stone-pocked eastern side, where they clustered together, finding some comfort in a community of misery. So, Ariadne and Troi's accidental choice of the sparsely populated western side had been fortunate. Despite the multitude of half-buried rocks scattered all around, it was quiet and isolated, which is how Troi liked it. Their belongings, such as they were, had not been disturbed, and Ariadne sat down on a rounded boulder with a sigh.

'Keep a careful watch,' he muttered urgently. 'If anyone approaches or seems to be watching, sound the salpinx.'

He concluded that his tone of voice had been a little authoritative, as she looked at him resentfully, but then nodded. He hastily pulled up a large flat stone, excavated a slight hollow, laid the dagger in it, and replaced the stone. Working as quickly as he could, he did the same with the more questionable of the other items he had collected, carefully memorising each rock and stone and what lay beneath it. Like a jay burying acorns, he thought. He blew out a long breath when he had finished.

Troi glanced over to the west. The wind was freshening, and he could see a low, thick band of dark cloud headed their way.

'It's going to get unpleasant,' he said, trying to be a little more emollient. 'Can you go and fill the flask and get a couple of bowls of water? I'm sorry, but I've a lot to do.'

Troi pointed out where the water was. She pulled a face, but rose readily enough and set off. The sun was already low in the sky, half-obscured by the threatening cloud. He took the two largest blankets he had found and the rather good sewing and repair kit he had chosen, of the sort soldiers commonly carried. He quickly and neatly overlapped the blankets and stitched them together.

Ariadne returned with the water. 'Can I use some of it to wash myself?'

He nodded, absorbed in his task. She took one of the bowls and scrubbed her hands viciously, then rinsed her face over and over again.

'Ugh. I shall never be clean again.' She looked across at him as he hammered the two spear shafts into the earth with a round cobble. 'And don't start that practical "oh, yes you will" rubbish.'

'I wouldn't dream of it,' he said, retrieving the handful of arrowheads from their hiding place.

Ariadne suddenly chuckled. 'Poor Troi. I bet you thought the knucklebones had fallen nicely when Aunt Euadne asked you to look after a pretty enough girl. And you've just ended up with the grumpy bitch from the Styx. You must find it a sore disappointment.'

He considered for a moment. 'Any comment, no matter how phrased, will be open to unfavourable interpretation. I respectfully decline to answer.' He attached the blanket to one of the shafts by hammering an arrowhead through it.

'You do realise that a refusal to comment is a comment in itself.'

'It's a dangerous world.'

She was silent. He glanced up from working on the second shaft, and she was crying.

'Sorry.'

'No, it's not you.' She rubbed her eyes savagely. 'Surprisingly enough. Sometimes a girl just needs to cry.'

He wasn't sure what to do, so he went on with his work, pegging out the sides of the blanket with arrowheads to complete the makeshift tent. She regarded it critically.

'It sags,' she complained.

He gave her an exasperated look. 'I'll make some guys. I'm sorry, but I forgot to bring my magic tent-making wand with me.'

'Typical,' she snorted. 'Forget the one thing that might have been of use.'

The sun had disappeared behind the grey bank of cloud, whose lower edge was beginning to smear and smudge. There was a distant rumble of thunder. Troi regarded his creation critically.

'You do realise that this may keep the worst of it off, but it won't be waterproof. Don't expect a comfortable night.'

Ariadne looked around ostentatiously at the barren and rock-strewn ground. 'Bugger,' she said. 'That's an unexpected blow.'

Troi grinned. He liked her sense of humour.

A salpinx sounded once, and he saw people gathering by the entrance. 'Come on. Dinner.'

Ariadne shook her head. 'I'm not hungry. I couldn't eat.'

'You have to eat. We get little enough. Now come along.' He tried to put authority into his voice. He should have learned his lesson earlier. It was a mistake.

'Don't you order me about,' she flared. 'You're not my keeper.'

He was dumbfounded. 'Euadne asked me to look after you—'

'Aunt Euadne may have, but I haven't,' she interrupted, her voice rising dangerously, 'and I'm the one to make any decisions that concern myself. Not you.'

'I have a responsibility.'

Ariadne snorted.

'Just be sensible,' Troi appealed. He knew it was another mistake the instant the words tumbled from his mouth.

'Sensible!' she said, staring angrily at him. 'Sensible! I see. I'm just a silly woman who thinks with her emotions. Which is why I need a sensible man to look after me.'

'I didn't say that.'

'You didn't need to. I certainly don't need to be told what to think by a so-called sensible man who is in the middle of fighting such an eminently sensible war.'

Troi began to feel anger rise within him. Her response was just illogical. 'So, you're better off without me? Shall I go?' He knew he sounded petulant.

'What a brilliant idea. Why don't you bugger off?'

Troi had another brilliant idea. Diomedes always said to do the unexpected. Make the enemy have to adjust mentally and physically. Redefine the battlefield. Troi turned, marched off about fifty paces and sat down on a rock, his back towards her. He grinned to himself. It was a good move. He had abandoned shelter, blankets, food in the face of the oncoming storm. She would be obliged to come and apologise and beg him to return. Which would be most satisfactory.

Then he began to think it through. Somewhat belatedly. Ariadne could just take her own blankets and go off into the rapidly approaching squall in a cuirass of self-righteous indignation. Or angrily come and dump some blankets next to him before stalking off back to shelter. Or even just wrap herself up in all the blankets within the tent and totally ignore him.

Dyaus's balls. Never cross swords with a woman. Aias had warned him. Her sword was in her tongue and would outreach his. Aias would follow up this sterling advice by claiming that when a woman has only two options, she will invariably choose the third. Or that a woman could twist the tail of a cow until it drank the milk. The old man seemed to have lived his life in accord with innumerable aphorisms. A saying for everything. And none of those concerning women boded well for Troi.

His mind shifted. It was the first time that he had thought of Aias for a very long time. A man whose memory outlasts the funeral meat is fortunate indeed. That, too, had been one of Aias's adages. Troi felt guilty. But he did not have the chance to fully ponder such unexpected feelings. So absorbed was he with these strange thoughts, he did not hear her approach.

'I'm sorry,' she said. 'I will eat.'

Troi was so taken aback by this unexpected capitulation that his rebellious words refused to form ranks. Women are most dangerous when they are apologising, Aias had always said.

SIXTY-SIX

THE WEATHER FRONT was worryingly close when they returned with their miserable bowls of soup and pieces of hard, dry bread. Beneath the approaching coil of cloud, the sun glowed for a few hekates like a hot coal, then fell from the sky, leaving them in chill gloom. Dyaus's anger rumbled almost continuously, and the sky was lit with the monochromatic flash of his thunderbolts. Troi took some of the filmy scarves he had collected and hastily tore them into strips, then knotted them together to make guys, gulping down mouthfuls of tepid soup as he did so.

'It still sags,' she said with a degree of satisfaction.

The storm was almost upon them. He bundled her into the apology for a tent, allowed her to ferret out the hip and shoulder holes, then tucked the layers of blankets and cloaks across her. He wriggled back against her and pulled the blankets over himself as well. Her arm slid over him, to his immense satisfaction. The rain began to patter down, then became a downpour.

'Try not to touch the blanket,' he said.

'How could I possibly do that? You have me cocooned like a caterpillar.'

'Do you always have to have the last word?'

'A discussion should always end on a reasonable note,' she declared stoutly.

The last word belongs to a woman. As does the first. And those in between. He could hear Aias intoning his maxim with lugubrious satisfaction. He could see him sitting on a low three-legged stool by the flicker of the small fire, carefully fletching an arrow, his wrinkled, weather-worn face a picture of concentration. Troi suddenly realised how much he missed him, and it caught in his throat.

The rain was falling in sheets now, seemingly frozen into immobility by the frequent flashes of godfire, the ground rapidly becoming a sea of mud and expanding puddles, their surfaces exploding into spume under the relentless bombardment. The first drops of water began to fall from the sodden blankets above their heads. The anger of Dyaus suddenly burst directly above them with a deafening roll, and the sky flashed an incandescent pure white that seared his vision. She was clinging onto him tightly. He rather liked that. A buffet of wind threw a fine spray of water through the tent.

'It's as wet in here as out there,' she grumbled.

'Would you prefer to be outside?' he muttered.

'Then who would be here to hold you when Dyaus bellows?' she asked sweetly.

Troi was obliged to smile. 'Bloody cheek.'

'I merely ask exactly who has got their arms round whom.' The sky lit up, and the crash followed several heartbeats later. The storm was passing. An annoying drip was landing on his head, and he tugged up a corner of a blanket to intercept it.

'And it's no good hiding,' Ariadne said gleefully, obviously pleased with her little victory. The rain was beginning to ease, and the anger burst ever more distantly. She seemed in a strangely happy mood, at odds with the horrors of the day.

He put his hand out and felt the top cloak. It was barely damp. 'We were lucky that it passed over so quickly.'

'Most people here weren't so lucky. They must be soaked and frozen.' It sounded like a criticism to him. She whispered in his ear. 'I'm sorry. I wasn't blaming you when I said that. I felt you tense. You're too sensitive, you know.'

Now that was a new one. No-one had ever complained of him being sensitive before. He squeezed her hand to reassure her, and she did not draw it away. The rain dribbled to a finish, and the moon came out to wash the desolate scene in its pallid light.

He couldn't get a firm grasp of her. She was so changeable. Like water that trickled through his fingers, refusing to take on a clear shape and identity, at one moment the gentle balm of a warm sea, placid and shimmering with light, at the next a turmoil of surging waves, tossing him in every direction.

She wasn't like him, trapped within constraints, not knowing how to change. It was her natural state of being. She was the water to his ice. She would flow to comfortably fill a space. He knew she had steel, but it was on the inside, not the carapace of bronze that encased him and held him rigid. Whatever it was he lacked, she had.

He lay there, listening to the receding sound of the storm and a steady drip from somewhere along the tent, and tried to make sense of his feelings for her. It wasn't simple sexual attraction. That he also felt this could not be denied. He was all too aware of the pressure of her breasts against his back, the animal warmth of her groin, her musky smell. But there was more. Her arm across him gave him a curious satisfaction and intimacy that seemed to have nothing to do with sex. There was a well of protective feelings, a measure of care and concern that he could not recall feeling before for anyone, and a puzzling feeling of... happiness, just to be with her.

She chuckled. 'I've just thought. Here we are, lying snuggled up together like an old married couple, and I don't know the first thing about you.'

'You know my name is Troilus, and that would seem to be the first thing about me,' he pointed out.

'I know that you say that your name is Troilus,' she immediately replied, and that ran him onto the rocks. He had almost forgotten that it was not his given name. 'Tell me about yourself.'

He stopped himself from groaning. For a moment he was back in Kalliope's andron. Were all women obsessed with dissecting you? So, he told her. The short, safe, expurgated version. The son of a simple hunter who had died a few moontides ago. He did not want to talk about Bogazkoi, so he simply described his home as a small town in the northwest of the Vale and said that he had been picked up by a patrol to be illegally sold to a slave trader. He sketched in his time as a slave and his career in the army. He made no mention of the driving need for revenge that still gnawed at his very being. She listened quietly. When he had finished, he waited for the interrogation.

She caught him totally by surprise. 'So, what was this Kalliope like?'

He floundered for a heartbeat. 'Nice,' he eventually said, somewhat weakly. 'She was kind.'

'Nice and kind,' she repeated sarcastically. 'She must have made a real impression. You can't stop going on about her.'

He made an effort. 'In her twenties. Average height. Slightly chubby. Round face. Brown hair. Nice smile,' and then a happy thought, 'and extremely well endowed.' Ariadne had nice enough breasts, but they could scarcely be described as large. And that elicited the first totally inaudible humph he had ever heard. Or not heard. Fascinating. He grinned to himself.

'Trust a man to become fixated on two lumps of body fat,' she grumbled. His grin grew even broader. 'But what was she like as a person, for Herakla's sake?'

'Nice,' he said again, clear evidence of his rhetoric tutor's total lack of success. 'Kind.'

'I think you've already said that.'

'She collected waifs and strays,' he continued. 'Everyone she took in was ill, or disabled or damaged in some way.'

'And which were you?' It was like sparring with Diomedes. The blow always came with bewildering speed, from an unexpected direction and with the pitiless accuracy of a Cretan archer.

'Just an unfortunate slave, I suppose.' This time the humph was audible, but strangely less powerful for being so. Women seemed to inhabit a world of illusion and paradox.

'And she gave you a scroll of manumission?' The question was gently phrased, but he had no doubts that she was moving in for the kill.

'Yes.'

'Why?'

'I suppose that she just liked helping people.'

'You seem to be doing a deal of supposing. How did you get back to Mykerenos?'

It *was* like sparring with Diomedes. 'By ship,' he answered reluctantly. 'From Leuctra.'

'Ships can't just drop in on a rebel-held coast. That would take some arranging.'

Troi said nothing. There was nothing he could say. She was manoeuvring for the coup de grace, and he had no defence. Perhaps if he shouted 'Fire!' that might work.

'Did she arrange it?'

'Yes.'

'Why? Was she so eager to get rid of you?'

'Well, I do seem to have that effect on women.' But it wasn't going to be that easy, and he knew it.

'You do indeed,' Ariadne said comfortably. 'But not in this case, I think.' There was a pregnant pause. 'Did you have…' She searched for the appropriate delicate construction. '…a relationship?'

'I was not her bedslave, if that's what you think.'

'No.' Her voice sounded surprisingly sad. 'I think the poor lady was in love with you.'

Troi was confused. He was embarrassed and uncomfortable with the questioning, but the gates had not shut as before. He still felt vulnerable, a hermit crab without a shell. The hurt could return.

'How can I know?' he said desperately.

'Because she told you so,' was the reasonable answer. His silence was confirmation enough. 'But you did not love her.'

'I really think that we should try and get some sleep.'

'Which, roughly translated, means shut up and leave me alone.'

'I thought it meant that we should try and get some sleep.'

'Men never know what they mean. That's why they need women to translate for them.'

That was one Aias had never used. He would have liked it.

SIXTY-SEVEN

THE KNIFE CREPT closer and closer to his heart. The maggots cascaded about him. Then he was awake, still bound by the unbreakable cords of his night hag, the scream clogging his throat, sweat cold on his brow.

Ariadne was shaking him urgently. 'Wake up, for Dyaus's sake.' She sounded almost hysterical.

Troi twisted onto his back, breathing heavily. The horror slowly seeped away. She was looking down at him, her face pale, its colour washed out by a combination of wan moonlight and fear.

'Thank Herakla. Are you all right?'

He nodded. 'Sorry. Bad dream.'

Ariadne collapsed alongside him with relief. 'You

went absolutely rigid, like a log of wood, and you were making the strangest noises.'

'It's called snoring,' he said, regaining his equilibrium.

'Don't joke about it,' she snapped. 'It frightened me near to death.'

'It damn nearly did for me, too.'

'Are you sure that you're all right?'

'It was just a dream.' He refound his hip hollow, and she tucked in tightly behind him, putting her arm across him as usual.

'Ugh, you're all damp and sweaty.'

'Sorry.'

'I suppose I should just be grateful that you weren't dreaming about what most men dream about.'

'Oh, you mean food.'

'I most certainly do not mean food. Now go to sleep. And no more of those dreams.'

'I'll do my best.' But nothing would stop the dreams.

Nothing.

SIXTY-EIGHT

TROI WOKE THE next morning as the grey light of dawn stole across a compound slick with mud and standing water. She was still fast asleep, breathing evenly. He slid carefully out of her embrace and looked down on her face, relaxed in repose. She looked beautiful, and he felt the now-familiar surge of tenderness for her.

Then he looked out at the dark fringe of woodland across the weed-choked and deserted farmland. In those woods, scouts would be watching. He had undoubtedly been seen and identified. He ought already to have escaped this place. He was betraying his comrades. He could get out. No trouble. What he could not do was take Ariadne with him. That would be risking not only his own life but hers.

He had made the Great Oath, but deep within he knew that was not what held him, what bound him to the rock like Prometheus, what could drive even Marsyas from his thoughts. Troi could feel the world shift beneath his feet, long moribund emotions stir and wake. How it would end, he had no idea. But for now the knucklebones had been thrown, and he must abide their fall.

He sighed and splashed his mud-spattered way across to the distribution area, where others were already gathering. He stopped, amazed. All along the rough palisade, within what had been the kill line, which had disappeared, large blankets and even tent leathers had been fastened to the posts and pegged out to provide crude shelters. People were emerging from them, looking relatively dry. He had expected everyone to be soaked, frozen and miserable.

The men arrived with the food. The guards wore saffron-coloured tunics instead of the dark green of yesterday, and with them was an officer he had never seen before, tall and well muscled, with a genial countenance and the typical black hair and blue eyes of a purebred Trog. The officer stood to one side as the waiting crowd was ushered into a line, saying nothing, but missing nothing. The guards were firm, but distinctly lacked the casual brutality Troi had come to expect. And there was none of the sloppiness either. It seemed they had a new guard unit with a decent officer.

He collected the thin porridge and returned to the tent. It was a fine day after the storm, the air washed so crystal clear that the serrated Ditykoians seemed to lie just beyond the trees like sharks' teeth gouging lumps from the sky. The sun was already beginning to warm the air, and swirls of mist rose from the multitude of puddles. Beyond the palisade, towards the trees, towards freedom, a low layer of mist lay, making the trees look as though they were growing out of a ghostly lake that lapped at their trunks.

Ariadne was awake and just crawling from the still-sodden tent. She surveyed the mud and pulled a face.

'Did *you* manage to sleep?' she asked acerbically as he handed her the bowl.

'Perfectly well, thank you. And you're very welcome.'

She brushed his response aside. 'Waking me up like that. You should have more consideration.'

'Sorry, but I was getting fidgety at the lack of complaints. It just seemed far too quiet.'

'Oh, you want more complaints, do you? Very well. Let's see. Number one…'

He hastily left. He grabbed another bowl and spoon and lined up with the laggards. As he held out the bowl for filling, a sun-browned hand fell across his.

'I think you've had your ration.'

He looked round to meet the steady gaze of the officer. 'That was for the girl, sir,' he said. He pointed to the distant tent where Ariadne was sitting on a boulder and eating her porridge.

The man glanced over at the young woman, took in the tent, made a speculative 'hmmm', then said, 'You're obviously a resourceful lad.' He recommenced his slightly unnerving scrutiny of Troi, looking thoughtful. 'Are you the one who saw off three thugs?'

Troi was surprised. 'I may have suggested to some unsociable young men that they go elsewhere, sir.'

The officer smiled, and the hand dropped away. 'Very well, but in future she comes for her own food.'

'I understand, sir.' He glanced back as he walked away. The officer's eyes were still upon him.

She had just finished her breakfast when he returned. 'And then there's two hundred and ninety-seven,' she said.

'Hades. I must have missed the first two hundred and ninety-six. Would you mind repeating them for me?'

Her mouth opened and closed for a heartbeat, then she laughed. 'Very well, we'll call it double tap.'

'Fair enough.' He squatted down and began to hungrily spoon down the lumpy porridge.

She looked away over at the mist, now a beautiful, shifting, pearlescent grey sea. 'You know. What Aunt Euadne said. I don't think that I need defending any more. You've done what you promised. Thank you.' Her tone was studiedly neutral.

'Dyaus have mercy,' he said. 'I thought you were protecting me!'

There was silence for a few long heartbeats. She seemed to be considering. 'Does that mean that I'm bloody well stuck with you?'

'I'm afraid so.'

'So, we will protect each other.' She finally looked round, and he thought there was relief in her eyes. 'A team?'

'A team,' he said with emphasis. 'Which means, by the way, that you will have to go and get your own food from now on.' She looked surprised. 'The new officer,' he explained. 'Seems a decent enough sort, but not a pushover.'

'I notice you waited to spring that one on me. It was the only reason for keeping you around.'

'I put up the tent, didn't I?'

She looked at the bedraggled, drooping wreck. 'This is an original use of the term "put up", I take it?'

'It was the rain. The ground got soft and muddy and the pegs shifted.'

'Well, I suppose we must make allowances for the totally unforeseeable.'

He spread his hands wide in a gesture of submission.

'What do you think they will have us doing today?'

'I've no idea.'

'Instant and complete elucidation of every question. I knew there was another reason for keeping you around.'

'And I thought it was my manly, rugged charm.'

'Not even close.'

He sorted out the tent. It was odd, he thought. He had never found social conversation easy. It had been laboured; there had always been that slight tension, the desperate search for something to say, the uneasy review of what he had said. Only with Aias had he been able to talk freely, without the interference of his internal censor and his querulous caution. He had been able to joke and seemingly be at ease with the scouts, especially Xanthos, but the censor had always hovered in the background, an admonitory finger raised and ready to wag. With Ariadne, he spoke as he thought and without care. It was a peculiar but pleasant feeling.

A salpinx suddenly sounded the double call. He grabbed the water flask, and they picked their way across between the puddles. A large cart had been driven just inside the gate, full of large water butts. That was better than amphorae lugged on shoulders. He clambered up, filled the flask, and jumped down beside the waiting Ariadne.

'Splash mud all over me, why don't you,' she grumbled.

'Thought I had done,' he responded cheerfully, 'but I can do it again if you like.' She gave him a hard stare. He even enjoyed it when she glared at him.

The officer appeared, caught Troi's eyes for a moment, then climbed onto the water cart, turning to face the crowd. He lifted a hand, and the murmur of conversation died away.

'My name is Sarpedon,' he said, his voice clear and carrying. 'As of today, I command the guard for this camp.' He looked round him. 'And I do not like what I see. So today we are going to make this camp a place where you can live in reasonable comfort while you support your Emperor's army.'

People were looking at one another, not at all certain what he meant.

'Firstly, I have arranged for proper leather tents and clean clothes sufficient for everybody. I have found some large stone troughs, which are being brought by cart. They will be placed at the lower end of the camp, where a channel can be dug to take waste water to the small stream beyond. I want the flattest part of the camp, the highest, cleared of stones so that all tents can be set up there.

'When the troughs arrive, I will erect some screens and the women will be able to wash themselves first and change, while the men clear the stones and erect the tents. The women will then wash their own clothes. Then the men can wash and change while the women rest, and the women will then wash the men's clothes too. They can be spread on the palisade to dry.'

He paused. 'I would remind you that I have removed the kill line, but anyone who attempts to cross the palisade will be shot down. Make no mistake.'

Everyone worked with a will, eager to create some shelter and comfort in this dismal place. The guards supervised and even helped, and Sarpedon seemed to be everywhere, instructing, exhorting and actually getting down in the mud and helping with his own hands. Troi was impressed. He sought him out.

'Ah, young Troilus.'

Troi looked at him in surprise. 'How did you know my name, sir?'

'I asked,' said Sarpedon simply, then took a deep draught from a water flask. He stoppered it and regarded the young man. 'A name of ill omen perhaps, but that's scarcely your fault. What can I do for you?'

'I have some suggestions, if you're minded to hear, sir.'

'I am.'

'The old abandoned farmhouse over there.' He pointed across towards the woods. 'I'm sure that we could scavenge sufficient paving slabs to put round the troughs and prevent the mud.'

'Good idea. I'll get a team on it straight away.'

'And could I suggest that we designate the four troughs for specific purposes? One for clothes, one for utensils and two for bathing. You can either make two separate areas for men and women or have different periods allocated.'

'The latter would be easier. We'll do it.'

'There's one more thing, sir.'

'No,' said Sarpedon definitively.

Troi shook his head in bemusement.

'You were going to ask for more food. The answer is no. The army itself is going hungry.'

'They're not getting enough, sir. They'll weaken and be of no use to you.'

'You may well be right, young Troilus, but the answer is no. I'm sorry.' He actually sounded it. It had been a long bowshot into the wind, but worth trying.

'Thank you, sir.' Troi walked away, conscious of the man's eyes still boring into his back.

SIXTY-NINE

THEY WERE ALLOCATED a tent in the very middle of the encampment, but, thanks to some of the useful items he had managed to secrete away, he negotiated an exchange with a couple whose tent was on the end of the outer row. Because of a large boulder, it was even displaced a little farther from the regimented lines. It was the best he could do by way of privacy.

He had furtively bundled up everything in his sleeping roll, the blankets now thoroughly dried, and had surreptitiously moved the knife from its hiding place, thrusting it down beside one of the palisade posts and covering it with a bit of moss.

Ariadne came across. Her hair was still damp and hung long and silky round her fresh face. She wore an overlong tunic and overshort leggings.

'Time for your bath.' She wrinkled her nose. 'In fact, it's well past time.'

He showed her where their tent was, and she happily began to organise its small cache of contents, hanging her old wet tunic over its ridge.

Troi returned after a while. Ariadne was sitting on the large boulder, running her fingers through her hair and holding it out to dry.

'Who are you?' she enquired.

He pulled a face at her.

'Give me your clothes, and I'll go and wash them.'

'Already done,' he said, hanging them across the tent, then joining her on the boulder.

'I'll wager they're not properly clean.'

'I'll wager they are.'

She leapt to her feet and took the offending articles to subject them to minute scrutiny. 'Well,' she eventually conceded, 'they're not too bad, I suppose; for a man, I mean.'

'Praise indeed.'

She suddenly brightened. 'Of course, you might have quietly lifted a new tunic and just dampened it. That would be a typical trick.'

Troi grinned. That was exactly what he had done. 'How could you think such a thing?'

'Remarkably easily.'

The salpinx sounded its two-note call. Troi stood. 'Come on. No more personal service from the diligent table slave.'

'When was there ever?'

They collected their food, eating it as they walked back to their tent. A gentle southerly breeze and unremitting sun had dried out the ground, and it was pleasantly warm. 'Is it my imagination, or is there more meat in this?' she asked.

'No, it's not your imagination. He said there was no chance of any more food. But he's found some way. Perhaps the last lot were taking the cream. Or, in this case, the scraggy horsemeat.'

'Who said?'

'Sarpedon.'

'You talked to Sarpedon?'

'Just some ideas to put to him.'

'Oh, very clever. Put yourself in his bowshot, why don't you? He'll start wondering what a man like you is doing in a place like this. And drawing dangerous conclusions. He looks like someone who knows which end of the horse eats the hay.'

'He seems a decent man.'

'He's a Trog,' she said with finality. 'And you're an idiot.'

'Thank you,' Troi said, with what he imagined was a dignified show of suppressed hurt. She obviously didn't see it in quite the same light, and was trying not to smile.

That really got to him, and he stomped off to the tent, sat down and finished the stew with an air of injured pride. She sat on the boulder and finished hers, then looked across at him.

'I'm sorry,' she said sweetly. 'Are all men so terribly vulnerable?'

He couldn't be angry with her. He relaxed and smiled. 'Most are. I'm the exception.'

'I'm sorry,' she said, this time seriously. 'Sometimes I let my mouth gallop before my brain's in a canter.'

'There are many responses to that,' he said, 'but I shall nobly refrain in the interests of harmony within the tent.'

'You see, you're not such an idiot after all.'

SEVENTY

PHOEBE WAS JUST drawing away from his kiss when he was snatched into blessed wakefulness by a noise outside. A man, en route to the latrines, had stumbled in the dark and sworn loudly.

'What is it?' A sleepy voice in his ear.

'Nothing. Some idiot fell over.'

Ariadne snuggled up a little tighter against the chill of the clear night. Troi heard her yawn. 'You've been dreaming again. Was it the night hag?'

'No.'

'Truth in a man is like a fish in a tree: you wonder how it could get there.'

He said nothing. Why were women so damned intuitive? Couldn't a man indulge in a meaningless bit of prevarication without being dragged before the Great Law Court of Absolute Truth?

He shifted slightly to ease the stiffness in his arm.

'Keep still. How can I get back to sleep with you bouncing around the place like a kitten after a ball of wool?'

He started laughing.

'Now what are you cackling about?' she demanded crossly.

'Nothing. Absolutely nothing.' He was wondering about that himself. He didn't usually laugh at all. It somehow felt right.

She snorted. There was silence for a while. 'Troi. Keep away from Sarpedon. If he gets suspicious, you won't have a parsnip's chance in a famine.'

'I love it when you talk root vegetables to me.'

'Don't be a clown,' she snapped. Then the tone of her voice changed. 'Promise me. Please. It frightens me.'

The fear in her voice made his heart leap. He brought his hand up to squeeze hers. She tensed momentarily, then relaxed. 'I will,' he said. He let go of her hand and fancied there was a slight movement of hers following his.

'Now go to sleep.'

'Absolutely.'

SEVENTY-ONE

THEY SPENT THE whole day toiling on the ramp of beaten earth that angled up and across the granite outcrop to the gate of the Akroakrai. The defenders had left it in a ruinous state, digging deep pits and trenches across it, and, towards the top, had managed to collapse it entirely. The work gang were given the backbreaking job of carrying baskets of rubble and soil up its long, shallow gradient, to empty them into the holes, and to pack down the fill with large, heavy wooden pile drivers.

The weather was cloudy, and a cool wind was blowing, so conditions were better than the first day. Sarpedon had arranged for ample water and a meagre ration of food at midday, and allowed rest periods. But the ever-present guards did not permit loitering, and were much more alert than their slovenly predecessors. The defenders of the citadel watched from the parapet but refrained from shooting. He wondered aloud why. An elderly man, who had been in the first group taken, told him. They were initially sent to bring out any wounded, guarded by the Bluecloaks. A defender fired a belly bow, injuring a guard. The others instantly grabbed the five civilians nearest the wounded man and slit their throats. Since then, they had been left unmolested.

He rarely saw Ariadne, as he was working on the ramp, and Sarpedon had given the women the less onerous task of filling the rubble baskets near its base. When the salpinx announced the end of the work day, he moved through the congealing crowd until he found her. She looked pale and tired, with dark smudges beneath her eyes. She gave him a weak smile.

'How are you?' he asked.

'Wonderful. It's been a great day. Do you think we could come here tomorrow as well?'

'I was thinking of a ride to the coast and a nice piece of fried sea bass washed down with some Pergamene white.'

'Just ride out.' Her tone was wistful.

'Well, a couple of horses might be useful.'

She was watching a heron flap its ungainly way across the dismal grey of the sky. She sighed. 'Did someone perhaps once, in an unguarded moment, suggest that you had a sense of humour?'

He chuckled. 'Well, my father used to laugh a lot when he bounced me on my head as a kid.' Father. A momentary vision of a bearded man swinging him round and round. Then gone.

'That might explain it.'

Her reply seemed listless, lacking her characteristic sharpness. He was uncertain how to respond.

She glanced across to the spare figure of Sarpedon. 'He's had his eye on you all day. Like a windhover watching a beetle.'

He laughed. 'So, I'm a beetle now.'

She made no reply.

A sense of unease made him fidget. She was right. He had noted the scrutiny and cursed himself for a fool.

The escort moved into position around them, and, at a sharp word of command, they began to trudge back to the camp.

She seemed distracted, and he caught an occasional, anxious glance in his direction. He made an attempt at conversation, but she gave him little encouragement. He was worried. It was not like her.

They arrived back as a fine drizzle began to fall, hastily collected their poor meal and retired to the cramped confines of the tent.

He could sense the tension in her and knew that she was at full draw. She laid her empty plate down and hooked her arms around her legs, then gazed out to where the dark line of the rain cloud floated just above the distant mountains. A truncated pyramid of sunbeams pierced the cloud, throwing the sharp summits and jagged ridges into black relief. She did not look at him when she spoke. 'Why are you still here?'

The question took him totally by surprise. 'I wasn't aware there was an option.'

'Don't pretend to be stupid. You're a skopos, a scout. You could be out of here without breaking sweat. Nicias used to tell me how good the scouts were, and you commanded Nicias, so you must be very good.'

He made no reply. She was right. He could not justify remaining in captivity, not when he could escape any time he chose. He had already loosened two stakes of the palisade that blocked a small gulley, so perfectly placed to provide an easy evasion route that it could have come straight from the basic training grounds at Naupactos. Or simply hide tomorrow. No problem. Wait until dark, approach the Akro, a double then triple kivick call of a tawny owl, and a rope would snake down for him. Nothing easier.

He knew that Harpalycus was in constant contact with the garrison. Xanthos had created a well-camouflaged access route that could be used by scouts, and Troi could leave along with the next one. He would see Diomedes first. He desperately wanted to talk to him again. There were things he was beginning to grasp, feelings starting to dominate his mind that he did not fully understand, an uneasy suspicion that Diomedes had read him only too well. But he could not leave her. The mere thought was unbearable. He was brought to the spear clash with his emotions and had to acknowledge them.

She was looking at him now. And had been doing so for some time. The light was fading, but there was something in her eyes. Her face was taut, and her hands gripped so tightly the knuckles were bloodless.

'So, when are you going? Back to your beloved war.' She spoke firmly, but there was a hint of desperation in her voice.

'I'm not.'

'You have to. I'm sure that Sarpedon has you in his bowshot. And your own side isn't going to be too happy with you.'

That's for sure, he thought. 'I was under the impression we were a team,' he said.

'There are bigger teams,' she said simply. 'Bigger responsibilities.'

'Not to me.'

'I'm well capable of looking after myself. You've no responsibility for me. If there ever was any, it's long since been discharged.' She looked away, a little too quickly. 'I want you to go.'

'I promised your aunt.'

She had been waiting for that. 'I have told you before, my aunt thought she was doing the right thing for me, but it was not her call. You cannot make someone oath-bound to another against that person's will. It is not my will.'

'It was the Great Oath. By the Furies.'

She swung back to stare at him. 'Heavenly Herakla save us.'

He grimaced and made a slight shrug.

'So that's why you're staying around.'

'No,' he said quietly.

She stared at him with discomfiting intensity, opened her mouth to say something, then shut it again. He wasn't sure what to say either. His denial had emerged without thought, a revelation that had slipped past the guards of his mind as easily as a wolf past a dozing shepherd. He felt exposed and vulnerable. Frightened.

She obviously chose not to question it. Which both relieved and disappointed him. 'It's the same,' she eventually said. 'All it needs is for me to swear to a denial.'

'But in a temple of the Furies. And the nearest one that I know of is in Plataea. Which rather leaves us in the same situation.'

'Why, by all the Gods great and small, did you make such an oath?'

'Euadne asked me. She was.' He stopped. His brain was betraying him. He took a deep breath. 'She was a persuasive woman. And I could not gainsay her.'

She winced slightly at the implications but did not react further. 'So, you won't go. I really am stuck with you?'

'I'm afraid so. You're a child of misfortune.'

She looked out at the sky, where the last vestiges of dull light were fading. 'I'm frightened, Troi.'

He wanted to reach out and hold her. 'There's nothing to be frightened of.'

'There's nothing!' she repeated incredulously. She shook her head. 'Perhaps you really were dropped on your head as a child. I wish you would go. Please.'

'No. I can't.'

'Then there is no more to be said. The knucklebones must fall where they will.'

He could not make out the expression on her face, but her voice seemed, to him, to hold a measure of relief. At least, he liked to think so.

It was dark now, though the moon was still visible low towards the western horizon and throwing its pale light directly into the tent, and the rain was becoming heavier, pattering on the leather skin of the tent.

'Let's to bed,' she said, and he wasn't at all sure that her tone did not carry a layered meaning.

They settled down in their now-familiar positions. Outside, the noise of the camp began to fade into the night.

'I've never slept with anybody before. It isn't nearly so exciting as it's supposed to be.'

He was utterly unsure how to respond, so took a defensive stance. 'Sleep is never that exciting.'

She was silent for a while, then spoke, very quietly. 'I don't want it to go any further, but would you kiss me?'

He lay still for a heartbeat, then rolled over. Their faces were fingerbreadths apart, and he could see well enough in the moonglow. Her eyes looked huge.

'Are you sure?'

She nodded. 'I have a bad feeling about this place, and I've never been kissed. I don't want to die never knowing how it felt.'

'You're not going to die.'

'You never told me that you were Hades himself,' she responded tartly.

'I've found that declaring oneself to be the God of the dead has a dampening effect on conversation.'

'Well, are you just going to lie there all night scrabbling around for something funny to say?'

He pressed his lips gently against hers. They felt cool, but there was no glimmer of response.

'Was that it?' There was a definite note of disappointment to her tone. 'Scarcely worth the bother.'

'You're supposed to work at it,' he said, struggling to keep the grievance from his voice. He tried again, bringing his hand up to tenderly caress the side of her face before kissing her again. He gently worked her lips, before pressing more firmly. He pulled away and took a long breath.

'So, the idea is that you suffocate one another. I think I'm getting the draw of this bow.'

'Look, why don't you try kissing me?'

She stretched forward, thrust her lips tightly against his, and held them there firmly for several hekates before retreating. She looked at him quizzically. He shook his head. Her mouth twitched slightly.

He smiled to himself. 'Let's try and relax. We'll just snuggle a little.'

He put his arms around her and drew her tightly to him. There was a moment's resistance, then she slid her arms around him as well. He massaged her back gently, then kissed her brow softly, then her cheek, and then her ear. She wriggled slightly. He began to nibble on her earlobe.

'Ooh,' she squealed, 'it's bringing me out in goosebumps.'

He immediately transferred his attentions to her slightly open mouth. The next moment, she was kissing him, tenderly and gently at first, then with increasing passion, until their mouths opened and their tongues intertwined. They parted and she was breathing heavily. She swallowed. He leaned forward and kissed her again, gently, nibbling on her lower lip. Then, another sudden burst of shared intensity. Almost without thinking, he slid his hand round and cupped her breast, feeling her nipple swell and stiffen even beneath the rough material of the tunic. She moaned quietly, then suddenly pushed him away.

'No,' she cried sharply.

Troi immediately pulled back. 'Sorry,' he said. 'Got carried away.'

'No, I should be the one apologising. It was a bad idea. It must be difficult for you.'

'It does have a momentum of its own,' he said ruefully, 'but it was nice.'

'Yes, it was, wasn't it? But perhaps we ought to just sleep now.'

He rolled back over and she clung to him tightly, lightly kissing the nape of his neck. 'I thought that you weren't after my body,' she whispered.

'I wasn't,' he whispered back. 'But it's actually a very nice body.'

'Just a sad lack of large mammary protuberances, wouldn't you say?'

'No, I wouldn't.'

After a while her breathing became slower and more regular. He timed it to perfection.

'Ari,' he said, 'who was the first boy you kissed?'

'What?' she asked sleepily. 'A boy called Tron who ate too much garlic and…' She stiffened. 'You bastard.' After a few heartbeats, she added, 'And if I were you, I'd stop that inane cackling. It could well be inimical to your health.'

He decided she had a good point.

SEVENTY-TWO

PHOEBE'S DEAD EYES vomited the heaving, squirming mass of obscene yellow maggots. Then he was awake in the claustrophobic confines of a small leather tent, and Ariadne was urgently shaking him.

'Troi, wake up. Wake up, damn you.'

He swallowed. The dream had not built to its full horror, and there was none of that petrifying rigor that froze his limbs and held him helpless, his insides turned to water, his mind gibbering with terror. He put a hand up to take hers.

'I'm all right, Ari. I'm all right.'

'You were dreaming again.'

'You woke me before it got too bad. Thank you.'

She lay down again and hugged him tightly. 'It's the same dream, isn't it? Every night. The same one.'

He stiffened. His instinctive fear of self-revelation clogged his mouth. But this time it was different. Something within him burst from its confines, and he found himself replying. Without thought. Without volition.

'Yes.'

'Do you want to tell me about it? It might help.'

He did want to tell her. Why, he did not know, but he did. He just did not know how to. He was quiet for a few hekates, struggling to form the words and force them past the barrier of his teeth.

She continued to hug him firmly. It reassured him.

He began, hesitantly. 'I'm with a… with a girl I knew, and…' She waited quietly, patiently. Their fingers were locked together. 'Suddenly she's a death's head, a corpse, and… maggots. Maggots falling from her. From her mouth. Her eyes.' Ariadne shuddered. 'And she's pushing a knife into my heart and I can't stop her because I'm frozen and can't move.' Sudden tears stung his eyes.

'Oh, my poor darling.' It was like the wash of cool water on a hot summer's day. 'Who is she?'

'Just a girl I knew in Koi.'

'Koi? Bogazkoi?'

She tensed with the shock. He cursed himself. Xanthos had warned him he was loose-mouthed, and he had caused enough problems back at the Villa. He should have learned. But it was too late now.

'The town where you lived. That was Bogazkoi?'

'Yes.' There was a feeling of relief, of yielding, of a crumbling.

'Just a girl?'

Troi said nothing, which said a great deal.

'Why the knife?' Ariadne asked intuitively. She was as bad as Klio.

He swallowed. 'I killed her with it. She had a gut wound.'

The grief was raw in his voice. It should have been impossible to hug him any tighter, but she managed it.

'You've never spoken of this to anyone, have you?'

'Not properly, no.'

'Tell me about it,' she demanded fiercely. 'You need to.'

So he did. The dam finally broke, and all of that dreadful day poured out in an unstoppable flood of words. And they were suddenly back in his mind, from whence they had too long been banished. Aias and Phoebe, Ourania and her daughter, his childhood friends, kindly old Elissa and gruff Erxander. And then, coming from a far distance, but looming larger until they dominated his memory, an elegant woman with long curly black hair and laughing eyes, and a tall, distinguished-looking man with a neatly trimmed beard.

Troi was crying, long, choking sobs, until his throat hurt. The grief seared him like acid. Ariadne clung to him desperately. Then, a memory of Diomedes asking a question about the guard he had killed that day of the ambush.

'They were brown,' he managed to blurt out. 'His eyes were brown. And it was surprise. A look of complete surprise.'

She did not understand, but never loosened her grip as he cried and cried until he could cry no more.

'Sleep now, my poor darling,' she whispered. 'You'll never have that dream again.'

And she was right.

SEVENTY-THREE

Troi woke, as always, with the dawn. Ariadne was stroking the side of his face tenderly.

'Are you alright, my darling?' she murmured.

My darling. It sounded like the windswept call of the curlew, the voices in the tumble of a mountain stream, the liquid song of the nightingale. But they were not as sweet, nor as beautiful.

He twisted round to face her.

'I'm sorry,' he said. 'I made a fool of myself last night.'

'No, you didn't. How you could have lived with that horror, I'll never know.'

'I feel different,' he said, uncertainly. 'As though I can breathe.' He paused. 'Like when they took the manacles off when I was a slave.' He shook his head. 'I can't really say what it's like, but I know it's good.'

She squeezed his hand.

'And I keep remembering Aias and the others. It's sad, and makes me want to cry, but I know it's what I should be doing. I should never have denied them all this time. I should have grieved for them.'

She reached out and cupped his face in her hands and gave him a long, lingering kiss.

'It's over. It's done with. You're back.'

'That's what Klio said, that I wasn't there. That she could bring me back. I just never gave her the chance. I never understood what she meant. I do now.' Then he shook his head. 'No, I still don't understand, but I know that everything is different.' He could not look at her, and he could not stop looking at her. 'And you did it.' He looked down instead. 'You called me your darling. What… I mean… did you…' He trailed away into an embarrassed silence.

She smiled. 'What are you trying to say, in your impressively articulate way?'

'I'm not sure,' he admitted lamely.

She put out her hand and gently ran her fingers down his face, through the fine stubble of his growing beard. 'Why do men have to get so hairy?' she asked.

'I've no idea.' He raised a tentative hand and touched her cheek too. His fingers felt strangely weak. She pressed her face against them. He wasn't sure what he felt. All he knew was that he was being tossed on a wild sea of uncertainty. He didn't know what he wanted, but that he needed something important from Ariadne was undeniable. And it wasn't sex. He took her fingers in his other hand and gently kissed them. Her eyes were bright. Slowly the distance between their lips lessened and they were kissing again, her hand hooked round the back of his neck and pulling him into her with feral urgency.

The salpinx sounded its double call.

'Bugger,' he said.

SEVENTY-FOUR

IT WAS A day of frequent showers, brief periods of sun and a cool northwesterly. He was unable to work with Ariadne, as the men were back to their hard labour on the ramp while the women filled the baskets at its base, but things had changed irrevocably. The earth had shifted. Neither said anything. But both knew. Whenever he had to return for more rubble, they could not help but reach out and interlock fingers, or just stretch to touch one another in passing, and each time it was like the rising of the sun. In the now-regular rest periods, they would quickly search for one another and sit, shoulder pressed to shoulder, hands twining and caressing, and talk. Ceaselessly.

Of hopes and fears. Of plans for the future. Anecdotes of their childhoods and silly stories. As if trying to compress a lifetime of experience into a dekate. They unobtrusively tested out one another's beliefs and attitudes. They subconsciously noted each other's sense of humour and natural idiosyncrasies. They interwove and bound together like hedge and honeysuckle. Despite the work and the situation, it was the most wonderful day of their lives.

At the end of the session, they had made but small progress on reconstituting the ramp. Troi estimated it would take a minimum of a fortnight to repair the damage. It was going to become a gruelling and familiar assignment.

When he found her waiting for him, she smiled with such genuine delight and held her hands to him so naturally that his heart almost physically lurched. They marched back through the light drifts of rain, hand in hand, hastily washed, grabbed their food and retired to the cramped confines of their tent. It was still light. The rain fell steadily but with no real venom.

The unspoken question that had hung between them all day loomed large as they set down their empty bowls. They looked at one another warily through the rapidly fading light.

'We might as well go to bed,' she said quietly, looking down and colouring slightly.

He nodded. He had been with women many times before, but this was different. He wasn't sure what he wanted. He couldn't deny the sexual attraction, but his thoughts were not about himself, but of her. That was new; he had never felt like that before, but it felt surprisingly right. She slid under the blankets in her usual position. He could see uncertainty in her face too. He found himself getting under the blankets facing her. Neither spoke. He tentatively put out a hand and gently stroked her cheek. He could feel that she was trembling, but she put her own hand up, grasped and stayed his, and pressed her cheek against it.

'Are you sure?' he whispered.

There was a moment's hesitation, then she gave a determined nod. 'We could be dead tomorrow. We should take the tide at the full.'

They lay for a few heartbeats, gazing into each other's faces, and then, simultaneously, came together and kissed.

SEVENTY-FIVE

In the early dekates of the morning, the storm of lovemaking had abated, and they lay quietly in one another's arms, fingers gently embracing, occasionally kissing, but tender and lingering, with none of the desperation of last night. It was not yet dawn, but a glimmer of pallid moonlight moulded her face from the surrounding shadows. It made her beauty ethereal.

She sighed. 'Another day of hard work.'

'After a long night of the same,' he agreed glumly.

She stared at him.

'Ah,' he said. 'Would that have been what we military folk term a tactical error?'

'It would. And it's up there vying for the laurel wreath.'

'And it could have repercussions tonight?'

'I would put an obol or two on it.' She suddenly looked serious. 'Do you think... Do you think Aunt Euadne knew?'

'What?' He was confused. Was she talking about Nicias?

'Us. Do you think she knew we would get together? She could see trout in a muddy stream. I wouldn't put it beyond her. I hope she did'. There was a long pause. 'These are strange circumstances. We've been thrown together. I just want you to know that I have no call on you.' There was a wistfulness in her tone.

'I love you,' he said.

Her eyes widened, but he was more surprised than she was. He hadn't meant to say it. His brain had slipped its leash, but he knew that it was true. Whatever love was, he had it. By the kraterful. All he wanted was to be with her, all he needed was her smile; his whole being hung on her needs, her happiness, her wellbeing. His life before had been sere and monochrome, a desiccated apology for living; now, it burst with vibrant colour and sheer exuberance. It was like climbing through cloud on the Eleans, when the grey murk would magically shred and dissipate, suddenly revealing the wonderful sunlit peaks and cols of the high mountains.

She gazed at him. 'I love you too,' she said, with such tenderness that he wanted to lie there within its echoes for ever. Then she reached for him.

The dawn found them intertwined, as though trying to meld into one.

Troi sighed. 'I suppose they wouldn't give us a rest day?'

'I can't see me getting much rest if they did,' she responded tartly.

'My thoughts exactly.'

‘In which case,’ she said, sitting up and reaching for her clothes, ‘we had better be up and about.’ She bent and kissed him. ‘There will be lots more nights.’

They scrambled out of the tent to a clear but blustery day. Ariadne bent to collect the bowls and spoons, and Troi glanced across at some unusual movement.

He froze. Ten men in triple-plumed helmets and rich blue cloaks were moving through the campsite. Marsyas’s personal guards. Led by a lanky, thin-faced officer with slicked-back black hair and a hook nose. Troi knew him instantly, and knew what they were doing. Already, a pretty, young, auburn-haired girl was being dragged roughly along by two of the guards. She was in tears.

‘Get in the tent,’ he hissed.

Ariadne stood up and looked at him, ‘What in Hades for?’

‘Get in the fucking tent.’

The frantic urgency in his voice was enough. She hastily ducked back in, but it was far too late. The bastard had seen her and was pointing in their direction. Troi was helpless. They approached like the knife to his heart. He was totally immobilised by shock and fear, held as rigidly as by any night hag.

‘Get her out,’ snapped the officer.

Two of the guards had fallen in on either side of Troi. They knew their business, though they apparently mistook his shock for craven cowardice and did not even bother to grasp him. A large man knelt, put in a huge, well-muscled arm and hauled Ariadne out by brute force. She screamed.

He reacted without thought. He savagely kicked down onto the side of the knee of the man to his right, breaking his leg, and planted an elbow in the face of the other, felling him immediately.

Then he launched himself at the astonished officer, who tumbled backwards. Troi was on him in an instant, his knuckled fist raised to crush the bastard's windpipe, when a huge hand closed round his, stopping its downward thrust in mid-air. A boot hammered into his back, and something hit him hard on the side of the head.

He fell forward across the officer, who was desperately trying to scramble away. Flashes of light erupted around Troi. He saw double and felt groggy, but he could still hear Ariadne's wailing cry.

He was hauled to his feet, helpless in iron fists, the officer screaming in his face and showering him with spittle. But it was nothing but the idle play of clouds across the sky. All reality was concentrated in Ariadne's harrowing sobs, torturing his mind with their rending echoes long after they had dragged him away.

SEVENTY-SIX

Troi was thrown into a small, pitch-black room with no windows and a hard-packed earthen floor. Otherwise, as he learned when he despairingly explored the impenetrable darkness with his outstretched hands, it contained nothing. His head ached abominably, and dried blood caked the side of his face. There was no stickiness, and his memories were uncertain, so he wondered if he had passed out for at least some of the time, and had no idea if it was still day, or whether the night had come.

The thought of the latter brought him out in a cold sweat, and a vision of Ariadne with that sadistic bastard tore his mind with savage talons.

He shut his eyes tightly, pressed his temples despite the blinding pain, and howled. But the images would not go.

They capered and laughed at his futile struggles. He knew he was a dead man, but the thought that he had not been able to protect her pushed such considerations from his mind. He huddled in one corner, drawn ineluctably to the agony like a fearful man to the very brow of a precipitous cliff.

Time passed. He drifted into an uneasy and febrile sleep. He woke. He roamed the cell like a trapped wolf. Time passed. He woke again to find Ariadne there, holding him, laughing, telling him that everything was all right, and the relief burst upon him like sunrise until he was brutally dragged awake for real.

Confused and groggy with exhaustion, his hands roughly tied behind him, he was hustled from the cell, down a long corridor and into a large room. He blinked against the searing light spewing through the large windows as he was forced down onto a rough wooden chair. He had been here before. He squeezed his eyes shut, then opened them blearily. The room slowly shifted into focus.

Two men sat behind a table looking at him. One was aged, jowly, thin grey hair plastered flatly to a squarish skull; the other, younger, quite handsome, with thick black hair and a short, neatly trimmed beard that accentuated his chin line. There was an unmistakable air of arrogance about him. To one side, standing quite stiffly, was the officer he had tried to kill, and he was aware of movement behind him, presumably his guards. Beside the officer stood Sarpedon, not looking at Troi, but with a strange expression on his face.

The old man glanced down at a wax tablet before him and looked up again. 'The charge is sedition,' he said in a monotone, 'in that the prisoner Troilus did wilfully attack and injure members of the Imperial Forces going about their lawful duties and attempt to assassinate an officer. Guilty.' There was not even a perfunctory pause.

The other man nodded gravely. 'Guilty.'

There was the scratching of a pen, and a tall, hunched clerk appeared from behind Troilus with a scroll, which he placed on the table. Both men signed it, and it was taken away.

'Sentence: death by hanging.'

'Agreed.'

More scratching. A second scroll was signed, and two burly guards hauled him to his feet, dragged him out and threw him bodily back into the tiny black airless cell. Imperial justice had been duly dispensed.

SEVENTY-SEVEN

TROI WAS HUNCHED in a corner, tortured by thirst, but far more by the thoughts that still mangled his mind and refused to be shifted, when the bolt was drawn with a juddering screech and the door opened to spill a dazzle of light across the tiny cell. He looked up. The dark figure who entered was somehow familiar. But he carried an oil lamp, and even this weak and flickering flame robbed Troi of his vision. Whoever it was, his time to die had come, and he was obscurely grateful.

'Troilus.' The man's voice was low, but now Troi recognised him.

'Sarpedon.' Surprise made him speak louder than intended.

'Keep your voice down,' hissed the officer.

This did not make sense.

'Are you all right? Can you walk?'

'Yes,' said Troi, with sheer bewilderment, staring up at the face slowly coalescing into clarity. He was even more puzzled to see that Sarpedon had mysteriously sprouted a full black beard.

'Then listen carefully. Come with me, and I'll get you to a place from which you should be able to make it to your own lines. If you're the kind of man I suspect you to be, there'll be no problem.'

'Why?' Troi's demand was blunt.

'I'm a soldier. I became one to fight for my country against other soldiers, not butcher and torture our own people. There's little I can do. But I can do this.'

'But you'll be held responsible. They'll execute you.'

'Not if I can help it. We're suffering a lot of desertions. Two men ran tonight. One was the guard who should have been here. The previous guard came and reported that he had not been replaced. He is someone I have reason to trust. He will claim that he was duly relieved, and that the deserter must have released you. The chance is too good to miss. It can only be a gift of the Gods. But you must hurry.'

'What about Ariadne?'

'I'm sorry. I truly am. But there is nothing either of us can do. She was taken to Marsyas's tent this evening. Staying here to be hung will not help her.' He stared intensely into Troi's eyes. 'Listen. I was based at Himera for a while. I became good friends with Rhea, the local healer. I can get your Ariadne to her. You'll be able to find her there.'

Troi felt the confirmation of his worst fears like a blow. His mind refused to function. It couldn't be true. The hope Sarpedon offered seemed but a shadow.

'You must come,' urged Sarpedon desperately.

For a heartbeat, Troi just sat there, his mind a vortex of images and terrors that were spinning down into some dark, deep place of pure horror. But, somewhere inside himself, he found the strength to do what was needful, and he clambered to his feet.

Sarpedon nodded with relief and led Troi out into the corridor, where he extinguished the flame of the lamp and quietly opened a door to the outside. It was a dark night, the moon overhung with clouds, but they were high and thin, and a faint wash of moonlight provided a modicum of illumination.

Sarpedon led him through the dark and silent buildings of the town on an obviously pre-planned route. They met no-one until they arrived at a small gate set within the curtain wall. A soldier stood waiting. Troi guessed him to be the guard who had alerted Sarpedon. There was a brief murmur of conversation and the gate was eased open. Sarpedon and Troi slid out.

They were in an encampment of leather tents, and Sarpedon led him through the stirrings and snuffles, coughs and snores, even past occasional solitary figures looming through the dark, though they took no heed of an officer and his companion simply passing through.

Beyond the tents, they bypassed horse lines and a guarded store dump, the sleepy sentinels barely acknowledging them, and then a stretch of empty ground until they came to the outer circumvallation palisade. Here the guards were alert, looking out vigilantly into the menacing darkness, conscious of the ever-present threat of the dreaded Agrianes. There were tents full of soldiers dozing, playing knucklebones, sitting quietly and talking, awaiting the call to arms. Sarpedon did not pause, but approached a group of guards and an officer at a gate. A bonfire blazed, casting flickering shadows in every direction.

Troi could not help but note the sheer stupidity of the defenders, destroying the night vision of their sentinels and making them easy targets, silhouetted against the background glow. No wonder the Aggies kept the Trogs in such terror. The fools made it easy for them.

The officer turned when he saw them coming, stiffened and immediately saluted Sarpedon. Troi belatedly realised that his companion was wearing the large ornate rank brooch of a chiliarches.

Sarpedon drew the youthful officer to one side. 'Chiliarches Melanpos with personal orders from the Satrap Marsyas,' he said quietly. 'A man is to pass through the lines. There is to be no mention of this to anyone. It is not to appear in the official report. You must not even report this to your immediate superior. Do you understand?'

The overawed young officer nodded. 'Yes, sir.'

Sarpedon turned to Troi and grasped him by the wrist. 'Good luck, Olus. A great deal rests on your shoulders. The Gods go with you.'

'Thank you, sir,' said Troi, playing his part, but meaning it.

The officer signalled to one of his men, who opened the gate. Troi turned and slipped through it to disappear almost immediately into the shadowed night.

SEVENTY-EIGHT

THE TREE LINE was barely fifty paces away as Troi rose from the shallow gully, along which he had been working his cautious way. The sky was lightening to the east. He put his left hand on his right upper arm, as though he was holding an injury, just three fingers on show, the thumb and small finger tucked beneath. In the arcane sign language of the scouts, this proclaimed that he was a scout in trouble, in the vicinity of the enemy, but not actually being pursued. Someone would have seen him emerging from the palisade and be waiting for him. He prayed that it be one of his fellows in the woods, and not a patrol of bloodthirsty Aggies.

His heart pounded as he walked steadily forward. Behind him, a cleft in the Boreads caught fire as the sun finally rose.

He passed between the first two trees and stopped, waiting. There was a soft thump to his left, and he turned to see the unmistakable face of Xanthos, grinning at him from beneath its slather of mud and moss.

'Well, you've taken your bloody time and no mistake. Harp is not at all amused.'

Troi extended his arm and they grasped wrists. He did not smile back. The turmoil in his head was still driving him almost insane. 'Things got difficult,' he muttered.

'I saw the difficulty,' said Xanthos, 'and I can appreciate the problem.'

'Perhaps not fully,' said Troi.

Xanthos looked at him in puzzlement.

'Marsyas took her,' Troi blurted out, not really meaning to, but unable to suppress the need to tell someone, to share his agony, to find some morsels of human understanding and comfort. Something he once would never have dreamed of doing.

Xanthos stared at him, devoid of words. 'Dyaus,' he eventually said, 'I'm sorry.' He saw the helpless despair in his friend's face. 'We'll get her out,' he said reassuringly.

'But what state will she be in?'

'We'll deal with that when we face it,' said Xanthos, more confidently than he felt. 'Time heals.'

'Perhaps.' And the tears rolled down Troi's face.

SEVENTY-NINE

HARPALYCUS WAS ANGRY. A stony, incisive anger. 'You should never have been in a village within the Troian area of influence to begin with.' His eyes were pure ice and transfixed Troi like a javelin. 'And to disregard your duty to rejoin the army at the earliest opportunity?' He picked up a wax tablet from the table before him and stabbed a finger down on it. 'Five,' he snapped. 'Five, including a woman, ran from the work detail that first day. They just walked out of the main gate. You were a skopos. You could have got out of there any time you chose.' He shook his head. 'It makes me wonder if the future planned out for you by Diomedes is achievable.'

Troi focussed on the wolf's-head banner that hung on the wall of the tent behind the young strategarch. Harpalycus had taken it as his personal sigil, and it was already known and feared by the Trogs.

'I love her,' he said obstinately.

Harpalycus brought his fist crashing down on the cross-legged table before him with such force that the majority of scrolls and tablets on it tumbled to the floor. He took no notice of the chaos at his feet.

'Love! Love has no place in a war for the survival of a people. We're not playing a game of tilia, where you can just wander off for a kiss and a cuddle when you feel like it. Men died while you were fumbling one another in a bloody tent.'

Troi felt the rise of anger, but curbed it with an effort. On one level, he knew Harpalycus was right. He would have said the same to any man under his own command. But he could not deny the irresistible force of his feelings. He should have done otherwise. He could not have done otherwise. He was in the fiery grip of iron tongs. So, he said nothing, but stared into the red eyes of the pendant wolf. The wolf stared back.

'You say this officer,' Harpalycus glanced down at the wax tablet in his hand, 'Sarpedon, promised to get her to Himera. You will not go there. Xan will arrange for a genuine civilian to go in and bring her out. You throw a discus like this again, and I'll have you shovelling shit for the rest of your military career. Do you understand?'

'I do, sir.'

Harpalycus laid the wax tablet on the now almost empty table. A sonorous note filled the tent as someone tapped the bronze cylinder hung outside. Harpalycus glanced up. 'Enter.' He looked back at Troi. 'You may go. And consider yourself bloody lucky that you're not on a charge of desertion.'

Troi turned to leave, surprised to see Xanthos coming in. The scout shot him a look that Troi could not interpret but which filled him with an amorphous sense of dread.

'This concerns Troilus, sir,' said Xanthos. He avoided Troi's eyes.

Troi swung back round, and Harpalycus nodded to him to stay. Troi stared at Xanthos, somehow already knowing what he was about to say, but fearing to even conceive of it.

Xanthos looked back, with sympathetic but haunted eyes. 'I'm sorry, Troi, I…' His voice died away like a wave seeping into the sand.

Troi sat down heavily on a small collapsible stool. 'Ariadne,' he whispered.

'We have a line of communication with the woodcutters who work for the Trogs. One reports that he saw a tall, brown-haired girl brought out from the Butcher's tent this morning.' He hesitated. 'She was on a shield. The side of her head had been caved in. She was dead.'

Troi did not respond. He just sat there.

Harpalycus gestured Xanthos over to one side. 'Are you sure it was her?' he asked quietly.

'I'm afraid so, sir. We watch the bastard. There were only two girls in his keep net. The other was short and auburn-haired. It was Troi's girl, all right.'

'Get him out of here and look after him,' said Harpalycus gently.

Xanthos took Troi by the arm. He rose obediently, almost like a child, and the scout led him from the tent.

Harpalycus watched them go, and swore.

EIGHTY

XANTHOS LED THE white-faced and benumbed Troi to the horse lines, pausing only to have a quiet word with one of Harpalycus's aides. Troi did as he was told unprotestingly, without any thought, scarcely aware of his surroundings. His eyes were unfocussed, his responses slow, his movements uncoordinated. Xanthos did not try to talk to him. He knew shock when he saw it. He took a couple of scout ponies, got his friend on one and quickly mounted the other. With a perfunctory nod to the guard officer, who knew to ask no questions of Xanthos and his doings, he ushered Troi off into the night.

The moon was waxing almost to full, and the sharp stars speckled the sky, but Troi was in a darker place, a moth circling ever closer to the flame that would eventually send it crackling and burning to the earth. Unless he could be coaxed back from the fire. And Xanthos knew of only one place where it might be done.

It took less than a dekate to arrive at a small, isolated farm, built alongside a stream that cut its muddy course through rough grassland. Black, shaggy cattle with wicked-looking horns lay quietly in crudely fenced enclosures, and a few small fields were given over to crops. A couple of dogs were heard to bark as Xanthos and Troi approached the farmhouse. A lamp flickered into life inside, spilling rivulets of ruddy light through the small gaps in the window covers. The door opened, and an elderly man stood there, two large mastiffs at his side and a young woman behind him, wrapped in a blanket.

'It's only me,' shouted Xanthos. The woman squealed with delight, pushed unceremoniously past the old man, and flew, barefoot, across the hard earth of the farmyard. The two mastiffs took off in hot pursuit, their tails windmilling, and the man emerged at a more sedate hobble. Xanthos was off his horse, and put his hand out to stop her onrush. She came to a halt, her mouth open, her eyes wide. The two dogs were not to be put off and launched themselves at Xanthos, crying their delight. The elderly man, a little portly, round-faced and grey-haired, arrived and studied the newcomer with ill-disguised suspicion.

To Troi it was a kind of trivial shadow show. He watched it with detached indifference. It had nothing to do with the pain that seared his mind, making him screw his eyes tightly closed from time to time in a hopeless attempt to shut out what could not be denied.

'Who's this?' the man growled, his tone so unfriendly that the dogs immediately bristled and transferred their watchful attentions to the figure sitting slumped on the scout pony.

For the first time, the woman realised that there was someone else and stared across at the stranger. She was tall and thin, fragile in build, with fine, delicate features and a halo of frizzy, dark brown hair. She looked back at Xanthos questioningly. So, he told them.

EIGHTY-ONE

All the time Troi had known Xanthos, there had never been the slightest hint that he was married. He never spoke about himself, and his somewhat anomalous position in the scouts, left totally to his own devices by Gwalchmai, meant that he came and went as he wished. Apparently, he had been married for three years when the rebellion broke out, and had a sturdy young son called Androcles. They had also had a daughter, but she had been sickly and died within the moontide.

His wife, Selene, was a kindly, loving and practical young woman, who somehow managed to accept Xanthos for what he was, and made no attempt to stop him joining the rebellion.

Her father, despite being taciturn to the point of rudeness, was a decent enough, well-meaning man, though he could not understand Xanthos's irrepressible thirst for adventure and freedom. He had thought a strapping young man to take over the small farm the answer to his prayers, but it was not to be. However, Xanthos had found a young lad to join the household, a little weak-witted perhaps, but a strong and willing worker, which meant they could get by.

Selene warmed up some broth and finally cajoled Troi into taking some, and they bedded him down in the guest room.

He did not sleep, rather willing himself to wake from this ride of the night hag, to open his eyes to the wonderful, cramped, damp confines of a malodorous leather tent, a drift of cold drizzle blowing in through the open end, his hip sore from the hard ground, his arm stiff and aching, but world enough for him, with a naked arm across his chest and her warm regular breath on the nape of his neck. But there was to be no waking from this. There had been little left of the night, yet it was the longest of his life.

When the chill grey of dawn finally seeped through the leather window covers, he rose, without thought, and wandered through into the large living area. Selene stood there, stirring a cauldron over the fire. A toddler with an unkempt mop of brown hair stood beside her, grasping a carved wooden horse. He turned and surveyed Troi with large, serious eyes. Selene turned too, and smiled.

'Good morning,' she said. 'Would you like some porridge?' He shook his head. Selene looked down fondly at her son. 'This is your Uncle Troi, Andro. Say hello nicely.'

'Hello, Uncle Troi.'

Troi tried to smile, but couldn't. 'Hello, Andro.'

'I got horse,' said Andro brightly and proffered it to Troi. Troi took it and admired it, though it merely threw an insubstantial shadow against the screaming hell beyond. 'Dada make it.'

'It's lovely,' he said mechanically, and gave it back to the boy, who began to push it across the floor, making surprisingly realistic neighing noises.

'He has a good ear.' She got a cloth to unhook the cauldron, putting it down on a well-scorched wooden stand. 'And, of course, his father encourages him. Xan has gone. He rarely stays long.' A lingering note of regret underlay her words.

Troi was a little surprised and confused. 'I must go too,' he said hesitantly.

'No,' she said. 'You're to stay here a while.'

She offered no explanation, but he understood. She busied herself round the kitchen, chattering to Andro. She made no attempt to engage Troi in conversation, so he sat down on a bench and withdrew into the dark place.

After a while, he said, 'They told me she was dead.'

'I know.' Her voice was soft and gentle.

He realised that she was sitting beside him. 'How can she be dead?'

She said nothing, but put her hand lightly on his arm. He saw Ariadne's long, elegant fingers resting there and began to cry, terrible wrenching sobs that tore at his throat and at his heart. Without a word, she put her arms around him and held him tightly.

EIGHTY-TWO

PERHAPS BECAUSE SOMETHING inside him recognised the danger and fought it, perhaps because Selene was naturally empathetic to an extraordinary degree, perhaps because the Gods are, ultimately, not without mercy, Troi did not fall again into the pit that split the earth at his feet. Instead of taking shelter within his own mind and shutting the doors on the painful world and those within it, he talked. He talked and she just let him, never questioning him, never advising him, never judging him.

She listened with such sympathy and silent understanding that he found himself telling her everything. He told her of his mother and Aias, of Phoebe's death and Amber rushing at the bear, of Gian and the soldier Troi had toyed with and slain at the ambush of the supply train, of Klio's desperate and awkward attempt at seduction. Of how she had said she loved him and he had walked away, but also of how, perhaps, if he had not met Ari, he might have returned to her. He told her how he had beaten poor, weak-minded Triopas and sent Nicias to his death without a second thought. He found himself telling her more than he would have ever told Ariadne.

But, above all, he told her of Ariadne herself, of her mercurial spirit and her luminous beauty, of her wry sense of humour, how her eyes crinkled when she smiled and the husky way that she told him she loved him that made his heart do handstands. Of the touch of her hand. More than anything else, the aching desolation of loss that bled all colour and savour from the world and left it a grey and hopeless void.

Meeting his pain face to face slowly brought a calm, an acceptance. The dreadful hurt did not go away, but he could live with it.

They sat in the late afternoon sun of a fine summer's day, on the steps leading up to the hay barn. He spoke hesitantly. 'I think I lost so much, so quickly, that I slammed shut the door on everything.' He was trying to make sense of the changes that spun him in a maelstrom of uncertainty. He was still not sure who he was.

As usual, Selene said nothing, but her large eyes were upon him, and she held one of his hands in hers.

He looked down. 'I denied them. All of them. I denied them their… their rights of grief. My mother and father. Aias. Gian. They deserved, they needed, to be mourned. And they weren't. Their tombs should have been watered with tears. But I'd none to give. No tears. None. And to deny them, I had to deny everybody. Each person around me was a sort of shadow, an insubstantial thing, a puppet playing a role, no feelings, no pain, nothing. Nothing that happened to them had any meaning.'

He looked at her, his eyes agonised. 'I was some kind of monster, Selene. Xan knew it. Diomedes knew it. Klio knew it, but she thought she could cure me.' He sighed. 'She might have too, if I'd only given her a chance.' He thought for a heartbeat. 'Poor Klio, how I hurt her and gave it no mind.' He scrubbed his hand through his hair. 'Only Ari didn't know it, and she somehow brought me back.' He paused. He dredged up his words with difficulty. 'And I could have fallen back into the same state; I would have, except for you.' He put his other hand on hers and held it tightly. 'Thank you, Selene.'

She smiled. 'You've spoken of Klio. She sounds like a kind and supportive woman who would be your friend. You could write to her. She might be a needed rock in a stormy ocean.'

'I… I hadn't thought of it. I might do that. I could tell her she'd been right all the time.'

'After all she tried to do for you,' said Selene quietly, 'she deserves that, at least.'

His eyes grew distant. 'It would be good to see her again.'

'Then consider it.' She paused. 'I'm sorry that I can't take away the pain.'

'Life is pain.' It was trite, and sounded trite, but he meant it. He stared unseeingly over the shallow stream. A sandpiper pottered along the muddy margins, and clouds of midges hung in the still air. 'If I knew, when I go to sleep tonight, that I wouldn't wake again, I'd be content.'

She cast a sidelong glance at him.

'Don't worry, Selene, I don't plan on killing myself. I wouldn't waste all your good work.'

He looked at one of the dogs, who sat up to inflict a highly satisfactory scratch on its ear, and then flopped down again. He did not see it. 'I've been thinking a lot about life recently. And I've come to the conclusion that, overall, life is tedious, back-breaking work, discomfort, disease and danger. Our greatest happiness always has worry at its heart, like the maggot in an apple. Even at its best, life is rarely more than tolerable. At its worst, it's torment and misery.'

There was a long silence. 'There are rare moments, of course,' he went on quietly. 'Sudden brief shafts of sunshine through the storm clouds, and we remember and cherish them. They colour all our memories so that life seems golden, when in truth it's drab and chill. I don't know why we fool ourselves so readily. It's some cruel joke of the Gods. To trick us into clinging, like a shipwrecked sailor, to the flotsam of life, when it would be so much easier to let go, to drown and simply end it.'

'Perhaps you will feel better about life in time,' she said. He realised that her eyes were on Androcles, who was sailing a little wooden boat along a cattle trough.

And how will your joy and pride survive the day he is brought back on his shield, red with blood and gasping his last breath? But Troi did not say it. 'Perhaps,' he agreed, without any conviction. 'But at least now I'm not alone in it. I can laugh with others, cry with others, feel for others.'

'Forgive others?' she asked. It was almost the first time that she had asked him a question.

'Most,' he said after a moment, 'but not all.' His tone was grim. 'I still have something to do. An oath I have sworn.'

EIGHTY-THREE

TROI RETURNED TO duty and threw himself into his work. He became the epitome of the dedicated officer. Every moment when the demands of duty occupied his mind was a time when the image of Ariadne could recede, when the dull ache of loss could be momentarily submerged beneath more pressing needs, and when he could forget, for hekates at a time, that his life had lost its very meaning.

The scrolls from Klio were no longer minor irritants, but seemed one of the few connections to another and better life. Her gossip about the enclosed microcosm of the Villa Antipatroi spoke of a world far removed from this brutal Hades of war and killing, and he would write back immediately. It was an anchor that held him fixed on a shifting sea.

But the nights remained. And he was dreaming again. The dreams were better than before. And worse. Ari would be there, her arm across him, laughing at him. 'You stupid man. But isn't that a tautology?' And he would roll over to the sunrise of her smile, the soft, sweet caress of her eyes and the gentle touch of her fingers on his cheek. The feeling of relief, that her death had just been a dream, would be… indescribable. And then he would awake to dismal reality, cruelly finding the dream had been but a mask for the night hag, which revealed itself only on his waking. The pain of losing her again would break his heart, so that he would weep to dream once more.

EIGHTY-FOUR

THE SIEGE OF the Akroakrai had continued. Fifteen days went by before the ramp had been repaired sufficiently to carry the huge, bronze-headed battering ram, hanging from its solid, wheeled protective shed, clad in dampened animal hides. It lurched forward painfully slowly, pushed by hundreds of men beneath covering shields, frequently stopping for long periods as the wheels stuck.

Halfway up the ramp, a salpinx blared from the ramparts above. The wary Troians halted, looking around them for whatever unpleasant surprise awaited them. At first, they could see nothing. Then curls of smoke began to appear from between the stones at their feet. The officers yelled to get the ram back, but it had scarcely started moving when the ground suddenly collapsed and the ram tumbled into the gaping hole, breaking into three pieces.

The two volunteers who had fired the pitch-soaked wooden supports in the cavern excavated beneath the ramp had already slipped quietly away, along a camouflaged route to a cleverly concealed hideaway. They regained the fortress that night via lowered ropes.

The new hole was tediously filled and two more rams were made, at the expense of valuable time, only to be destroyed by the rain of rock and fire from above. The fourth ram eventually brought some of the masonry down to reveal packed earth beyond. The sappers quickly began to burrow through it, only, to their dismay, to find themselves stopped by another masonry wall. The Mykerenaeans had built no fewer than four well-buttressed walls, interspersed with solidly packed earth, and were prepared to build more if necessary. But enough was enough.

Marsyas, after an abortive and spectacularly disorganised night attack, decided to starve them out. It would occupy his entire army. His advisors told him that to lead the larger part of his army elsewhere would result in any masking force left behind falling prey to the Mykerenaean army, prowling about them like wolves in the shadows beyond a campfire, and then the Boreas would be closed for good. As it was, the supply convoys were taking a considerable proportion of Troian troops to get them through, and one in five was not making it.

Throughout the short, dark days of winter and well into the greening of spring, Marsyas stayed quiescent, doing nothing but blockade the Akroakrai. Eventually, his strength and army morale inexorably weakening, though not as rapidly as the fragile patience of Laomedon, he was obliged to return to direct assault. Harpalycus conducted spoiling attacks in support of the dwindling band of defenders. Every night became a terror as the Agrianes slipped stealthily about their murderous business, every day a series of alarms as the Thracians launched their highly effective hit-and-run raids. Every se'ennight brought a long list of lost patrols, ambushed reinforcements and destroyed supply trains. Above all, the incessant drain of desertions and defections that weakened the Troians and strengthened the rebels.

Nevertheless, Diomedes' men were becoming fewer every day, each assault was more difficult to beat back, and there was now an inevitability that could not be denied. But the price of blood had duly purchased immeasurably valuable time. In Pelium and Naupactos, the new phalanxes were perfecting their drills, more mercenaries arrived each day, trained units were beginning the long march across the Vale to join Harpalycus, and volunteers continued to flood in. The balance of power was shifting. Akrai had indeed been the deciding factor.

EIGHTY-FIVE

Diomedes clambered up onto the fall of broken stone and looked out across the dark masses of assault troops forming up. It was a beautiful morning, still and sharp, with a golden sun pulsing warmth from the cerulean sky, just a few wisps of high cirrus marring its perfection. A robin hopped amongst the blocks of stone and stopped to regard Diomedes with a beady eye. Everything was so clear and bright and… perfect.

The occasional zip of a catapult-fired bolt reached his ears, but the Trogs would be lucky to hit him at this distance. Behind him, the tired, grimy and bandaged remnants of his command were making their final preparations to meet the oncoming tide that would wash them to oblivion. None would see nightfall.

It had finally come. The Troians must have scoured the Empire for engineers, and some clever bugger had identified a thin stretch of wall that had been awkwardly built over a difficult outcropping of limestone. Large catapults had launched grapnels attached to winches, and the previous day they had finally succeeded in partially collapsing the section. Now they were coming. He had hoped the defenders would have longer, but thought it would be enough. He rolled his shoulders and began to do stretching exercises.

There was a scramble behind him, and Praxis appeared, a dirty, blood-stained rag bound around his temples. He glanced at the assembling hordes.

A bolt struck a masonry block some distance away and shattered. The robin flew off with its sharp tick of alarm. The crew of the catapult began the laborious task of winding back the bow against the powerful resistance of the twisted ropes.

'Three hundred and twenty-seven days,' observed Praxis. 'I told you we wouldn't make the year. Pay up.'

Diomedes had been expecting this. He fished in his pouch for an obol and tossed it to the small red-bearded man. His comrade caught the coin deftly and regarded it triumphantly. 'Pays for the crossing.' He turned to go.

'Prax,' said Diomedes, still watching the Troian preparations, 'we've had our differences, but you're a fine soldier, and I'll be proud to die in your company.'

Praxis stopped and gave a wry smile. 'And I—'

There was a thump and Diomedes flew backwards to crash into a tumble of fallen blocks. Praxis was down and kneeling by his side immediately. The heavy bolt had penetrated the bronze cuirass as if it were cotton. Blood was bubbling at the corner of his mouth, and his eyes desperately sought those of his companion and caught them in an unbreakable grip. He coughed up blood and tried to speak. It sounded something like 'Al', and then he was gone.

The little man looked down on him for a few heartbeats, then, surprisingly tenderly, closed the eyes. The mouth was slightly open. Praxis took the obol and slipped it under the tongue.

'We'll meet on the other side,' he said, then stood and walked back up over the partially collapsed curtain wall.

Behind him, salpinxes sounded. Before him, the last defenders manned the new structure they had built to seal off the breach. But it was weak and would not hold.

'Right, you lazy bastards,' he roared. 'Time to earn your fucking pay.'

EIGHTY-SIX

On the twenty-first day of Mounichion, in the year 512, three hundred and twenty-seven days after the Troians had first arrived at the gates, the ancient fortress finally fell. There were no survivors. The naked and mutilated bodies were hung from the walls in spite.

But Marsyas's moment of triumph was the flight of the mayfly. More terrified of the increasingly exasperated Laomedon than of the Mykerenaeans, he uncharacteristically flung his entire army over the Scyllan Mountains, via the Andros Pass, against the provincial capital of Plataea. Thirty-two days after the fall of Akrai, Harpalycus joined battle beneath the walls of the town. The Troians still held a significant advantage in numbers, and for a time it seemed numbers would tell, but the four phalanxes proved unstoppable and ground a bloody gap into the Troian frontage. The young strategos threw the Hetairoi, his elite heavy cavalry, across the grain of the battle, against the now-exposed flanks of two isolated speiroi. Their collapse created panic, and the Troians crumbled. They fled precipitously back across the pass, pursued and harried mercilessly by the Agrianes and Thracians.

The Troians tried to reform outside Akrai, but the advance of the now-powerful Mykerenaean army was too much for the craven spirit of Marsyas. He sacked and burned Akrai, long his base, and withdrew through the Boreas. Mykerenos had finally achieved its dream of freedom.

EIGHTY-SEVEN

HARPALYCUS LOOKED DOWN from the shadows of the pine forest at the long, shambling and dispirited column that slowly wound along the wide valley. It was an army in defeat. The units were intermingled and impeded by the overloaded supply wagons, discipline appeared to be collapsing, and the huge, stricken, writhing slug left a slick of abandoned equipment in its trail.

Every night, deserters stumbled up to the dark, terrifying tree line, white-faced, their hands high. Every morning, the Troians left a forest of improvised gibbets from which swung the bodies of those that had not made it past their own guards. Every evening, the Aggies crept down with their fearsome knives. They had taken to decapitating their victims and delighted in leaving cairns of their trophies in the path of the Troians. Every day, the Thracians would erupt from the trees to swoop on some group that had strayed from huddled safety, and leave yet another mound of dead and dying, transfixed with javelins like the spines of a hedgehog.

It was a race. Tortoise against tortoise. Moving through the difficult terrain of the flanking woodland, the great bulk of Harpalycus's forces could not be brought to bear. Much of the rebel army was following through the Boreas, but the best that it would be able to do was to tear and rend the Troian rearguard. It would be unable to stop Marsyas's retreat.

But Harpalycus held a weighted knucklebone. Immediately after Plataea, he had presciently sent Medraut and a phalanx, with supporting troops, along a high ridge route, the Broken Steps, that wriggled across to join the valley of the North Anopus, and then dropped down to cut the Boreas. If they could get there in time, they could block the Troian escape. Arrow riders were reporting that they were just not going to make it. Medraut was driving his men unmercifully, but the Troian van would pass the Anopus before they arrived.

There was yet hope. Marsyas, surrounded by a thick shield of his personal guards and best units, had placed himself in the very centre of the retreating army. Medraut estimated that his phalanx would be in position to cut the long column within two dekates. The pursuing forces, under Brasidas, were already in sight of the Trog rearguard, and Harpalycus had his light troops stationed along the forest edges.

A coordinated attack across such a distance was fraught with danger, not least if the Troian van should turn and trap the phalanx between the two halves of their army. But Harpalycus was confident that, given the poor morale and leadership of the Trogs, those beyond the jaws of the trap would depart post-haste, thankful for their deliverance.

He turned to Simonides with some crisp orders. The Chief of Staff hastily transcribed them to wax tablets, and arrow riders plunged away in various directions. It was approaching noon. The day was warm with fair-weather cumulus sailing serenely across the sky before a southerly breeze. Birds sang and called from the trees around them, and the long snake writhed and twisted below. As arrow riders arrived and left, Harpalycus sat patiently, estimating distances, rates of progress and time. He nodded in quiet satisfaction. The phalanx would, after all, be able to launch its attack downstream of the Butcher. The reckoning would be paid. At last. In full.

EIGHTY-EIGHT

TROI DROVE DOWN with three tetrarchia of the elite hypaspistai and light infantry support, tasked with taking the Butcher himself. The day of vengeance had finally arrived, though his lust for it was no longer the consuming blaze that it had been. In the gathered twilight, it had lost its much of its blistering intensity, but it still burned.

They had a hard fight of it. The Bluecloaks resisted with desperate courage and broke the rebel shield line. The fighting became fierce and individual. Troilus walked through the screams and clash of steel, the voided waste and the broken bodies, the sobbing of the wounded and the blood. Above all, the blood. But he took no more note of the carnage than the skylark still singing high overhead. He was looking for but one person as the mêlée surged back and forth around him.

Then he recognised the Bluecloak before him. He had watched Marsyas long enough to be able to immediately identify one of the three notorious Daemons, a thin man with a long chicken neck and a narrow face. Blood from a scalp wound ran down one side of his head, he was limping slightly, and there was a dark stain on his armour below his right arm. His face was pale and slick with sweat, but he still carried shield and sword. Unusually, he held the sword in his left hand. All three had always sparred right-handed. Troi immediately suspected that he was a natural left-hander who tried to keep it secret to give himself an advantage in a real fight. Behind the Daemon lay two blue-cloaked bodies encircled by a dozen or so dead hypaspistai. His eyes fixed on Troi, and he moved towards him.

Xan's words rang in Troi's mind. 'They know every dirty trick in the scroll.' He yanked his helmet off and tossed it to one side—he could not afford to have limited vision in such a fight—pushed his shield forward and gripped his spatha tightly.

Then the man was upon him. Troi had been taught well, and the Daemon was already wounded, but the savage onslaught of blows took him totally by surprise. He had to give ground, desperately blocking with shield and sword. They came with dizzying speed, and watching the man's cold eyes was no help at all. There was no warning of where the next blow would fall, no barely perceptible shift to signal its direction, just a frantic blur of speed and fear and instinct. Troi had no time for conscious thought until there was a moment's pause as they separated.

Three times he had been too late with a parry, thankfully never of a full blow; twice the man's sword was stopped by Troi's bronze cuirass, but there was a stinging cut across Troi's thigh, and the blood flowed freely. He could not feel it but knew it would tighten up and slow him down. This man was too good. He came at Troi again.

Troi retreated again before the whirlwind. Then his heel hit something and he stumbled backwards, only belatedly conscious that the Daemon was aiming a kick at his groin. The stumble saved him, as the Daemon's foot merely caught the inside of Troi's shin, but he lost his balance. He staggered back, reflexively spreading his arms to keep himself from falling. His assailant's shield swung quickly, trying to catch the inside of Troi's and knock it farther away, while his sword thrust forward at Troi's unprotected chest. Troi threw his own shield up to allow the Troian's shield to pass beneath it, catching it a jarring blow as it went. The buffet caused him to lose his balance completely, crashing downwards onto his back, the sword thrust flashing over his face.

He hit the ground hard enough to knock the air from his lungs, and looked up to see his death held high against the pure blue of the sky and about to descend with brutal finality. The blade flashed with reflected sunlight, and a drop of blood hung from the tip. The man grinned. A warping of his lips that never touched his soulless eyes. The momentary pause was all Troi needed. He kicked upwards and hit his assailant full in the testicles.

The man screamed, and Troi, flat on his back, swung his heavy sword round at full stretch across his body and caught him hard on the ankle. He collapsed in a clatter of metal, and Troi released his shield and rolled away before scrambling to his feet. The Daemon was trying to rise, but his foot was hanging from the end of his leg by tendons, and he was helpless. Troi chopped down swiftly and severed the man's sword hand, then stood beside him, seeing nothing in the cold, emotionless eyes that stared up at him. But only for a heartbeat—he wasn't going to make the same mistake as the Daemon—before burying his sword in the man's throat. A gush of blood, a horrible gargling noise, a shuddering, and the eyes stared at him with that same indifference and then went still.

Troi leaned on his sword, breathing heavily, and looked around. It was all over. Mel's Aggies had come swarming down the valley side from the tree line and smashed into the rear of the Bluecloaks, finishing them for good. The last few were being hunted down when Troi spotted his aide some distance away, obviously searching for him.

The aide saw him at the same moment and ran across, a stocky, ruddy-faced youth with a mess of straw-coloured hair, obviously very relieved to find Troi.

'Sorry, sir, got waylaid by a Bluecloak or three.' He stopped and stared at the blood-soaked, spread-eagled corpse at Troi's feet. 'Did you do that?'

Troi nodded.

'Remind me never to annoy you, sir.' He looked to the scatter of bodies beyond. 'Was he one of the Daemons?'

'Certainly fought like one. More importantly, any news of Marsyas?'

'I'm afraid not, sir. The bastard's disappeared.'

Troi sighed. 'Let's get back to the horses.'

EIGHTY-NINE

A HEAVILY BANDAGED TROI guided his horse through the detritus of battle. Behind him rode his aide and his guards, along with a brace of arrow riders. In most places, the corpses were remarkably few in number. Huddles of dispirited prisoners stood around, each under the careless watch of a few bowmen or a small squad of hoplites. The overwhelming majority of the Troian forces had surrendered the instant they saw the Mykerenaeans break cover. The van of the army had taken one brief look, then disappeared down the pass at the ram. Behind them, standards had fallen to the ground in swathes like trees before a tempest, weapons discarded, hands raised.

Only in one place did Troi find bodies lying in drifts and heaps, the air thick with the stench of death and the ceaseless moans and cries of the wounded. Only here, where Marsyas had surrounded himself with his personal guard, had they fought, and fought desperately, knowing there would be little mercy for those who wore the blue cloak.

Most of the Bluecloaks had died, though a small group of thirty or so, many clutching bloody wounds, sat nervously to one side, under the close scrutiny of some Agrianes. The Aggies not only looked as though they would happily slit their throats for a bent obol, but actually would. Meleagros was sitting by, chewing on a bit of boustria. He raised a hand in greeting to Troi.

Troi got down stiffly from his horse. 'No sign?'

'Not yet, but he can't be far. We'll have the fucker. My Aggies are searching up to the tree line. I've sent for scouts. My lads won't go in until Gwalchmai's boys have had a good look.'

'You've checked those prisoners, I presume? He isn't pretending to be a common soldier?'

'Been there before you, laddie. Unless he's managed to lose fifty minae overnight, he's not part of that sorry bunch.'

Troi glanced across at the dejected group and stiffened. 'By all the Gods great and small.'

Meleagros looked up enquiringly, but Troi simply stalked across to the prisoners and stared down at the nearest man, who wore the sash and brooch of an officer. The man looked up, fear clenching his narrow blue eyes, his long face pale. Black slicked-back hair, pointed chin, hooked nose. Troi slowly removed his helmet. The man sprang to his feet. His face, pale before, lost all colour. His mouth hung slackly open, his eyes suddenly wide.

'It c-can't be,' he stammered. 'You're d-d-dead.'

'I must look worse than I thought.'

'You were hanged.'

'Obviously some administrative mistake,' said Troi comfortingly. 'If a hanging is required, I'm sure we can rectify the situation.'

The man stepped back. 'No,' he said. 'No.'

Meleagros had joined them, still chewing on his boustria. He glanced curiously at Troi. 'Friend of yours?'

'Let's say that I know him. But I don't know his name.' He cocked a quizzical eyebrow at the ashen-faced officer.

'Sicinnos, son of T-T-Telekles,' the man finally managed to get out.

'That's a bad stutter, my friend. There was no sign of it at Tegea. You remember Tegea, don't you?' The man shook his head violently. 'You know, that lovely little village in the water meadows with the clapper bridge. You must recall. Bridge. Village. Bridge. Bridge. Village. Bridge. It's a little pastoral scene that has stuck in my memory for some reason.'

'It must have b-been another officer,' cried Sicinnos desperately.

'Oh, no, it was definitely you. You must remember.' His voice hardened gradually. 'The one where you took all those able to work, then left orders to burn the place and slaughter the old, the sick and the children. That one.' He was spitting venom. 'You must remember it.'

'I was f-f-following orders. I had no choice.' His voice was choked.

'You always have a choice.' Troi glanced across the battlefield, to where a supply wagon had been tipped on its side against a boulder, its oxen, their traces cut, placidly grazing on the rough grass. The shaft was angled high against the sky.

'Hang the bugger,' he said.

'You can't,' said Sicinnos weakly.

'Really? Why?' Troi's voice was harsh but controlled. 'Because it's against the law of arms? Because it's immoral? Because it's forbidden by the Gods? Which of those arguments would you dare to choose?'

Tears were pouring from the man's eyes. He fell on his knees. For a heartbeat, Troi actually felt sorry for the snivelling, snot-nosed, cringing apology for an officer. Then he remembered Ariadne. Her screams as they dragged her from the tent. It would be over too quickly for him.

He gestured to two of his guards, who dismounted and hauled the shaking man to his feet. Troi's aide rode over to the wagon, leaned over and triumphantly drew forth a length of rope. Sicinnos could not speak. His mouth opened and closed, but no sound came out.

Meleagros shook his head. He spoke softly. 'Can't be done, laddie. It's not right.'

'What he did wasn't right,' snarled Troi. 'I promised him a bad death, and a bad death he shall have.'

'You know Harp's orders.'

'I don't give a fuck. He was the bastard who took Ariadne.' His voice broke for a moment. Then strengthened. 'And I want him to remember that as we haul him off the ground. I've seen men take a long time dying on the end of a rope, and I'll savour every heartbeat.'

Sicinnos was swaying on his feet and looked about to collapse. His face was bloodless and slick with sweat. He was moaning weakly.

'Listen to me,' said Meleagros. 'If he did what you say he did, and I'm not questioning it,' he added quickly as Troi threw him an angry glare, 'then he'll hang. No question. The sorry bastard will just have that much more time to look forward to it.'

Troi looked at him, wavering.

'If you kill without trial, you would be harnessed to the same chariot as that piece of shit, Marsyas.'

Troi stared at him. The memory of his own 'trial' suddenly rose vividly in his mind. Then a vision of Diomedes, sitting across from him at the small table, looking at him with sorrowing eyes. 'You will become Marsyas.' For a few heartbeats, Troi was at war with himself; then he slumped slightly, conceding defeat.

'You're right, Mel.' He eyed the uprearing shaft regretfully. 'Pity, though. Never mind, it will come.'

He turned to his aide. 'Phorbas, your sole duty, until further notice, is to keep that evil whoreson in confinement, and to get the witnesses to build a case that will hang him. No failure and no excuses.'

'Yes, sir,' Phorbas acknowledged crisply. 'No problem.' He yelled across to a squad of hoplites moving past. 'Dilocho, here, with your men, ramming speed.'

The men broke ranks and ran across.

'Pinion that piece of vomit.' Phorbas threw the length of rope to the ektaktos. The dilochagos cut the rope with his knife, and began to bind the trembling prisoner, just as an unmistakable yell of triumph rolled across the battlefield. Troi instantly turned in its direction. Some hoplites were standing round an ox cart, gesticulating wildly.

It could only mean one thing.

NINETY

TROI FLUNG HIMSELF onto his horse and urged it forward. Meleagros, who disdainfully eschewed horses when he was with his beloved Agrianes, ran alongside. Galloping down the valley side came a group clustered beneath the red and black wolf's-head banner. Other small clumps of officers were converging from every direction. Everyone knew what it meant.

Troi arrived first and slid from his horse before it had stopped. A bearded lochagos, his red face split with a massive grin, saluted. 'The bastard's under there, sir.'

Troi crouched down and peered beneath the wagon. Hanging desperately, his ankles hooked painfully over the rear axle, his podgy fingers clinging onto the front one with white-knuckled determination, was a fat man whose black hair was plastered to his skull with sweat. He was making strangled, whimpering noises. His terrified eyes stared into Troi's.

Troi felt a surge of relief, followed by sheer elation. It was over at last. He grinned. 'Well, well, my Lord Satrap. Isn't it more usual to ride on top of the cart? More befitting your lordly status.' Marsyas began blubbering. Troi straightened up, still grinning, as Harpalycus arrived and dismounted.

'Marsyas?'

'Indeed.' Troi was unable to keep the delight from bubbling in his voice. 'The Butcher himself.'

Harpalycus nodded. 'Good. Get the sod out.'

Troi gestured to the lochagos, who crawled beneath the cart. There was a thump as he unhooked Marsyas's feet, followed by a few hekates of straining and grunting.

'Bugger won't fucking let go, sir.'

'Allow me,' said Troi, reaching into the ox cart's toolbox and withdrawing a suitable mallet. He slid underneath and smashed Marsyas's fingers without a moment's hesitation. The man screamed and fell to the ground. Troi and the lochagos grasped his ankles and hauled him bodily from under the cart, his broken left hand leaving a thin trail of blood.

A circle of officers and soldiers looked down at the quintessence of evil, the interloper who had ruled their homeland with terror and cruelty, the bugbear that frightened child and man alike. He was a short, fat man, bawling his eyes out, laid in a pool of his own urine. A paltry thing that evoked contempt rather than fear. There was a murmur of demands that he be hung, crucified, flung on a burning pyre. The suggestions escalated rapidly. Harpalycus raised a hand, and the voices died away.

'We cannot kill him without a trial. And a trial he will have.'

'We can let him go, though,' said Troi suddenly. The incredulous silence that followed was almost tangible. 'There's no requirement that we take him prisoner.'

Harpalycus was looking at him and frowning. Meleagros's mouth was hanging open.

Troi gave a savage smile. 'There's a village only ten or twelve stadia back. Or, rather, there was a village. Until this bastard—' He kicked Marsyas hard in the side, who howled with pain. 'Sorry, foot slipped—decided to wreak his so-called vengeance on it. Women and children slaughtered. The place burned. But they had time for a lot to get away. They'll be back now. I suggest that we leave him there for his faithful subjects to lovingly tend his wounds.'

Meleagros grinned wolfishly. 'It would save a lot of bother.'

'You're serious,' said Harpalycus.

'I bloody well am,' agreed Troi. There was a rising murmur of support from all round.

Harpalycus surveyed the angry mob and considered. 'No-one has more right than you, Troi. It will be just.'

The lochagos and Troi quickly bound the ankles and wrists of the struggling, gibbering Marsyas and threw him bodily across the withers of Troi's horse. Troi mounted, as did Harpalycus, who surveyed the burgeoning crowd. 'We're not taking this lot.' He looked round, quickly naming the senior officers present. 'Sim. Bras. Medraut. Tereus. Xander. Sorry, Mel, you don't have a horse.'

Meleagros reached up and hauled a surprised cavalryman from his mount to fall in a heap on the ground, and launched himself onto the vacated saddle cloth. 'Yes, I fucking well do.'

Harpalycus grinned. 'Hektor,' he added. Then he shifted his gaze to the edges of the now-seething mass. 'Xan,' he called. 'You deserve to come.' Xanthos pushed through the throng on his shaggy pony and slapped Troi on the back. Harpalycus looked down at the lochagos. 'Report to me tonight with your squad. You did well.'

'Sir,' said the delighted man, his teeth white amidst his bushy black beard.

'The rest get about your duties. This day sees the freedom of Mykerenos.' There was a tremendous cheer, probably heard as far as Tanagra, as the small group manoeuvred their horses through the throng and set off at a steady trot towards the once-prosperous and picturesque sheep-farming village of Paros.

The terrified Marsyas just would not stay quiet. He wept and cajoled, made blood-curdling threats and vindictive curses, offered vast sums of money. He even had the nerve to claim he was innocent. That finally angered Troi.

'Do you recall Bogazkoi?' he said eventually, once the boiling in his blood had subsided slightly. 'My father, my friends, my neighbours: all slaughtered.'

'The men got out of hand. It wasn't my fault.' His desperate cries, interspersed with sobs, were difficult to make out.

'You ordered the beheading of Elissa and the others.'

'I had to. It was the only way to prevent further bloodshed.'

'And the deliberate murder of the old, the lame and the children at the village of Tegea.'

‘The officer exceeded his orders.’ Marsyas’s words seemed more confident. The whimpering was less insistent. He was beginning to hope that he had found someone who would listen. He had answers.

‘Above all,’ said Troi quietly, ‘a few days after your first attack on the Akro, you took to your loathsome bed a young girl and then smashed open her skull.’

He remembered. There was a moment’s silence. ‘She attacked me,’ he cried desperately. Troi drove his elbow into the man’s kidneys. Marsyas screamed. Harpalycus slowed his horse and looked round, questioningly.

‘Elbow slipped,’ said Troi innocently. ‘Seem to be all feet and elbows today.’ Simonides gave one of his famous humphs. Alexandros and Meleagros laughed out loud. Marsyas whimpered and sobbed and moaned. They rode on.

Troi leaned forward. ‘I hope you’re a very long time dying, you sick bastard. If it was a hundred years, it would be but a pebble alongside Olympus. But think on. When you finally cross the Styx, there will be thousands awaiting your arrival on the farther shore. And you can’t die in Hades. Only scream.’ That quietened the monster. For a short time.

NINETY-ONE

When they arrived, the fires were still burning. Some men were hooking the burning thatch down from a cottage. A line of corpses, many tiny, lay in a row in the small agora, covered with roughly woven cloaks. A few women were tending to some wounded in the shade of a half-collapsed porch. All stopped and stared. Marsyas, who had started blabbing again, all but incomprehensible in his terror, fell silent.

Harpalycus spoke, loud and commanding. 'People of Paros. Nothing can take away your grief and suffering. But I bring a gift that may assuage it just a little.' He nodded slightly to Troi, who slit the bonds round Marsyas's wrists and ankles and dumped him unceremoniously onto the ash-

and blood-smeared ground in a blubbering heap. 'I give you Marsyas, the Butcher of Mykerenos.'

The villagers stood and stared. More were quietly arriving. Some were drifting away and returning with knives, mattocks and scythes. Harpalycus looked around at the gathering crowd. Troi could see tears in his eyes. 'May it give you some comfort.' He turned his horse and walked off, followed by the others.

Marsyas scrambled to his feet. 'Please,' he wailed. 'You can't leave me.'

He began to stagger after them. There was not a sound from the villagers as they slowly converged on their erstwhile satrap. Harpalycus urged his horse into a trot, and the rest followed suit. Marsyas began to run, his belly wobbling, sobbing with terror, screaming for them to wait. They began to canter. The villagers inexorably moved in. None of the officers looked back. The almost inhuman screaming began as they left the ruined village, and it continued thereafter, constantly, until it eventually faded into the distance. Xanthos glanced across at Troi. He had no need to ask.

'No,' said Troi sadly, 'it doesn't make me feel any better.' His mind was full of faces that looked upon him with sad eyes and tore at his heart. But for some reason, the screams reverberated in his skull. For all that Marsyas had done, they were still the screams of a living creature, and they brought no satisfaction. Troi did not regret his part in Marsyas's end. It had been deserved and as just as anything could be in this unjust world. But it changed nothing.

And he would be there when they hanged Sicinnos, but he would gain no pleasure from it. In his pain and anger, he would have hanged him then and there, but Mel had been right: he would have looked back on it in shame. Nothing would bring back Ariadne or Aias. Nor would it give Nicias life once more. Where he had seemed to be following so simple, so clear a sunlit route, now he was adrift on the fog-hung deep. The one guiding fire that was to bring him through the writhing sea fret had been extinguished. The only constant in his life for two and a half years was gone, and there was little left, save to go on fighting. Laomedon remained.

They were re-entering the fringes of the battlefield. Troi looked down at a white-faced speiros, his face awash with sweat, his eyes glassy, his hands vainly trying to hold in a tumble of entrails. Troi got down from his horse, drawing his long knife. He knelt by the man and put his hand gently on his brow. The man's eyes focussed on Troi's face.

'It is time for Elysium, for peace,' said Troi.

The man's hand came up, waving feebly.

Troi took it in his left hand and gripped it strongly. 'Sleep well, my friend.'

'Thank you.' A breath so faint that he could hardly hear it.

He efficiently thrust the dagger straight into the heart. The man shuddered and died. Troi closed the man's eyes and looked around at the flotsam of death, listened to the clamor of groans and anguished cries for help, smelt the unmistakable stink of blood and sweat, urine and faeces, and swore the Great Oath for the third time, his hand on the bloody blade of his dagger. When they had gained the victory, when Gea was free once again, when Laomedon lay as still and cold as this spearman, when his ghosts were finally laid to rest and the night hag rode no more, he would walk away and never fight again. He owed Ariadne. "Then let's do away with officers. Do away with soldiers. With war." He would war no more.

He still needed the peace and time to heal fully, or, at least, as much as he ever could. He dreamed of a place of rest and tranquillity, as far from strife as possible, and he thought he knew of such a place.

NINETY-TWO

TWO MOONTIDES LATER, and Harpalycus had stopped a half-hearted Troian excursion from Tanagra, while Phormio had won a spectacular victory over the Troian fleet when they had attempted to descend on Pelium. He had ambushed them, using newly built triremes with reinforced rams. His highly trained crews rammed and backed water, instead of using traditional boarding tactics, and all but annihilated them. The Propontis had effectively become a Mykerenaean lake. In the next meeting of the High Command, Phormio was particularly expansive about the battle, still smarting as he was from the loss of a squadron of triremes that had been trapped and burned in the Bay of Nestor.

Troi had been engaged in mopping up the last vestiges of Troian presence in the Vale, the units and garrisons abandoned to their fate by Marsyas's cowardly scuttle. It had been easy enough. The Troians, terrified of the revenge of the local population, were only too ready to surrender to a suitable force, and they had little need for guards. But sometimes Troi had arrived too late, and the results were not pretty.

It was early in a cool, blustery and rather grey afternoon as his tired men, with a long, shambling line of prisoners bringing up the rear, entered Akrai. The town was being rebuilt, chosen as the strategic centre for the now-impressive Mykerenaean army. The Akroakrai was under repair, and a mausoleum had been erected over the graves of the dead, long since removed from the walls and entombed with due ceremony and honours. Troi had bespoken a golden sword to be buried with Diomedes. He was now at peace.

The war was not over, and Harpalycus was already planning a strike at Leuctra, at the head of the Scyllan Gulf, to wrest the entire east of the country from Laomedon's grip. But there was a lull, and they would soon be into autumn. Winter would stanch the bloodletting with its icy grasp, but only temporarily.

Troi ordered his deuteros to see to the prisoners and wearily dismounted, handing his horse over to the waiting groom. He had a room in the town, and the quickest way was through the training ground. Several squads were there, wilting under the verbal lash of their drill masters. An officer was standing, watching his hyperetes berate an unfortunate soul who was apparently uncertain as to the difference between right and left. Troi recognised the officer immediately and went over.

'Sarpedon, well met.'

The Troian swung round, startled, but to Troi's mind did not seem at all pleased to see him.

Troi put his hand out, and there was a moment's hesitation before Sarpedon took his wrist.

Troi was a little disconcerted by Sarpedon's attitude. 'So, you decided to jump from ship to shore. I hoped that you would.'

'I was given the chance.' He appeared strangely reluctant to speak.

'Tell all,' urged Troi.

Sarpedon seemed to consider, then spoke. 'When you hit us in the Boreas, there was no option but to surrender. Now I can tell myself I did my duty and start afresh. Have done with Laomedon once and for all.'

'Well, we're pleased that you're aboard.'

Sarpedon turned away from him to watch his men shuffle together into a somewhat disorganised shield wall. 'Get closer, you useless prats,' yelled the exasperated hyperetes. 'Tighter than a porna's grip on your obols.'

Troi tried again. 'I've never properly thanked you for what you did. Were there any problems?'

Sarpedon shook his head. 'Just filled in a report that nobody read.' He glanced significantly at Troi's sash and chiliarches' brooch. 'Nobody guessed that they had a full-maned lion in their grasp.'

'Well, I thank you nevertheless. I owe you.'

Sarpedon was back to watching the squad attempt a reverse line. He nodded in an offhand manner.

Troi was puzzled, then suddenly angry. 'What in Hades is it?' he demanded. 'You're making me as welcome as a whore at a wedding feast.'

Sarpedon turned and looked at him. His eyes were hard. 'Dyaus's balls. What do you think? You abandon the girl because Marsyas brutalised her. Too grand to take another man's leavings, no matter her needs?'

Troi stared at him. In shock. 'Abandon her?' Then he slowly picked sense out of the reeling confusion. 'You can't mean that she's alive?'

'Of course she's alive. In Himera. As I told you she would be.' It was his turn to stare at Troi. 'You didn't know?'

'They said she was brought out a corpse, with her head smashed in.'

'She had certainly been hit hard, but Rhea has the touch of Aesculapes. She recovered.'

Troi just continued to stare. Something was bubbling up inside. An ineffable feeling that rose, glistening and free, like a dolphin surging from its cool, dark element to cartwheel gleefully through the sunlight in a shower of spray. It was a feeling he had never felt before.

'She's alive,' he whispered. 'Alive.'

NINETY-THREE

TROI STOPPED HIS horse and looked down. It was a perfect early autumnal day, the blue vault of the heavens unmarred by any cloud, the air fresh and cool, the trees burning to ochres and golds, and the distant mountains as sharp as a Thracian's dagger.

The diminutive, willow-fringed stream that ran past Himera's small cluster of buildings was crystal clear. The long waving fronds of waterweed were alive with the silver flash of fish, a heron stalked the shallows with slow and stately deliberation, and grey wagtails fed busily along the stream's margins.

She was sitting on a large boulder, knees drawn up within the compass of her slim brown arms, gazing meditatively across the waters. He could see the ugly scar on the side of her head, just behind her ear, imperfectly hidden by thinner hair.

'Ariadne,' he called quietly, sliding down from his horse.

She swung round, and the smile on her face was the sun, the moon and the stars.

NINETY-FOUR

A COLD NORTHERLY WIND drove the thick grey clouds before it. It was not actually raining but threatening to. Klio shivered and drew her cloak more tightly around her. She stood and waited at the gate to the garden that fronted the villa. She did not know what to make of the scroll Troi had sent.

He had written that he was coming "home", though just for a brief visit. And he would have someone with him. But she was not to worry. It was not as she might think. He would explain all.

Her favourite hound had recently whelped, and one of the puppies had followed her and was busy excavating a hole in an empty flower bed. Otherwise she was alone. She had sent everyone away, only wishing Ilus was here with her;

but he had died in battle outside Plataea. The anxiety and uncertainty inside her were building to intolerable levels, so that she closed her eyes tightly and rocked back and forth, desperate to relieve the tension. She prayed silently to the Lady Herakla.

When she opened her eyes, there was a small group climbing the track from the river. She almost stopped breathing. As they approached, she saw that amongst the expected escort of guards and aides were two women. One looked elderly, but the other was far from it.

She was benumbed with shock, her mind racing like a chariot wheel spinning eerily along on its own, broken from the wreck of the chariot that scarred the neatly raked sand of her life. They were closer now. Even though wrapped within a cloak, the younger woman was manifestly beautiful, slim and tall, and Klio hated her. She wanted to turn and run, but could not move. She was scarcely even aware of Troi as they rode up.

'Klio,' said Troi. 'It's good to see you. This is Ariadne. Ariadne, your Auntie Klio, whom I told you about.'

Ariadne gave her a huge smile. 'Hello, Auntie Klio,' she said in a strangely childish voice. Then her eyes suddenly widened. She was gazing beyond Klio. 'Ooh, a puppy.' She looked round at Troi beseechingly. 'Can I play with the puppy, Uncle Troi?'

'Of course, darling. But you must be careful and gentle with it.'

'I promise.'

She almost tumbled off her horse in her haste. Troi turned and made a slight hand signal to the tiny, elderly woman, grey-haired and rose-cheeked, who nodded, then got down from her horse with more than a hint of stiffness. She was clearly tasked with keeping an eye on Ariadne.

Klio watched in bemusement as the young woman swooped on the puppy, picked it up, tickled its small, round belly, made cooing noises, and then broke into giggles.

Klio looked at Troi for the first time, her eyes questioning.

'We need to talk,' he said.

NINETY-FIVE

THEY WALKED A well-worn path beside the river, past the reed beds and weeping willows that clung desperately to their last few leaves, past the clumps of hawthorn and the small coppices of alder and oak.

Ahead of them, Ariadne was with Rhea, throwing sticks into the water, and then clapping her hands delightedly as they swirled and twisted downstream, racing each other on the current. The fat puppy, presented to a delighted Ariadne and imaginatively rechristened Fat Puppy, bumbled along in their wake, lost in a wonderful world of new smells, until he came across a red squirrel and clumsily chased it up a tree. When the squirrel chittered angrily, Fat Puppy sat down with a bump and a surprised expression, and Ariadne laughed. She laughed a great deal.

'She's a very good-natured kid,' said Troi, though it sounded odd to describe the lithe, graceful and beautiful young woman as such. 'But she is physically mature, so she gets the moon sickness. She can get a little grumpy then.' He smiled. 'Surprisingly enough.'

'Will she…' Klio sought for the right word. '…improve?'

'Rhea is positive that she will be like this all the rest of her life. There has certainly been no change in her so far.'

'Does she remember anything?' Klio was nervous and tended to speak rapidly.

'Not a thing. She had no idea who I was.' There was a world of regret in his voice. 'Rhea had to teach her her own name. But not remembering is a blessing from the Gods.'

'What if she does begin to mature?' she asked hesitantly.

Troi knew her underlying concern well enough. 'I don't know, Klio,' he said honestly, 'but I really don't think she will.'

'She is physically a young woman.' She struggled with what she wanted to say, what she needed to say. 'Is there…? Have you…?' She flushed, and her voice died away in agonised embarrassment.

He immediately divined what she was trying to ask. 'No, she's a child. And she's not even Ari as a child. Don't ask me how I know, but I do. The Ariadne I loved is dead. Gone. But I feel responsible for the child, for Ariadne's sake.'

'I'm sorry.'

'Don't be. You had a right to wonder.'

Ariadne stopped and gave Rhea a big hug. The old lady returned it with real affection.

'She loves Rhea. That's why I asked her if she would come and be her nurse. Ari needs security, familiar people round her. If that's all right with you, of course.'

She took his hand. 'Of course.'

'She can get very bad headaches, but Rhea makes her a tisane of willow bark, and they pass.' He paused. 'The worst is that she sometimes has bad dreams. Not often, but they're bad. I've some feeling of what she's going through, though she's unable to describe them. She just says "the bad man came". I've a pretty good idea that the bad man is short and fat. And dead,' he added grimly.

Klio looked across sympathetically and squeezed his hand.

'It's important that there should always be someone with her at night, to wake her immediately and comfort her. It can take some time. She occasionally wets the bed.'

They stopped to watch a moorhen paddle furiously into the reeds.

'Get her whatever she needs. Whatever it costs. It may surprise you to find that I will be a very rich man once this is all over.' He held up a hand to forestall her response. 'I know. You would do that anyway. I don't intend any insult, Dyaus be my witness. But I need to provide for her. You will give her the love she needs, and that's what's most important by far. Allow me to know that I'm giving just a little too. Please.'

'I'll look after her,' Klio promised.

'I know you will. It's the essence of your being.'

Klio smiled.

'She can't remember much from day to day. It will be a long time before she remembers that you're Auntie Klio. She still forgets my name. Though she never forgets Rhea.'

He seemed to be searching for words, so she just walked quietly alongside him. Eventually he spoke. 'I can't help it, and it's irrational, but I'm haunted by the idea that somehow she has taken on my burden, freed me from my night hags by accepting them herself.'

She squeezed his hand even more tightly. 'Now that you've come back to me, don't lose yourself again in a web of guilt. What happened, happened. There was nothing you could have done, and, if you hadn't been there, it would have been far worse.'

He nodded, unconvinced. Two woodpigeons burst from an oak tree in a clap of wings. Ariadne pointed at them and shouted with glee. Fat Puppy watched them go with his head cocked quizzically to one side. Then they walked on, Fat Puppy determinedly trundling along behind.

The sun was but a faint glow through a sheet of grey stratus, and the cold wind still blew, but they were warm enough in their thick woollen cloaks. Klio suddenly stopped and looked at him. She took a deep, shuddering breath and braced herself.

'What about us?' she said. The terror rose in her. He could see it in her eyes.

He took her other hand and softly massaged them both. 'I don't think I understand love, Klio,' he said slowly. He had been expecting this moment and had thought a great deal about what he should say.

'I know that I loved Ariadne, but that was a thing of passion, almost a madness. That kind of love is burned out in me. It won't return.' His eyes were sad. 'But there may be other kinds of love. I have found myself thinking about you a great deal. I don't know whether it's love, but I would like to be with you.'

He could see hope flare in her eyes like a signal beacon on the Boreads and felt her hands tense. 'You're the kindest person I've ever known,' he continued. 'I like you. I can talk to you. I enjoy being with you.' He shook his head. 'I don't know whether that's a different kind of love and I don't know if it will satisfy you, but it's all I can offer. When this war is over, I'd like to come back here, to you, if that's what you would like. You wouldn't be getting the best part of the bargain, not by a very long bowshot, but there it is.'

'I would like that very much,' she said quietly.

He leaned forward and kissed her, gently.

Ahead, Ariadne shouted with delight as her stick swept triumphantly past Rhea's.

Afterword

THE LONG INVESTMENT and eventual bloody storming of the Akroakrai, in which the defenders died to a man, has long been identified as the pivotal point in the Mykerenaean Rebellion. It certainly became a potent symbol of resistance, and Diomedes remains known to history as the Rock of Akrai.

Troilus duly achieved the rank of strategos, as foreseen by Diomedes, and proved a good one. He fought under Harpalycus at Hattusas, then spent most of the war as military governor of Mykerenos, concentrating on training and reinforcement. Despite rarely taking to the field, he supported Arctos in his northern thrust, capturing Tanagra, and was present at the misnamed Battle of the Sands. Under Medraut, he commanded a wing at Delos, the culminating victory of the Mykerenaean Rebellion in 518, and then, true to his Oath, retired to the Villa of the Antipatroi, where he married Kalliope. He never fought again.

Kalliope and Troilus had but one son, born in 530, after several stillbirths. He was called Pyrrhus after his father's proper name.

Tragedy struck in 537, when Rhea and Ariadne walked down to the river. Rhea was found dead on a stone bench, gripped by Herakla, and Ariadne had wandered off to play and drowned. They were buried together in a small coppice of cypress trees. Kalliope died of lung fever in 543, and Troilus of Poteidan's trident in 549.

Pyrrhus is for another story.

Glossary

aegis : Protective cloak of Pallas Athen. To be under someone's aegis is to be mentored and protected by them

Aesculapes : Gean God of healing

Aggie : Nickname for an Agrianian

Agriania : Mountainous Gean province in the southeast

Agrianian : Wild and fierce mountain men who inhabit Agriania

agora : The central open area and marketplace of a Gean town

Akrai : Town in Mykerenos dominating the exit of the strategic Boreas Pass (3B3)

Akroakrai : Ancient fortress built near Akrai

alalalaloi : Traditional Gean war cry

alpha : The letter A, the first letter of the alphabet; the number 1

Amber : Troilus's childhood dog

amphora (e) : Storage jar

andron : The main social area within a house

Andros Pass : Important pass linking the Vale of Mykerenos with the Mykerenaean Littoral and Plataea (4B2)

anger of Dyaus : Thunder

anger of Poteidan : An earthquake

Anopus : River that runs from the Hydran Breasts and down the Boreas Pass to join the Aegospotomai (a formidable river running north from Dryopia to the Tirynian Estuary; see Mykerenos map)

Antenopolis : Troian naval base on the eastern coast of the Chalcidikian Peninsula (3B2)

Antipatroi : Once-important aristocratic family from the Vale of Tempe

Apamea : Gean city and enclave in Thrake, on the eastern side of the Scyllan Gulf (4B2)

Apollon : Gean god of light, poetry and prophecy. His attribute is a rayed sun disc

archon : The chief official of a town or village. Equivalent to a mayor

Aresia : Gean God of war. His symbol is a sword

Argos : Capital of the Argolid, a north-central Troian province (3B3)

Argos : Aias's hunthound

Arkosians : Guild of assassins with a stronghold on Mount Arkot in southern Keltia

arrow rider : Despatch rider

aspis : Heavy round wooden shield faced with bronze

Artemisia : Gean goddess of hunting and of the moon

Athen Parthenos : Capital of Attica, a Gean coastal province

Athos : Major river marking the western border of Gea, running to the Scyllan Gulf at Leuctra (B1, B2, C2, C3)

aurochs : Wild cow

Basilides : Aristocratic family from Thessalia, claiming descent from Apollon

Battle of the Sands : The annihilation of an ill-prepared Troian invasion from the Argenusae Islands in 518

belly bow : A crossbow drawn by pressing down on the crescent-shaped crosspiece with the stomach and fired with a simple trigger mechanism

beta : The letter B. Represents the number 2

black-figured : Style of ceramic decoration in which figures are painted in black on a red or natural ground

bloody flux : Dysentery

Bluecloak : Household guard of Marsyas with a reputation for brutality

Boeotian helmet : A helmet of open design, allowing good vision but less protection

Bogazkoi : Town set in the northwest of the Vale of Mykerenos (3B3)

Boreads : The southern range of the Mykerenaean Mountains. Split by the Boreas Pass into western and eastern ranges (see Mykerenos map)

Borean Way : The track from Tanagra, through the Boreas Pass and across the Vale of Mykerenos to Pelium (see Mykerenos map)

Boreas Pass : Strategic pass in Mykerenos, leading from Tanagra to the Vale of Mykerenos (see Mykerenos map)

boule : The ruling council of a settlement of any size

boustria : Jerky; dried meat

breast band : Strip of linen bound around the breasts

Broken Steps : High-level ridge route that connects the Andros Pass with the Boreas Pass (see Mykerenos map)

Butcher : The name given to the brutal Troian satrap Marsyas

Carthago : Important Troian naval base on the eastern coast of the Chalcidikian Peninsula (3B2)

cast the discus : To point the finger, to make aspersions

Chalcidike : Gean province. Northeast of Greater Troia

Chalcidikian : An inhabitant of Chalcidike or pertaining to Chalcidike

Chenoi : Wild Geese. Volunteers fighting for Mykerenos, wearing dark green uniforms

Chief Scout : Or Skoparches. Commander of all skopoi or scouts

chiliarches : Commander of a thousand men or more. Equivalent to a brigadier. Dark red sash with a silver boar-on-laurel-wreath brooch

chiton : Long pleated garment, open at one side

Ch'n : Land in the far east of Ionia

circumvallation : The besieging of a town or fortress by building an enclosing wall or defensive work; such a wall or defensive work

cog : Small merchant ship

Cretan (s) : Inhabitants of Creta, famed as mercenary archers

crow : A wooden cross on a tripod upon which armour can be hung

cuirass : All-round body armour constituting chest and back protection, made of bronze or linen

curtain wall : Defensive wall surrounding a fortress or town

cut farther from hoof and horn : Of a better standard. Idiom derived from the best cut of meat being from the haunch

daemon : A spirit, often protective and individual to a person, but can be maleficent. Also the nickname of Marsyas's personal guards

dekate : The tenth part of the night or day. Thus there are twenty tenths in a complete day. The actual length varies with the season

Delos : Town and army base in Thalassa. Site of the final battle of the Mykerenaean Rebellion in 518 (2B2)

Delium : Site of battle in Phthia, 454

Demetra : Gean earth Goddess; Goddess of crops and fecundity. Her symbol is a sheaf of corn

Demetrius : Fortress. One of the Five Fetters. Situated on the Attic coast (2C1)

deuteros : Second-in-command

dilochagos : A double file leader, equivalent to a sergeant
dilocho : Diminutive of dilochagos
Dionysia : Annual festival in celebration of Dionysius, Gean God of wine
discus throw, same : As bad as
Ditykoians : Part of the western rim of the Mykerenaean Mountains (see Mykerenos map)
Dog Star : The star Sirius in the Canis Major constellation, the brightest star in the sky
double tap : An expression from a child's game that means to agree that things are equal
drachma (e) : Unit of currency. Worth six obols
Dryopian : Pertaining to Dryopia, an area of forest in southeast Gea still not under Gean control. The Dryopian people are noted for their fierceness
Dyaus (Pitar) : Chief God of the Geans. His attribute is a keraunos, or stylised thunderbolt
Dyaus's anger : Thunder

eilarches : Commander of a cavalry eile of 256 men. Equivalent to a major. Dark green sash with a bronze laurel-wreath brooch
eile : Unit of 256 cavalry
Eiris : The messenger of the Gods, who usually brings a dream
Elaphebolion : Month. March 22 – April 20
Elean (s) : Savage tribesman inhabiting Elis
Eleans : Northwest region of Mykerenaean Mountains, constituting the hill region of Elis (4A1)
Elis : Region of the northwest Mykerenaean Mountains (4A1)
Elysian Fields : Or Elysium. Part of the Gean otherworld inhabited by the blessed
embrasures : The openings between raised stone merlons that creates the crenellation, or tooth-like pattern, of battlements
Enkos : Tributary of the Athos (8B1)

Eretrian : Inhabitant and language of Eretria, a country to the west of Gea

Erotes : Gean God of erotic love

Evinian Pass : Pass through the Elean Mountains from the Northern Thebeaid to the Vale of Mykerenos (4A1)

falling sickness : Epilepsy

file : The basic unit of 16 men

Five Fetters : Five fortresses: Kerakos, Gla, Demetrius, Ithome and Akrochalcis

flutes, play the : To totally control someone. From the use of flutes to provide the marching rhythm for heavy infantry

Furies : Spirits of revenge that hunt to death a man guilty of murder, hubris or oathbreaking

gamma : The letter G, the third letter of the alphabet and the number 3

Gea : Area in north-central Ionia (the largest continent on Xenos), located on the southern shores of an inland sea, the Pontis; inhabited by a people with a single language and culture

Gean (s) : Inhabitant and language of Gea

Gean Thrake : A mountainous province inhabited by Thrakoi. Separated from Thrake by the Scyllan Gulf

Gla : Fortress; one of the Five Fetters. Set in the Vale of Tempe (8A1)

Goat's Way : Difficult high-level pass between the Vale of Tempe and the Mykerenaean Littoral (4B3)

god guard : Amulet of the symbol of a chosen protective deity, usually hung round the neck

gorgon : Mythological monster whose look turns men to stone

gorytus : Combined bowcase and quiver

graphotrapeza (e) : High writing table with an angled top

Greater Troia : Gean province. Centrally situated and the richest and most populous

Great Oath : A vow by the Furies. A terrifying oath

Great Reef : A chain of islets running from Mykerenos to the entrance to the Gulf of Scylla (4B2, 4C2)

Great Revolt : The usurpation of the throne by Laomedon, 500–502

greave : Thin bronze shin guard that clips round the leg

Hades : Gean God of the dead. Attribute a skull. Also, the place of the dead; by extension, any state of chaos or misery. Also, an intensifier to indicate disgust, surprise, etc.

Haloea : Midwinter solstice festival

Hattusas : Village in the Boreas Pass. Site of a battle in 514 (See Mykerenos map)

hedgehog : Slang term for a speira

hekate : Unit of time. The hundredth part of a dekate and so theoretically variable. Generally taken as a hundred heartbeats and so just over a minute

hekaton : Shortened form of hekatonarchia, a unit of 256 psiloi or peltastes

hekatonarches : Commander of a hekatonarchia

Herakla : Queen of the Gods. Her symbol is a pomegranate

Herakla's grip : Heart attack

Herea : Large fortress dominating the Hook of Mykerenos and the entrance to the Gulf of Scylla (4A2)

Hetairoi : Elite Mykerenaean shock cavalry. The name means 'the companions'

Himera : Village north of Akrai (see Mykerenos map)

holder : The designated official in command of a large town or fortress

Holokauston of Bogazkoi : The total destruction of a Mykerenaean town by Marsyas in 510

Hook : Or Hook of Mykerenos. A long narrow peninsula extending into the Gulf of Scylla (4C2)

hoplite : Gean heavy infantryman armed with stabbing spear and large shield hypaspist (ai) : Elite, fast-moving infantry armed with spear and shield

hyperetes : Senior file closer. The equivalent of a sergeant major

Ikaros : Small Mykerenaean village. Temporary base for Mykerenaean field army (see Mykerenos map)

Ilios : Largest city and capital of the Troian Empire (3A4)

Imbros : Large lake in the Vale of Mykerenos (4A1)

Iphikrates of Kos : Historical general who developed the peltastes in 457–9

Iron Rock : Battle in 501 resulting in victory for Laomedon and death of Troilus IV

Iyalissos : Village in the Vale of Mykerenos, close to Bogazkoi

Kallisthenes : Makedonian strategos 374–423

Katane : Main base for the Mykerenaean army during the latter stages of the struggle for Mykerenos (see Mykerenos map)

Keltos (oi) : Inhabitant of Keltia, a country south of the Debateable Lands. The language of Keltia

klismos : Chair with back, arm rests and curved legs. Often ornately carved

knucklebones : Primitive dice. Sheep or calf ankle bones that can come to rest with one of four faces uppermost, each given a value

Kodros : Capital of a small Agrianian kingdom

Koi : Diminutive of Bogazkoi

kopis : A single-edged, single-handed slashing sword that is widest towards its tip

Korinthian helmet : An enclosed helmet that affords good protection but poor vision

Kratelos : Theban general 410–454

krater : Large bowl for mixing wine and water

Kriptia : Aias's misspelling of Krypteia

Krypteia : Laomedon's feared secret police force

kyklopean : The use of massive stone blocks for building. Of ancient and unknown origin and associated with the ancient race of the Kyklopes

Kyklopes : Race of Titans who fought the Gods

kylix (es) : Drinking vessel

Leuctra : Large port at the end of the Gulf of Scylla (4B3)

lochagos : Gean file leader, equivalent to a corporal

lung fever : Pneumonia

Maimakterion : Month. November 22 – December 21

manumission : The legal freeing of a slave

Massalia : Free city on the coast of Euxinia, a grain-growing region on the eastern shores of the Pontis

Megara : Town in the Argolid famous for its rug manufacture and home of the Military Academy (3A4)

Mickey (s) : Slang term for a Mykerenaean

Military Academy : Situated in Megara. Academy for officer training and military history

mina (e) : A unit of weight equal to a little over half a kilogram

Moesian Gorge : A long, deep ravine that lies across the Pass of Anchises (see Mykerenos map)

Monotheite : Monotheite : Member of a monotheistic cult that attempted a theocratic putsch in 500; of or pertaining to this cult

moon sickness : Menstruation

moontide : Month

Morrigan : Keltian death Goddess

Mounichion : Month. April 21 – May 20

Mykerenaean : Inhabitant of Mykerenos, or pertaining to Mykerenos

Mykerenaean Littoral : The wide, fertile 'shelf' of coastline between the Mykerenaean Mountains and Great Reef Bay (4B1, 4B2, 4C2)

Mykerenos : Gean province in the northeast of Gea

Naupactos : Mykerenaean port in the Great Reef Bay (3C4)
navarches : Admiral
night hag : Nightmare

obol : Small coin. Six obols to a drachma
Oenone : Small town between Gla and Leuctra (see Sea of Grass map)
Olympus : Highest mountain of Agrianian range. Traditionally the home of the Gods (8B4)
Order of the White Rose : Proscribed underground Mykerenaean organisation dedicated to a free Mykerenos
Ossa : Highest mountain in Mykerenos. See also: pile Pelion on Ossa

Pan : Minor God. Spreader of panic
pankration : A combination of boxing, wrestling and kicking. Only eye-gouging and biting are not allowed
Paleius : Eretrian philosopher 461–502
Paros : Village in the Boreas Pass sacked by Marsyas during his retreat
Pass of Anchises : Little-used and difficult pass between the Northern Thebeaid and the Vale of Mykerenos (see Mykerenos map)
pavise : Mobile wheeled shield
Peace of Poteidan : A small merchant cog
Pelion : Mountain in Mykerenos. See also: pile Pelion on Ossa (4B1)
Pelium : Port and naval base on the north coast of Mykerenos (3C2)
pelta : Small, light shield, usually of wood, circular or crescent-shaped, carried in the hand
peltaste : Light infantryman, usually armed with a small pelta shield and javelins
peplos : A draped dress, usually gathered at the waist
Pergamene white : A very sweet white wine from Pergamon
phalanx : Mykerenaean unit of heavy infantry armed with sarissae. A full phalanx has over a thousand men
Phraidos : River rising below Mount Thrax in the Rhodopians and running into Great Reef Bay (4B2, 4B3)

Phthian : Inhabitant of Phthia or pertaining to Phthia, a Troian province in the northwest. Also a breed of heavy horses bred in Phthia, fast and powerful

pile Pelion on Ossa : To make something too large even bigger; to take excessive measures

pilos helmet : Simple conical bronze helmet

Pindus : Large, slab-shaped massif in the Agrianian Mountains

Pinopsion : Aias's misspelling of Pyanopsion (the month from October 23 – November 21)

plag : Diminutive of plagiophylax, a unit of 128 cavalry troopers

plagiophylakes : Commander of a plagiophylax. Equivalent to a captain. Light green sash and bronze crossed-spears-and-helmet brooch

Plataea : Mykerenaean capital (3C3)

porna : Prostitute

Poteidan : Gean God of the sea. Storms and earthquakes were known as the Anger of Poteidan

Poteidan's trident : Stroke (i.e. apoplexy)

Priamos : Town on the Aegospotomai river in eastern Greater Troia (7B1)

Prometheus : Divine hero who stole fire from heaven for mankind and was punished by being chained to a rock while an eagle tore at his liver

Propontis : The sea to the east of Chalcidike and Mykerenos

psilos (oi) : Missile infantryman, usually armed with bow or sling

Pterseus : Mythological hero who saved the Princess Andromeda from a sea monster

pteruges : Leather strips around a kilt that act as protection

Pyrrho : Theban philosopher 307–78. Founder of the Skeptic School

ram speed : Or 'at the ram'. To move as quickly as possible

read the entrails : Predict the future

red-figured : Ceramic decoration with paintings in red on a black ground

Rhodian red : Fine wine produced round the town of Rhodos in southern Lesser Troia

Rhodian slingers : Famed mercenary slingers from the island of Rhodos in the Eastern Pontis

Rhodope : Culminating mountain of Rhodopian range

Rhodopians : Mountain range north of the Vale of Tempe, in Gean Thrake (4B3, 4C3)

rhomphaia : A two-handed sickle-shaped weapon with a fearsome reputation

Ring of Mykerenos : The Mykerenaean Mountains that encircle the Vale (see Mykerenos map)

Rock of Akrai : Name given to Diomedes after the siege of Akrai in 512

roll up in blanket bag : To have control over, to have someone 'in your pocket'

salpinx (es) : Gean trumpet for conveying orders

sarissa (e) : Long spear about sixteen feet in length

satrap : Governor of a province

satrapy : A province of the Troian Empire

satyr : Demigod of the woodland, with the horns and legs of a goat

scuttle : Slang for a rapid retreat

Scyllan Gulf : Or Gulf of Scylla. Long inlet from the Propontis to Leuctra (4C2, 4C3)

Scyllan Mountains : Part of the eastern rim of the Mykerenaean Mountains (see Mykerenos map)

Sea Door : A gap in the Great Reef through which ships can enter Great Reef Bay (see Mykerenos map)

Sea of Grass : The Vale of Tempe

se'ennight : A week

Selenes : Day of the week. Monday

shatang : A strategy board game in which pieces are moved to control space

sigil : An identifying symbol of a unit, officer or family

sigma : The letter S, used as a brand to mark a slave

sistrum : A musical instrument with a handle attached to a loop of metal upon which loosely fitted rings rattle when shaken

Skoparches : Chief Scout

skopos (oi) : Scout

snatch and bag : A surprise assault or a kidnapping

speira (i) : A Troian 'hedgehog' of 1,000 to 2,000 spearmen

speiros (oi) : Troian spearman, wearing a leather jerkin and carrying a medium-sized oval shield

sphairai : Oxhide thongs worn round the fists of boxers. To 'don the sphairai' is to take on a difficult task

stade (ia) : A distance of approximately 1/10 mile

steader : Inhabitant of a steading, an isolated homestead, particularly in the Vale of Tempe

strategarch : Senior general. Equivalent to a field marshal

strategion : Army headquarters

strategos (oi) : General. White sash of office with a golden eagle-and-snake brooch

strophion : A band worn under the breasts to lift and emphasise them

Stymphalian Campaign : Genocidal campaign led by Laomedon when warden of the Debateable Lands to clear the Stymphalian Marshes 498–500

Styx : The river that borders the Underworld. To cross the Styx is to enter the Land of the Dead

summer godfire : Sheet lightning

swordmaster : Expert swordsman, usually employed for personal protection or training

symposium : A social gathering for food, wine and conversation tag : Diminutive for a syntagma, a unit of 256 hoplites or phalangites (infantrymen who fight in an ordered phalanx)

talent : Large unit of currency. A silver talent is 6,000 drachmae, a golden talent 15,000

Tanagra : Strategic town on the River Anopus, in the Northern Thebeaid, dominating the Boreas Pass (3B3)

taxiarches : Commander of a taxis of 128 heavy infantry

Tegea : Small village north of Akrai

Tenedian wine : Cheap wine from the area round Tenedos in Greater Troia

Tenos : A small town used as the Troian winter quarters, and the site of two battles (see Mykerenos map)

tetrarches : Commander of a tetrarchia. Equivalent to a lieutenant. Yellow sash and bronze crossed-spears brooch

tetrarchia (tet) : Unit of 64 men

Thebeaid : Troian province, east of Greater Troia

Thematis : Free city on the coast of Thrake

Thessalian : Inhabitant of Thessalia, a Troian province in the west, famed for its light cavalry

Thrak (s) : Slang term for Thracians

Thracian (s) : People of Thrake, or pertaining to Thrake

Thrake : Land inhabited by the Thracians. Part independent and part Gean Thrake, a Gean province

Thrax : Mountain in Gean Thrake (4C3)

threnody : Solemn lament sung as a memorial to the dead

tilia : A popular board game in which stones are moved round or taken off according to dice throws

tisane : An infusion of herbs in hot water, often with medicinal properties

trireme : Warship with ram and three banks of oars

Trog (s) : Nickname for a Troian. Often used a synonym for Imperial troops regardless of their actual origin

Troian : Inhabitant of or pertaining to Troia. Often used as a synonym for Imperial troops

Troian Empire : Period of Troian hegemony controlling all of Gea except for Dryopia, Agriania and the Stymphalian Marshes

trooper : Common term for a cavalryman

Tirynian Estuary or Shore : The mouth of the Aegospotami, separating Chalcidike and the Northern Thebeaid

Vale of Tempe : Eastern area of Thebeaid, the Sea of Grass (8A1, 8A2, 8B1, 8B2)

Villa Antipatroi : Kalliope's home above Leuctra

wand : Thin stick set up as a target for expert archers. A target

wasting sickness : Cancer

waycastle : A fortified camp situated for supply trains to take shelter

which end of the horse eats the hay : Idiom for something simple and straightforward

windhover : A kestrel

woodwose : A legendary spirit of the forest given to mischievous spells

xyston (oi) : Short thrusting spear with a long blade used by shock cavalry

Zagria : Town in Greater Troia on the Scamander and on the Troian-Korinthian border (6C1)

Main Characters

Abantes : Slave and bully
Aias : Putative father of Troilus in Bogazkoi
Alexandros (Xander) : Mykerenaean chiliarches, commander of the Hetairoi. Known as Alexandros the Golden
Ariadne (Ari) : Young woman from Tegea, cousin of Nicias

Brasidas (Bras) : Mykerenaean strategos

Diomedes (Dio) : Strategarch. Once swordmaster to the holder of Gla

Gian : Thessalian slave and friend to Troi

Harpalycus (Harp) : Troian eilarches, later Mykerenaean strategos

Ilus : Advisor and guard commander to Kalliope

Kalliope (Klio) : Young widow, the last of the Antipatroi

Marsyas : Troian satrap of Mykerenos, noted for his cruelty
Meleagros (Mel) : Mykerenaean chiliarches, later strategos, commanding the Agrianes

Nicias (Nici) : Young Mykerenaean scout

Phoebe : Girlfriend of Troilus in Bogazkoi
Phoebus : Bondservant at the Villa Antipatroi

Sarpedon : Troian officer
Selene : Xanthos's wife
Simonides (Sim) : Chief of Staff of Mykerenaean Army

Troilus (Troi) : Cover name of Pyrrhus, son of Aglaia and Perikles

Xanthos (Xan) : Mykerenaean scout. Son of Phyllida and Dymas
Xander : Diminutive of Alexandros
Xarchon : Glycon's slavemaster

Minor Characters

Adrastus : Miltiades' secretary during the Monotheite Plot
Aglaia : Mother of Troilus, daughter of Kalliste and Miltiades
Alexa : Slave girl at the Villa Antipatroi
Androcles (Andro) : Xanthos's son
Antinous : Troilus's uncle, son of Kalliste and Miltiades
Arctos : Mykerenaean strategarch
Aristippus : Swordmaster at Ikaros
Aristobulos : Mykerenaean chief engineer
Aspasia : Elderly neighbour of Troilus in Bogazkoi
Auntie : Nickname for Eirene

Cari : Cowardly follower of Evenios
Chileos : King of small Agrianian kingdom of Kodros; son of Neritos
Chrysaor : Real name of Harpalycus

Danae : Troi's mistress at Ikaros
Diocles : Survivor of the Holokauston of Bogazkoi
Doreios : Member of the Order of the White Rose in Ialyssos

Eirene : Housemistress to Kalliope
Elissa : Priestess of Herakla in Bogazkoi
Erxandros : Town archon of Bogazkoi. Equivalent to a mayor
Eubalos : Chiliarches in command of the northeast quadrant of the Boreas
Euadne : Mother of Nicias
Evenios : Thuggish villager from Tegea

Glycon : Slave owner in the Vale of Tempe
Gwalchmai : Mykerenaean Chief Scout

Hektor : Mykerenaean chiliarches
Herm : Slow-witted follower of Evenios
Hermione : A friend of Kalliope

Inaros : Injured survivor of the Holokauston of Bogazkoi
Iphiclus : Kalliope's major-domo

Kalais : Leader of a rebellion against Laomedon in 509
Kalliste (Kal) : Troilus's grandmother, married initially to Miltiades and then to Diomedes
Kittos : Thuggish guard at Glycon's Villa
Koinos : Simple-minded slave at Kalliope's villa
Koronos : Slave trader

Ladon : Mykerenaean chief of logistics
Laomedon : Emperor of Troia

Mad Mel : See Meleagros

Manannan : Keltian slave
Mardonius : Mykerenaean eilarches at the First Battle of Tenos
Medraut : Mykerenaean strategos
Melanpos : Name adopted by Sarpedon during Troi's escape
Miltiades : Father of Aglaia and grandfather of Troi

Neritos : Agrianian King of Kodros, now dead

Olus : Name adopted by Troilus during his escape
Onomastus : Strategos under Marsyas
Ourania : Neighbour of Troilus in Bogazkoi

Palaemon : Chiliarches in command of the northwest quadrant of the Boreas
Parmenio : Troian strategos
Patrobas : Eilarches in the Hetairoi
Perikles : Troilus's father
Philemon : Mykerenaean officer at Ikaros
Philomena : Name of Troilus's mother according to Aias
Phoinos : Aide to Diomedes
Phorbas : Aide to Troi
Phormio : Mykerenaean admiral
Phyllida (Phyll) : Mother of Xanthos
Poteidonius : Senior plagiophylakes in Chrysaor's eile
Praxis (Prax) : Senior Mykerenaean officer at Ikaros
Pyrrhus : Son of Troilus and Kalliope
Pyrrhus : Troilus's given name

Rhea : Healer from the village of Himera

Shark : Nickname of Poteidonius
Sicinnos : Brutal Troian officer responsible for the massacre at Tegea
Sinon : Mykerenaean spymaster

Tereus : Thracian tribal chief fighting with the Mykerenaeans
Themistocles : Mykerenaean chiliarches
Triopas : Bondservant at the Villa Antipatroi
Troilus III : Troian Emperor. Son of Idomeneus II. Succeeded his brother Aristogeiton
Troilus IV : Troian Emperor. Son of Troilus III. Usurped and murdered by Laomedon
Tron : Ariadne's first boyfriend
Tros : Mykerenaean eilarches at the First Battle of Tenos

Xenarches : Troilus's military tutor
Xenon : A scribe

Measurement

Time:

Each night and each day are divided into ten dekates each, so there are twenty dekates in a day, and they vary in length according to the seasons. They are roughly equivalent to hours. A hekate is theoretically the hundredth part of a dekate and therefore around three quarters of a minute. Practically, it is taken as a hundred heartbeats. A se'ennight is a week and a moontide a month.

Length:

Mostly intuitive, paces and finger lengths; but a stade (plural 'stadia') is about one tenth of a mile.

Money:

Seven obols to a drachma.
One hundred drachmae to a mina.
A silver talent is 7,000 drachmae and a golden talent 15,000.
Gold coins are valued according to weight, but the stater of the Free Cities is by far the most common and is equivalent to fifty drachmae.

Days of the week:

Selenes	Monday
Areos	Tuesday
Hermou	Wednesday
Dios	Thursday
Aphrodites	Friday
Kronou	Saturday
Heliou	Sunday

Months of the year:

Poseidion	December 22 – January 20
Gamelion	January 21 – February 19
Anthesterion	February 20 – March 21
Elaphebolion	March 22 – April 20
Mounichion	April 21 – May 20
Thargelion	May 21 – June 19
Intercalary Days	June 20 – June 24
Skirophorion	June 25 – July 24
Hekatonbaion	July 25 – August 23
Metageitrion	August 24 – September 22
Boedromion	September 23 – October 22
Pyanopsion	October 23 – November 21
Maimakterion	November 22 – December 21

RANKS IN THE GEAN ARMY

Number of men	Arm	Rank	Modern equivalent	Unit name	Modern equivalent
		Hegemones	Commissioned Officers		
as required	All	Strategarch	Field Marshal	Stratia	Army
as required	All	Strategos	General	Keras	Division/Corps
as required	All	Chiliarches	Brigadier	Meros	Brigade
1024	Infantry	Phalangarches	Colonel	Phalanx	Regiment
1024	Cavalry	Hipparches	Colonel	Hipparchia (Hip)	Regiment
512	All	Telarches	Lieutenant Colonel	Telos	Battalion
256	Infantry	Syntagmarches	Major	Syntagma (Tag)	Battalion
256	Cavalry	Eilarches	Major	Eile	Battalion
256	Light Infantry	Hekatonarches	Major	Hekatonarchia (Hekaton)	Battalion
128	Infantry	Taxiarches	Captain	Taxis	Company
128	Cavalry	Plagiophylakes	Captain	Plagiophylax (Plag)	Troop
64	All	Tetrarches	Lieutenant	Tetrarchia (Tet)	Platoon
		Ektatoi	NCOs		
64	All	Hyperetes	Company Sgt Major	Tetrarchia (Tet)	Platoon
32	All	Dilochagos	Sergeant Major	Dilochos	Platoon
16	All	Lochagos	Sergeant	Lochos	Squad
8	All	Hemilochagos	Corporal	Hemilochion	Section

Commands in the navy:
keulestes : Lighter ships such as biremes or cargo ships
trierarches : Triremes
kataphractarches : Heavier ships such as hexeres
thalassarches : A squadron of vessels
navarches : The equivalent of a strategos i.e. an admiral

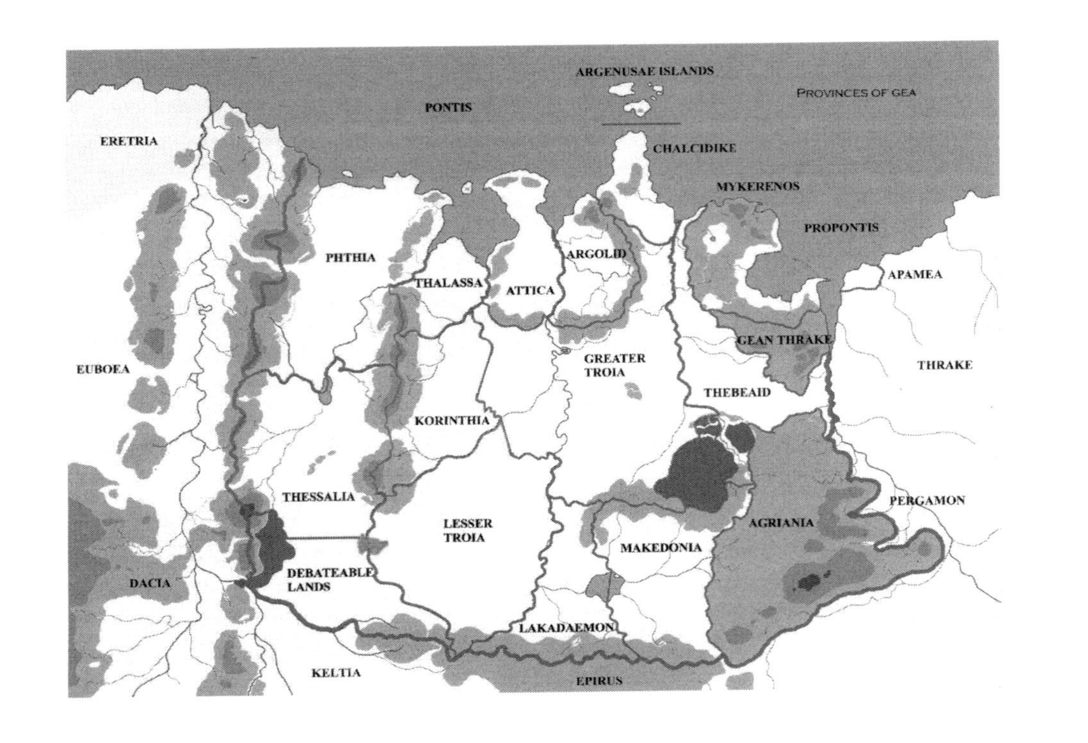
ARGENUSAE ISLANDS
PROVINCES OF GEA
PONTIS
ERETRIA
CHALCIDIKE
MYKERENOS
PROPONTIS
PHTHIA
ARGOLID
THALASSA
ATTICA
APAMEA
GEAN THRAKE
EUBOEA
GREATER TROIA
THRAKE
THEBEAID
KORINTHIA
THESSALIA
PERGAMON
AGRIANIA
LESSER TROIA
MAKEDONIA
DACIA
DEBATEABLE LANDS
LAKADAEMON
KELTIA
EPIRUS

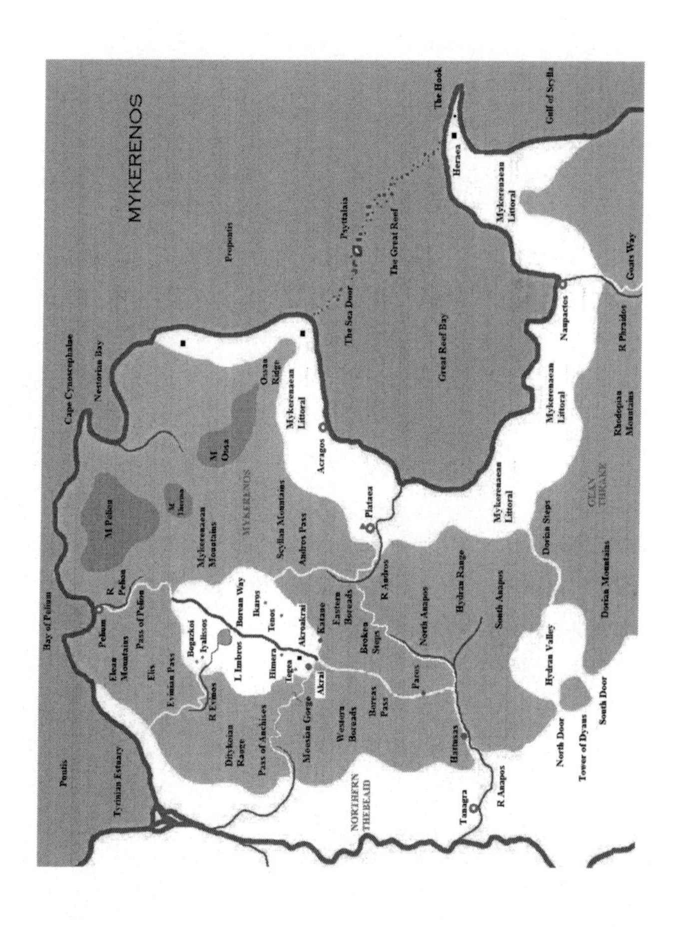
MYKERENOS
Bay of Pelium
Pontis
Cape Cynoscephalae
Nestorian Bay
Tyrinian Estuary
Pelium
R Pelion
Elean Mountains
M Pelion
Pass of Pelion
Elis
Evinian Pass
M Therma
Bogazkoi
Iyalissos
R Evinos
Mykerenaean Mountains
M Ossa
Proportis
Ditykoian Range
L Imbros
Borean Way
MYKERENOS
Ikaros
Pass of Anchises
Ossan Ridge
Himera
Tenos
Scyllan Mountains
Tegea
Mykerenaean Littoral
Akroakrai
Andros Pass
Moesian Gorge
Akrai
Katane
Acragos
Eastern Boreads
Western Boreads
The Sea Door
Psyttalaia
NORTHERN THEBEAID
Broken Steps
Plataea
Boreas Pass
R Andros
The Great Reef
Paros
North Anapos
Great Reef Bay
The Hook
Hattusas
Heraea
Tanagra
Hydran Range
R Anapos
South Anapos
Mykerenaean Littoral
Mykerenaean Littoral
Hydran Valley
Dorian Steps
Gulf of Scylla
North Door
Mykerenaean Littoral
Naupactos
Tower of Dyaus
South Door
Dorian Mountains
GEAN THRAKE
Rhodopian Mountains
R Phraidos
Goats Way

The Chronicles of Gea

What Dreams May Come is the second of a series of related but standalone novels in this setting. The others, in chronological order:

None So Blind (Matador, 2019)

The year is 499. The Troian Emperor is inept and ineffective. Dissatisfaction and disloyalty taint the political air, and Diomedes, an aging swordmaster, finds himself unravelling a plot against the Emperor, while struggling with his feelings for his friend's wife, whose life is in peril.

When First We Practise

Eugenia, the niece of the new, tyrannical Emperor, observes a battle against the rebels. It does not turn out as anticipated. She decides to manipulate her captor, Telamon, to regain her freedom, but manipulation is a two-edged sword.

The Key

The rebels are stopped by the impregnable fortress of Gla. Perhaps Thallia, the daughter of its commander, might prove to be the key? Harpalycus (*What Dreams May Come*, *When First We Practise*) attempts to use her as such but unlocks far more than he planned. She becomes a helpless pawn in dangerous power plays.

The Initiate

Civil war erupts. When Andro, son of Xanthos (*None So Blind*, *What Dreams May Come*), is conscripted, he is still a virgin. Seeing this as bad luck, his file members take him to a brothel. He is entranced by Theodosia, but she humiliates him. In battle, his phalanx is broken and he runs away. Hidden deep in the woods, he finds a fleeing and desperate Theodosia with a deadly secret. Are his feelings genuine? Are hers?

The White Prince

In yet another struggle for hegemony in the tortured land of Gea, the young Belisarius, illegitimate member of a royal family, becomes Emperor in all but name after his abduction of a princess and the subsequent forced marriage. Although Belisarius falls for the princess, Iphigenia, the great niece of Thallia (*The Key*), she does not reciprocate, and he is faced with the deadly threat of invasion by the Dokari Horse Lords.

Shadow Wolf

A new Emperor attempts to conquer neighbouring Keltia. His chief of scouts, Hermolycus (son of Andro (*The Initiate*)), is captured. Kern, an old ally, frees him on the agreement that he will protect his daughter, Branwen, against the threat of the insulted king's son. But Branwen finds herself torn in two directions, and Hermolycus has to face the ultimate test.

Beholder's Eye

Pyrrhus, son of Troilus (*What Dreams May Come*), defending Gea against a Keltian invasion, arrives at a waystation run by Zoe, a young woman whose face has been smashed by the Dokari. After her waystation is destroyed, he offers her the post of housemistress at his villa. There she is accused of embezzlement and murder, but Pyrrhus is determined to find the truth.

Huntress

Bran (*Shadow Wolf*) becomes a bounty hunter. She takes on a mission to find the son of Belisarius (*The White Prince*), a previous king, now seen as a threat to the youthful new Emperor. Numa, a young trainee tags along, and Bran and she are mutually attracted. Then they find Belisarius's son, and Bran is faced with a dreadful decision for the second time.

The Epigoni

The final novel is an immediate sequel to *Huntress*. The search for Belisarius's son transmutes into a race against time to stop Lysander, the increasingly psychotic and out-of-control young Emperor. Individuals from earlier books come together in this dangerous and desperate attempt.

The opening sections of all these novels can be downloaded and read at harpalycus.com

Matador